Running Away

Book Four of the Just Say Yes Series

Author's Note

While this is book four of the Just Say Yes series, it can be read as a standalone. This book is a spin-off from Andy and Zoey's story, which takes place in books 1–3. Characters from the first three books will be mentioned throughout, but *Running Away* is written in such a way that there are no questions as to who everyone is. If you'd like to delve deeper into the James family dynamic and the wonderful characters, I recommend reading the first three books. Thank you!

The following story contains mature themes, strong language, and sexual situations. It is intended for adult readers.

Dedication

To every person who has had their dreams squashed, ignored, laughed at, and degraded. Anything is possible when you learn to ignore the hate and jealousy and live YOUR life the way you want to. You're only given one life, live it like there's no tomorrow.

Author's Note

While this is book four of the Just Say Yes series, it can be read as a standalone. This book is a spin-off from Andy and Zoey's story, which takes place in books 1–3. Characters from the first three books will be mentioned throughout, but Running Away is written in such a way that there are no questions as to who everyone is. If you'd like to delve deeper into the James family dynamic and the wonderful characters, I recommend reading the first three books. Thank you!

The following story contains mature themes, strong language, and sexual situations. It is intended for adult readers.

Dedication

To every person who has had their dreams squashed, ignored, laughed at, and degraded. Anything is possible when you learn to ignore the hate and jealousy and live YOUR life the way you want to. You're only given one life, live it like there's no tomorrow.

Acknowledgements

Lorrie Anson, Editor, Flaming Pen Editing
www.flamingpenediting.com

Sarah Foster, Cover Designer, Sprinkles On Top Studios
http://sprinklesontopstudios.com

Tami Norman, Formatter, Integrity Formatting
http://integrityformatting.wix.com/integrity-formatting

To my lone beta reader, Becca Dawn from Prisoners of Print Book Blog. Thank you so much for the time you took away from your busy schedule to read this book for me. Your medical feedback is much appreciated.

April Stanley, you delivered in a big way when I randomly posted on Facebook asking friends to name a naughty sounding drink that you'd get at a bar. When you commented with "Redheaded Slut" I knew that second you'd hit the nail on the head. The name of the drink could not have fit any better for the scene where it's used in this book. Thank you!

Thank you to Enticing Journey Book Promotions for handling my blog tour and release day blitz!

The Indie Erogenous Zone ladies! I would not be sane(ish) without you and I love you all.

My blogger friends! Thank you for everything you do for me. I wouldn't be here without every single one of you!

Special thanks to every single person who has purchased the books in this series. I wish I could write a book about all the characters you loved, and maybe someday I will.

~ Jen

Teagan

January 2013

This was the absolute worst part of my job. Mr. Johnson's pulse was getting weaker by the hour. His time was definitely near. As a registered nurse, currently working in home hospice, I was only two hours in to my twelve-hour graveyard shift with my patient who was dying from pancreatic cancer.

I loved my midnight to noon job through Denver Home Hospice, in Colorado, but my feelings about mortality were beginning to take a toll on me. I'd lost two patients in the last three weeks. Mr. Johnson would be my third.

Before waking his wife, I straightened his blankets, combed his hair to the side, and left his room. A minute after I knocked, she eased open her door. Her drooping shoulders and heartbreaking expression confirmed she was aware of the reason I was here.

"Is it time, Teagan?" Her weary eyes closed briefly as she drew in a ragged breath, waiting for my response.

My lips pursed and I gave her a nod. "I believe he's close, Mrs. Johnson. I'm sorry. You might want to gather your children as quickly as possible."

She pulled her robe from the hook on the back of the door, slipping it around her shoulders. A wracking sob broke free from her as she returned to the bedside table for her phone.

While she contacted her children, I packed away all the spare medical supplies in Mr. Johnson's room to make extra space for them once they'd arrived. Still alone with Mr. Johnson, I pulled a chair close to his bedside, and sat resting my hand on top of his.

"Mr. Johnson, it's been a pleasure taking care of you these last few months. You are a good man, a good husband, and an amazing father. Your wife is calling your family now. Please hold on just a bit longer for them. They'll be here soon."

The bedroom door opened without a sound, and Mrs. Johnson took a hesitant step into the room. I went to her. She was grief-stricken with tears in her eyes and seemed scared to death. My heart clenched inside my chest for her and the pain she was going through.

She wrapped her arms around me and sobbed uncontrollably on my shoulder. At that moment, I was all she had and held on to her as her tears soaked my scrubs top. She was about to lose her husband, the father of her children, and the love of her life. I had no idea what that felt like, nor did I want to imagine.

"H-how long do you think he has l-left, Teagan?" She gasped between each sharp intake of breath.

I pulled back slightly, and rubbed my hands up and down her arms. "I can't say for sure, but based on my experience— maybe a day or two at most." Fortunately, all of their children lived in Colorado and would be here within a few hours to support her.

"Sally?" The ragged voice of Mr. Johnson calling for his wife echoed quietly through the room.

A knot formed in my throat, knowing this might be the last time she would hear his voice. He had been in and out of consciousness for the last few days, occasionally waking up and calling for his wife or one of his children.

Stepping away, I slipped into the hallway and shut the door behind me, giving them privacy. In the kitchen, I transferred dirty dishes from the sink to the dishwasher to keep busy. Washing dishes wasn't part of my job, but I didn't want the Johnsons to worry about unimportant chores like this for the next few days.

They were going to have a hard enough time while Mr. Johnson passed from this life to the next.

In some ways, I wanted my patients to live longer to spare their families the agony of losing them forever, but at the same time, I wanted their pain to end. I hated to think that way, but who wanted to see someone suffer continuously?

Thus the reason for my job choice: I aided my patients in hopes of easing their pain, and tried my best to help the families who were watching their loved one die. It was a double-edged sword. Both parties were suffering, from either physical pain, or emotional pain.

As I scrubbed a few dried-on bits of food from a plate, a soft knock sounded at the front door. Drying my hands, I glanced through the peephole, finding the Johnsons' daughter, Evie, on the step. She attended the University of Colorado, living in a dorm on campus, and was their only daughter who lived close by. I swung the door open and she stepped in hesitantly then hugged me.

"Thank you, Teagan, I was in such a rush when my mom called I forgot my house key." Evie's bottom lip quivered and tears filled her eyes while she shrugged off her coat and hung it on the rack beside the door. "Thanks for taking such good care of my dad. I don't know what we would have done without you."

"You're welcome. I understand this isn't easy for your family, but I'm here to help any way I can."

Evie offered me a crestfallen smile before making her way to her father.

Even though I couldn't fully relate, I knew the sense of helplessness when someone you loved dearly was fighting for their life. My own father, who was technically my stepfather, but had raised me from age three, had been diagnosed with colon cancer when I was in my teens. We hadn't been sure if he would survive, so I'd spent every spare second with him—just in case. Fortunately, my dad had survived and was back in my hometown of Sacramento, California, with my mom, sister Shannen, and my nanna. The way the doctors and nurses had cared for him during his treatment had inspired me to choose a career in nursing. As a nursing intern, I had specifically asked to work with an oncologist and found myself drawn to the families with loved ones losing their battles with various types of cancer. I found that I wanted to ease the pain of my patients, as much as I wanted to take care of their families.

Once I had nothing left to do around the house, I sent a text to my best friend and coworker, Katie. She was Mr. Johnson's day nurse and I wanted her to be prepared before she came to work.

We worked five days per week, and each of us worked three twelve-hour shifts with Mr. Johnson. On our other two workdays, we were on call and filled in for other nurses who had the day off from their patients. That was how I'd lost two other patients in three weeks. I had been assigned to work at their homes while their regular nurses were off duty.

One of the patients who had passed away on my shift was a young man diagnosed with Non-Hodgkin's Lymphoma, and the other patient was a six-year-old girl with a brain tumor. Those particular deaths had hit me hard because both patients were so young and hadn't even begun to live their lives yet. I had attended both funerals, as I would Mr. Johnson's.

Katie texted back saying to call her if anything had changed before her shift, and she would come to help me. We were supportive of each other when it came to our jobs. Only another hospice nurse would know how much of an emotional toll the job took on us.

My boyfriend, Gary, couldn't understand why I loved my job so much when all of my patients were going to die. He thought I should work on helping to save people instead of caring for the dying, but he'd never had anyone close to him get sick or die, so he didn't grasp the helpless feelings one went through when a loved one was deathly ill.

During the last several months, Gary and I had hit a rough patch, and I was almost positive he was cheating on me again.

I'd been working the day shift until three months ago, when I was transferred to care for Mr. Johnson. Gary worked Monday through Friday, from eight to five, with weekends off. We barely spent time together anymore, and hadn't slept in the same bed together in months. I slept during the day while he was at work, and woke in time to get ready for work as he was heading off to bed.

I hated to admit, but living with Gary felt more like a convenience now, than because of love.

I headed back to check on Mr. Johnson. When I finished notating the changes in his condition, I asked Mrs. Johnson and Evie, "Can I get either of you a cup of hot tea or anything?"

Evie jumped quickly from her chair, shaking her head. "I can get it Teagan. Thank you, though." She turned to her mom. "I need a minute, Mom. I'll bring some tea when I come back." Evie exited the room with tears in her eyes.

As soon as she stepped into the hallway, she broke down crying. Mrs. Johnson stared down at her hands folded in her lap, and in a comforting gesture, I reached over and squeezed her hand. "Do you want to talk about anything Mrs. Johnson? Do you have any questions for me?"

Her tired eyes met mine and she began rambling. "It wasn't meant to end this way, Teagan. We were supposed to grow old together." Tears escaped her eyes and rolled down her cheeks.

I squeezed her hand again and listened as she told me how she and her husband met, fell in love, and married all within a year.

Evie came back into the room with a tray full of teacups and a teapot. She poured us each a cup, and I added sugar to mine. While Mrs. Johnson was sipping her tea, she reminisced with her daughter about their family life.

"Do you remember the camping trip we took to Patrick's Point in California, Evie? We froze our butts off. It rained all night, and we were in tents! That was the worst vacation ever. All we wanted to do was see the ocean." Her eyes lit up as she recalled the memory. Evie nodded along and giggled as they shared their favorite stories.

Just after six a.m., the Johnsons' three other children arrived after traveling together from Boulder. Once I'd given them an update on their father, I excused myself from the room. Gary should be awake by now, and getting ready for work. I scrolled through the contact list on my phone and called him.

"Hey," he said when he answered. His voice sounded strange with a slight hint of annoyance.

"Good morning, babe. How did you sleep?"

He sighed. "I slept well, actually. I was getting out of bed when you called. Look, Teagan, I need to get in the shower because I have to be to work early for a meeting. Can I speak to you later?"

"Um, sure . . . I guess. I wanted to call and say hi and that I missed you. My patient had a bad night and I just needed to hear your voice."

"Okay, sure. I'll talk to you later, then."

He ended the call without giving me a chance to say anything else. What happened here? He seemed distracted and blew me off when I needed him. I sat on the couch trying to figure out if I had done something wrong.

Well, something *other* than his usual complaints about me. Thoughts from earlier came back to me. Was he cheating again? Why did I continue to be his doormat and stay with him? *Because I have nowhere to go, no family nearby to help me, and I don't have the guts or confidence to leave.*

The rest of the morning, I weighed all of my options with Gary, and still ended up not knowing what to do.

Right before noon, Katie came in to relieve me. "Hey, Teags, how'd the rest of your shift go?"

"Fine, I suppose." I was a little grouchy after spending the morning stewing over my call to Gary, in addition to being worried about the Johnsons. I took out Mr. Johnson's chart and went over the changes in his condition I had noted throughout the night.

"All their kids are here now too, so you'll have a house full of people all day." I handed his chart over to her.

The family was gathered in the kitchen to make lunch, so I was able to sit and chat with Katie for a while.

"What's going on with you? You're acting strange," Katie said. "Are you upset about Mr. Johnson?"

"I think something's going on with Gary again. I called him

earlier and he acted like he didn't want to talk to me."

Katie's eyebrows rose and she looked away. "Maybe he was busy or something, Teagan."

I frowned at her. Was she defending him?

"Whatever. I'm going home. I'm tired and hungry. I'll be back tonight. Call me if anything changes with Mr. Johnson." I left Katie and went into the kitchen to say goodbye to the family.

I gathered my purse and headed out into the cold Denver winter to my poor old car. I stuck the key in the ignition of my Dodge Neon and prayed to the car gods the engine would start. Fortunately, it did. I shifted into gear and began my slow drive home.

On the way, I stopped at a fast food drive-thru and ordered a combo meal. When I pulled into the driveway at home, I noticed a pile of that stuff that looked like kitty litter covering the large oil spot in my parking space. I made a mental note to schedule an appointment to get the leak fixed on my next day off during the week.

I took my food, purse, and my soda and headed inside the house. I pulled out a barstool at the kitchen island and sat to eat my bacon cheeseburger and fries. On the countertop, I found a note from Gary. He was kind enough to say he would be home late and he'd appreciate it if I would find the time to get my car fixed so it would stop leaking all over his driveway.

My car was a high school graduation present from my parents, which I refused to part with. The odometer recently turned over one hundred sixty seven thousand miles. I took great care of it, but my Neon was going downhill fast.

Gary griped constantly about me spending money on repairs. Since he was an accountant, he handled all the finances and with my crazy work schedule, I was more than okay with the arrangement. Gary paid my bills on time, but I wished he would cut me a break when it came to my car.

When he'd asked me to move to Denver with him two years ago, I'd had to wait a few months to join him because I'd been under contract with my previous employer. By the time I arrived in Denver, he'd already bought the house we lived in. The only thing that was truly mine was my Neon.

As I ate my food, I called and made an appointment for the following day to drop my car off after my work shift ended. I dragged my tired butt up the stairs, stripped down, and pulled on flannel pants and a thermal shirt. As soon as my head hit the pillow, I was out cold.

My alarm went off at ten that night. I rolled over and slammed my hand down on the snooze button. After showering and dressing in clean scrubs, I twisted my long, wavy red hair in to a knot, and headed downstairs to find something to eat before I left for the Johnsons.

The house was dark inside, and I realized Gary still wasn't home. Although his note had said he'd be working late, he'd never worked this late before. I pulled my phone from my purse and since there were no messages, I called him.

"What's up, Teagan?" Again, he sounded like he didn't want to talk to me.

"Gary, what's going on? Where are you?"

He sighed and I waited for an explanation.

"I'm still at work. We have a big account that one of the idiot entry-level accountants messed up royally, and guess who gets to fix it? That would be me," he muttered.

"I'm sorry you're stuck fixing their mistake, Gary. I only wanted to check in and make sure everything is okay since you weren't home yet. Thanks for taking care of the oil on the driveway. I made an appointment tomorrow after work to drop my car off to be fixed."

I heard him typing frantically on his keyboard and wondered if he was paying any attention to what I was saying. "Gary, are you still there?"

"Look, Teagan, I don't have time for this. I need to fix this account and you're making me lose my concentration. I'll see you when I see you."

Wow . . . what a jerk! "Alright, I'll talk to you later. I love you," I said, to see if he'd return the sentiment.

"Whatever," he mumbled and then hung up the phone.

In my gut, I was certain there was something going on.

Once I arrived at the Johnsons' house, I let myself in and headed toward Mr. Johnson's room. I found Katie standing in the hallway outside his closed bedroom door, talking on her cell phone.

She smiled when she noticed me coming down the hallway then returned to her call. "I gotta go for now. Teagan is here. I'll be at your place later." She slipped her phone into the front pocket of her scrubs top. "Hey, girlie." She looped her arm through mine and we went to the living room. We sat on the couch and she filled me in on our patient.

After she left, I checked on Mr. Johnson. According to Katie, he'd taken another turn for the worse. He would pass away soon so I prepared myself to handle the grief the family would no doubt go through within the next several hours.

Around two in the morning, they decided to try to get some sleep. I settled into the recliner in Mr. Johnson's bedroom and pulled a book out of my purse to read. After an hour, the machines around Mr. Johnson began beeping indicating his heart had stopped. I tossed my book down and shut off the machine.

After I confirmed his death, I unhooked all the tubes and the IV then pushed the IV stand to the corner of the room. I said a quiet farewell to Mr. Johnson then went to wake his family.

Once everyone was awake and in the room saying their own goodbyes, I called the funeral home for them to pick up Mr. Johnson's body. I'd prearranged with Mrs. Johnson to call them if he passed on my shift, so they could spend time with him instead of having to make calls.

When I returned to the room, the family was standing in a circle around the bed, holding hands, and praying. Mrs. Johnson looked over and held her hand out for me to join them. I stepped between her and her daughter, Maddie, took their hands, and bowed my head right along with them. I felt the love from them filling the room.

While Mrs. Johnson led the prayer, my mind drifted back to my own family in Sacramento. I missed them terribly. I missed our bi-weekly get-togethers, the holidays, and I just missed . . . them. Over a year had passed since I'd been to Sacramento. Because Gary hadn't been able to take time off work, I had flown home alone as a surprise for Nanna's eightieth birthday and had been thrilled to spend two weeks with them. I needed to visit them again, soon.

Right after five, the funeral home van pulled away from the house. I met with everyone in the living room where Mrs. Johnson hugged me one last time.

"Thank you again for everything, Teagan. We never would've made it through this without you. Why don't you head on home, sweetie. There's no reason for you to stay until the end of your shift," she said.

I gave my condolences and left. My Neon started on the first try and I made my way home. *Thank you, car gods!*

The house was dark when I arrived, but it was almost time for Gary to get up and get ready for work. I wanted to speak to him face to face and see what was going on with him. I dropped my purse onto the couch and headed to our bedroom.

As I walked down the hallway, I heard the radio playing through the open door and knew Gary would be awake. Assuming he would be in the shower, I flipped on the light when I entered the bedroom.

What I saw in front of me would be burned in my brain forever. On the bed was my best friend, Katie, buck-naked and screwing my boyfriend.

I gasped and slapped my hand over my open mouth. I stood, staring at them, not knowing what to do. Katie turned and screamed as she jumped off Gary. She pulled the sheet over herself as Gary sat up to see what was going on.

"What are you doing here, Teagan?" Gary asked.

"The last time I checked, I lived here." I still didn't believe what I was seeing. "How could you two do this to me?"

Katie immediately began crying. She flung the sheet off, picked up her clothes off the floor, and put them back on. "Teags, I'm so sorry. It just happened," she cried.

Gary covered himself and then leaned back against the headboard. He was cheating on me in our bed! In our home! But instead of cheating with one of his coworkers like the last time, he was cheating on me with my supposed best friend. Why was he acting like this was no big deal?

Katie ran past me through the bedroom door, crying her apologies as she went by. I walked to the edge of the bed and glared down at Gary.

"What's going on, Gary?" I wasn't sure why I asked because I knew he was going to blame me like he always did.

He gawked at me with an indignant expression on his face. I hated that expression and it made me want to smack him upside his stupid-ass head.

"What does it look like to you, Teagan?"

I stepped closer.

He was relaxed and acting like what I'd just caught him doing was completely acceptable.

"It looks like my boyfriend of three wasted years, is screwing my best friend while I've been at work watching a man die and his family grieve!"

Rolling his eyes, Gary huffed out an annoyed breath and threw the sheet off himself. He picked up his underwear from the floor, shoved his feet through the leg holes, and pulled them on as he stood.

He brushed past me, went into the bathroom, and slammed the door. I stood in disbelief for a minute before I went and retrieved my luggage. I tossed my suitcases onto the bed, and started packing my clothes. I was filling another suitcase when Gary came out of the bathroom freshly showered for work.

"I don't know what I did to deserve this, Gary. If you wanted me to leave, you should have said so, and not screwed my best friend. I forgave you for the other women, but no more!" I was trying not to cry.

Besides my good friend, Reese, Katie was the only other true friend I had made since moving to Denver. Sure, I had acquaintances, but I hadn't really connected with anyone like I had with Katie and Reese.

Gary turned and looked me up and down as if I repulsed him. "You should be thinking about what you didn't do, Teagan. Look at you! You completely let yourself go and I don't even recognize you anymore." He smirked and brushed past me to his dresser for clothes.

I turned to face the full-length mirror on the closet door

and scrutinized my body. I hated to admit it, but he was right. I didn't know how much weight I'd gained, but each time I went shopping for clothes, I needed a bigger size. My five-foot-two frame was no longer visible. I didn't need to take my clothes off to see that.

Yet, I did. I yanked my shirt off over my head and dropped it to the floor then turned from side to side. My face was full, my cheekbones hidden. A layer of fat covered me giving me the dreaded muffin-top spilling over the waistband of my scrubs pants.

Gary stood behind me and glared over my shoulder, making eye contact with me in the mirror. "See what I mean? You make me sick," he muttered, and then he did the unthinkable. He gripped the fat around my middle with both hands and shook it.

I watched in disgust as my belly fat and boobs jiggled like Jell-O.

My heart pounded in my chest as my eyes filled with tears. My body trembled, but not from being hurt. I was downright mad and tired of his insults. Before I realized what I was doing, I turned and slapped him across the face. "You son of a bitch!" I seethed.

He touched his reddening cheek.

I attempted to slap his other cheek, but he grasped my arm, and we struggled.

He finally twisted me around and tossed me onto the bed then straddled me, with his hand gripping my neck. "You're a crazy bitch, Teagan! I want you out of here by the time I get home from work." Gary released his hold on me and shifted off the bed.

Gasping for air, I stared at the ceiling, wondering what had just happened. The fight drained out of me, and the tears flowed freely.

"Why are you doing this again, Gary? Why did you have to pick my best friend this time?" I sat up to find my shirt.

"Look at her, and look at you!" he yelled. "Besides, what difference would it make who it was? I can't stand to touch you anymore. You're never home because of your stupid job. You never want to go out to do anything because you're always tired. I can't live like that anymore, Teagan."

What he and Katie had done to me wasn't right. I'd lost my best friend. What was I going to do now? Where was I supposed to go? The only other person I knew here was Reese, but all I wanted was to go home to Sacramento. Unfortunately, there was no way my car would make the twelve hundred mile drive without a major overhaul.

I turned and stomped to the bathroom, locking the door behind me. I sat in there until I heard Gary leave for work. Once he was gone, I pulled all my dirty clothes out of the hamper and dropped them into the washer then finished packing up the rest of my clean clothes. *What am I going to do about a place to live?*

While I waited on my clothes to wash and dry, I gathered my personal items and packed them into a few boxes I found in the garage. Once my clothes were done, I packed them too then crammed all my belongings into my car.

I drove straight to the bank where my joint bank account with Gary was and withdrew the money from my last two paychecks, plus another thousand dollars from our savings. I had myself removed from the account and opened my own account.

From the bank, I drove around aimlessly and decided to rent a motel room for the time being. I pulled my car into the cheapest, but safest looking motel I saw and paid for a week in advance. I would give myself that time to figure out what to do.

Jeremy

March 2013

God, I hated hospitals. Yet, here I was, in the elevator headed to the maternity floor to see my sister. The halls smelled like antiseptic, and the lights were too bright.

I didn't know why I hated them, really. I'd been in the hospital once to have my appendix removed when I was ten. It hadn't been a traumatic experience or anything, so my dislike made no sense.

When the doors slid open, I stepped out onto the floor that housed the maternity wing and nursery. Across from the elevator was the visitors' waiting room. I checked it, but no one in my family was there. Shit. I didn't even know my sister's room number.

A cute blonde-haired chick with fake tits popping out of the V-neck of her scrubs top came bouncing through a door and nearly ran in to me. I grinned down at her, sneaking a peek over the rest of her body.

"You look lost. Are you here to visit someone?" she asked in a flirty tone. "Your wife maybe?" She blatantly checked my left hand for a wedding ring.

I shook my head and grinned. "No, no wife or girlfriend. My sister is here actually. She had a baby yesterday. Can you help me find her?"

I turned on a little charm, hoping she'd help me, and then maybe give me her number so we might hook up later.

"Sure thing, handsome. Follow me."

She turned and walked toward the nurses' station. She had a nice ass, and the sway of her hips made my dick twitch.

Damn, I desperately needed to get laid.

All of my go-to girls had boyfriends now, except Nicole who was completely off-limits to me after a run-in with my sister Zoey.

Nobody was more important to me than my family, and I would do anything for them. That included distancing myself from people who tried to hurt them.

She sat at the desk behind the nurses' station and asked, "What's your sister's name?" She batted her eyelashes and tapped the tip of her pen on the desk while she waited for my response.

"Zoey Tate." I leaned across the counter on my elbows and had a nice view down her shirt from that angle. She had a great rack. Not too big, not too small. Yet, definitely fake.

After a few mouse clicks, she scribbled something down on a piece of paper. "Your sister's in room 405, down the hall behind you, and to the left. This is my number. Call me sometime. My name's Cammie." She held the paper between two fingers.

I took the paper and shoved it in the front pocket of my jeans. "I'm Jeremy. What time are you off tonight, Cammie?"

She looked at her watch and smiled. "I'm off in an hour. Meet me here then?"

Hell yes. I thumped the top of the counter with my fingers. "See you in an hour."

Zoey's was the first room I came to when I made the left turn at the end of the hall. The door was open, and I walked in only to find the room empty of visitors. My sister was lying on her side, staring down in awe at the pink bundle beside her on the bed.

Her eyes shot up to mine when the bottom of my shoe squeaked on the floor. I stopped in my tracks, so I wouldn't do it again. "Sorry, Z, did I wake her?"

She shook her head after she checked Hannah. "I didn't think you were going to come see us, Jer. Do you want to hold her?" she asked quietly then motioned for me to come closer.

I walked over to the bed and stood, staring down at my new niece, Hannah. She was sleeping peacefully, so I didn't want to wake her by picking her up.

Zoey smirked. "Just pick her up you chicken-shit. She won't bite," she whispered.

I let out a quiet chuckle and slipped one hand under Hannah's body, and the other hand under her head and neck. I very carefully picked her up and cradled her against my chest. My tiny new niece was perfect.

"Hey, sweet pea," I said softly and kissed her on the head before making myself comfortable in the rocking chair near the bed. "Andy was right, Z. She does look exactly like you. Where is he anyway? I didn't think you'd be here alone."

A guilty expression washed over her face. "Um, he went to get me some real food. I can't eat any more hospital food—it tastes funny."

I stifled a laugh so I wouldn't wake Hannah. "That sounds about right."

My sister's aversion to anything out of a box or pre-made came from being neglected by her birth mother for the first eight years of her life, then spending the next six years in foster care before my parents adopted her.

"So, what do you think, Jer?" Zoey grinned at me expectantly then looked from me to Hannah and back.

"Think about what?" As soon as the words left my mouth, I figured out what she was asking me. "Not now, Zoey. I'll find the right girl when she comes along."

She was always bugging me about settling down. I was going to be the big 'three-oh' on my next birthday. Holy shit . . . thirty! *Fuck, I'm getting old.*

I looked back over at her. "Just because you found the love of your life, doesn't mean it's in the cards for the rest of us, Z."

She rolled her eyes at me like she always did when she thought I was being dumb. "Are you even trying to meet anyone?"

Ignoring her question, my gaze drifted back down to the baby in my arms. She was getting squirmy and let out an adorable whimper. I started to get up and take her back to my sister, but she quieted down and remained sleeping.

"I happen to have the phone number of a cute nurse I met when I got here."

Zoey perked up at my admission. "Oh yeah? What's her name, Jeremy?" she asked as she narrowed her eyes at me.

Shit . . . What the hell was her name again? Candy? Carrie? I had a sleeping baby in my arms; it's not like I could reach into my pocket to pull out the slip of paper she gave me.

"Uhh . . . shit. Okay, you got me. It begins with a C though. That I *do* remember."

She snorted and then winced. "Don't make me laugh asshat. I have staples in my gut."

I smiled back at her. "You did it to yourself, jerk, so don't blame me."

"What did you do to my wife?" Andy asked, strolling through the door carrying a plastic bag full of food containers.

Glancing up at him, he had his usual love-struck grin on his face.

"I didn't do a damn thing to her, bro. She's just being her usual, nosy-self and was teasing me."

When he reached Zoey's bedside, he leaned over to kiss her. "Hey, beautiful, I hope you're hungry."

He unpacked her dinner and set it on the table next to the bed.

The way they took care of each other and seemed to know exactly what to do for one another made me want to gag sometimes. They'd been through so much in the short time they'd been together, but they loved each other and now had a new baby girl. For some reason though, today, they didn't make me want to gag. Something had changed between them. They both seemed so content and happy. As if they were truly living the life they were supposed to.

"You hungry mate?" Andy asked me, thankfully breaking my train of thought. "There's more than enough food here."

"Nah, you two go ahead. I'll hold Sweet Pea so you can eat."

I still had about twenty minutes until I was supposed to meet what's-her-name, so I might as well stay put until then.

Hannah became restless again, so I stood and walked around the room with her. It settled her right down, so I swayed back and forth with her.

I watched as Andy hoovered his food down, while Zoey ate hers slowly and enjoyed every single bite. That dude packed away the food and never gained a pound. I didn't think he even worked out or anything. I didn't have that luxury. Jesus, I sounded like a bitch. What guy worried about their weight?

Oh, yes. That would be me.

"Jeremy has a date, baby. With a nurse he met when he got here. Can you believe it?" Zoey looked over and stuck out her tongue at me.

God, she was a brat sometimes.

Andy raised his eyebrows. "A date, huh? Like an actual date?" He stood from his chair and put his empty plate and fork back in the bag, then washed his hands.

I ignored them and rocked my niece. "Your parents are assholes, baby girl," I whispered in her ear.

"You'd better go, so you're not late for your date." Andy came over to get Hannah. "And quit teaching my girl bad words already. She's gonna learn enough of them from her mother."

"Hey! I'm sitting right here, you know?" Zoey said.

"Goodnight, Sweet Pea." I kissed her on the head again then handed Andy's daughter to him.

With a few minutes to kill, I pulled the paper out of my pocket and unfolded it. "Her name is Cammie."

Zoey smirked at me again. "You're lucky she wrote it down for you."

I flipped her off and watched as Andy kicked off his shoes and eased onto the bed. He cradled Hannah in his arms protectively and once he settled next to Zoey, he brushed her hair back over her shoulder.

They were the perfect family, and for once in my life, I thought maybe my little sister was right about me settling down.

Shit! I needed to get the hell outta here. These two were rubbing off on me.

"I'd better go meet *Cammie,*" I said, pointing to Cammie's name and phone number on the paper she'd given me.

Quickly, I walked over and shook Andy's hand. "Congratulations, man."

I leaned across the bed and kissed my sister on the cheek. "Good job cooking that baby, Z. She's beautiful."

"Thanks, Jer. Let me know how your date goes." She air-quoted the word "date" and playfully smacked my cheek, scrunching her nose up at me.

"Smartass," I muttered and straightened to leave.

"Manwhore," she retorted.

Andy just sat with his eyes fixed on Hannah.

We said our goodbyes and I gave one last kiss to Sweet Pea then headed out to the nurses' station.

On the way there, I thought about Z calling me a manwhore. I hated that my family assumed the worst of me when it came to women. Little did they know, I'd only been with four women in the last five years. I wasn't a manwhore; I just had female friends with benefits.

I found Cammie waiting for me with her purse slung over her shoulder.

"I was wondering if you forgot about me," she said.

"Nah, I was holding my niece so my sister and brother-in-law could eat their dinner. You ready?"

I followed Cammie to the elevator and down to the first floor.

"So, where to Jeremy?" she asked when we reached the parking garage.

"That depends on what you have in mind." I was planning on asking her if she wanted to go home and change so I could take her out and get to know her a bit when she turned, and dragged me around the corner behind a concrete support wall. I pushed her farther into the corner where nobody would see us if they happened to walk past. By the time I backed her against the wall, my pants were undone, and she was yanking them and my boxers down my legs. Once they were at my knees, she grabbed my dick and pumped her hand up and down, getting straight to business.

Apparently, she wasn't expecting anything but a quick fuck from me. I wasn't usually a one-night stand kind of guy, but I was horny as hell so I was going to make an exception tonight.

I let my mind drift back to the task at hand, kissed her neck, and slipped my hand up her shirt to check out that fake rack of hers. I reached around and undid her bra, then pulled up her shirt to bury my face between her tits.

Briefly, I paid attention to her nipples, and then pulled her pants and lacey panties down. I ran my hand down between her legs, sliding my fingers through her wetness. She was ready to roll and let out a throaty moan when my fingers made contact with her clit.

"You need to get inside me right now," she said as she exhaled. "I'm on the pill, hurry."

"Condom," I muttered, reaching into my pants pocket to pull out my wallet. No condom, no sex. That was my cardinal rule, and I never, ever broke it.

I ripped open the package and rolled the condom down over my dick. Cammie kicked her pants and underwear off one leg, and I hoisted her up against the wall. She wrapped her legs around my hips.

"Fuck me hard," she commanded as I centered against her.

With one swift push, I slammed inside her. "Aghh, shit . . ." I groaned. She was hot and tight, and had said to fuck her hard, so I pulled my hips back and rammed into her again. With her body pinned between the wall and me, she was making these sexy grunting noises each time I pounded into her, and I could feel her tightening around my dick.

"Ohh, right there, Jeremy. Keep doing that. Mmm, almost there," she murmured against my neck.

Her back arched away from the wall and her inner muscles clenched around my dick. "Oh, that's good . . . it feels so good," she whispered as she rode out her orgasm.

The tension in my body increased, my dick thickened, getting harder and more sensitive the deeper I drove into her. My thigh muscles burned and constricted with each movement and my brain focused on the contact of where our bodies joined. The pressure built up in my balls, they tightened then released as I came. I gave two final thrusts until the head of my dick was too sensitive and I had to stop. The rush of blood flowing back to the rest of my body made me hot and the tension quickly dissipated. *God, it's been too long . . .*

Taking in several ragged breaths, I kept her against the wall for another moment while my body relaxed from the exertion. Once I pulled out of her, I helped her get her feet back on the ground then let go of her. I slid the condom off and set it aside while I pulled up my boxers and pants.

Cammie pulled her pants back on and re-hooked her bra. She looked at me with no hint of embarrassment in her expression. "That was fun. Call me, and we can do it again sometime."

She was going to make this easy on me. "Yeah, I definitely will. It was um . . . nice meeting you, Cammie."

She picked up her purse, slung it over her shoulder and left. I picked up the used condom and wrapper then tossed them into the trash.

The strangest feeling washed over me when I sat in my car, and for the first time in my life, I felt like I needed something more. I quickly brushed the feeling away and drove home.

April 2013

Almost every day at lunchtime after I cleaned up, I grabbed my lunch from the break room fridge then headed up the stairs to my sister's temporary apartment above the shop. Spending time with Zoey and Hannah when Andy couldn't make it home for lunch was one of my new favorite things to do.

Today, only halfway up the stairs, I could hear Hannah crying. I knocked, and Zoey opened the door a few minutes later while trying to calm a now screaming Hannah. She looked like she was about to cry, so I stepped inside the apartment and set my lunch on the table.

I turned back to my sister. "Let me try, Z," I said calmly, reaching out to take my niece.

"I've tried everything, Jer. Feeding her, changing her diaper, singing to her—nothing works. What am I doing wrong?" Her bottom lip quivered slightly as she stared at the screaming baby in my arms.

"Sounds like you've done everything you're supposed to, Z. It's just one of those things. I've got her now."

I hated seeing her stressed out, and with Andy working two jobs and overseeing their apartment renovation, he wasn't able to come home often throughout the day. Z had gone through a lot the last few years so I felt it was my brotherly duty to do whatever I needed to help her.

Her ex-husband, Rob, had accidentally killed himself by getting high and setting a fire in the back of the store Zoey and Andy owned. Although he was no longer a threat to her, she was my only sister, and I was very protective of her, especially now that she had a baby. Besides, protecting her was second nature to me and would always be part of my job.

She took Hannah's hand in hers and kissed it as I cradled her to my chest. "Hey Sweet Pea, quiet down for Uncle Jeremy," I said soothingly in her little ear. She pressed her soft forehead against my neck, taking in a deep breath. A wave of relief washed over Z's face, but she was completely frazzled. "Zoey, I'll take care of her. Go take a hot shower or something."

She stepped closer to me and threw her arms around my waist, squeezing me tight.

I hugged her back one-armed and patted her on the shoulder.

"Thank you, Jer." She jogged down the hallway to her room, grabbed some clean clothes, and shut herself in the bathroom.

I sat down at the kitchen table and ate my lunch one-handed while I rocked my niece to sleep. At just over a month old, she still looked exactly like my sister.

I felt bad because Z was having a shitty day so I sent Andy a text.

Z's having a bad day. I got Hannah to sleep and sent Z to the shower. I can cover your job at the shop. Get home ASAP.

Not even five minutes later, he came through the door of the apartment. He stopped when he saw me sitting at the table. "Where is Zoey? Is she alright?" He scanned the apartment for her.

"She's still in the shower. I'll take care of Sweet Pea. You go check on Z."

"Thanks, mate."

Andy walked over, kissed Hannah, and headed down the hallway. He knocked on the bathroom door and a moment later, he went in and closed the door behind him.

I really liked Andy. He was good to my sister and would do anything for her and my family.

He'd screwed up royally last summer when he'd left Zoey after freaking out over some bad news he'd received. They had worked everything out, got married, and were living the life they'd always dreamed of.

I felt a minor pang of jealousy shoot through my gut. Not in a bad way—I was happy for them. But ever since noticing at the hospital how perfect they were for each other, and now seeing every day how happy they were, I'd realized spending most of my free time hanging out with my friends was getting old. And when I wasn't with them or my family, I was at work.

Although I hadn't dated anyone in a few years, I had decided to give it another shot. No more friends with benefits for me. It was time to get serious. So a few days after I'd hooked up with Cammie in the parking garage of the hospital, I'd asked her out on an actual date.

Zoey and Andy came into the kitchen as I was putting my lunch dishes back in my lunchbox. She looked much better and Andy had changed out of his work clothes. I didn't dare ask why his hair was wet though because I didn't need to know what had gone on after he went in to see my sister. The big grins on both their faces told me way more than I wanted to know as it was.

I stood and handed Hannah off to Andy.

"Thanks, mate. I appreciate your text and watching out for my girls when I can't."

I nodded and clapped him on the back. "Anytime, man."

He dipped his head and kissed Hannah on the top of her small head. "Hey beautiful girl, Daddy missed you today," he whispered.

I left them to their family moment and returned to work. Once I tightened some bolts and cleaned up the import car Andy had been working on when I'd texted him, I was done for the day.

Thank God it was Friday—MMA night at the bar with the guys. I hadn't been to MMA night since I'd started dating Cammie and I was ready for a night with no female drama. There was probably going to be enough of it on Sunday when I took Cammie to meet my family for the first time.

Two days later, as Cammie and I arrived at my parents' house for dinner, I noticed Noah and his wife, Jess, had parked right behind us. We got out and waited for them.

"Hey, bro," I said, smacking Noah on the back. "This is Cammie. Cammie, this is my brother Noah, and his wife Jess."

Cammie shook their hands, and mumbled "hello" to them.

Noah looked Cammie and I over, and I could tell he was holding back a smirk.

Jess came over and hugged me, and Cammie glared at us.

What the hell was that about?

"What are we gonna do with you Jeremy James?" Jess whispered into my ear. "That girl is going to be nothing but trouble."

In my heart, I knew Jess was right. But, we were already at my parents' house so it was too late to turn back now.

I threw my arm over Jess's shoulder, grabbed Cammie's hand, and escorted them up the sidewalk.

Jess was super sweet. She never cussed, and was a perfect angel according to my brother.

As soon as we walked in the door, every female in the house descended upon Cammie and me.

Once she'd met all the women, I introduced her to my

parents, my brothers Jason and Adam, and Andy.

Throughout dinner, Cammie picked at her food, complaining because it was "too fattening" and she didn't really like Mexican food.

My mom noticed, but didn't say anything. All the women in the family tried to make Cammie feel welcome, but the constant scowl on her face showed that it wasn't working.

Finally, after dinner, I cornered Cammie when she came out of the bathroom. "What's the problem, Cammie? I brought you here to meet my family and you're being rude."

She huffed. "They're making me uncomfortable asking all those questions about me. Make them stop!"

Was she serious? "Cammie, they're trying to get to know you. That's what people do, they ask questions."

"Please take me home. I don't want to be here anymore."

Because I didn't want my family to witness an argument between us, we said our hasty goodbyes and left. I dropped Cammie off at her apartment and went home. I had a lot of thinking to do, and I needed space from her.

It was time for me to figure my shit out.

3

Teagan

May 2013

"Come on, Teagan," Reese growled in my ear as he squatted on the mat next to me. "Ten more, then you're done."

I was close to completing a series of crunches that would end my workout, but I didn't know if I had *two* more crunches in me, let alone ten. My stomach muscles were on fire. My roomie must be trying to kill me.

After my weeklong motel stay, I'd gone straight to the only friend I had left in Denver. Reese.

Once I'd told him what Gary and Katie had done, he'd insisted I move in with him. I didn't hesitate. I couldn't afford to rent my own place and had nowhere else to go.

We'd made a pact then to get me back into shape—the shape I was in when I moved to Denver. He'd taken me quite literally when I'd told him to kick my ass in the gym. Not only did he create an exercise regimen and hold me to it, he'd outlined a diet, too. No more fast food. No more being lazy. But most of all, no more excuses. Now I was down twenty pounds, with only fifteen left to lose.

This was my life, and I was done standing in my own way of living it. I was getting *me* back!

Reese chanted the final countdown for me, and the second I finished the last miserable crunch I threw myself backward onto the mat to let the burn in my muscles subside. I slowed my breathing and relaxed for a few minutes.

"I hate you," I muttered to Reese as he threw a towel at me. I didn't have the energy to block it or catch it, so it landed on my face.

"Honey, you love me and you know it, don't try to lie." He smirked, grabbed my hand, and pulled me up from the mat.

Reese was dressed in his black shorts and T-shirt with the gym's name stretched across his muscled chest, and I couldn't help but notice all the women around us take notice. Too bad for those women that he batted for the other team. *Great news for the other team, though.*

I laughed as my body trembled from the vigorous workout he had put me through for the last hour and a half.

"You're right, I do love you. I'm gonna hit the showers. I'll see ya at home tonight," I said, and made my way to the locker room for a shower. Once I was dressed in my scrubs and had my hair twisted back in a knot, I headed to work in my Neon.

After my shift ended, I went home, got ready for bed, and crawled in next to Reese. His apartment had only one bedroom, so we'd decided to share rather than take turns sleeping on the couch. With his being gay and us being such good friends, our sleeping arrangement was like a slumber party. Some nights we'd watch movies or crazy videos on YouTube, eat popcorn in bed, or gossip about men.

To anyone else, our relationship might have seemed odd, but it worked perfectly for us. Reese called me his "snuggle buddy" which I thought was hilarious. There was only *one* issue with our sleeping situation.

"Reese, if I didn't know any better, I'd say you have feelings for me," I teased one day as his morning wood pressed against the back of my thigh. I wiggled my hips, so he'd know what I meant.

Reese laughed quietly and moved back. "No offense sweetie, but *Reese junior* hasn't seen a vajayjay since the day I lost my virginity twelve years ago. Pretty much guaranteed he'll never see another because that one terrified him."

Later, after Reese had gone to work, I was in the kitchen cooking an egg white omelet when my cell rang with "Mama," by Flyleaf. I answered, "Mornin,' Mama, how are you?

"Hi, honey," she said, her voice unsteady as she spoke. "I'm not doing so well this morning. I'm afraid I have some upsetting news."

"Mama, is it Dad?" I feared the day I would get the call that my dad's cancer had come back.

"Teagan, Dad's fine." She took a breath and let it out. "It's Nanna. She's had a stroke."

Oh God, no. Not Nanna. I was very close with her. My mom had even named me after her. Dread spread like wildfire through my body, and I swallowed around the lump in my throat.

"Is she alive?" I asked hesitantly, squeezing my eyes shut until she responded. I would never forgive myself if she passed away without me there to say goodbye first.

"Yes she is, honey. They're running tests right now to see how bad it is. She is conscious, but she's very confused. Her right side is numb, and she's having a hard time speaking."

"Mama, as soon as I can get my things together I'm coming home. Will you please keep me updated? I'm going to pack now."

She promised to keep me informed on Nanna's tests and any changes in her condition. I hoped I would get to see her one last time if this were the end.

I shoveled in my breakfast and took a quick shower. Then I called my job, to quit. With the type of work I did, they were very understanding about why I needed to go home. After I packed, I drove to the gym to say goodbye to Reese in person.

When I entered the gym, Reese excused himself from the client he was working with and jogged over to me. With the way his brows furrowed and his face paled, he knew something wasn't right with me.

"Teagan, what happened? What's wrong?"

"It's Nanna. She's had a stroke. I'm going home, Reese, but I needed to see you and tell you goodbye." I felt the tears prick my eyes.

He hugged me tightly. "Oh sweetie, I'm so sorry about Nanna. I'm going to miss you so much," he said sadly. "But, you need to go and be with your family."

I nodded and wiped the tears off my face. "I love you, Reese. Thank you for everything. I promise to keep in touch, and you better come visit me."

"I definitely will, Sweets. I worked damn hard for this body and I'm tired of covering it up during the winter. It could benefit even more from some of that Cali sun."

Two nights later, I pulled in my parents' driveway. I'd been keeping in touch with my mom during the trip. Nanna was still stable and would be released from the hospital the next day. Really, nothing could be done for her condition with the exception of physical therapy and speech therapy. Fortunately, she lived in a retirement facility with round the clock medical staff, so we were all comforted to know she would be looked after constantly and would start her therapy once she returned.

I hopped out of my car and ran up the sidewalk to the door of my childhood home. The door flew open as I reached for the knob, and my dad was standing there waiting for me.

"Teagan's home!" he called excitedly over his shoulder.

"Dad!" I was so happy to see him. He looked perfect and healthy.

He pulled me into a hug, and my mom and sister Shannen joined us. I'd missed them all so much.

During dinner, we discussed Nanna's prognosis, and I finally told my family about Gary and Katie. They had known he'd done something unforgivable, but I hadn't told them the details. I didn't tell them about the other women, though, because I was ashamed of how I'd forgiven him too many times before Katie.

When the hospital released Nanna to the retirement home, I helped her settle back in, but I had ulterior motives. I wanted to make sure the staff caring for her was competent. I was impressed with what I saw, so I felt better about leaving her there.

After she was comfortable, I sat down on the chair next to her bed to visit with her. "Nanna, it's Teagan, can you hear me?"

Her green eyes were vacant, but suddenly, she blinked and her mouth moved. "P. .p. .peach . . . Peaches?" she said as she recognized me. She had a difficult time speaking because the stroke had paralyzed the right side of her body.

"Yes, Nanna," I giggled at my nickname. "It's me, Peaches." I squeezed her hand and thought back to when I was small, and I'd asked her why she called me Peaches.

She'd said, "You have peaches and cream skin. Anytime you get worked up about something or embarrassed, your skin blushes to the color of a sweet, ripe peach. A little peachy, a little red."

Knowing Nanna should rest and save her strength, I grabbed her book of poetry by Yeats. The volume was so tattered and worn, I had no doubt she'd read it hundreds of times.

I read to her until she fell in to a deep sleep.

June 2013

I'd been living in California for a while now and had found a great job at one of the local hospitals. Since I was an RN, I could work almost anywhere in the hospital. The Emergency Room was where I seemed to be scheduled most of the time. Today was absolutely insane. We had patients with bogus illnesses, stabbings, a shooting, and everything else imaginable.

We even had to remove a small rock from a four year old's nose. I wished I could say this was the only time I'd ever seen such a thing. But it wasn't. And probably wouldn't be the last either. Kids put strange crap up their noses. A lot.

Thankfully, my lunch break finally came around because I was starving. I took my place at the end of the line of nurses to wait for my turn to clock out. I didn't know all of the nurses, but I had made good friends with some who had worked at the hospital for years and they had taken me under their wing.

"Hey, Teagan!" My friend Natalie called from the line behind me.

"Nat, what's up?"

"Save me a seat!"

I gave her a thumbs up. Once I clocked out, I found my lunch in the fridge and took a seat at one of the tables. I pulled my salad and grilled chicken out of my lunch bag, then tossed them together with salad dressing. I pushed my lunch bag across the table to hold the seat for Nat.

Eventually she dropped down on the chair across from me. "Fuck me running," she groaned as she laid her forehead down on the table. She raised her head a few inches then dropped it back down with a thump.

I chuckled and patted her on the back. "Bad day, Nat?"

She sat upright and scrubbed her hands over her face. "You could say that. I swear, if one more kid pukes on me, I'm gonna go hide in the janitors' closet and curl up in the fetal position on the floor. I've changed my scrubs three times today."

Oh, crap that sucks. There was nothing worse than being puked on. Okay, there were worse things, but that was the most common occurrence for the nurses in the pediatrics unit. I shook my head and laughed. "Sorry, Nat, might I suggest changing in to a Hazmat suit?" She didn't laugh but glared at me instead. I smiled back at her.

"Alright ladies, I don't know about the rest of you, but I have had a shit day," Nat whined to the other nurses at the table. "I am ready to go out for a drink after work. Who's coming with me?"

Nat and I laughed when all five groaned and raised their hands. Everyone seemed to be having a crap day except me. That worried me, because it meant I was either going to be puked on, or get a horrible patient before my shift ended.

Everyone agreed to meet after work and head over to Dub's Sports Bar for a drink. I questioned aloud why seven women would be going to a sports bar. One of the other nurses, Rhonda, spoke up.

"Oh, girl, there are always some sexy men at that bar. I'm thinking about becoming a cougar if I can find me a fresh piece of young-man ass tonight!" Rhonda went on and on about what she was looking for in her future boy-toy.

It took me a minute to figure out she was describing a famous actor. "Rhonda, you do realize Brad Pitt is actually *older* than you, right?" I asked.

She laughed. "Honey, I know. If I found a Brad Pitt look-a-like from the *Thelma and Louise* movie, I'd kidnap his hot, little ass and keep him in my basement to service me whenever I saw fit!"

All the girls around the table agreed in unison that it was a grand idea. I laughed and shook my head. Brad Pitt, *so* not my type.

We chatted to finalize our plans while we finished our lunches then headed back to our work areas.

The rest of the day, I ran my butt off in the ER. Thirty minutes prior to my shift ending, Jackie, my other good friend, called me over.

"Can you help the doctor over in bed three, Teagan? I know you're off duty soon, but it's a simple suture you can assist with," she said. "I'm already in a shitty mood and don't want to deal with Dr. Asshole again today." Then she smiled as she wiggled her eyebrows and pushed me toward bed three. "The patient is hot as hell!" She leaned in and whispered, "Move your ass girl, get in there and help that fine man!"

"I'm on it, Jackie. Thanks for giving me something quick."

When I entered the exam room, I found a very good-looking man holding a white, bloodstained towel to his forehead. Quickly, I washed my hands and retrieved a pair of medical gloves from the box.

The man was casually resting back on the exam table as if being there was no big deal. In fact, he appeared to be sleeping. He was wearing a dark blue work uniform so he must have been hurt on the job.

"Hey there," I said quietly, stepping closer to him, and pulling my gloves on. "Looks like you have yourself a nasty cut from the amount of blood on that towel."

His body jerked slightly as if I'd startled him. He opened his eyes slowly and rotated his head to face me. *Holy crap, he is gorgeous.* I stood in awe for a moment and stared at him.

The funny thing was, he was staring back at me. *Interesting . . .*

Our stare-a-thon lasted for several long seconds before he swallowed and let out a quiet laugh. "Please don't tell me I got the only nurse in the entire building who's afraid of a little blood."

Okay, so maybe he *wasn't* staring at me and I imagined the whole thing. This man was so out of my league, but a girl could dream. Even a girl with a few extra pounds left to lose.

I laughed with him so he didn't think I was a freak for gawking at him. "No, not me. Definitely not afraid of blood," I replied. "Sit up and let's see what's going on under that towel."

He'd barely pulled off the towel before a fresh trail of blood ran down his face.

"Whoa, better put that back on and keep pressure on it until I'm ready," I said. Crap, he was bleeding a lot. I picked up a square package from the tray, ripped it open, and pulled out the sterile gauze. "When I say go, pull the towel off and I'll put this gauze pad on it. Then we'll get it cleaned off and see what we're dealing with."

"Ready when you are, Red," he teased.

Yeah, like I'd never heard *that* before. Freaking red hair! It was a curse and a blessing.

The towel he was holding against his forehead had come unfolded to cover half of his face, but from what I'd seen of my patient, he had a nice smile.

"One, two, three, go!" I counted rapidly while we both laughed. He yanked off the towel, and I pressed the gauze over the cut as more blood ran down his face. I held the gauze against his forehead with more pressure to stop the blood flow.

"What exactly happened to you?" I asked him while I put my other hand on the back of his head to hold him steady. *He has nice hair.*

"I got in a fight with the exhaust system of a car and lost," he joked and relaxed somewhat. He had long thick eyelashes that rested against the skin of his face when he closed his eyes. *Nice.*

"Are you having any pain in your head, other than the cut?"

"Nope, no pain," he replied. "I didn't even want to come

here, but I was forced to since it's work comp. I was going to slap a Band-Aid or two on it and call it good."

He was getting fidgety, and seemed uneasy for some reason, so I continued my questions trying to take his mind off his injury. He'd been joking with me, so I figured it was safe to tease him a bit.

"Well, I didn't see any of your brain coming out, but I think it's a pretty safe bet you'll need a few stitches," I said.

He turned to face me so abruptly, it caught me off guard, and I almost took the pressure off his cut.

"Stitches? Seriously? Fuck me," he muttered.

I gasped and let out a quiet giggle at his reaction.

He looked mortified. "Oh, I'm so sorry," he said. "I didn't mean to cuss in front of you."

I laughed at his sincerity. He really seemed to feel bad for his outburst and rubbed his palms up and down his thighs like he was nervous. What was with this guy?

"Don't apologize. You wouldn't believe what I hear on a daily basis in this place. Let's check your cut again. The doctor will be back in a few minutes to stitch you up, but in the meantime, let me get it cleaned up for you."

I pulled the gauze back and the blood had slowed enough, so it was no longer gushing. "So, you're a mechanic then?" I asked, remembering what he'd said caused the injury.

He nodded, and I noticed he was pale. He had gorgeous olive colored skin, so his paleness was quite obvious. He also had the most beautiful blue-gray eyes I'd ever seen. "Are you sure you're okay? You're looking kind of pale."

He stared at me. "I'm fine. I hate hospitals."

I washed the laceration and was finishing when Dr. Robinson came in to do the stitches. He was a complete jerk and all the nurses hated him because he frequently berated them in front of staff and patients. Dr. Asshole was definitely a fitting nickname.

The doctor injected a local anesthetic to numb the area around the cut while I assisted with the procedure. As soon as the stitches were in, Dr. Robinson tossed his instruments and used gloves down on the tray.

"Clean this mess and get the room ready for the next patient," he muttered and hurried from the room. He didn't look me in the eyes once the entire time he was in the room barking orders at me.

"Asshole," I smirked.

I turned back to find my patient leaning up on his elbows staring at me with a sexy grin on his face. I laughed at having been caught calling the doctor an asshole, but knowing he thought it was funny, I decided I didn't feel bad about it.

"Well, he *is* an asshole!" I whispered.

"Yes, I can see that. Are we finished here? I need to be someplace," he said, his tone a bit brusque.

Inwardly, I flinched remembering the way Gary often spoke to me. He wanted out of here, and I didn't want to keep him from where he was supposed to be. However, he was a mess. "Almost. I need to clean you up first because you're covered in blood. You can't leave here looking like the victim of a slasher movie."

He chuckled. "Point taken."

As I cleaned the dried blood off his face, he closed his eyes and relaxed. Occasionally, he let out a quiet moan that was barely audible in the noisy ER. While I worked, he sat up abruptly and leaned forward, resting his elbows on his thighs.

"Are you sure you're okay?" He was acting strangely and seemed almost . . . embarrassed?

"Positive, I swear. I uh . . . just needed to move. That's all."

I shook my head and cleaned the blood off his cheek and jawline. "You really bled like crazy. Head wounds are always bleeders though. It went down your shirt. Do you want to clean it off before you leave?"

I definitely wasn't sticking my hand down his shirt. Although, he was *really* good looking and I wouldn't mind seeing what was underneath it. *Out of your league, girl . . . Get it together.*

"Actually, I probably should clean it off. If my mom sees me like this when I go back to work, she'll go ape-shit and think I'm dying."

"You work with your mom, and you're a mechanic?"

"I work at my family's business. She might be there when I go back to get my car. She works in the office, but was gone when I left. I'm not sure if she even knows what happened yet."

"Ahh, I see. Yes, we do not want to scare Mom. That never ends well."

He unbuttoned his shirt and slipped it off. Instead of letting it drop to the exam table behind him, he wadded it in a ball and set it on his lap. He was wearing a black tank top underneath. The blood had gone down the front of his shirt onto his chest, and had seeped over his shoulder and down his back.

"Well, looks like you get to clean the front, and I'll get your back since you can't see it," I said, and grabbed us each a new wet wipe.

I took notice of how lean and muscular he was. He wasn't a *big* guy, but he definitely took care of himself physically. At least that was what I could tell by the part of him not covered by his tank top and work pants.

I wonder if he has a girlfriend. Jesus, Teagan, you have no business thinking about this guy like that. He probably has a supermodel for a girlfriend. Why would he want you?

Tears pricked my eyes and I shook the self-demeaning thoughts from my head, refocusing on my job. "You really did a number on yourself. The blood ran down under your shirt, so I need to lift the back. Do you mind?"

He laughed nervously and pulled the neck of his tank away from his skin. "Um, it's down the front too."

In one swift movement, he pulled his tank top off and set it on his lap with his other shirt.

As I was wiping the blood from his back, I found even his back and shoulders were ripped with muscles. I didn't dare look at the front of him. He had the most amazing olive colored skin and I couldn't get over his skin and blue-gray eyes combo. And his hair! Dark brown, short on the sides and long on top. I bet he has great bed-head and after sex hair.

Did I really just think that? Either way, it was hot and something I'd never see for myself.

Most men his age, which I guessed was close to my age,

had at least one tattoo. Not this guy though. There was not a drop of ink on him.

After I finished cleaning his back, I stepped in front of him to make sure he'd washed all the blood off. He did a good job getting it off his chest, but had missed a few spots on his neck.

I reached up and gently cleaned the blood from his neck. "You missed a spot," I said softly, completely mesmerized after finally getting a good, long look at him.

He closed his eyes as I wiped away the blood, and I heard another rumble escape him. His body tensed, his gorgeous eyes blinked open meeting mine, and my hand froze in place on his neck. He slowly let out a breath and relaxed.

Holy crap, was it *me* causing him to make those incredibly sexy noises? Was he feeling what I was feeling? There was no way this man would want me.

We stared at each other without saying anything. My hand was still resting on him, but I noticed my fingertips were curling back and forth, lightly kneading his neck.

"You have pretty eyes," I blurted out, breaking the awkward silence. *Well, that was embarrassing!* I knew my traitorous cheeks flushed red because I felt them getting warm.

"I love your hair, and the flush on your pretty face," he replied in a hushed tone. He touched my face, running the back of his fingers delicately over my cheekbone.

My eyes instinctively closed when I pressed my cheek against his hand. *How long had it been since a man had touched me like this? And why did it have to be this guy?* A moment later, I felt the absence of his warm hand. I opened my eyes and found he had folded his hands together on his lap, probably regretting his words to someone who was clearly not his type.

"Wow. I am really sorry about that," he said as his own cheeks flushed. "I don't know what's wrong with me. Maybe I did get knocked in the head harder than I thought." He ran his fingers through his dark hair.

Jackie came into the room. "Hey, girl, are you finished in here, or do you need some help?"

When I realized I was leaning against his legs, I stepped

back and looked away from the amazing, sexy man who I would never see again. "Uh, yeah," I mumbled to Jackie. "I mean no, I'm finished. I don't need help."

Not with work anyway, but I wondered if I needed mental help. This guy was turning me in to a mumbling idiot. *What floor is the psych ward on? I can't remember . . .*

Jackie's eyebrows rose as she looked between my patient and me. I noticed the smirk on her face before she turned and left the exam room. I turned back to him and found him grinning at me.

Remembering what I was supposed to be doing, I applied a dab of antibiotic cream to the gash and put a small piece of gauze and tape over it to keep out germs. I gathered the empty gauze packages and tossed them into the trash along with my gloves. I dropped a few supplies he would need into a small bag for him. By the time I turned around, he was putting his tank back on. *Bummer.*

"Thanks for um . . . taking good care of me," he said, slipping his toned arms into his work shirt. "I really appreciate it."

"No problem. It was my pleasure." And it really, truly was. "Promise me you won't fight with any more cars, okay?"

He laughed and gave me a gorgeous smile. "I'll try, but that's not something I can promise with my profession."

He stood and looked at me again without saying anything. Although I didn't know him, I felt he was acting unusually. "Did someone come here with you? I'm not sure you should be driving. You seem a little out of it still."

He nodded. "Yeah, thanks. My brother-in-law is in the waiting room. Besides, I'm quite sure now my head injury is not the problem."

What did he mean?

He continued smiling, not taking his eyes off me.

"Okay, then. Well, good luck with your head. Keep it clean and use antibiotic cream and the bandages I gave you over it for today so it doesn't get infected. Keep it dry after that—no getting it wet in the shower or anything—for forty-eight hours. Make an appointment with your doctor to have your stitches removed in about a week."

He took the bag from my hand. "Thank you, again." He didn't make a move to leave. He stood staring at me with an odd expression on his face.

"Let me walk you out to your brother-in-law so I can speak to him." I wanted to make sure someone knew to keep an eye on him, just in case.

He didn't question me and obediently followed me out to the waiting room. I noticed another man who wore a uniform identical to my patient's and walked toward him.

The man stood when he saw us and headed in our direction. *Holy crap, he's huge.* He towered over me by at least a foot, and he was easily as good looking as my sexy patient.

The two men stood next to each other waiting for me to speak, while all I wanted to do was pull out my cell and snap a picture of them so I'd remember what they looked like.

"Are you with this guy?" I asked the taller, gorgeous blue-eyed man.

"Yeah, unfortunately I am. Is he gonna live?" His blue eyes sparkled in amusement.

Oh, he has an accent. Maybe he's from Australia or New Zealand. I could never tell the difference because I hadn't been around many people from either country.

I smiled. "Yes, I do believe he will. He did take quite the knock to the head and needed stitches. Can you keep an eye on him or let his family know to keep an eye on him after he goes home?"

"Oh, I am sure he can find someone to take care of him," Mr. Accent said as a sly grin eased over his face. He looked back and forth between my patient and me, and I wondered if he could tell something had transpired between us in the ER.

"Thanks a lot, asshole," my sexy patient muttered, clapping Mr. Accent on the back rather roughly. He seemed embarrassed by what Mr. Accent had said.

"Sorry about my brother-in-law. He's an ass. Don't mind him," he said dryly.

I laughed at the two men in front of me as they bantered back and forth. I didn't see a shop logo on their uniforms so I wouldn't be able to find out where they worked. *Crap.* I glanced at the clock on the wall—almost five fifteen.

"Well guys, my shift is over, so I need to get out of here. I hope your head heals quickly, and remember what I said—no more fighting with cars."

"No promises. Thanks again," patient-guy said.

I watched as they turned around and walked their fine asses through the emergency room doors. As soon as they were out of sight, I jogged back to the nurses' area and clocked out, then found Jackie and Nat waiting for me at the nurses' station.

"You lucky little bitch," Natalie said when I walked over. "I saw those guys you were talking to. Now let's go so we can go find a few more at the bar."

I let out a sigh. "Yes, they were both rather good looking, weren't they? And I am definitely ready for that drink." I needed to get my mind off sexy-patient guy and his Mr. Accent sidekick.

Jeremy

As soon as Andy and I walked out the door, the Northern California heat blasted me like a torch and I felt like I was going to keel over. I'd barely made it ten feet out the door before I needed to stop and lean against a pillar. I had no idea what had happened while I had been in the emergency room, but now I felt like I was having a panic attack. I was dizzy, hot, and sweaty, and my heart was racing so fast I couldn't catch my breath.

The strangest sensation was feeling like I was outside of my own body and looking down on myself. I leaned against the pillar for a few minutes, but that didn't help. I bent over at the waist, my head hanging, and my forearms resting on my thighs. I shut my eyes and willed myself to take deep slow breaths. In through my nose, out through my mouth.

Jesus Christ, was this what my sister went through for all those years when she had panic attacks?

"Jeremy! Are you okay? Do you need to go back inside to see the doctor again?" Andy gripped my shoulders and maneuvered me back to a standing position.

No, but I wouldn't mind going back in to see the redheaded nurse.

Andy pushed me upright against the pillar. I drew in another deep breath and let it out while he pretty much held me in place. My heart rate slowed and I was feeling slightly better, but my head was pounding. "No, man, I think I'm good now. I need air though, lots of cold air."

We walked across the parking lot to the shop truck and got inside. Andy started the engine and blasted the A/C as high as it would go. I aimed every vent in front of me directly at my face, but I was still too hot.

Once I pulled off my work shirt and pointed one of the vents toward my body, I felt some relief.

"What is with you?" Andy asked. "Are you sure that exhaust system didn't hit you in the head harder than you said it did?"

"I'm fine. This has nothing to do with the damn car." But it had *everything* to do with the gorgeous nurse and her telling me I had pretty eyes. I'd heard that my entire life and it never meant a goddamn thing to me.

Not until *she'd* said it.

As soon as the words had come from between her pink, full lips, my mind had gone off on its own. Did I really tell her I loved her hair and the flush on her pretty face?

Holy fucking shit. I really did that. It's official. I'm brain-damaged, just like Adam. What is happening to me?

The last thing I remembered distinctly, was working underneath a Mustang. I'd tack welded an exhaust hanger onto the cross-member for the new exhaust system I had custom built. I'd moved to the back of the car to weld another hanger, then Jason had asked me for help and I'd removed my welding helmet. The next thing I knew, the tack weld I'd just finished broke loose and the entire exhaust system had come down on my damn head.

The end of the tail pipe smacked me right on the forehead about half an inch below my hairline. I thought I was fine until I'd felt the warm blood running down my face and into my eye.

"Are you sure you're alright?" Andy asked, breaking the silence.

I shook my head no, but "yes" came out of my mouth.

"Well, which is it?" Andy asked, shooting me a cocky half-grin.

I needed to know what the hell was going on, and why the redheaded nurse was getting to me. When she'd come in the room and said "hey there," my entire body had reacted to her voice.

And I truly meant my *entire* body. My heart had felt like it stopped when she spoke. Once I'd pulled the towel back and opened my eyes to look at her, my heart had resumed beating. My damn toes had even curled inside my steel-toed boots.

Fuck!

I didn't respond to Andy, instead, I opened the door. I had to do something. I couldn't leave without getting her name and number.

"Where the hell are you going?" Andy asked.

"I'll be back," I said over my shoulder, practically running from the truck.

I went through the ER doors and over to where the receptionist sat behind the safety window. Thank God nobody was around. I was too antsy and nervous and might have chickened out if I'd had to wait.

The receptionist pulled open the window. "Can I help you?"

"Yeah, I hope so. I was just in here for stitches and . . . um . . . well, the pretty nurse with the red hair that helped me . . ." *Shit, what was I supposed to say?* "Look, I wanted to see if I could talk to her again. Is it possible for you to see if she is still here?"

Then I remembered her saying her shift was over when she'd walked me back out to the waiting room. *Shit!*

The receptionist smiled and pushed her glasses back to their rightful position on the bridge of her nose. "Sorry, sweetie, I know who you're talking about, but she's gone for the day."

"Can you at least tell me her name so I can come back to see her another day?" She frowned and I knew she was going to say no.

"Sorry, but I can't give out that kind of information for confidentiality reasons. I'm sure you understand," she replied.

Yes, it made sense, but I still didn't have to like it. "Do you have a pen and a piece of paper I can use to leave her a note? Can you make sure she gets it when she comes back to work?"

She smiled and found a notepad and a pen then handed it to me.

After I thanked her, I found an empty seat to sit on to write the note. I had no idea what to say to the nurse without coming across as a creeper so I kept it short.

Dear Red,

Thanks again for taking care of the cut on my head today. Please don't take this the wrong way, but I'd like to see you again. Without having to get more stitches in my head, though. If you want to get together for a drink or dinner sometime, give me a call or text. My cell number is 555-0102. Hope to hear from you soon.

Jeremy James

I'd never written a note to a girl in my life, so I read the damn thing six times before I took it back over to the receptionist. After reading what I had written one last time, I decided it wasn't too stalker-like, folded it in half and handed the paper through the window along with the notepad and pen.

"I'll make sure she gets this," the receptionist said. I watched her scribble a name on the paper then tack it to the bulletin board next to her desk.

I tried like hell to read the name she'd jotted down, but it was too small and too far away. *Shit.* If I at least knew her name, I wouldn't be feeling so helpless right now.

She would have my name and number as soon as she got the note, and I hoped she would call. It was up to her now, and I didn't like it one bit. Usually it was the other way around—a woman was waiting on my call. Now that I'd given her my number, I was the one waiting in limbo.

I walked back to the truck and hopped in. It was nice and cold inside as Andy had been blasting the A/C while he waited for me.

Halfway back to the shop, Andy finally broke the silence. "Do you have something you want to talk about, mate?"

I couldn't ask my brothers or my friends about what was

going through my mind because they'd all give me shit. Andy was the only person that wouldn't. Well, not too much anyway.

"Dude, please don't think I'm a total pussy when I say what I'm about to say. Something happened in the ER. I'm not sure if what I *think* it was . . . is really what it was. Does that make sense?"

"Just spit it out already, mate. Then I'll decide whether or not you're a pussy."

Here goes. "What did it feel like, and what were your first thoughts when you met my sister for the very first time?" I blurted out.

I had overheard Zoey's version of the story when she was talking to Jess, and she'd described it as an instant connection. Like she was drawn to Andy almost magnetically and had no control over it. From what I'd seen over the nearly two years they'd been together, she was right.

When we had our family dinners, they were always within twenty feet of each other. They gravitated around each other, like one of them was the sun and the other the moon. I had a feeling that they both thought of the other as the sun.

Shit, I sound like a total pussy right now, but I have to know.

"Dude, are you going to answer me?" I asked, staring over at him. He seemed to be deep in thought.

"I'm not telling you my *first* thoughts of your sister," he said dryly without looking at me.

"What the fuck. Why the hell not?" I needed to know if what I felt was similar to what happened with them when they met.

"Because the first time I saw your sister she was on her hands and knees, with her ass in the air cleaning my bathtub . . . that's why." He shot me a sideways look with a devious grin on his face.

"Okay, okay, Andy! Shut the fuck up now. I don't need to know that."

He smirked. "You asked, asshole. What's going on? You're acting strange."

"The nurse. I uh . . . felt *something* when I met her. I need to know what it was. It's never happened to me before when I've met a girl."

Andy took a deep breath and eased the blasting of the A/C. "I scared the hell out of her the first time I met her. She had her earbuds in and didn't hear me when I tried to get her attention. When I finally did, she stood and turned around to face me . . ."

He stopped talking so I stared at him, waiting for him to finish. I had no idea what had just happened to him, but he had so many emotions rolling over his face, it was almost too hard for me to watch.

I knew he'd gone through a lot before he moved to the States, and life hadn't gotten much easier for him once he'd moved here. He'd had several losses in his life and I knew my sister was his anchor, as he was hers. He had a great life now that he had Zoey and Hannah.

I'd never experienced that with anyone, so I had no idea what it felt like.

"Do you know what they say about what happens right before you die? How your life passes before your eyes?" He looked over at me and I nodded my response.

"That was what it felt like when I saw her for the first time, except it happened backward. Instead of seeing my past, all I saw was *her*. My future, my wife—the mother of my children. The only family I had left was my aunt and uncle. But then I saw Zoey . . ."

I swore his eyes were watery. *Fuck me.*

"I knew I loved Zoey and that I wanted to spend the rest of my life with her a week after meeting her."

Holy shit. A week?

"Thanks for telling me, man," I said to Andy. "You have to swear to me this conversation will go no further than this truck. Don't even tell Z, please."

"Sure thing, mate."

He pulled around to the back entrance of the shop and parked. As soon as we were out of the truck, Zoey came out with Hannah to check on me.

"How's the head, Jer?" she asked as Andy kissed her cheek then took Sweet Pea from her.

"I had to get stitches!" I groaned as my sister pushed my hair back to inspect my head. "I gotta go guys. I am already late for fight night. Now I've gotta show up with this stupid thing on my head." I pointed to the small piece of gauze that Red had taped over my stitches.

I hugged Z and told her goodbye. When I kissed Sweet Pea on her cheek, I was close enough to Andy to talk without my sister hearing me. "Not a word man. I swear if you tell my sister, I will kill you in your sleep."

Andy let out a loud laugh and nodded. "Understood."

I jumped into my car and hauled ass back to my apartment to shower and change.

After removing the bandage from my head, I inspected my stitches, and hoped the scar wouldn't be too noticeable. I stepped into the shower, careful to keep the cut dry, and let my mind drift back to my encounter with Red in the ER.

When she had come in the room, my heart had freaked out on me and I could not take my eyes off her. She was gorgeous. I didn't normally date redheads because of a bad experience, but I'd sure as hell date her if given the chance.

That's when I remembered I was already dating someone—and she worked at the same hospital as Red, just on the fourth floor. I hoped they weren't friends.

I thought about my relationship with Cammie and felt guilty for being attracted to Red, but I couldn't help it. Every time she'd touched me, my heart had pounded faster and my palms had gotten all sweaty.

When I thought how I would love to see all her pretty, red hair spilling around us, while naked in my bed, my dick had betrayed me and pitched a tent in my pants so I'd had to sit up.

Jesus, when she cleaned the blood off me . . . I hadn't been able to control my reaction. I'd slammed my eyes shut, but I hadn't been capable of suppressing the noises coming from me. *God knows I tried.*

Her touch had been soft and gentle. Although she'd worn latex gloves, I'd felt the heat of her hands on my skin and couldn't concentrate on my job of cleaning the blood off my chest and neck.

After she'd stood in front of me and told me I'd missed a spot, something had shifted between us. She'd pressed against my legs as she cleaned me off. I'd died and gone to heaven by the time her hand stopped, and her fingers were stroking the back of my neck.

We'd sat for several long seconds staring at each other. Then she told me I had pretty eyes. It'd seemed like an out of body experience when I reached up and stroked the soft skin on her cheekbone.

I stepped out of the shower, and as soon as I was dressed, I put ointment and a new bandage over my stitches. Shit, my friends were gonna give me crap all night about it, so I decided to wear a hat.

Once I left my apartment, I hopped into my Cadillac CTS-V, cranked up some Motorhead, listening to "Ace of Spades" blaring through the speakers as I headed to Cammie's. The shop had been crazy-busy this week, and I'd worked late a few nights with Jason, helping him meet a deadline on a sick-ass motor he was building for a drag racer from Southern California. That had sent Cammie into a tizzy, which was why I was taking her with me to my Friday nightspot to watch the MMA fights with my friends, John, Sonny, and Eric.

When I knocked on the door of Cammie's apartment, I heard that stupid dog of hers barking like crazy.

Her roommate, Jasmine, opened the door wide. "Come on in and sit down, Jeremy. She's nowhere near being ready to go yet," she said with a knowing smile.

Fuck. I rolled my eyes and stepped through the door as Jasmine laughed.

Cammie's lateness drove me crazy. She was never on time for anything. I had to wait for her to finish putting on her makeup, finish the episode of the stupid reality show she was watching, or I had to wait for her to get off her cell phone.

Thirty minutes after I arrived, Cammie was finally ready to go. She was in a pissy mood based on the scowl she wore on her face when she came into the living room. I didn't care though because we were already well over an hour late and had missed the first of the MMA fights.

She yanked the hat off my head and pushed my hair back to examine my wound. "Why did I have to find out from my friends that my boyfriend was in the ER today? What, you couldn't call me and tell me?"

I grabbed my hat back from her and carefully put it back on my head. "For your information, I didn't have time to call you since I was bleeding from the head and needed stitches. That's why. By the time I got out of there, I was already running late and something came up." That something being writing a note to a pretty nurse who took care of me, and who I wanted to see again.

"Well one of my friends saw you leave. You could have called me then."

Jesus, she wasn't going to give up. So I did. "You're right. Can we go now? We're already late."

She grinned like she'd just won a prize, and we finally left her apartment.

I opened the passenger door for Cammie and she slid down onto the seat. Once we were on the road, she began changing stations on the radio. Several stations later, she still hadn't settled on one.

"Cammie, that's enough." I pushed her hand away from the radio and turned it off. "We'll be at the bar soon anyway."

She sat back in her seat, letting out a huff of annoyance and crossed her arms over her chest. "I hate the music you listen to. It's old people music," she whined. "Can't you put some music on your iPod for me?"

Um, hell no. There will be no boy bands or crap like that on my iPod. *Not gonna happen.*

Z was in charge of adding music to my iPod. She knew what I liked to listen to and I was good with that. All I had to do was hand it to her and the next day I'd get it back loaded with more music.

"I'd rather listen to nothing than that crap you call music, Cammie. They all sound like Charlie Brown's teacher."

She glared over at me. "Who's Charlie Brown? Someone you went to school with?" she asked, seriously.

Holy shit, she is a fucking moron. She was actually trusted to take care of sick people at a hospital. *Scary.*

"Never mind," I muttered as I pulled into Dub's parking lot. I was still shaking my head when we walked through the front doors.

My friends were at our usual couch close to the bar and big screen TV's. I bought myself a beer and Cammie ordered something called a "Redheaded Slut" which instantly made me think of the nurse from earlier. Not that I thought she was a slut, but just the mention of red hair caused my heart to skip a beat. I also found it highly coincidental that the day seemed to revolve around redheads. Drinks in hand, we weaved our way through the crowd to where my friends were sitting.

"Hey douchebag, you're late!" John bellowed when he saw us. John and I had been best friends since we were in diapers because we had grown up next door to each other.

"Sorry, man. I had an issue at work." I shoved Sonny over on the couch to make room. I took a seat, and Cammie sat her ass right down on my lap, blocking my view of the TV. After introducing her to my friends, I took a long swallow of my beer then set it on the table. Eric caught me up on what I'd missed on the fights.

Within ten minutes, Cammie had taken out her cell phone and was texting back and forth with someone. I decided to ignore her even though it bugged me. We were supposed to be "spending time together" according to her, and she was more interested in her phone.

I downed the rest of my beer and wanted another. "Cammie, I need to go back to the bar for another beer."

"Okay, baby," she cooed. "I need another drink too. I'll come with you."

Inside, I cringed as each one of my friends called me "baby" before they gave me their beer orders. We both went back to the bar where I asked for four bottles of Sierra Nevada.

"I'll have a strawberry margarita this time," Cammie said to the bartender. "That Redheaded Slut was nasty."

Rolling my eyes, I pulled out my wallet to pay and left it sitting open on top of the bar while we waited for the bartender to bring back my card.

Cammie snatched my wallet off the bar and laughed at the picture I kept in the slot where my driver's license should have been.

"Who is this fatty?" She smirked and giggled like an idiot.

The picture was of me wearing a pair of swim shorts and no shirt when I was seventeen years old. I weighed two hundred and twenty pounds at five-feet nine inches tall. Granted, I was not that size or height anymore, but the photo was my daily reminder of how I used to look, and never wanted to look again.

I jerked my wallet out of her hand. "It's none of your fucking business, Cammie."

"What's your problem Jeremy? You've been acting like an asshole all night. Do you need some extra-special attention from me?" she asked with her fake, sweet voice as she slid her hand over to my crotch and squeezed.

It felt good, but not good enough to deal with all her crazy-ass shit.

I looked her over, trying to figure out what I had ever seen in her. Everything about her was fake. From her tits, her voice, her attitude, to her blonde hair.

Once I had my card back, I turned to Cammie. "Actually," I said, removing her hand from my dick and setting it back on her own lap. "I don't need anything from you. We're over. I'm taking you home now."

She slid off the barstool and ran to the bathroom crying.

"Shit," I growled and slid from my seat. I grabbed the four beers I'd just ordered, left the margarita on the bar and took the beer to my friends.

"Looks like I'm leaving guys," I said. "I'll catch you later."

Before I could turn to leave John asked, "Damn! Hey, Jer . . . isn't the redhead over by the door that bitchy chick from high school?"

Please do *not* let it be her. I hadn't talked to Sabrina Roberts since the day I got the nerve to ask her out my last year of high school. John was the *only* person who knew what happened because I'd been so embarrassed.

I'd had a slight infatuation with Sabrina since we were

freshman. She was my dream girl and had gorgeous red hair. When I finally asked her out, she laughed in my face, and said she would never go out with a fat ass like me. She was the reason I didn't date redheads.

"Well, is it her or not Jeremy?" John asked.

When I finally looked, it wasn't Sabrina, but Red, and she was still dressed in her work clothes. What were the odds?

She was looking around the room for something. Was she trying to find somewhere to sit? The place was packed and I didn't want her to leave, so I waved my hand in the air.

"Hey, Red!" I called out.

She instantly recognized me and smiled, waving at me excitedly.

I quickly made my way to the end of the bar near the door.

"Well, I never thought I'd see you again," she said and climbed onto a barstool that I'd pulled out for her. "Thank you. How's the head?"

If I didn't know any better, I'd say she was as happy to see me as I was to see her. "It's good. Do you mind if I buy you a drink?"

She smiled. "I'd love a beer. Thank you."

"What are you doing here, Red?" I tossed some bills down to pay for our drinks. "This isn't really a place where many ladies hang out."

She took a swig of her beer straight from the bottle. "What makes ya think I'm a *lady,* blue eyes?"

Holy shit, I loved this woman. She was quick witted and gorgeous.

I stared at her in awe for a moment because I still couldn't believe she was *here.* She had pretty, green eyes with tiny flecks of gold in them, and long, thick lashes.

"Um, let's see." I examined her from the neck up. "Pretty green eyes, amazing hair, a bit of makeup on your face—seems pretty lady-like to me."

She smirked. "Wow, I'm not sure if I should be thanking you, or offended."

I raised my eyebrows in question.

"Most guys would have gone straight for the obvious tits

and ass," she clarified, and then burst out laughing.

Holding in a laugh at her boldness, I nearly choked on my beer. "I'm gonna keep my mouth shut about your tits and ass for now. But, I am sure they're as beautiful as the parts of you that I *can* see."

She smiled sincerely. "Thank you. I will definitely take *that* as a compliment, blue eyes."

Okay, enough with the nicknames, I needed to know her name. I didn't want to keep calling her "Red."

"I'm Jeremy, by the way." I held my hand out to her, officially introducing myself.

She placed her small hand in mine and gave a gentle squeeze. "Teagan."

Finally, I knew her name.

"Teagan." Her named rolled easily off my tongue. "A beautiful name for a beautiful woman." The barstool next to Teagan opened up and I sat down. We talked about nothing in particular until John came to the bar for another beer.

"Dude, I thought you were leaving." His brows rose and he glanced between Teagan and me.

I realized that he was trying to tell me something. *Shit! Cammie is still here.* "That's right, I was, but this pretty girl sidetracked me." Casually, I glanced around before bringing my eyes back to Teagan's. I hadn't seen Cammie anywhere.

Suddenly, Teagan seemed uncomfortable.

I was about to ask her for her number when she abruptly stood. "I need to run to the ladies room. I'll be right back."

She walked in the direction of the restrooms but stopped to chat with some other women dressed in scrubs. I hadn't realized she was here with them, but I recognized one of the women as the nurse who had come into the exam room earlier that day. They both looked back at John and me and smiled while John stole Teagan's barstool.

Teagan turned and headed toward the bathroom. After fifteen minutes, I became worried because she hadn't come back yet. I went to look for her. When I didn't see her anywhere, I approached the nurse I'd recognized from the ER.

"Have you seen Teagan?" I asked.

"Yeah, she left about ten minutes ago," she said.

What the hell? Why did she leave?

"I'm Jackie. What's your name?" she asked.

I held my hand out to her to shake. "Jeremy. It's nice to meet you."

"Are you ready to go, Jeremy?" I spun around to face Cammie. Son of a bitch!

Teagan had apparently gone home, but I couldn't risk asking any more about her because Cammie was standing right there. *Fuck my life!*

Cammie folded her arms across her chest and tapped her foot on the floor, waiting for me to do something.

I turned back to Jackie and said, "I need to go and drop her off." I didn't want to give the impression that I was going to be spending the rest of the evening with Cammie when I definitely wasn't.

She nodded then turned back to the bar, dismissing me.

In the parking lot, Cammie walked around to the passenger door, and waited for me to open it for her. Instead, I clicked the unlock button on the key fob and sat in the driver's seat.

She stood outside her door waiting for me to come back around and open it for her.

I pressed the button on my door that rolled the window down on her side. "Cammie, if you don't want to walk home, I suggest you get in."

She stomped her foot, pulled open the door, and threw herself down in the seat like a two year old throwing a tantrum. She glared over at me as she purposely slammed the door shut. Guess she wanted to play some games with me. If she wanted to act like a brat—game on!

I rolled up her window and found my favorite metal band, In This Moment, on my iPod. I hit play, shifted into first gear, and cranked up the volume to an ear-splitting decibel. I tortured her with all the screaming, loud guitars and complete insanity the band and their singer Maria Brink could muster up. Ahh, Maria Brink. Now there's a hot-ass chick!

It was immature, but I enjoyed every second of the ride

back to her apartment. I pulled into a parking space and hit the button, unlocking her door. I didn't bother helping her out or turning down my stereo.

As soon as she slammed the door, I backed out and left, hoping I would never see Cammie again.

Teagan

I was an idiot. I'd been having a great time, but now I was in the Dub's parking lot in my car, wondering what the hell had happened, and why I'd ever thought a guy like Jeremy would be interested in me.

Before running into Jeremy, I'd kept thinking back to my favorite patient of the day and realized I didn't even know who he was. I had completely forgotten about the chart that held his name when I had seen just exactly how gorgeous he was.

Inside the noisy TV room at the bar someone had called out, *"Hey, Red."* When I realized it was sexy patient-guy, I had to admit I was so excited to see him again I'd waved back like a hyperactive schoolgirl.

Sitting at the bar having a drink with him, I had found him easy-going, funny, smart, and cool to hang out with.

Even when I'd made the comment about my tits and ass, he'd rolled with it, but then had complimented me again. He hadn't turned it in to anything other than what it was, *a simple joke*. He'd been flirty, but he hadn't gone overboard with it.

I'd flirted right back, startling myself for being so forward with him. Although I felt I looked decent, I still had a bit of weight to lose, and I probably didn't measure up to his standards.

On my way to the bathroom, I'd thought about how extraordinary Jeremy was. I was undeniably interested in him and had just enough confidence to hint at a date when I returned from the bathroom. I definitely didn't have the guts to ask him out.

Everything had gone south in the bathroom though. While I'd been standing at the sink in front of the mirror, rearranging my hair, two younger women had come in. I'd recognized them as medical assistants from the hospital, but they worked on a different floor than me.

One girl was still wearing her scrubs. The other one, dressed in street clothes, had gone into a stall and shut the door behind her. I thought I remembered her name as being Tammy. The girl in scrubs had stood at the sink and stared at me.

"Can I help you?" I'd asked. She'd kind of creeped me out with her staring.

She'd folded her arms across her chest and took a breath. "Are you dating Jeremy?"

What the heck? "No, I only met him today. We just happened to run into each other here." Then I wondered where the line of questioning was going.

She'd smirked. "Well, so you know . . . he's a total manwhore. You probably shouldn't get mixed up with him. He's been with quite a few of the MA's on our floor. Needless to say, none of us knew about each other, but he was stringing a few of us along at once."

"He's a total asshole," the other girl had echoed from her bathroom stall.

I'd felt nauseous by what they were saying and I had thought, *Um, that's gross. Did he really do that?* He didn't seem like a sleaze ball, but I'd known him less than a day.

"Okay . . . um thanks for letting me know," I'd said as I picked up my purse from the counter and pulled the strap over my shoulder.

Still, she'd stared at me. "We might as well introduce ourselves since we do work at the same hospital." She laughed—a clearly fake laugh. "I'm Tiffany. What's your name?"

"Teagan," I'd said. "Sorry, but I need to go. It's been a long day."

I'd brushed past her to exit the bathroom then had stood in the hallway trying to decide whether to go back out to Jeremy and pretend nothing was wrong, confront him about what Tiffany had said, or leave? In the end, I'd snuck out.

So here I sat, in my car, thinking about how much fun it'd been getting to know Jeremy, and comparing that to what I'd been told. I had a hard time believing what Tiffany had said, but why would she say that if it weren't true?

I'd seen firsthand what assholes men could be after Gary had cheated on me with Katie. I had also seen how deceitful girls could be, too. I wasn't sure whom I could trust.

Except Reese.

He was my best friend and my sounding board. I needed to hear his voice and definitely needed his advice, so I called him. Luckily, he answered.

"What's up hooker-face?" he said.

I couldn't help but laugh at his nickname for me. It stemmed from one of our nights drinking and watching funny videos online.

"Oh, you know . . . the usual. Kinda got my heart broke a little . . . again."

"What? By who?"

"I met someone today."

No sooner had the words left my lips, Jeremy came out the door with the medical assistant, Tammy, and went toward what I assumed was his car. My hopes that he was a decent guy were dashed that second. I let out a defeated sigh and slumped farther down in my seat. Well, that just proved to me that the girls in the bathroom were telling the truth.

"Reese, I thought he was a good guy, but I was told a few not-so-nice stories about him from two girls I work with. I don't know what to do." I sighed and let my head fall back against the headrest of my seat.

"I'm sorry, sweetie," Reese cooed. "But if you just met him, how do you know if what you heard is true?"

He brought up a good point.

What if it's not true?

But what if it was?

"Well, considering he just got in his car and left with one of the girls doesn't look too promising for him."

"I'm sorry, hooker-face. You'll find someone who's right for you. Just forget about that guy and move on."

He was right. I definitely didn't want to risk getting my heart broken again, especially since I barely knew Jeremy.

"You're right Reese, I don't want to go through this. From what I was told, he's a liar and a cheater. I think I'm gonna go home now." Trying to change the subject, I asked, "When are you coming to visit?"

"Good news, sweets! I applied for a job at the same gym chain where I'm working now. But guess in which city."

"I have no idea, which city?"

"Sacramento, beeotch!"

"Heck yes! Oh my God, I hope you get it!" I squealed. "Maybe by then I'll have my own place. We can be roomies again!"

"Yes, you need your own place, Teagan. Reese junior misses his snuggle buddy!"

"Aww, tell junior I miss his good morning pokes to the back of my thighs."

"I sure will," he said. "Now you go home and get to bed young lady. You are out too late on a work night!"

He was right. I was suddenly feeling exhausted after my long workday. And hungry. I realized I hadn't even had dinner yet.

"Thanks for listening, Reese. I'll talk to you soon," I said.

"Goodnight, sweets."

I drove home and found that my mom had covered a plate of leftovers for my dinner. I'd lost my appetite since I'd thought more about Jeremy leaving Dub's with the chick from the bathroom. But, I knew if I didn't eat something, I'd never make it through my workout in the morning.

After I pulled my dinner from the microwave and added a small salad to the plate, I took my food to the living room where I plopped down next to my sister who was watching a movie. She was sprawled across the couch, leaving me only half a cushion to sit on.

"What are we watching?" I asked when I didn't recognize the movie.

"Some dumb-ass chick flick," she groaned, which caused me to snicker.

"Why are you watching it if it's dumb?"

"Brian dumped me," she said quietly.

Oh, crap. She and Brian had been together for over a year. Suddenly my issue didn't seem as bad. At least I wasn't in a relationship with Jeremy.

I set my fork on my plate and turned to face her. "Sorry, Shannen. Are you okay?"

She nodded. "Yeah, I suppose. I'm still in shock. I mean— I know our relationship hadn't been going well for some time now, but—I think it's really over."

"Did he give you a reason?"

"He says he found someone else more compatible."

"Well, if it's any consolation, I met someone today then it blew up in my face."

Shannen sat up and I told her about Jeremy, and what Tiffany had said about him.

"Are you sure you can trust that Tiffany chick though?" she asked.

"I don't know what to think, or who to trust. He seemed nice and genuinely interested in me. We had a good time tonight, Shannen. I mean a *really* good time. But after he left with Tammy—I just don't know. I am not going to think about it anymore. He obviously can't be trusted." I picked up my fork and stabbed it into the center of my pork chop. Cutting off a big chunk with my knife, I shoved the meat into my mouth. It was not what I wanted to eat and immediately felt like binging on an entire tub of chocolate and peanut butter ice cream.

Thank God there wasn't any in the house.

The whole situation was depressing and Shannen being dumped by her longtime boyfriend wasn't helping to restore my faith in men.

Shannen smiled. "Let's make a plan to go out to a club dancing soon."

"That sounds like a great idea. But no men allowed!"

Shannen agreed and I finished my now cold dinner. I wasn't going to think about Jeremy anymore and decided that bed was the best way to get my mind off the day. I would think about it tomorrow when my head was clear, and my heart wasn't achy.

Unfortunately, I woke completely drained. I had dreamt of Jeremy all night. What was with this guy that I couldn't stop thinking about him? I needed to run and clear my head.

Forcing my butt out of bed, I threw on running clothes and pulled my hair up in a messy bun. I glanced over at the clock, and found it was already after six. Well, at least it was still cool enough outside for my run. I brushed my teeth, and headed out the door.

I walked to the end of the sidewalk and turned right, instead of left like I usually did. By the time I reached the other end of the block, my tight muscles had loosened, so I picked up my pace.

We lived in an older subdivision, but it was a relatively safe place. As I ran up one street and down another, I found myself looking at all the houses in our neighborhood. Several houses had been remodeled or were currently in the process of being remodeled.

One house, which was for sale, always caught my attention, because it was exactly what I dreamed of in a house. Yes, I was your typical girl. I wanted the big house with the white picket fence. Didn't every girl?

Remembering I wanted to visit Nanna before work today, I ran home fast and hopped in the shower. Since I had to work, I'd only have time to stop in for a few minutes.

Once I pulled into a parking space at Nanna's home, my mind drifted to Jeremy. I had avoided thinking about him all morning, but now, he consumed my thoughts. I speculated how he could be so cool to hang out with then leave with Tammy right after he had been with me at the bar having what I felt was a great time.

With all the sweet things he'd said, all the compliments he'd given me, and all the fun we had been having, was I that dumb to think he was interested in me?

He had to be an expert at playing games if he was stringing multiple girls along like Tiffany had said. *Ugh. What a jerk!*

I cleared my head of Jeremy and went into Nanna's room. She was sitting up on her bed, and when I came in, she turned her head to look at me. "Peaches, hello," she said quietly. Two words in a row, spoken clearly, was music to my ears.

"Good morning, Nanna. How are you today?" I asked, hoping she'd be able to respond easily again.

She tried to speak, but was having a difficult time getting the words out. Finally, she said, "Good to see Peaches."

I smiled at my sweet Nanna and hugged her. She was doing well since her stroke, but at times, her mouth wouldn't cooperate with her brain. Especially when she became frustrated or anxious. Her daily therapy seemed to be helping, and I was confident that her speech would continue to improve as the days went on.

I took her hand in mine. "I can't stay very long, Nanna, because I need to go to work. I missed you and wanted to come by and see how you were doing."

I grabbed the Yeats book then took a seat in the chair I pulled up next to her bed. As I read to her, she drifted off to sleep. When it was time for me to leave, I stood looking down at my frail Nanna and my heart clenched in my chest. I hated seeing her so fragile.

My nanna used to be a feisty thing when she was younger. My poor Papa had a hard time keeping her reined in at times. I laughed when I thought back to when I was around ten years old. She'd had a *Fried Green Tomatoes* movie moment at the grocery store one day.

Shannen and I had been staying with them for a few days during our summer break from school and they had taken us grocery shopping. The parking lot had been packed and she had already circled it three times before she finally saw a car backing out of a space. Mind you, at the time, Nanna drove a gigantic 1967 Impala.

She arrived at the space first, but this small car driving the wrong direction down the row, snuck into the space right at the last minute. She got out and yelled at the man for cutting into the parking space since it was *rightfully* hers. He told her she was crazy then walked away from her.

Well, that had not set well with Nanna. It just so happened the car parked in the spot opposite of the man's car backed out as we circled the lot, once again. So what had Nanna done? She'd pulled into the recently vacated parking space and pushed the space thief's car out of the space so she could park where she'd wanted originally.

So now, this man's car was not only *out* of the space he *stole* from Nanna, it was blocking the entire driving lane, causing a minor traffic jam in the parking lot. Nanna and Papa had laughed the whole time we were in the store.

Checking the time, I kissed Nanna and headed to work. Once I pulled into the hospital parking lot, I noticed a black car pull in down the row from me. As I gathered my purse and my identification card, the door of the black car opened and a man stepped out.

Crap. It was Jeremy. I briefly wondered if he was here to see me, but then another thought crossed my mind. *What if he is here to see one of his many conquests?*

I couldn't say why, but it made me feel a little better to see he was alone.

I still didn't want to talk to him, so I waited in my car until he made his way through the ER doors, then jogged to the employee entrance, flashed my ID in front of the card-reader, and stepped inside the building.

My curiosity got the better of me, so I snuck to the ER and stood behind the half-wall near the receptionists' desk where he couldn't see me. I had to know what he wanted.

He was speaking to Margie, the receptionist.

"Sweetie, like I told you yesterday, I can't give you that kind of information," Margie told him.

I wondered what he'd asked her yesterday.

"Did you give Teagan the note I left?"

He left me a note?

Margie looked sideways briefly when she noticed me hovering nearby. I shook my head at her letting her know I didn't want to speak with him. Thank God she understood what I meant.

"Not yet, sweetie, I haven't seen her today. But I promise I'll get it to her when I do," Margie responded.

"Okay," Jeremy said. The tone of his voice told me he was clearly disappointed.

But why? Hadn't he spent the last part of his evening with Tammy? Why would he be here asking for me? This situation was so confusing.

I crossed my arms and continued to listen as he spoke.

"Will you at least tell me one thing?" he asked Margie.

She sighed loudly. "I will if I can. What do you want to know?"

"Does she have a boyfriend?" He sounded anxious for some reason, which further confused me since he'd left the bar with another woman last night.

"Well, that I can answer honestly," Margie replied. "I don't know if she does or not. All I can say is I'll get your note to her as soon as I see her."

"Alright, thanks again for your help," he said.

He must have left because Margie closed the window and turned to me. "Teagan, what is going on with that man?"

I shrugged my shoulders and smiled. "I wish I knew Margie. I wish I knew . . . so what's this about a note?"

"He came in after you left yesterday and said he wanted to talk to you. He left you a note. It's right here." She scanned the bulletin board next to her desk. A moment later, she turned back to me. "Well, it was here, but now it's not. Are you sure you didn't get it?"

I shook my head. "Maybe whoever worked reception after you last night put it in my locker. I'll go check there. Thanks Margie. Have a good day!"

I went to the locker room to stash my purse, but found no note when I opened my locker. Crap. I was very curious to know what it said.

Several nurses and MA's came through the door, including Tammy and Tiffany. I groaned inwardly at the sight of them. They started talking loudly, about Jeremy. Naturally, I wanted to hear what they had to say, but I didn't want them to know I was listening so I stepped into a bathroom stall on the other side of the lockers from where they stood talking.

"It was awesome! We were all over each other as soon as we got inside my apartment. He is so hot and has an amazing body. Oh, his dick is huge, and he fucked me so hard! He has a cute birthmark on his hip, right here," Tammy said.

Deciding I didn't want to eavesdrop any longer because their conversation was making me sick, I flushed the toilet to alert them to my presence. I paused before opening the door then went to the sink to wash my hands.

Tammy and Tiffany both looked over when I walked past them, and they burst into giggles. I felt my face flush, and it pissed me off because I was letting them *and* Jeremy get to me.

He was nothing to me, right? I didn't even know him. Now, I never would.

Once I clocked in, I headed to the ER to work. The first person I ran in to was Jared Peterson. He was an ER resident and had asked me out a few times, but I'd declined.

"Hey there, pretty lady," he said when he saw me.

"Please don't call me that, Jared. People can hear you," I said a bit too brusquely.

"What's with you today? Bad night?" he asked, taking a step back.

He seemed genuinely concerned, and I felt bad. Had I taken his comment the wrong way because I was upset about what I'd heard in the locker room? "I'm sorry, Jared. I had a bad night and a bad morning. I visited Nanna before work and it upset me."

Well, at least that was all true. It did upset me to see her, but I didn't want to tell him what else was going on. Jared and I were friends and he knew all about Nanna's stroke.

He pulled me into a hug and rubbed his hands up and down my back to comfort me. "Sorry, Teagan, I know you're close with her. Let me know if you want to talk. Maybe we can get together for dinner tonight?"

I pulled back and looked up at him. What did I have to lose by having dinner with him? He was a nice guy, good looking, and he honestly seemed interested in me. "Thanks Jared, that sounds good. Text me when you get ready to eat, and I'll meet you."

Jared tilted his head down and kissed the top of my head. "I will. Have a better day Teagan."

I would definitely try. No promises . . .

Jeremy

What the hell was wrong with me? I'd been pissed ever since Teagan had ditched me at Dub's last night. But why? I barely knew her. So *why* was I still so pissed? Yeah, she was adorable, pretty, sexy, perfectly curvy, and positively the most gorgeous woman I'd ever—*Jesus H. Christ! Who thinks shit like this?*

Not Jeremy James.

She was adorable? Really?

Evidently, I thought shit like that. Now.

I'd never been more pissed in my life than when Jackie told me Teagan had left. After that, all I'd wanted to do was go home and be alone. Unfortunately, I'd still had to deal with Cammie even though I'd broken up with her literally *minutes* before Teagan had come into the bar.

Actually, now that I'd thought about it, I wasn't really *pissed*. I was . . . hurt.

This was *not* a normal feeling for me. Especially when it involved a girl.

I had to see Teagan and find out why she'd left. Fortunately, I was off work for the weekend, but would she be working on a Saturday? I knew her work shift ended around five because she'd mentioned it when I'd left the ER the day before. I checked the time on my phone, and it was only six a.m. She probably wasn't even at work yet. I had plenty of time to run off some of my anger before I tried to track her down.

Later that morning, I left the hospital with a sick feeling in the pit of my stomach. *What the hell is wrong with me?* Teagan wasn't at the hospital according to the receptionist, and I was disappointed because I didn't get to see her. And I still didn't have her number. I needed to find something constructive to do with my time, so I headed over to the shop to finish the exhaust on the Mustang.

When I arrived at the shop, I welded the exhaust hangers that had come loose yesterday and sent me to the ER. This time I gave it a tug to make sure it was sturdy before moving on to the next one.

I did not need another trip to the emergency room, but if the exhaust did fall on me again, I might get to see Teagan.

"Fuck!" I yelled in frustration. I ripped off my welding helmet and hurled it across the shop. It bounced off the wall and skidded across the floor.

Was I seriously hoping to be knocked in the head again so I could go back for more stitches? What the hell was this chick doing to me? I was an idiot.

I threw my welding gloves on the floor and went to the break room to get a bottle of water. The second my ass hit the couch, my phone buzzed with an incoming text.

It buzzed two more times before I could get it out of my pocket to see who'd texted. All three texts were from Cammie. I didn't give a shit what she wanted after the crap she'd pulled last night and only opened the texts to delete them. But the picture she'd sent caught my eye. Although taken from a distance, I could see it was of Teagan.

She was wrapped in the arms of some douchebag in a white coat with a stethoscope around his neck. It seemed Teagan had a boyfriend, and it seemed this boyfriend was a doctor.

Of course he was. Like I stood a chance in hell against a *doctor*.

I couldn't stand to look at it so I moved on to the next text— a photo of Teagan looking up at the doctor while he looked down at her—both wearing contented smiles. In the last picture, Teagan's arms were wrapped tightly around him and he was kissing her on the head.

"Fuck!" I growled and chucked my almost-full bottle of water out the break room door. *What is wrong with me?* I scrubbed my hands over my face and through my hair.

"Jer, is everything alright?" I heard my sister's quiet voice ask from the doorway.

Zoey stood at the entrance with Hannah cradled protectively in her arms. She looked worried and Hannah's bottom lip was quivering like she might cry at any moment.

"Yeah, Z. No. Hell—I don't know." I had no clue what I felt. I just knew it was messing with my head in a way it never had before.

Hannah started crying. I jumped up, went over to them, and held my hands out to her.

"Sorry, Sweet Pea, I didn't mean to scare you." I felt horrible when she buried her face against Z's neck and refused to come to me. Zoey stared at me in confusion. Hannah had never done that before. She always came right to me.

Right then, I felt like the biggest piece of shit. I stepped closer and pulled them both into a hug so Hannah would see everything was okay and she didn't need to be scared of me. Resting my cheek on her shuddering back, I talked to her quietly until she calmed down.

I pulled away from them, and as soon as I did, Hannah raised her head and looked at me. The sight of my baby niece with big tears rolling down her face tore me in two. It was *me* who'd made her cry. At that very moment, I felt like crying.

That was until she held her arms out to me. My Sweet Pea had forgiven me.

I reached out and took her from Z and she immediately snuggled into the crook of my neck. She took in a deep breath and let out a big shaky sigh.

"I know exactly how you feel, baby girl," I said, breathing in her sweet baby scent. At only three months old, I was wrapped around her little finger.

I went and sat on the couch then rocked her while I talked quietly to her. I told her again, how sorry I was for scaring her, and I would never do it again.

I was teaching her to play a game. I held her tiny hand over my mouth so I could kiss it. I always kissed it nice and loud because that made her smile. We would do it over and over, until she grew bored and would smack me on the cheek instead.

Z went over to the fridge and pulled out two bottles of water. She opened both, and handed me one. I nodded a thank you.

"Jer, what's wrong?" Zoey asked after a few more minutes of silence.

I really didn't want to talk about it, so I handed her my phone with the last picture of Teagan still on the screen.

"Who is that?"

"The girl of my dreams—and her boyfriend." She *literally* was the girl of my dreams. I'd dreamt of her all night last night, which was probably the reason I woke up in a bad mood. I usually slept like the dead, but not last night. I'd tossed and turned the entire night.

"That sucks," Zoey whispered.

"Yeah," I agreed.

"Why is Cammie, of all people, sending you pictures of her?"

I shrugged my shoulders. "Does it matter who sent it? She has a boyfriend . . . and he's a *doctor.* I can't compete with that."

Z glared at me. "Jeremy Douglas James, don't you ever say that in front of me again."

Right now, I really felt like shit, but I knew better than to let her get started on how nobody was better than anyone else regardless of how they lived, what they did for a living, or how much money they had.

Teagan was turning me in to some kind of freak. This whole thing was new to me and I didn't know how to deal with it. I had never felt an attraction to anyone like I did with her.

"Come home with us, Jer. I was getting ready to make lunch when I saw your car out the window. Andy and I have something we need to talk to you about anyway."

I nodded and stood. Zoey turned off the welder and closed the valve on the gas tank for me because I was still holding

Hannah. After she locked the door behind us, we walked up the stairs to their temporary apartment above the shop.

"Hey, how's it going today, mate?" Andy asked when we walked into the kitchen. It seemed he was fixing lunch now, not my sister.

"Not so good, man. You're not gonna poison me are you?" I asked motioning to the sandwiches he was putting together.

"Nah, not today. Maybe another time," he replied casually, piling the giant sandwiches onto plates.

Freakin' Andy. He always had a witty comeback. But you needed one ready at all times in our family.

Zoey pulled a bag of chips from the pantry and some drinks from the fridge. I followed her to the table, still holding a sleepy Hannah. We sat, and Andy brought the sandwiches to the table, setting them on the place mats in front of us.

Z smirked when she saw her huge sandwich and immediately took half of it and put it on Andy's plate. "Baby, I'm eating for one now . . . not two," she noted.

Andy kissed her on the cheek before sitting down. "For now," he said.

Jesus, he's already talking about another baby. Z shook her head at him and took a bite of her sandwich.

"What's going on?" Andy asked me after he sat in his chair.

Since he already knew about Teagan, but he didn't know what had happened last night, I merely said, "I saw Red last night. Just found out she has a boyfriend."

"Shit. Sorry, mate."

I shrugged it off and carefully shifted Hannah to my left side to eat my sandwich with my right hand. "So what did you want to talk to me about?"

Zoey looked over at Andy and set her sandwich back on her plate. She took Andy's hand in hers as she swallowed her food.

"Jeremy, we have something really important to ask you. We'll totally understand if you say no, but we hope you'll say yes. I know it's going to be a shock for you, but we don't want anyone else."

This was serious because she used my whole first name. She only calls me Jeremy when she's pissed at me. "What do you want me to do?"

"We want you to be Hannah's godfather."

If I'd had food in my mouth, I would have choked on it.

"*Me?* Are you *insane?* I don't know anything about kids."

They both laughed at me.

"Are you sure about that?" Zoey asked as she pointed to Hannah, who was now sacked out on my shoulder. "Let me plead our case before you say no. Please, Jer."

I nodded, so she continued.

"First off, our baby girl loves you. Look how she is with you. She's been like that with you since you held her the very first time at the hospital. She trusts you. *We* trust you, Jer. You've been my biggest protector since I was fourteen, and I know you'd protect her with your life if . . ." She took a long pause before she spoke again and her eyes got a bit watery. "If anything were to happen to both of us."

I had no idea they felt that way. They trusted *me* with the life of their child?

Their child.

Z was right though, I would do anything to protect Hannah, including dying to keep her safe, and I'd do anything to make her happy.

"I'll do it," I whispered. "I would be honored."

Not surprisingly, Zoey let the waterworks fly after I said yes. She stood and hugged me as tightly as she could without squeezing Hannah.

"Z, you wake up my goddaughter and I'm kicking your ass."

"Jesus, don't go all Marlon Brando on me," she replied and smacked me on the back of the head.

Andy reached over and shook my hand. "Thanks, Jeremy."

"You're really serious about this bro?" I asked Andy, because I was still in disbelief.

"Yeah, mate. Your sister makes a pretty good argument when it comes to you."

After we finished our lunch, I strolled down the hallway and put Sweet Pea in her crib to finish her nap. I kissed her on the head and ran my fingers over the blonde curls forming in her hair.

"I love you, Hannah," I said softly as I pulled a thin blanket over my new goddaughter.

On the way back to the kitchen, I ducked into the bathroom to absorb what my sister and Andy had just asked of me.

Me . . . a godfather, who would've thought?

I turned the water on in the sink as cold as it would go, and splashed some on my face. After I dried off, I went back to the table and sat down.

"Thank you. I don't know what else to say . . . just . . . thank you," I said to my sister and her husband. "This means so much to me. I swear on my life to take it very seriously."

I choked up a little so I stopped talking before I embarrassed the hell out of myself.

"We'll need to go see our lawyer sometime next week so we can sign the papers. Make it all legal," Andy said.

I nodded. "Name the time and the place. I'll be there."

The rest of the day, I was on cloud nine. I was still hurt after seeing the pictures of Teagan, but after lunch with Z and Andy, I felt better.

I didn't feel like a loser anymore. They had given me the best gift I'd ever received.

I would be the best-damned godfather who ever lived.

I was on my back in a tattoo shop, of all places, getting my first tattoo. It hurt like a bitch.

A few hours ago, I had been signing papers giving me the legal right to care for Hannah if something happened to her parents, and in celebration, was now getting it commemorated on my body.

I had her handprint inked on my chest over my heart. Above it, I had the words 'Property of' and below it, her nickname 'Sweet Pea', all in a script font. My heart was officially 'Property of Sweet Pea.' I'd chosen her tiny handprint because she had me wrapped around every single finger.

It was cool when the tattoo artist actually rubbed washable ink on Hannah's hand and made the template directly from it.

Andy came into the room and sat in an extra chair to watch the tattoo artist finish my tat. "Yours all finished, bro?" I asked him.

"Yeah, all done," he said, holding up his hands, showing off his new ink.

Andy had gotten not one, but two tattoos today—Hannah's initial and the initial of his first daughter, Emma, on the insides of his wrists.

"So how many does that make?" I asked. Andy's body was plastered with tattoos from the waist up.

He smiled proudly. "Zoey's name was number twenty-eight, so these two make it an even thirty. But, since the New Zealand and Maori tats are all combined into one large design, technically, I only have four," he said with a sarcastic grin.

Holy shit, he had thirty tattoos. I was barely making it through the one I was getting.

"You must have an extremely high tolerance for pain," I said.

Andy smirked. "You have no idea."

"Shit, man. I didn't mean it that way," I said.

He shook his head. "It's fine. I know how you meant it."

The artist finished my tattoo and rubbed ointment on it as Z and Hannah came in.

She and Hannah took a seat on Andy's lap. "I got my snowflake tattoos drawn up. Now I just have to wait till this little girl isn't breastfeeding, then I can get it!"

"Jesus, Z. Quit talking about shit like that in front of me. I don't need to hear about it," I muttered as I sat up. Not the visual I was wanting of my *sister,* of all people.

Everyone in the room laughed when I shuddered. I think Sweet Pea even giggled, but I wasn't sure.

"Z, can you take a picture of me and Hannah showing off my tattoo?" I asked.

She handed Sweet Pea to me and I held her on my lap while Zoey snapped our picture with my phone and then snapped another with hers. When I put my shirt back on, I changed my screen saver to that photo.

July 2013

To keep my mind off Teagan, I'd added an extra mile to my morning run. Running was the only time during the day I could clear my head. I'd helped Andy and Z move back to their place when the renovation was finished, and took on more jobs at work to keep busy.

I also made a promise there would be no more screwing around with women *before* getting to know them. That hadn't worked out so well for me with Cammie.

Hence the reason for my current state of blue balls. I'd fucking cock-blocked myself.

On the way back to my apartment, I noticed that the neighborhood that I'd lived in for years was deteriorating. There were houses with boarded up windows, trash everywhere, and graffiti covering several flat surfaces.

I slowed my running down to a jog about a half-mile from my apartment. The neighborhood wasn't getting any better. At a quarter mile away, I slowed down to a walk. Even the street I lived on had turned to shit. I needed to get the hell out of this neighborhood and find a real home. I was going to be thirty in November and all I owned was my car. Plus, now that I was Hannah's godfather, I needed a safe place for her to play and an upstairs bachelor pad was definitely not the right place.

As soon as I rounded the corner of my building, who did I find waiting for me on my steps?

Nicole.

Not who I was expecting to see at my place before seven in the morning. I stopped in front of her, and noticed she'd been crying.

"What are you doing here, Nic?" I asked, getting straight to the point. I hadn't seen her in several months and was still angry with her.

"Can I speak to you Jeremy?" she asked timidly. "It's important."

Shit, this can't be good. But, I'd known Nic for years and she obviously had something serious on her mind. No matter what she told me, I'd be honest and upfront with my sister about her visit. "Yeah, sure. Come on up." I held my hand down to her and helped her off the step. She followed me up the stairs, and I let us inside my apartment.

We took a seat on the couch after I got us each a bottle of water from the fridge. I loosened the cap on hers before handing it to her, and then uncapped mine.

"Thanks," she said softly. She took a sip and put the cap back on the bottle. "I wanted to say I'm sorry for everything, Jeremy."

I knew she was talking about Zoey and Andy because she hadn't personally done anything to hurt me. "I'm not the person you should be apologizing to Nic and you know it."

Her eyes filled with tears. "I know. I tried to talk to Zoey, Jeremy. I really did. But when I saw her, I chickened out. It was right after Rob . . ." She broke down at that point and cried.

I hated seeing women crying, so I moved closer to her and squeezed her shoulder, but I didn't do anything beyond that because I didn't want her to mistake my being nice, as anything other than that.

She calmed down and resumed talking.

"I went to her store and saw her walking in the front door. I didn't know she was pregnant, Jeremy. Not until I saw her. I didn't want to stress her out more than she probably already was. Will you please tell her I'm sorry?"

I nodded. "Yeah, I'll tell her Nicole. But you have to promise me you'll stay away from her and Andy. That whole thing with Rob was really shitty." I didn't want her causing waves where there didn't need to be any.

She looked truly remorseful. "I know. I don't know why I made Zoey think I was having sex with Andy, other than doing it for Rob. He was mad because she was seeing Andy. We were doing meth together, and I didn't know what I was doing. I swear . . ."

Holy shit, I wasn't aware she'd been doing drugs with him. "Nic, are you clean now? Or are you still doing meth?" I felt like I needed to help her if she were still doing it.

She smiled weakly and shook her head. "No, I'm good. After Rob died, my parents sent me to rehab. I've been clean since January."

"That's great, Nic. Look, I'll talk to Zoey and Andy, but don't expect anything in return from them okay? They're at a great place in their lives and don't need any drama."

She nodded and stood. "Thank you. I knew I could count on you. For what it's worth, I always thought you were a great guy and a good friend. I know there can't be anything between us ever again, but I hope we can still be friends."

"Sure Nic. We'll see what happens," I said as we walked out to her car. I opened her door for her.

She started to get in and then turned back and threw her arms around me. She seemed to need it, so I hugged her back.

She pulled away from me and laughed quietly. "You're all sweaty, go get in the shower."

"Sorry," I chuckled as she stood on her toes and kissed my cheek.

"Thanks again, Jeremy. Have a good day at work."

I pulled in through the back gate of the shop thirty minutes late to work. As I stepped out of my car, Z was walking across the lot from the store to the shop.

She was packing a now four-month old Hannah on her hip, while juggling her giant purse and Hannah's diaper bag.

Hannah let out a loud squeal when she saw me jogging toward them. She was yanking hard on a handful of Z's hair. I laughed when I saw Zoey wince and attempt to shuffle her purse and the diaper bag to reach Hannah's hand.

"Sweet Pea, are you torturing your mama?" I asked, freeing Zoey's hair from her grip. "That's my good girl."

Zoey laughed and passed Hannah over to me. "Morning, bro," she muttered before she backhanded me hard in the gut.

After we went in through the back door of the shop, I followed her to the office. "Hey, Z, I need to talk to you about something important if you have time."

She sat behind her desk while I sat in the chair next to it, settling Sweet Pea on my lap. She grabbed at the pockets and collar of my work shirt then smacked me on the face.

"What is it Jeremy? You look pissy," Zoey replied.

I smirked as Hannah moved on to pinching my nose. "Guys don't get pissy, sis. That is strictly a woman trait . . . but speaking of pissy women . . . Nicole came to see me this morning."

Zoey's expression immediately soured. "What did she want? Please tell me you aren't screwing her again, Jer. You can do so much better than her."

I shook my head. "No. Trust me. There will never be anything like that with her again. She wanted me to tell you she was sorry for everything. She wanted to tell you herself, but I think she knew you wouldn't speak to her."

Choosing my words carefully so I wouldn't upset her, I told Zoey all about Nicole's visit, how sorry she was, and that she'd been to rehab. I really, truly thought she was telling me the truth, but I kept that to myself.

"Okay, Jeremy," she said finally. "Thanks for telling me. I'll talk to Andy about it later. What else did you need to talk to me about?"

I smiled big and rubbed my palms together. "You interested in a project?"

Zoey was only working part time between the shop and the store so she could take care of Hannah full time, but I knew she was getting antsy being home too because she did most of her work while Hannah napped in the portable crib we'd set up in the office for her.

"You have my attention," she said as she arched her brows.

"I want to buy a house, Z. This dating thing isn't working, and I'm too old to be living in a bachelor pad apartment. I want something that is mine. A real *home*."

Z's expression went from interested to elated. "I'm in."

We sat in the office for the next forty-five minutes while I told her what features I wanted in a house. She scribbled notes like a mad woman while I played with Hannah.

Adam poked his head through the door as Zoey and I were finishing up. "Hey, asswipe, you gonna work today or fuck around and let us do your work for you?" He smirked.

Zoey spun her chair around and chucked her pen at him, hitting him in the side of the neck. He flipped her off.

I handed Hannah off to Zoey then stood, and pretended to stretch.

"You are so dead!" I said, lunging at Adam. I picked him up and tossed him over my shoulder then carried him out to the shop.

Thank God he was small. He struggled and punched me the whole way to the shop. I had a hard time keeping hold of him between the punches, and because I was laughing so hard.

"Andy! Get the duct tape!" I yelled when I saw him standing at his toolbox. "Jay, get his feet! Noah, you get his arms!"

I dumped Adam down by one of the support beams of the shop, as my brothers captured his hands and feet.

Andy pulled the end of the duct tape out from the roll as we pinned Adam to the beam. Starting at his feet, Andy wrapped the tape around the beam and Adam's body clear up to his neck.

"What should we do to him now?" Jason asked as we eyed Adam and contemplated our next move.

Zoey came over holding Hannah, and a small girly-looking bag. She looked us all over from head to toe.

"Here, Jer. You're the cleanest, hold my girl. I need to get our baby brother here all pretty for his photo shoot."

Andy and my brothers pulled out their cell phones and snapped pictures while Z did a very nice job putting makeup on Adam. Once she finished with his makeup, she found two rubber bands, and pulled Adam's chin length hair into two pigtails. If he were wearing a dress, he'd look like a male prostitute posing as a female prostitute.

"You're all assholes!" Adam muttered, whining like a little bitch. "Oh man, now I gotta take a piss. Cut me down you bastards!"

After we sent a few pictures to his girlfriend Angie, I handed Sweet Pea back to my sister and went to work.

We left Adam duct taped to the beam for over an hour

before he became so annoying and loud we had to cut him loose. We should've duct taped his mouth shut when he started singing. After his tenth time singing *God Bless America,* we'd had enough of him. If anyone knew how to be irritating and drive us up a wall, it was Adam. He'd been perfecting it since he was born.

A couple weeks and several houses later, I received a frantic call from Zoey while I was installing new headers and an exhaust system on a 2012 Camaro.

"Jeremy, you need to come and look at this house, right now! I was going to look at another house in the same neighborhood and found this one on the way there. It's for sale by the owner and perfect for you." Zoey finally took a breath and waited for my response.

"What's the address?" I jogged to her office and wrote down the address she gave me. "I'm on my way." I ripped the paper off the notepad then went out and let everyone know I was leaving for the afternoon.

I washed up and changed my shirt, then went to my car where I typed the address of the house in to my GPS. Twenty minutes later, I parked my car behind Z's black Tahoe in a nice, older neighborhood.

Hello, suburbia! However, the house was closer to the shop than my apartment—which was awesome—but the white picket fence surrounding the front yard was throwing me off. I wondered why Zoey thought I might like this place. I wasn't the white picket fence type of guy.

Zoey and Sweet Pea met me on the sidewalk in front of the house and she laughed when she saw the look on my face. "I know what you're thinking. Try to ignore the fence for now."

I looked over the outside of the house, which had been updated and looked brand new. The attached two-car garage was a great aspect. We walked through the gate and up the sidewalk, where we found a covered front porch.

"It's a three bedroom, with two full baths, Jer. And there's an in-ground pool!" She went through the front door then stopped and turned, looking a tad worried. "Okay, it needs *some* work."

"*Some* work?" I lifted an eyebrow.

"Wait till you see the potential."

"That sounds like *a lot* of work, Z."

She shifted Hannah to her other hip. "Did I mention it has an in-ground pool?"

"Yes, you did." I put my hands on her shoulders and turned her. "Now show me what the big deal is, already."

I entered the house behind her, into a decent sized living room. The hardwood floors were recently redone and built-in bookshelves lined the back wall.

After looking over the living room, we walked in to what I assumed was the kitchen. It was completely gutted. Next, we checked out the dining room, two bathrooms that were in the same gutted condition as the kitchen, and then the three bedrooms.

"It needs a lot of work," I said as we walked through the house again.

"I know it *seems* that way, but the owners have everything to put the house back together. One of them lost their job here, so they're moving back to Texas," she said. "All the cabinets for the kitchen and the bathrooms are still in boxes in the garage. The only thing we have to do is put it all back together, Jer."

That intrigued me for sure. If all I had to do was install everything, it wouldn't take long at all. And I could most likely do it on my own.

Standing here, looking all around the house again, everything clicked in to place. It felt right. "Where are the owners, Z? I am definitely interested."

She smiled brightly and clapped her hands. "They're waiting for us on the back patio."

I grinned at my sister as I faced the possibilities of my new life. "Let's do this."

Teagan

"You ready to run, Shan?" I asked my sister as I stuck my head in through the open bathroom door. She was pulling her long black hair back into a ponytail. She'd recently dyed the entire underside of her hair hot pink, so when she pulled it up, the hot pink stood out boldly.

I would love to do something like that to my hair, but unfortunately, nothing really matched my dark red hue.

"I still have to get dressed," she groaned. "I still can't believe I let you talk me in to this." Shannen brushed past me and went back to her bedroom to change, so I went to the living room and waited for her on the couch.

After Shannen and Brian's break-up, and whatever it was that happened between Jeremy and me, we'd decided to stick together and keep each other's spirits up. I'd admit I was still confused about Jeremy, especially since I couldn't stop thinking about him.

He'd sent flowers to Tammy twice since that night in the parking lot at Dub's. She made sure to rub it in my face, so to speak. Even though I'd told Tiffany I'd only met Jeremy that night and wasn't dating him.

I was baffled. If he wanted Tammy, why had he come looking for *me* at the hospital? It made no sense. But he'd made his choice, and his choice was Tammy.

Yes, I realized I was the one who left the bar first, but now I wasn't sure it was the right thing to do. Would Tammy be in the picture if I stayed? *Who the hell knows?* Ugh, I groaned. There was no point in dwelling on it.

Besides, I was dating Jared, and I'd decided to let things get a *little* more serious. We were seeing more of each other now, and had gone out on several dates outside of the hospital.

Shannen came into the living room dressed in her running clothes. She and I couldn't look any more different if we tried. She was about five-five, had naturally black hair that was stick straight and thick, and gorgeous snow-white skin. She had the biggest, palest blue eyes I'd ever seen. However, I had peachy skin and crazy red hair that reached my waist when I stretched it out straight and was a whopping five foot two in height.

My cheating prick father and my mother hadn't married, because it turned out, my dad had already been married and had a family in Ireland. He'd left my mom before I was even born. He was a piece of shit cheater, just like Gary, and I was the product of an affair.

When I was two, my mom, Belinda, met and then later married Lucas Jennings. A year later, my sister Shannen came along.

Lucas legally adopted me as soon as they were married, but they hadn't changed my last name because my mom had named me after my nanna to keep a part of our Irish heritage. So here I was, Teagan Shea Donnelly. When I was older, they had given me the choice to change my last name to Jennings, but I loved my nanna so much, I'd declined.

Nanna Teagan was born and raised in Dublin, Ireland. She and my papa immigrated to the United States when my mom was six. I had no idea how they ended up in Sacramento of all places, but they had.

"Yo, space cadet," Shannen said as she waved her hand in front of my face. "Are we going or what? You're the one who got me doing this shit every morning, you know?"

She was right. I had dragged her out running with me every morning after Brian had dumped her. She had a hard time keeping pace with me, and only made it a block or two before she slowed down to walk, but she was working on it, and I had no doubt that within a few more weeks she would be able to keep up with me.

We ran down the sidewalk for almost two blocks before she fell behind. She always made me go ahead of her so I could get in my full run. I would go to my stopping point then turn back and meet her wherever she was along our regular route.

Today we met in front of my favorite house. The "For-Sale" sign was gone, and someone was working on the house. The yard was freshly mowed and the sprinklers were on, watering the grass. It didn't seem like anyone had moved in yet though.

We jogged home and I hit the shower first since I had to be to work before her. Shannen was a hairdresser at a trendy place uptown, and didn't have to be to work until ten.

After I showered and dressed, I ate breakfast, packed my lunch, and went to work. When I entered through the secure employee entrance, I headed straight to the locker room to drop off my purse.

As soon as I walked through the door, I saw Tiffany and Tammy waiting to give me my daily dose of "Jeremy did this, and Jeremy did that." Frankly, I was getting tired of it.

"I wonder if he'll send me more flowers today. Last night was amazing!" Tammy said.

I rolled my eyes as I put my purse into my locker.

"The two T's," as Jackie, Nat, and I referred to them, continued their discussion as I left the locker room. I tried my hardest to ignore them.

I knew I needed to stop thinking about Jeremy, but I was still having a hard time believing everything they said was true. The guy I'd briefly gotten to know didn't seem like he would do the things they said he had.

I could see him sending flowers, for sure. But, to have multiple "girlfriends" at the same time? That was a tad much. He seemed smart to me, and that many girls at once . . . not so smart.

If Tiffany had been one of them, and thought he was an asshole like she'd said, why was she okay with her friend Tammy dating him now? It made no sense.

In my opinion, neither of the two girls seemed very smart. They were young; I'd say around twenty-three or so, and they were immature. Granted, I was only twenty-seven, but still.

I hurried down the hallway toward the ER to clock in, and when I passed the residents' room, a hand snaked out through the doorway and pulled me inside. I yelped as the door swung shut behind me. When I realized it was only Jared, I playfully smacked him on the chest.

"You scared the hell out of me!" I giggled.

"Good morning, sexy lady," he said and backed me against the closed door.

I hated it when he called me that. We hadn't even come close to having sex, but we'd had some heavy make-out sessions.

"Good morning to you too, Jared." I checked around the room to make sure we were alone.

"We're all alone for now, Teagan," he murmured, kissing a path from my collarbone up my neck to my ear. It felt good, but it also kind of irritated me.

When Jared pushed his hips forward, I felt him growing hard against my stomach. Did he really think I was going to get it on with him in here?

He kissed across my jawline to my lips. He sucked my bottom lip into his mouth and bit down lightly. My lips parted for him freely, so he slipped his tongue inside, probing and exploring. Not thinking clearly, I kissed him back.

Apparently, he took it as an invitation to proceed. His hands wandered from my hips back around to my butt. His hands gripped me tightly, pulling my hips forward, pushing his very obvious erection against me.

I wasn't about to have sex with him in the residents' room. Someone might come in at any time. Not to mention, I needed to get to work, and honestly, I was not the type of person to have sex in a public place.

"Jared, stop. I need to get to work," I said after I broke our kiss.

"Come on, Teagan. Nobody will come in, I swear." He groaned, and then pushed his hardness against me again. "Can you feel what you do to me?"

I put my palms on his chest and slowly pushed him

backward. "Jared, I really need to get to work. I'm still a temporary employee here for another three months. I can get fired simply for being late."

My job at the hospital had a six-month "trial" period during which my abilities were being assessed to see if I was a competent employee. During that time, I could be let go for minor infractions.

"Don't you think it's time we took this relationship to the next level?" he asked, closing the distance I'd put between us.

Seriously, was this a joke?

"No, actually I don't, Jared. Last time I checked, we were merely dating. I'm not even sure I'm the only girl you're seeing anyway since we haven't made anything *official* regarding our relationship."

"You've been the only one for the last month Teagan. That's pretty exclusive in my opinion." He grinned and pulled me toward one of the beds.

Unwilling to let this go any further, I locked my feet in place, halting his momentum.

"Jared, this is not going to happen right now . . . and honestly, it's not going to happen any time soon. I'm not the girl for you if you expect to have sex here, plus I'd prefer to be in an actual relationship."

"That's not what I heard," he smirked.

"I guarantee you, whatever you heard isn't true. Now if you'll excuse me, I need to get to work. I'm late now," I said, gritting my teeth.

I was pissed. Pissed that I was late to work, and pissed that someone was saying crap about me that wasn't true.

"How about a blow job then? I heard you like to give those," he said, his tone filled with spite.

"What's gotten in to you, Jared?" I was disgusted with the way he was acting.

"Nothing. I think we've been fooling around long enough, and it's time for you to do a little more."

He was trying to intimidate me and I was prepared to knock him on his ass if he touched me. No man would ever lay his hand on me again like Gary had. Regardless, I needed to end this now because Jared had just proved he was as big of a jerk as Gary. I deserved to be treated like a human being, not a play toy for a man who obviously had no respect for me.

"Goodbye, Jared. If you really want a blow job, I hear there are a couple of MA's on the fourth floor who are more than willing."

"Where do you think I got this tidbit of information, Teagan?" He huffed out an irritated breath and scowled at me. "The girls on the fourth floor were very forthcoming with what they know about you."

Tammy and Tiffany—I should've known. "I think they were talking about themselves, not me. Maybe you should try there. I really, really need to get to work now." I spun and left the room.

After clocking in ten minutes late, I went to the ER and spent the morning running around like crazy. A kid came in with a burst appendix then a construction worker who'd cut off his thumb. That one made me queasy!

Sure enough, our day wouldn't have been complete without the various bogus illnesses, and addicts coming in trying to get more drugs for pain that didn't exist.

Overall, it was a typical day.

When it was lunchtime, I clocked out and headed back toward the break room. As I neared the residents' room, the door opened and Jared peeked out the door before ushering Tiffany out when the coast was clear. He squeezed her ass as she passed him.

It was obvious what they had been doing. I guess Jared had taken my advice. Good for him. I rolled my eyes and kept on walking.

After I entered the break room, I said hi to my friends who were saving me a seat and went to the fridge to find my lunch. I searched it three times before I gave up. My lunch was gone, and I was so hungry I was ready to gnaw off my own arm.

I went to Jackie and Nat, frustrated and on the verge of tears. "I'm leaving to get lunch because someone stole what I brought. I need to get the hell out of here, anyway."

Jackie and Nat gathered their lunches and followed me out the door to the cafeteria.

Once I had made a salad, we sat down and I told them all about my missing lunch and what Jared had done.

Several days later, when I arrived for my shift at work, I found a message taped to my locker asking me to come to the Human Resources Department at ten for a meeting. I wondered all morning about the meeting, but I couldn't think of a reason for being summoned. I had a bad feeling about it though because I was still on my six-month probation.

I was so nervous I pulled Jackie and Nat aside to tell them about my meeting. Both of them tried to say something positive, but the expressions on their faces told me I should be worried.

At five minutes before ten, I was waiting in the HR office and at ten on the dot, a woman stepped through the door behind the receptionist's desk and made eye contact with me.

"Teagan Donnelly?" she asked, extending her hand.

I stood and shook her hand. "Yes, I'm Teagan."

Introducing herself as Jan Edwards, she asked me to follow her into her office then shut the door behind us.

"Please, have a seat," she said motioning to the chairs in front of her desk. I sat, and she stepped around her desk and took a seat in her chair.

She flipped a folder open on her desk and then folded her hands together, setting them on top of the folder. She leaned forward. "I'm sure you're wondering why you were called in here today."

I nodded. "Yes, I am. Is there something wrong with my job performance?"

"Not at all Teagan, that's not why you're here," she said.

Her assurance still didn't calm my nerves.

"As you know, you're in a mandatory probation period as a new hire here at the hospital. Two recent accusations have been brought against you," she said.

I appreciated how she was being straight to the point because I hated it when people beat around the bush. "What am I being accused of?"

"The first accusation is simply a minor issue with clocking

in late, Teagan. It's not that big of a deal. I verified that you made up the time by working late," Jan stated. "The next accusation, however, cannot be taken lightly."

I nodded once. "Please, what else am I being accused of?" I was about to freak out.

Jan pulled a few pieces of paper out of the folder and then set them side-by-side on the desk in front of me. I picked them up and looked them over. They were pictures someone had taken of Jared and me hugging in the ER.

I swallowed hard and set the papers back on Jan's desk. Shit. This is not good.

"Are you having a romantic relationship with Jared Peterson, Teagan?" she asked.

I knew the rules about the no fraternization policy when I'd started dating Jared. I had been trying to move past what had happened with Jeremy, honestly. But, I'd also known of several other people working at the hospital who were dating, so it didn't seem like the rule was enforced. Apparently, I was wrong. Very, very wrong. I wasn't a snitch, so I kept my mouth shut about the other couples who were dating.

"I will admit I was previously dating Jared, but I broke it off," I said quietly. I had messed up . . . bad. I was going to lose my job.

"Can you explain these photos?"

I nodded because I knew exactly when they were taken. "Yes, I can. They're from a morning I came straight to work after visiting my grandmother. She suffered a stroke a few months back, and is the reason why I moved back here from Denver."

Jan paid close attention, made notes, and nodded as I talked.

"I was upset after visiting her . . . she and I are very close. Jared was the first person I saw when I arrived at work and he could tell I was upset. He was comforting me. Nothing more," I said. "We were just friends at the time, though."

Jan finished writing before she looked back across the desk at me.

"Thank you for your honesty, Teagan. As I am sure you're aware, we do have a three-strike policy here during your probationary period. You will have two strikes in your personnel file since you admitted to your actions. May I suggest you be extremely careful during the remainder of your probationary period? Your supervisor has nothing but good things to say about you, and we'd hate to lose you over infractions such as these."

I felt tears sting my eyes, and I tried desperately not to cry in front of Jan. I was embarrassed and scared I was going to lose my job.

"I'm very sorry for causing problems, Ms. Edwards. I promise I will be extra careful about my behavior from here on out," I said. "There won't be any more accusations brought against me, I can assure you."

Jan stood and walked me to the door. "Thank you again, Teagan. I am sorry to put the tardiness in your file because you did make up the time, but rules are rules, and we must treat everyone equally, no matter how well they perform at their jobs. I'm sure you understand."

"Yes. I do. Thank you," I said as Jan opened the door for me to leave. "Have a nice day, Ms. Edwards."

As soon as I left the HR department, I practically ran to the locker room. By the time I pushed through the door and ran into an empty bathroom stall I had tears rolling down my face. I backed up against the wall of the stall, and cried as loudly as I dared.

Later that night when I got home, Shannen and I made our plans to go out and let loose.

I knew just where to go. Dub's Sports Bar, next Friday night. I needed an MMA fix . . . and some tequila. And if I happened to run in to Jeremy, I had a few words for him—and they weren't going to be nice words.

8

Jeremy

August 2013

It had been weeks since I'd seen or talked to Teagan. To put it bluntly, it sucked. She hadn't called or texted me to acknowledge my note or the flowers I'd sent her.

Then on Monday, shit hit the fan at work when Jason opened the big, bay door in his work area to pull a car inside. The doors were kept closed during the August heat and each bay was kept cool by a portable A/C unit.

"Oh shit! Andy!" Jason yelled from across the shop.

I turned to see what was going on and saw he was jogging out the open bay door. We followed him outside to find a tow truck with what appeared to be Zoey's old black Chevelle on it.

"What the fuck?" Andy grumbled and went to speak to the tow truck driver. After arguing with the driver, he came back over to us. "I need to find a place to put that car before your sister sees it." He held out an envelope to me.

I snatched it from his hand. Inside was the pink slip to the car and a note.

The note was from Rob's parents, saying they were sorry for everything Rob had done to Zoey and they thought she should have her car back. They were also sorry for the condition in which Rob had left the car, but they'd signed the pink slip relinquishing all rights to the Chevelle.

I walked over to the back of the tow truck and found that every body panel and piece of glass on the car was smashed to hell.

"We can't let Z see this." I scrubbed my hands up my face and through my hair. Everyone agreed. "I'll ask the driver to take it to my house and I'll lock it in the garage. Andy, you tell Z about it later. She can go see it when she's ready."

He nodded and pulled some money from his wallet and handed it to me. "It's for the tow to your house. Thanks, mate, I really appreciate it."

I didn't have any cash on me, so I thanked him and took the money. I had the tow truck driver follow me to my new house and we locked the car in my garage.

This was going to be a long week.

The last of the renovations on my house were complete, and Zoey was now taking her time decorating. Just as we had done with the apartment above the shop when Andy moved to Sacramento, we worked on furnishing my house room by room. By the time escrow closed, we had a game plan in place, and we were sticking to it.

She'd dragged my ass shopping nearly every night after work for the last two weeks. I never wanted to see another paint sample, comforter set, or accent pillow again. I didn't even know what the fuck half the shit was she made me buy. And I really didn't want to know either. If she said I needed it, it went into the shopping cart. I'll admit my sister was a miracle worker. Wherever she put that crap in my house, it looked great.

The three bedrooms had been done first, since they were the easiest. She'd found some kick-ass furniture for my living room, which wouldn't be delivered until the following week, so the living room was being used as a storage area for all my moving boxes until then. Now she was working on the bathrooms and would work on the kitchen and dining room next.

Since she spent so much time at my house while continuing to work part time, she'd turned the empty dining room into a space for Hannah, complete with one of those play pen things to keep her corralled. She'd brought over so much baby stuff the house looked like a baby actually lived there. I didn't mind though. If it kept Sweet Pea happy while we worked on the house, then so be it.

Since the living room furniture wouldn't be here until next week, I could put off the unpacking until the weekend. After checking that Zoey didn't need my help at the moment with anything inside the house, I went to work on the front and back yards, setting up the new gas grill and patio furniture I'd bought. I cleaned the pool. Given the August heat, I couldn't wait to use it.

Now, Thursday night had arrived, and my buddies, John, Eric, and Sonny, were coming over to help me arrange the garage. I called to have a few pizzas delivered then iced down a case of beer in a cooler and set it on the back patio in the shade. Since I needed to find my stash of paper plates and napkins for the pizza, I found some boxes labeled "kitchen" and moved them to the countertop and began unpacking.

I'd only made it through one box when someone went apeshit ringing the doorbell. It could only be one person. John. I went and opened the door and found all three of my friends standing on my front porch.

"Hello suburbia! Jeremy James has gone to the fucking dark side!" John bellowed and clapped me hard on the chest with the palm of his hand.

I tripped him as he walked past. "Thanks a lot, dickhead. Glad you came by."

Eric and Sonny came through the door behind him. "We brought housewarming drinks!" Sonny called out, raising a paper bag in the air. I could only imagine what was in it. Eric was carrying a case of Sierra Nevada.

"Dude, you said 'housewarming,'" John said to Sonny. "Are you going to the dark side with this idiot?" John pointed at me with a smirk on his face then shook his head in what appeared to be disbelief.

John was the ultimate bachelor of our group with Eric coming in a close second, and neither of them would consider settling down any time soon. Sonny was picky with women, but he had a lot of female friends. He was the guy who could hang out with anyone, and everyone liked him.

For me, settling down was a priority, and I wouldn't let my friends deter me no matter what. When I glanced at Sonny, he stood at the end of my kitchen island staring down into the bag he'd brought with him. He was gripping the edges of the countertop so tightly his knuckles were white.

"You good, man?" I asked, because something was definitely going on in his mind. He'd been acting a bit off lately, but I'd been so busy with getting the house ready I hadn't had a chance to hang out with him as much.

When I bumped his elbow with mine to get his attention, his head jerked up.

"Yeah. Just got a lot on my mind, that's all," he said, his voice unsteady and quiet.

"You know you can talk to me, right?"

He gave me a quick, awkward nod then pulled two bottles of silver Patrón tequila from the bag he'd brought.

"Okay, enough with the gay, male-bonding shit you two have going on over there," John muttered to Sonny and me. "Let's get this party started."

Sonny stormed across the kitchen, shoved John against the counter, and fisted his hand in the front of John's T-shirt. "Shut up!" he growled, his face just inches from John's.

Eric stood in shock watching the exchange, his bottle of beer halfway to his open mouth.

John's hands shot up in surrender and his face distorted in shock and confusion. "Easy man, it was just a joke."

"It wasn't funny."

Sonny released John's shirt and took a step back. He seemed just as surprised at his outburst as the rest of us were. He returned to stand next to me and pulled the cork from the Patrón bottle. "Shot glasses?" He pointed questioningly to various cabinets.

I shook my head because I had no idea where they were and my brain was still reeling from what had just taken place between John and Sonny.

"We can't drink this if we don't have shot glasses," Sonny

said, his voice back to normal. Apparently, whatever had been on his mind was forgotten and he was ready to drink.

"Help me unpack these boxes so we can find them faster. We're looking for paper plates and napkins too. Once the pizza gets here, we're set," I said.

Twenty minutes later, the doorbell rang again, and I went to pay for the pizzas.

I set the plates and napkins that John had located on top of the pizza boxes, and the guys brought the shot glasses and one of the bottles of tequila out to the patio. We piled our plates with slices of greasy pepperoni pizza and downed a couple tequila shots.

When we started working on the garage after eating, I was glad I had left my Caddy parked outside on the driveway. With Zoey's Chevelle taking half the space in the two-car garage, we needed the extra room to move around my toolbox, cabinets, and shelves.

At least with the Chevelle smashed to shit, it wouldn't hurt if anything fell on it. Every time I looked at the car, I got pissed off again at what Rob had done to it. Zoey had *not* taken the news about the condition of her car well. Still, she refused to go inside the garage to look at it. I didn't blame her really. But as soon as my garage was set up, and I was settled into my house, I planned to fix the car in my spare time.

The tequila flowed as we worked on the garage and soon, I forgot how I wanted to arrange everything. I hoped that when I looked at the garage tomorrow, everything would be in one piece and in the right place. After I went outside and pulled my car forward into the garage for the night, we went back to the patio.

Sonny thought it would be funny to jump in the pool fully clothed. John and Eric followed shortly, but were smart enough to take everything out of their pockets first. Sonny had drowned his cell phone and his wallet. The air was warm and muggy outside, so I emptied my pockets, stripped down to only my shorts, and hurled myself off the low diving board into the deep end of the pool.

We each floated on air mattresses and finished off the rest of the beer and a bottle of tequila before we got out of the pool and sprawled ourselves on the patio to dry off. The guys were too drunk to go home, so everyone decided to crash at my place.

The next morning, I woke up outside on my patio. Fortunately, I'd taken my air mattress from the pool to lie on. *Unfortunately,* the air mattress had completely deflated overnight, so I had slept on the concrete.

Sonny was sleeping on the hammock. *Lucky bastard.* I glanced down at the man I'd known since I was eight years old and wondered what had gone through his mind the previous night when he'd shoved John. I gave him a push to wake him up and it startled him so badly he almost flipped the hammock over, but I grabbed it just in time.

"Shit! Sorry, man. I wasn't trying to dump you on the ground," I said with a laugh.

Sonny laughed and carefully stood without tipping the hammock over. "It's all good," he replied. "No harm, no foul."

"Thanks for coming to help last night, Sonny." I wanted him to know that we were solid. Whatever he had going on in his head, he would bring up eventually.

"Sorry about that incident with John last night." His brows furrowed and he swallowed hard, but never broke eye contact with me. He opened his mouth to say something else then quickly closed it. After another few seconds, he said, "I gotta go."

"Look, man, John was being a dick last night, okay? He shouldn't have said what he did. I've known him my entire life and I know how he is. He's just pissed because I've decided to settle down and he'll never grow up."

Sonny nodded in agreement. "Don't tell him, but I think I'm heading that direction too, Jer. I need to get my mind right first, though." He reached out to shake my hand and we clapped each other on the back before he left.

Once he was gone, I wandered around the house and found all of John's wet clothes in a heap on my kitchen counter. I picked them up and took them with me while I searched for him and Eric.

I found Eric on the bathroom floor and woke him up.

John was sprawled facedown across my fucking bed.

Buck-ass-naked.

"Dick!" I hollered at John as I chucked his wet clothes at him. "Get your dick off my bed!"

John groaned and rolled over. Thank God I turned away when he did. I had already seen his bare ass, and I didn't need to see any more of him.

"Now I'm gonna have to wash my comforter again!"

"Dude, you just said '*comforter*,'" John joked as he pulled his shirt over his head. "You're turning in to a pussy. Did you grow a vagina in the last month too?"

"Fuck you," I muttered. *Damn, he is really taking this shit personally.*

I glanced over at my alarm clock. It was after nine in the morning, and I was over an hour late to work. I located my cell and found I'd missed two calls from the shop. I called the office, and prayed Z would answer, and not my mom.

"*Hola, Mijo,*" my mom said when she answered the office phone. "Are you planning on coming to work sometime today?"

Shit. *Busted.* "Sorry, Mom," I said, hoping she would forgive me. "Um, the guys helped me with the garage last night and we had too much to drink. I overslept. I'll be there as soon as I can."

She sighed into the phone. "Sure, *Mijo.* Hurry though, we're busy."

Shit. I pushed my friends out the door, took the quickest shower known to man, and threw on a uniform.

I swung through Dutch Bros. for coffees then stopped at Burrell's Bakery for a box of pastries for everyone so they would forgive me for being so late. It was after ten-thirty when I pulled into the parking lot of the shop.

"Oh, my son," Mom said when I dropped into the chair next to the desk. "You look like dog shit."

"Gee, thanks, Ma. I love you, too. Do you have aspirin or something?"

She laughed as she dug through her purse to find some pills for my hangover and the aches in my body from sleeping on the concrete.

I stood and pushed the intercom button for the shop. "There's food and coffee in the break room. Sorry I'm late," I said through the microphone.

My mom handed me three ibuprofens, and I swallowed them with a big gulp of my coffee. I took my cinnamon roll to the shop and ate it while I found the tools I would need for the job I had scheduled.

Work sucked. Thank God it was Friday.

My asshole brothers wouldn't let me get through an hour without making puking noises at me to see if they could get me to barf. My cinnamon roll sat like a lead weight in my stomach, so the thought of puking didn't sound like a half-bad idea.

By the time five o'clock rolled around, I was feeling somewhat better. I went to my apartment, packed the last few remaining boxes, and hauled them over to my house. I was actually hungry by the time I got to the house, so I ate a few slices of leftover pizza.

I was unpacking a box of clothes when Eric called. "What's up, man?" I asked when I answered the phone.

"You coming to Dub's tonight?"

"Nah, you guys go ahead. I'm gonna stay here and get all this shit put away."

I had forgotten Z was having a barbecue tomorrow night for Andy's thirtieth birthday, so I had less time than I'd originally thought to unpack.

"Alright, bro, come by if you change your mind, we'll be here. Looks like it's just me and John tonight," he said.

I said goodbye to him and unpacked a few more boxes of crap.

While I was unpacking, I let Teagan slip into my mind, which pissed me off. I'd made an ass of myself by sending her flowers when she had a boyfriend. Every time I passed by the extra bottle of tequila Sonny left sitting on the counter in the kitchen, I wanted to drink it to forget about Teagan.

After I unpacked my bathroom boxes and hopped into the shower, I only wanted to crash for the night. I finished my shower and pulled on some shorts and a T-shirt. After running a comb through my wet hair, I headed to the kitchen for the tequila and a shot glass.

I didn't want to keep thinking about her and her doctor boyfriend.

The house was eerily quiet for a change. Tonight was the first time I had been here alone for a lengthy period of time. It was too quiet, so I took my pity party out to the patio to listen to the noises of the neighborhood.

I was halfway through the bottle of tequila, and I was feeling pretty good. Drunk again, but good. My cell rang. Looking at the screen, I saw John was calling.

"What's up, dickface?" I asked, my words slightly slurred from the tequila.

"Dude, you need to get your ass down here!"

I jerked my phone away from my ear because my head hurt from drinking two nights in a row.

"Fuck no, man. I'm staying here with my bottle of tequila," I mumbled. *My tequila wouldn't leave me for a douchebag in a white coat.*

"I'm not gonna say it again. Get your ass down here. Red is here with her friends. She's all sorts of pissed off and dropped some dude to his knees when he grabbed her ass!"

All I heard was that Red was there, and some asshole was putting his hands on her. "What do you mean she dropped him to his knees?"

"It was fucking awesome. She keeps looking for you, I think. Oh, shit!" he yelled and then it sounded like he covered the phone with his hand.

"What's going on now?" I asked, hoping Teagan was okay.

"Cammie and her friends just came in. Shit's gonna get real. *Get your ass down here right-the-fuck now!*" he yelled before hanging up on me.

Whatever was happening had him all excited. I'd drunk too much tequila to drive, so I called a taxi. Because I wasn't driving, I took two more shots and slipped my feet into the only pair of shoes that were not in a moving box somewhere.

They happened to be the black, rubber flip-flops I'd bought for when I was cleaning out the pool. It was either those or my work boots, and since I was wearing shorts . . . ugly flip-flops it was.

When the taxi pulled into Dub's I paid the driver and went inside where I found my friends at our usual couch. There were four girls with them. One of the girls was Teagan. She was sitting as far away from my friends as possible and not speaking to anyone. Her friends and my friends appeared to be having a great time though.

I walked toward them, never taking my eyes off Teagan. Her back was turned toward me, so she hadn't seen me yet. None of my friends had either. They were too engrossed with the four pretty women surrounding them.

I was only five feet from my friends when a pair of arms wrapped around me from behind. I felt like I was being squeezed to death.

"Jeremy, there you are!"

I cringed when I heard Cammie's voice behind me.

My friends turned toward me when they heard someone call my name. Teagan turned and made eye contact with me and the expression on her face turned lethal.

I seized the hands that were around me and pulled Cammie off me. She tried to throw her arms around my neck, but everything happened so fast, and I'd had too much to drink, I only halfway blocked her advance. She jumped up and planted a kiss on my cheek.

"What the hell, Cammie?" I growled. I was tired of her pulling this shit with me. I gripped her elbow and pulled her through the bar and into the parking lot.

"What is your problem? We've been over for months now. Why do you do shit like that?" She tried to snake her arms around my waist, and I grabbed her wrists to stop her.

"Come on baby," she whined. "You know we're good together. Let's try it again. I promise to be a good girl this time. Unless you want me to be a *bad* girl." She pressed herself against me in an attempt to entice me.

"Cammie, I told you we were done and I meant it. You need to get over it and find someone who's willing to deal with your shit, 'cause it's definitely not me."

"*Asshole,*" she seethed. "You'll change your mind and come crawling back to me." She turned and went back inside the bar.

Yeah, that's not gonna happen. I followed her back in, but only to find Teagan.

I found her sitting at the bar with four shot glasses in front of her. I sat next to her, not really knowing what to say. Teagan downed all four shots, one right after the other, barely taking a breath in between each one. She didn't even look over at me when she spoke.

"Shouldn't you be with your girlfriend?" she asked so quietly I almost didn't hear her.

"I don't have a girlfriend. Shouldn't you be with your boyfriend?" I countered.

"I don't have a boyfriend, Jeremy."

"Are you sure about that, Red?"

She finally looked over at me. "Yes, I'm sure. Are you sure you don't have a girlfriend? One you might send flowers to at work and one you took out to dinner last night?"

She turned back to the bartender and ordered four more shots of tequila.

What was she talking about? "The only girl I've ever sent flowers to is *you*."

"I'm sorry, what did you say?" She stared back over at me in disbelief, her eyes bloodshot, and her eyelids heavy.

Shit, she was drunk. She definitely didn't need the additional four shots she'd ordered. "I said the only girl I've sent flowers to is you, Teagan."

"When?" She was still staring at me.

"I left you a note the day I met you and sent the flowers a week or so after that. You never called me," I said. "Didn't you get them?"

She shook her head and looked down at the bar. Something was definitely wrong here. She picked up a shot and tossed it back, then slammed the glass on the bar. Then she started crying. I was not expecting that.

"Hey, what's wrong? Talk to me." I turned her bar stool so she was facing me.

"God, I'm so stupid, they've been playing me all along."

What was she talking about? "What do you mean? Who's

been playing you?"

She huffed loudly and did another shot, then wiped the tears from her face with a napkin from the bar. "The Two T's," she muttered.

I wasn't sure what that meant. She stood from the bar and swayed on her feet. I steadied her before she turned around and stomped over to the couch where our friends were sitting.

She said something to the girls then they stood and walked into the other room with Teagan leading the way, and she looked pissed.

I walked toward my friends as they were scrambling off the couch to follow the girls.

"Bro, there's gonna be a catfight right now. I suggest you go get Red before she scratches somebody's eyes out," Eric said, giving me a push toward the other room.

What the fuck? I jogged to the other room to find Teagan beating the living shit out of Cammie. There was no catfight about it. She had her pinned on the floor and was straight up punching her.

It took me a few seconds to comprehend what was *actually* happening and spring into action. While I pulled Teagan off Cammie, she called Cammie a lying bitch and mumbled something about her job.

As a horny guy, seeing Teagan with her skirt bunched up around her muscular, yet feminine thighs as she straddled Cammie was officially the hottest thing I'd ever seen. The vision of her smooth legs wrapped around my waist damn near had me dropping to my knees.

"Teagan, stop!" I gripped her upper arms when she tried to go after Cammie again.

She freed one arm and slapped me.

Holy shit she was feisty, and I loved it.

"This is *your* fault!" she growled and tried to do it again.

I dodged the next slap, but not the kick to the shin. Son of a bitch! She was wearing pointy shoes. That hurt like hell.

"Ow! Calm down, Teagan!"

Fortunately, my face was slightly numb from my tequila stupor, so the slap had no effect, but her pointy shoe to my bare shin hurt like a motherfucker. She finally stopped struggling, and I was trying my damnedest not to laugh because I didn't want to be slapped or kicked again.

Cammie's friends picked her up off the floor, and checked her over. She looked fine to me, but I didn't really give a shit about her. I turned my attention to Teagan.

"What the hell was that about?" I asked her.

Teagan was shaking and breathing heavy. Her hair had slipped free and was hanging in loose curls all around her. She looked beautiful and sexy as hell with it all down and wild.

"Fuck you Jeremy," she muttered as she turned away from me.

She took two steps before she ran in to the chest of a bouncer who was the size of a small car.

"You're outta here, Red." He took her by the upper arm and led her toward the door.

That sobered me up momentarily. I followed them out the door with our friends close behind me.

Teagan leaned against the front of a Dodge Neon, crying. Her friends gathered around her trying to calm her down.

"Does someone want to tell me what just happened?" I said to the group of girls, hoping someone would tell me what was going on. A woman with jet-black hair came over and pulled me aside.

"I'm her sister, Shannen. I assume you're Jeremy?"

I nodded. "What's going on with Teagan and Cammie?"

Shannen looked confused for a second. "Her name is Cammie? Not Tammy?"

Again, I nodded.

"Look, I think Teagan and you need to talk. There's been something going on with those two at work, and it's about you."

Fuck me. "I'm going to get a taxi and take her to my place so we can talk. Is that okay with you?" I asked. "I swear she'll be safe with me."

Shannen looked unsure, but after John and Jackie stepped up and said they would vouch for me, she agreed. I gave her my cell number and told her to call to talk to her sister anytime.

I needed to get Teagan away from here so she could explain to me what was going on. I walked over to her, and her friends left us alone.

"Teagan, I'm not sure what's going on with you and Cammie, but we should really talk about it if it has something to do with me. Come home with me so we can talk . . . *please.*"

She started to say no, but her sister spoke up. "Teags go with him," Shannen pleaded.

I watched the exchange between the two sisters and eventually Teagan nodded. Thank fucking Christ.

We left our friends, and I called a taxi to come and get us.

While we waited for our ride, she explained that two girls named Tammy and Tiffany had been screwing with her at work.

I was confused as to who Tammy was, and then I remembered Shannen had been confused about Cammie's name, as well. I explained to Teagan that her name was Cammie and that she was my ex-girlfriend.

"So you didn't take her out to dinner last night?"

"Definitely not. Ask my friends. We were at my house last night working in my garage," I said.

I felt like shit for whatever Cammie and her friend had put Teagan through.

The taxi still hadn't arrived, so we stood near the side of the building waiting. I reached out and took her hand in mine, hoping she wouldn't pull away.

She didn't.

Instead, she interlaced her fingers with mine and then did the same with my other hand. I leaned back against the building, and she propped herself against me, still holding my hands.

I was thrilled when she rested her cheek on my chest and took in a deep, calming breath then let it out. I let go of one of her hands and entwined my fingers in her hair. I'd wanted to get my fingers in those strands since I'd met her, and I wasn't going to miss my chance.

"Teagan," I said softly. "I'm sorry about the flowers and everything else. I would've stopped Cammie and her friend if I'd known what they were doing to you."

She tilted her head back and looked me in the eyes. "I'm sorry for slapping you."

I nodded, accepting her unnecessary apology.

"Jeremy, what did the note say?"

"It said thank you for taking good care of me, and that I wanted to see you again. I left my name and number and asked you to call if you wanted to get together for a drink or dinner."

She reached up and pushed my hair back off my forehead. "You got your stitches out . . . I would've called if I'd gotten the note."

As the taxi pulled into the parking lot, she gently took my face in her soft hands and pulled me down to kiss me.

The instant our lips touched, it was as if everything around us stopped. There was no sound, no traffic, and no noise coming from inside the bar. It was only her and me.

The taxi honked twice, forcing us apart. I opened the door and slipped inside after her.

After I sat down, she moved closer and threw her legs over mine. By the time she was comfortable, she was fully on my lap and resting her head in the crook of my neck.

Although she was drunk, I went with it. After not seeing her for so long, she was exactly where I wanted her. With me.

I rattled off my address to the taxi driver, and we were on our way.

By the time we made it to my house, she was asleep in my arms. I couldn't have been happier. I paid the driver and woke Teagan. I didn't think she even opened her eyes as I carried her to my door.

At my door, I had to stand her on her feet to get my keys out of my pocket. As I slid the key into the lock, she suddenly pulled me back down to kiss her. This time it wasn't a sweet kiss like we'd shared while waiting for the taxi. This kiss was blazing hot and demanding.

Our lips parted, our tongues touched and we devoured each other while standing on my porch. She slid her hands under the front of my shirt, and the instant she touched my skin, a breathy moan escaped her.

I couldn't help it, I hadn't been with anyone since Cammie, and now the woman who'd consumed the majority of my thoughts was all over me. I leaned back against the door and pulled her closer.

After kissing for another minute, she reached down and turned the doorknob. I felt the door swing in, throwing me off balance. I lifted my foot to take a step inside, but my flip-flop caught on the threshold and I fell backward.

I landed flat on my back after hitting one of my moving boxes on the way down. That was gonna leave a mark, but I didn't care. Teagan landed on top of me, kissing me again within seconds.

"Teagan, the door," I murmured against her mouth.

She giggled, crawled on her hands and knees to the door, and slammed it. She crawled right back on top of me and was kissing me again.

No matter how badly I wanted her right then, I would not have sex with her. I was doing it differently this time, and we still had too many issues to discuss.

Then Teagan turned the tables on me. She took my hands in hers and slid them along her bare thighs up under her skirt. When my palms were on her hips, over the top of her panties, she removed her hands and lifted my shirt.

"Touch me, Jeremy," she whispered as she continued pushing up my shirt, kissing and licking her way up my body as she went.

Jesus, this was going to be a lot harder than I thought if she kept talking like that.

I didn't move my hands, and I didn't sit up for her to pull my shirt off, but my fingers instinctively caressed her hips as we kissed. After a moment, I was finally able to concentrate. Just as I moved my hands to take them out from under her skirt, I realized her panties were tied at each hip with satin ribbons.

Oh Jesus, what I wouldn't do to see them.

She put her hands over mine to stop me, and together we tugged the ribbons loose. I felt her panties fall open at her hips.

"Jeremy, *please* . . . touch me," she begged. "Just for tonight."

Oh God, my body was betraying me. I wanted to be inside her so badly I was about to burst. She rocked her hips forward, rubbing herself along my fully hardened dick. *Fuck, I cannot do this. I cannot mess this up.*

I wasn't going to have sex with her, but there was no reason not to give her what she was asking for. I slid my hand between her legs and slowly began stroking her. She was hot and so, so wet.

She was sitting up, straddling me, and looked so perfect. Her long, red hair spilling all around her, with her chin tilted down toward me, her eyes closed.

It was exactly like my dreams about her.

"Teagan, you're so beautiful," I said as I plunged my finger inside her.

She panted with each thrust from my finger. "No I'm not," she whispered. Her bright, green eyes opened and she sucked her bottom lip between her teeth.

Why would she say that? Does she not see how perfect she is? "You're the most stunning woman I've ever met." Knowing I needed her to finish before I did something stupid like have sex with her, I slid a second finger in and she hummed in pleasure. Her eyes closed and her brows furrowed as she rocked her hips, moving herself against my hand.

Oh fuck, now she was riding me. She was moving back and forth across my dick and it felt amazing even over my clothes. My free hand slid around to her ass. I gripped it tightly and guided her hips to move just a bit faster. The sounds that came from her mouth astounded me. She was practically purring like a cat.

God, please do not let me do something stupid.

Teagan quickened her pace, so I did too, moving my fingers in and out, now rubbing my thumb in circles over her clit. She was making the sexiest moaning noises, and I was barely able to contain myself.

Her eyes shot open and her green eyes stared down into mine. When I felt her body tightening, she slowed her movement down, never looking away. She threw her head back and let out a long, breathy moan as her body pulsed around my fingers.

I loved the weight of her small body on mine, and her hair falling over her shoulders. She rode out her orgasm then fell forward on top of me, resting her cheek against mine. Her breath was quick and warm against my ear, but still it sent chills right through me.

With the most beautiful girl I'd ever seen draped over me, I laid on the floor of my new house unable to believe what had just happened. Teagan moved down and pressed her cheek against my chest, and I wondered if she could feel how fast my heart was beating for her.

Easing my hand away from her, I let it fall to the floor beside me, as my other hand moved slowly up and down the soft skin under the back of her shirt. Eventually, her breathing slowed and I thanked God she had fallen asleep.

That definitely stopped me from doing anything else with her. I maneuvered her off me to the floor, and stood. I slipped off my shoes, walked quietly to my bedroom, and pulled back the blankets on the bed then grabbed a T-shirt and some boxers out of a moving box for her.

Back in the living room, I carefully picked her up and took her to my room. I set her on the edge of the bed and woke her long enough for her to strip out of her clothes. She did as I asked, and slipped into my T-shirt and boxers.

My eyes were closed the entire time, because seeing her completely naked would be my undoing. I was not going to screw this up.

When she was dressed, she curled up on my bed and I pulled the covers over her. I wished then that I'd had her take some ibuprofen. She was going to have one hell of a hangover tomorrow.

I turned off the light and laid on the bed fully clothed. I needed to keep my distance, so I didn't get under the covers with her, but I wanted to stay with her in case she woke up and needed something, or got sick.

Tomorrow, we would have a long discussion about how to deal with the Cammie situation. When she curled her body into mine, all I could do was hold her close and breathe her in. Whispering *goodnight,* I kissed her sweet lips and closed my eyes.

Teagan

My body jerked in my sleep and instinctively braced itself for impact. It was one of those dreams where you felt like you were falling and woke up just before you landed. It wasn't a good dream to have when you already felt like you'd been hit by a bus.

My head was throbbing and felt too heavy when I tried to lift it. I slowly opened one eye and had no idea where I was. I stretched and took in a deep breath through my nose. It didn't smell like I was in my bedroom at my parents' house.

I smelled the faint scent of cologne and freshly washed sheets. *Cologne? Why do I smell men's cologne?* I opened both eyes and let them adjust to the darkened room.

Once my eyes adjusted, I turned my head and saw the silhouette of someone lying next to me. If it weren't for the windowed French doors, the room would be too dark inside to see anything.

Think Teagan . . . think! Dub's, Jackie, Nat, Shannen . . . Tequila . . . lots and lots of tequila. Blue eyes . . .

Oh, crap. Jeremy. Kissing him, being on top of him, sliding my hands under his shirt, his hands up my skirt. All extremely pleasurable memories . . . but . . .

This was not happening. Oh my God, what had I done? I had sex with Jeremy . . . *I think*. I didn't do one-night stands. Obviously, I did with the way it appeared right now. I looked again at the man sleeping next to me and groaned.

Getting my bearings, I took a quick look around and found a digital clock on a nightstand next to me. Its glowing red numbers told me it was five thirty-two in the morning. I had to be to work at eight, had a hangover from hell, and no idea where I was.

Except I was in a bed with Jeremy. The man who was the cause of all the crap I had been forced to endure at work. I shouldn't be here.

Careful not to wake him, I eased the covers back and found I was at least wearing clothes. They were, however, not mine. They appeared to be his. As I sat up, I felt my hair snag on something. I ran my hand down the thick section of trapped hair until it bumped another hand.

Jeremy had a thick lock of my hair curled around his fingers. As I tried to free it, he stirred and gripped it tighter. *Crap.*

"You're not trying to make your escape are you?" he murmured, half asleep.

I could hear the smile in his voice and the breath caught in my throat at the sound. *Dang, he was sexy.* But it didn't make up for all the things that had happened since I'd met him.

"Um, I need to use your bathroom," I whispered. It was partly true. I did need to pee, but I also needed him to go back to sleep so I could get the hell out of here. Gently, I pried his fingers from my hair.

He let go of my hair but not my hand. He brought my hand to his lips and kissed it.

My stomach fluttered from the sweetness of it.

"Bathroom's the door on the left," he said then released my hand. "Hurry back."

It was light enough that I caught sight of two doors at the other end of the room. I assumed the other door was a closet. I sat up slowly, lowering my feet to the floor, and let my foggy brain catch up to the rest of my body before I stood.

Once I was up, I walked across the cool hardwood floor and went through the door on the left. I quietly shut it behind me and felt around on the wall for a light switch. When I found it, I flipped it on and immediately wanted to shut it back off as I caught sight of my reflection in the mirror.

I looked like hell. My hair was a rat's nest and my eye makeup was running down my face. I looked like a crazy, redheaded raccoon.

I used the facilities then washed my hands and face with the hand soap on the counter. When I finger-combed my hair, long strands came out in small chunks. What the heck? As I combed, I pulled against a knot, and my scalp felt tender.

That's when it hit me. Tammy. No, *Cammie*. I'd attacked her.

Memories were coming back from last night. I screwed up . . . bad.

All because the man in the other room couldn't keep his pants on. Not that I had room to talk. It appeared that he was able to coax me out of mine, and I didn't remember a thing about it.

I shut off the light and stepped out of the bathroom. "Jeremy?" I said it loud enough to wake him. He didn't answer, so I said it again, much louder this time. After he gave no response, I assumed he'd fallen back to sleep.

Not wasting any time, I searched around for my clothes, and found them draped over the footboard of the bed. Making my escape from his bedroom, I found my purse and then cringed when I located my panties on the living room floor. My shoes were nowhere to be found and I wasn't going back to his bedroom to look for them. His living room was empty of furniture, but there were stacks of moving boxes lining the opposite wall.

After I shoved my clothes inside my purse, I bolted out the front door with plans to call a taxi once I'd figured out where the heck I was. I jogged barefoot down the sidewalk toward the street and had the strangest feeling of déjà vu.

Once I reached the end of the sidewalk, I noticed the white picket fence around the yard. I stepped through the gate and looked back at the house.

Jeremy was the new owner of my favorite house and lived only three blocks away from my parents. *What are the odds?*

While I stared at the house in surprise, a light came on inside. Jeremy was awake and probably looking for me. *Crap, gotta run!*

At least I knew where I was now and didn't have far to go to get home. I jogged down the sidewalk toward my street. Once home, I went straight to the bathroom and into the shower. I hoped nobody had seen me running through the neighborhood with no shoes, while wearing a man's shirt and boxer briefs.

Jesus, I had been wearing Jeremy's freaking underwear. The boxers were light gray, with narrow, dark gray stripes and very, very sexy. I imagined him wearing them and nothing else. The visual of that alone made me sigh.

Oh, and I'd kicked his ex-girlfriend's ass. *That* made me smile, but only because of the crap she had pulled on *me*.

Who are you and what did you do with Teagan? I smirked at my dumb joke as more hair came out while I washed it. Cammie must have really been yanking on it hard.

I stepped out of the shower, wrapped my hair in a towel, and pulled on my robe. I rummaged through the medicine cabinet for some ibuprofen then swallowed four of them with a cupped handful of water from the tap.

I picked up Jeremy's clothes from the floor and took them to my bedroom. I tossed them into my laundry hamper along with the clothes I'd worn the night before.

Crap, I was going to miss the shoes I left at his place. I'd splurged on them when I lived in Denver, and they were my favorite pair.

I was getting dressed when there was a quiet knock on my door. "Teags?"

"Come in," I called.

Shannen stepped inside my room and shut the door behind her. "Holy shit, Teagan. What the hell got in to you last night?" She sprawled across my bed, making herself comfortable.

I shrugged. "I'm still having a hard time remembering everything, honestly. Did I really hit that girl?" I asked then said, "Oh, thanks for bringing my car home."

Shannen nodded, "Yeah, yeah. No prob," then grinned. "You didn't hit her, you beat her ass, and the bitch deserved it. From what John was saying, she's been calling and texting Jeremy since he broke up with her."

Great. I flopped down on my bed and hugged my knees to my chest. "I think I had sex with him," I blurted out.

Shannen shot up to a sitting position. "I'm sorry . . . you *what?* What do you mean *you think?* Either you did, or you didn't. I can say that if you had sex, I'm gonna kick his ass because he told me you'd be safe with him. That means he's not supposed to have sex with you!"

I frowned. "I really don't know. I woke up in his bed, wearing his clothes and I found my panties on the living room floor."

Shannen's mouth dropped open, and her eyes grew big. "Teagan, do you like him? Like, *really* like him?"

Did I? Without a doubt, yes. "I do, a lot. I can't trust him though. I've heard too many bad things about him and with all the problems at work . . . I can't deal with that. I have two strikes against me now, and I can't lose my job."

"What are you talking about, Teagan?"

I hadn't told her about the disciplinary meeting at work, so I explained my visit to HR and then told her Jeremy had sent *me* the flowers, not Cammie. We talked until it was nearly time for me to leave for work.

"I really don't know what to say, sis. I know those girls were saying and doing some nasty things, but it's not really his fault. Cammie got what was coming to her last night, so maybe she'll stop screwing with you."

She was right. Technically, it wasn't his fault. However, because of my non-relationship with him, they'd made my life a living hell.

I didn't know what to believe about him, but I *did* know I wasn't going to live my life being put through that kind of hell because of someone else's actions. I wanted to be in a relationship where I didn't have to worry about lying, cheating, crazy ex-girlfriends, or losing my job. Being in a relationship wasn't worth that type of stress or drama.

After I was ready for work, I tossed a salad together for lunch and put it in a plastic grocery bag. My stolen lime-green lunch bag was still missing, and I wasn't expecting to see it again. It was probably in a landfill somewhere by now.

I arrived at work early and was the first person in line to

clock in. As I was heading toward the floor where I'd be working today, I ran in to Nat and stopped to chat in the hallway.

"Wait till you see Tammy today," she said. "She looks so *pretty.*"

I knew she was being sarcastic, and it really made me want to see what I had done to her.

"I found out last night her name is Cammie. I guess she is Jeremy's ex-girlfriend. They broke up a while back," I said.

Nat rolled her eyes. "That explains a lot then. Nice job kicking her ass last night." Nat snorted and laughed. "Can we still call them the two T's?"

My brows rose in question. "Why?"

"Because the initial still fits," she said, and continued, "they're both twats."

I nodded. "Abso-freaking-lutely."

We made plans to meet for lunch and headed our separate ways.

For a change, I spent the morning working ordinary nursing rounds. It was rather nice not running around the ER from one emergency to the next. After attaching a new IV bag to a stand for a patient, I stepped out of the room, and my cell vibrated in my pocket. I snuck into the bathroom and entered an empty stall, locking the door behind me. I couldn't risk getting caught texting someone. I pulled my cell out and found a text from Shannen.

10:15 AM- You didn't have sex with Jeremy. FYI.

What? How the hell would she know that? I texted her back.

10:16 AM- And you know this how?

10:18 AM- He told me. He also wants me to tell you he's mad at you for leaving before he talked to you.

She spoke to him?

10:19 AM- Why are you talking to him?

10:20 AM- Because I knew you wouldn't, but you should.

Yep, my little sister . . . big pain in the ass.

> 10:25 AM- Tell him thank you for taking care of me last night, and we're even now. He'll understand what I mean.

I'd taken care of him in the ER, and he had returned the courtesy by taking care of me when I was drunk. Questions ran through my mind. If I didn't have sex with him, why were my panties on the living room floor? How did I get in his clothes? Where had he put my shoes?

Ugh, who cares? It was all over now. I could get on with my life and try to keep my job. I shut off my phone, shoved it back inside my pocket, and went back to work.

At lunchtime, I took the stairwell down to the first floor to meet Nat and Jackie. I found my lunch still carefully hidden where I stashed it in the fridge, so that made me happy.

I took a seat to wait for my friends and pulled my cell out of my pocket. Once I turned it back on, I had eight new texts from my sister.

I scrolled to the oldest and read them in order.

> *10:28 AM- He says you are not getting away that easy, and he wants your number.*

> *10:30 AM- Gonna give him your number if you don't text me back, bitch.*

> *10:36 AM- Now he wants to know why you don't like him. I told him it's not true, and you do like him.*

> *10:45 AM- Where did you go?*

> *10:47 AM- Teags, this guy really, really likes you. Give him a chance.*

> *10:53 AM- He wants you to go to a barbecue with him later.*

> *11:00 AM- Don't believe everything you hear. Only believe what you see for yourself.*

> *11:15 AM- I'm done being the go-between. Text me back when you can.*

Holy crap, my sister had become BFF's with him. I tapped reply on my phone and texted her back.

> 11:30 AM- I'm saying no. I can't deal with all the ex-girlfriend drama.

She replied to me within a minute.

> 11:31 AM- You're already dealing with it. At least go out with him to see if he's worth the trouble. You might be surprised.

She was relentless. Now I was frustrated, so I didn't respond to her. There was a lot to think about and I wasn't about to do it with a hangover.

Nat and Jackie joined me for lunch, and we recapped what had happened the previous night. Well, not *all* of it. I'd left a few parts out, mainly the part after I'd left with Jeremy. They'd both seen Cammie this morning, and said she had a black eye and a split lip.

Thankfully, I finished out the day without anything going wrong. I saw Cammie from a distance as I was leaving, but she was wearing sunglasses.

The next morning I woke in the midst of a mind-blowing orgasm. I was moaning quietly and clutching my sheets in my fists. *That's never happened to me before.*

I'd been having a great dream about Jeremy. Only, I realized everything in the dream had actually happened. I hadn't had sex with Jeremy, but I had done *something* with him.

Everything that had happened was at *my* instigation. He hadn't coaxed me in to a thing.

I'd been the one to kiss him first. I remembered the feel of his skin, the coarse hair on his legs against my legs while I had been on top of him in the middle of his living room floor. Most of all, I remembered the way his thick fingers felt inside me, and the feel of his erection pressed against me.

I had begged him to touch me, and he had. Jeremy could have taken it further, but he hadn't. He'd given me what I wanted and then he'd put me to bed.

Thinking back to when I woke up in his bed, I'd been under

the covers. He hadn't. He'd been on top of them, fully clothed.

All he'd wanted to do was take me somewhere private to *talk,* and I'd ended up throwing myself at him. What the hell was wrong with me?

And what had I done afterward? I'd run away . . . like a scared animal. Now I felt like a jerk because I hadn't given him a chance to talk.

Parts of that night were still fuzzy, but I remembered him telling me Cammie was his ex, and he would've stopped her if he had known what she was doing to me at work.

I thought back to one of the texts from Shannen. She said not to believe everything I heard, but to believe what I saw personally. That's what I was going to do.

So far, I'd felt the crazy connection we'd had in the ER, I loved the way he looked at me, and I craved the way he touched me. *Oh God, that part I love the most.*

He'd written me a note asking to see me again. He'd come to the hospital to talk to me. *He'd sent me flowers.* Gary had never sent me flowers. Jeremy had told me I was the first girl he'd ever sent flowers to. That had to mean something, right?

Then the man did just the opposite of what any other man would have done when I was crazy-ass drunk and throwing myself at him; he didn't take advantage and have sex with me. He'd only touched me when I'd begged him to, and now my body hummed in blissful remembrance.

But, I was embarrassed by my drunken behavior and I felt like apologizing to him. And I owed it to him to hear his side of the story.

Finally, I gathered the nerve to go see him after Shannen and I had seen him one morning when we were out running. As we'd turned onto his street, he'd been leaving his house dressed only in shorts and running shoes. The sight of him had stopped me dead in my tracks. And because I'd still been so embarrassed, I'd ducked behind a parked car to avoid being seen by him.

Now, here I was, standing in front of his house with his clothes in my hand, trying to gather enough courage to go to the door. I mentally kicked myself in the ass, walked to the door, and knocked. A few minutes passed before the door swung open.

Standing in front of me talking on a cell phone, was a tall blonde-haired woman in her mid-twenties. Her eyes grew big when she saw me standing there. *Was she expecting someone else? Did she know who I was?* She motioned for me to come into the house. I stepped inside, and she closed the door behind me.

"I'm sorry," she said, pointing at her cell. "Give me a sec to finish this up."

She was wearing an engagement ring and wedding band that was hard to miss because of the size of the center diamond. The gem was easily two carats, and absolutely stunning.

She turned and went into the room next to the kitchen. I could hear her conversation clearly.

"It's horrible. I've only been here twenty minutes and now that I've seen it with my own eyes, I am sick about it. Why would he do that to me?"

She was upset about something a man had done, that's for sure. I didn't want to eavesdrop, but I had nowhere else to go, and she was speaking loudly enough for me to hear her from the other room.

"I should have known that asshole would screw it up. He's not even here, and he's still hurting me."

Oh my God, who was she? Jeremy's wife? Was he lying to me? She came back into the living room and tossed a bag of some kind to the floor next to the moving boxes. *Is that a diaper bag?*

"I'm so sorry, just one more minute," she whispered to me.

This time when I looked at her, tears were forming in her eyes. Something was definitely wrong here. I nodded and swallowed hard. She wasn't acting weird toward me, but still I wondered what she was going to do, or say to me when she was off the phone.

She continued talking as she went back into the other room. She was pacing back and forth in front of the entryway, as she listened to the person on the other end of the line.

"Jason, hang on a sec," she said to the person on the phone, then said, "Good morning, beautiful girl, how was your nap?"

The next time she paced by the doorway, she was cradling a baby against her shoulder. The little girl was adorable. She had blonde curls and big blue eyes. *Big blue eyes.* Oh God, was she Jeremy's daughter? Had I stepped into Jeremy's reality? The one where he had a wife and daughter? Why else would this woman and her baby be in his house?

Glancing around the living room again, I noticed a few items I hadn't the last time—a high chair, diaper bag, and a playpen. And of course, the pretty woman with her baby. *I am such an idiot!*

The things she was saying . . . she was talking about him. The girls at work had to be right about him. I tossed his clothes on top of one of the moving boxes and left.

Tears of guilt streamed down my face as I ran down the sidewalk. As I was fumbling with the gate latch, the woman came out the door with her baby still in her arms.

"Wait!" she called out. "Come back!"

There was no way in hell I was going back in there. I turned to her and took a shallow breath. "I'm so sorry," I mumbled as I pushed the gate open. I ran home as fast as my shaking legs would carry me.

In the safety of my bedroom, I curled up in to a ball on my bed and cried. I'd spent the night with not only a married man, but also one with a baby. I was a horrible person and he was a lying sack of shit. How could he cheat on her and their perfect little girl? Jeremy was exactly like Gary—no, he was worse because he had a child. He was like my cheating prick of a father who'd deceived my mom and his own family in Ireland. I felt so horrible I cried until I fell asleep from exhaustion.

The next day at work, after I had been walking around as if someone ran over my dog, Nat and Jackie cornered me in the locker room. Too upset to care who was around, I told them about the married woman and her baby in Jeremy's house. Shannen had been right on one account. I needed to believe not what I heard, but what I saw. And the possibilities of what I'd seen made me sick.

Later that day, when I was in line to clock out I heard someone whisper from behind me, "I heard you met his wife and daughter."

Craning my neck around, I saw Cammie. Of course. I turned away without responding to her.

"That's how I met him. Here at the hospital. He wasn't even here when his own daughter was born. He came afterward. Then an hour later he was fucking me in the parking garage."

She sounded prideful—like screwing Jeremy had been some great accomplishment for her.

My stomach clenched and I swallowed back the vomit that was threatening to come up. Jeremy and Cammie were equally sick. And I was ashamed for what I'd done with him. I should have listened to the voice in my head that told me not to trust him. Now, I would never forgive myself.

For the next few days, I lived in a guilt-ridden stupor. I went to work. I came home. I barely ate and I didn't run in the mornings because I didn't want to run in to Jeremy. My family was getting worried about me. Shannen tried to get me to tell her what was wrong, but I refused. I was so ashamed, that every time she brought it up I couldn't keep from crying. Finally, she forced me to go grocery shopping with her to get me out of the house.

As we were walking around the store, putting groceries in the shopping cart, a familiar person entered my view. Jeremy. He was carrying the sleeping baby in his arms and gently rubbing his hand up and down her back.

His wife was next to him, pushing their cart, and filling it with food to take to their home behind the white picket fence, and prepare their meals. When he kissed the baby on the top of her head, I decided I had seen enough.

Shannen was still comparing prices on pasta and I was grateful she hadn't noticed them.

"Shannen, I'll be in the car," I muttered then snuck out of the store as Jeremy and his family took a spot in line at one of the registers.

By the time I was in my car, I was hysterical because I'd seen them all together with my own eyes now. I hated him, and I hated myself for what we'd done to his family. They didn't deserve treatment like that and for us to put a sweet baby in the middle of this mess was unconscionable.

To add insult to injury, the trio came pushing their cart across the parking lot and stopped at the back of a big black SUV—the same SUV I'd seen parked in front of his house.

I watched them laughing and talking as they put their grocery bags into the back of the SUV. The baby was still in his arms, but she was awake now. In between helping his wife, he was being playful with his daughter. She was pressing her hand over his mouth and he was kissing it in return. When his wife pushed the cart over to the cart corral while he strapped the baby in her car seat, I reclined my seat and closed my eyes so I didn't have to see them anymore.

Jeremy

I was living in utter confusion. Teagan refused to speak to me, and I missed her like crazy. I barely knew her, but couldn't stop thinking about her. We'd had something going the night I'd brought her home from Dub's. Her leaving the next morning felt like someone had rammed their hand into my chest and was squeezing my heart.

It fucking hurt.

These feelings were unfamiliar for me. I was miserable, and I couldn't do a damn thing about it. Whatever had happened had been bad enough in her mind to ditch me. Again.

A few days after she'd left me, she'd come back to see me, but I had been at work. I remembered the phone call from Zoey very clearly because she'd been having one of her panicky moments.

"Teagan was just here. I don't know why, but she ran away crying."

"What happened, Zoey?" This was so, so bad. On every level of bad, this was the worst level.

"I don't know, Jer. I was on the phone with Jason talking about how smashed and broken my car was, how it was so much worse than I thought it would be."

Her voice was unsteady, but she kept rambling like she did when she became overwhelmed.

"When she knocked at the door, I knew it was her because

she looked exactly like you'd said. I let her in because I wanted to meet her and get to know her, but Jay was still rambling on and on about the car, then Hannah woke up . . . and I picked her up from the playpen . . . then I heard the front door slam."

She took in a deep breath, and her voice was raspy from crying. "There was just so much going on all at once and I got overwhelmed a bit. She was at the gate when I called for her to come back. She told me she was sorry and ran away."

Shit. This is not good. "Z, did she say anything else?"

"Nooo," she said. "Jer, I'm so sorry, I should have hung up the phone with Jay, but I was upset. I asked her to wait, and she did for a few minutes, but then she took off."

She paused again briefly. "She did leave your shirt and boxers here though. Do I want to know why she had them?"

Great, even my own sister thought I was an asshole. "She didn't have them for the reason you think, Zoey. It's not that way with her, trust me. I need to do everything right this time. That is, if she'll even give me a chance. It's not looking too promising though."

"Jer, I believe you. What are you going to do?"

I had no idea then, and still had no idea now. That conversation was almost two weeks ago.

I'd tried texting and calling Shannen, and even she wasn't talking to me now. What happened to make Teagan hate me so much she wouldn't even speak to me?

So many thoughts ran through my mind. Did she regret coming to my house? Oh shit, did she regret what had happened between us that night?

The thought made me sick to my stomach. What if Teagan thought I'd taken advantage of her? I should've put her straight to bed without touching her, but we'd both been drinking—Fuck. I am an asshole.

But what if it had nothing to do with that? What if Cammie had done something else to her?

I'd never know if I couldn't speak to Teagan. I still didn't know her cell number or her last name. The only thing I knew was her sister's number. I was at a loss as to what I was supposed to be doing right now. I'd never chased a girl before, because I never had one run from me.

I hated that she was running away.

I wanted her to run *to* me, not *away* from me.

I had no choice but to go back to my regular life until I ran in to her somewhere, or Shannen took my calls again. I worked at the shop every day, unpacked all my boxes, lounged around my pool . . . and waited. The thought of Teagan hating me had me stressed and worried.

My living room furniture had arrived and the room was now complete. Zoey was finally working on decorating the kitchen and dining room. She'd sent me a text after lunch telling me she had a surprise in the dining room for me when I came home from work.

Honestly, I was hoping she'd cooked me dinner. She was a great cook, and I was tired of living off sandwiches. One day, I'd even tagged along with her to go grocery shopping, so I would actually have food in my house. Instead, I'd spent most of my time packing Sweet Pea around and had forgotten half the shit I was planning to buy.

My phone pinged with a text from John. Since it was Friday, I assumed he was checking to see if I was meeting the guys for MMA night. But that's not what his text said.

> *Shannen messaged me and says she's getting your texts, but she has no info for you yet. Red won't talk to her, so she's giving her time until she's ready to talk. She doesn't want Red to find out she's talking to you, so she asked me to tell you, and she's sorry. She'll let you know when she finds something out.*

Well, that was better than hearing nothing at all. I texted him back.

> I need to see Teagan. This sucks. I don't know what I did to hurt her, but I can't fix it if I don't know what I did. Tell Shannen thank you. Gonna skip out on MMA tonight. Zoey has something planned.

Shannen said whatever it is, it's really bad. Every time she tries to talk to her, Red starts crying, so she's not talking to her about you anymore.

What the hell did I do to her to make her cry? The thought of upsetting her that badly made my chest hurt. I wanted to leave work to try to see her, but the only place I was confident I would find her, was the hospital. And I wasn't about to go there and give Cammie any reason to harass Teagan. I felt like shit enough as it was for what Cammie and her friend had done.

After work, I drove home and found Zoey's Tahoe in the driveway. I pulled in and parked next to it. As soon as I opened the front door, I smelled food cooking. Thank God.

"Z? I'm home!" I called out. I didn't see her in the living room or the kitchen.

She jumped through the dining room doorway into the living room, very excited about something. "Surprise!"

Oh boy, someone was in a good mood. I laughed when Andy stepped out of the dining room behind her holding my Sweet Pea. He was shaking his head and smiling at his wife's enthusiasm.

"What's the surprise?"

Andy and Z stepped aside and she motioned for me to go into the dining room. When I walked in, I found she'd not only painted it, but the entire room was completely furnished. She'd decorated the brand new table with place mats, my dishes, and a long, wooden centerpiece, shaped kind of like a canoe or something with these funky round ball things in it. It looked awesome.

Everything was neutral with "little splashes of color" as Zoey liked to say. It looked like a family lived here, not a bachelor. I was thrilled with the results. "Z, thank you." I looked around the room again. She'd made the entire house perfect for me—well almost perfect. One thing was missing. One major thing. The house needed a woman.

No, *I* needed a woman.

Zoey handed me an envelope. Inside along with a funny

congratulatory card, was a personal note.

Congrats on your new house. The dining room
furniture and decor is our housewarming gift to you.
Love you, brother. Zoey, Andy, and Hannah.

"Seriously, guys? That's awesome, thank you so much." I shook Andy's hand and hugged Z. "What's for dinner?" I inhaled deeply. "It smells delicious."

"All of your favorites," Zoey replied with a smile. "Now go take a shower. It'll be ready when you're done."

"Yes, bossy. Jesus, man, how do you put up with her?" I asked Andy.

He laughed and shrugged his shoulders. "I just say yes. It doesn't get any easier than that."

After I showered, I put on shorts and a T-shirt and headed to the kitchen. Zoey was pulling a glass baking dish out of the oven. She'd made her famous mac and cheese. I would be happy eating only that, especially if she put jalapeños in it.

"You know you're my favorite sister, right Z?" I asked as she set the dish on top of the stove. I pretended to wipe the drool off my chin from the sight of the mac and cheese . . . *with jalapeños.*

She glared at me then threw a potholder at me. "I'm your only sister, dipshit."

I saw through the French doors that Andy was out on the patio taking something off the grill. Hannah started crying from another room. I found her in the guest bedroom in her playpen, so I picked her up and took her back into the kitchen.

"You need to quit putting my Sweet Pea in that playpen thing, Z. She probably feels like a zoo animal."

She smiled and tickled Hannah's bare foot, causing her to giggle and bury her face in the crook of my neck. "I know, but you were in the shower, Andy had to get the lemon chicken off the grill, and I was making the salad. We didn't really have a choice."

Andy came through the door and we sat down for dinner in my new dining room. I settled Sweet Pea in the high chair I'd bought for her, and Z set some baby food in front of her. It was hard to believe she was six months old now and eating solid foods.

Halfway through dinner, my phone rang. When I looked at the screen, I was surprised to see Shannen's name. I panicked. She finally had news, and I was scared shitless as to what it might be.

"Shannen, is everything okay?" My heart was racing.

"I'm not sure," she said. "Depending on what your answers are to the next few questions, I'll let you know."

I walked to the living room for some privacy. "I'm ready."

"I finally know what happened, Jeremy. Teagan confided in Nat and Jackie and I forced them to tell me what happened since she wouldn't."

"Please, I'll tell you anything you need to know." I needed to fix this. I would do anything I needed to. *Anything*.

"Jeremy, are you married?" she asked bluntly.

What the hell? "No, why would you think that?"

"Teagan went to your house and there was a woman and a baby there. She thought it was your wife and baby. When she talked to Nat and Jackie about it, that Cammie chick or one of her friends overheard the conversation, so Cammie told Teagan it was true."

Fuck me. "Shannen, the woman who was at my house is my sister. This is insane. Where's your sister? I need to see her. This has gone on long enough." I was pissed at Teagan for not talking to me and running away without an explanation. And I was furious with Cammie for lying to her.

"She's here with us at Dub's. She allowed Nat and Jackie to drag her ass down here after I told her you wouldn't be here. You need to make this right, Jeremy. I'll do whatever I can to help you. I can't stand to see her thinking she is a part of you cheating on someone who is actually *not* your wife."

"Alright, thank you. I'm coming to get her. Make sure she stays there, please." We ended our call and I went and told Zoey and Andy I was going to get Teagan. "Can you both stay here? I'm going to need your help with this. I can't let her see you're here until the time is right. Can you park your Tahoe in the garage, Z?"

Zoey jumped up and snatched her keys from the kitchen counter. "Yes. I'll do anything, Jer. We need to fix this." She hurried out the door.

When she said *'we need to fix this,'* I knew she was still feeling guilty about the day Teagan left crying.

"Good luck, mate," Andy said as I gathered my keys and wallet then slipped on my shoes.

"Thanks, man. I'm gonna need it." Then I realized I had no idea how to handle the situation. "Wait, what am I supposed to say to her? Every time I see her she disappears on me and she has made it abundantly clear she doesn't trust me at all."

"You just have to be honest with her. That's all you can do. Put her needs before your own because she's the one who's been hurt the most with all the lying and stories."

Zoey came back in as Andy finished his sentence. "Jer, he's right. But most of all, she needs to know she's who you want and no matter what, you'll do anything to prove that to her," she said.

With a nod of understanding, I jogged out to my car and hauled ass over to Dub's. I found my three friends, and the four girls hanging out at our usual couch. If Teagan decided to hate me forever, this could get awkward.

Teagan was perched on the very edge of the couch. I knew by the look on her face that she did not want to be there. She looked like she was ready to run. In fact, when she looked over and saw me, she did run.

My heart sank. She hated me. She'd made it into the other room by the time I caught her. She refused to face me, so I slipped my arm around her waist and rested my hand across her flat stomach.

"Teagan, *please,* stop running away from me. Can we talk?" I pleaded with her.

She turned to face me. "I have nothing to say to you, Jeremy. After everything that's happened, I can't even stand to look at you." Her eyes filled with tears—her words crushed me.

"Please," I begged. "What you think you know, and what Cammie told you is wrong. Please come with me so we can talk. It will all make sense if you'll let me explain. It's not what you think, I swear."

She crossed her arms over her chest and glared at me. She was so freaking adorable when she was infuriated, and I couldn't help but smile at her. I knew I was getting to her when her expression softened.

"We can do this the easy way, or the hard way, but it needs to be done. You decide," I said, challenging her.

"None of this has been the easy way, Jeremy. Why start now?" she countered. She was being a smartass, and the corners of her mouth turned up slightly.

Thank fuck. We're making progress here, people.

"Fine, then. Don't say I didn't give you a choice, though. The hard way it is."

I bent at the knees, picked her up, and tossed her over my shoulder.

She squirmed and yelled, "Put me down you freaking caveman!"

"Hell no." I walked to the other room where our friends sat on the couch. "We're leaving. Have a good night, guys."

Everyone on our couch laughed and cheered, which in turn, pissed Red off even more. She jabbed me in the ribs several times with her fingers. When that did nothing to deter me, she slapped me on the ass repeatedly.

Shaking my head, I made my way to the front door of the bar. She begged me to put her down and smacked me the entire way.

"Knock it off, Teagan, or you're gonna regret it," I warned.

My ass was stinging from her spankings, but all it did was turn me on. I was about to smack her on the ass when she stopped struggling and started laughing. I knew right then I was in trouble.

She stuck both hands down the back of my shorts and twisted the waistband of my boxers.

Abruptly, I stopped. "You wouldn't dare," I muttered. That little shit was playing dirty.

"Oh yes, Jeremy. I definitely would." She twisted the waistband tighter to prove her point.

Fine, two can play this game. I slid my hand up her bare

thigh and beneath her skirt to clutch the top of her panties. "Teagan, if you pull mine up, yours are coming down. The choice is all yours."

"Well, since we seem to be doing everything the hard way . . ."

She tugged on my boxers.

I pulled her panties down an inch.

We were at a stalemate, and people were watching our exchange. Actually, it was kind of amusing.

"On the count of three, we both let go," she finally said.

I turned to face the bar full of people, in case she tried to trick me. She wouldn't want her bare ass shown to everyone in the bar. "Okay," I agreed.

"One, two, three, go!" she said.

Neither one of us let go.

I turned and left the bar with her hands still down the back of my shorts. I let go of her panties and wrapped one arm around the back of her legs to keep her steady as I hit the button on my key fob to unlock my car. I stopped at the passenger door. "Let go of my boxers and I promise I'll put you down."

She gave them a slight tug then let go. I carefully set her down and as soon as her feet hit the ground, she tried to walk off. I grabbed her hand and pulled her back to my side.

"Teagan, I swear if you run away from me again, I will tackle you and drag your ass back. So don't even think about it."

She sighed loudly and dropped onto the seat after I'd opened her door. I belted her in so it would be harder for her to get out and run while I walked around to my side of the car. To be on the safe side, I locked the doors, too.

I kept my eyes on her as I walked around the front of the car. She was quick and feisty, and I didn't trust her for shit right now. I grinned and she crossed her arms over her chest as she glared at me.

When I reached my door, I hit the unlock button. As I went for the handle, the locks clicked again. I bent over and eyed her through the window. She was staring straight ahead. I gripped the handle and hit the button again. This time she let me in. I got in and started my car.

"You're a feisty little shit, you know that?" I asked her as I pushed in the clutch and shifted to first gear. When she ignored me, I drove to my house without saying another word to her.

At my house, she sat in the car until I came around to open her door for her. She took off her own seatbelt, and when I reached my hand in to help her out, she smacked it away.

When she stepped out of the car, I took her hand again. This time, I laced my fingers through hers, and couldn't help but grin when her small fingers closed around mine.

Once in my living room I said, "Wait here, Teagan. Please don't leave. Everything will be okay, I promise." I was ecstatic when she agreed and sat on the couch.

Andy and Zoey were at the dining room table eating dessert.

"Where's Hannah?" I asked quietly.

"She's asleep on your bed since she's not a zoo animal. Is Teagan here, Jer?" Zoey asked.

"Yeah, I'll bring her in here in a few minutes." I wanted her to meet Sweet Pea first.

Zoey clapped quietly and danced in her freaking seat.

Laughing at my dork of a sister, I left the dining room and was relieved to see Teagan still sitting where I'd left her on the couch. I offered her my hand and reluctantly, she took it, following me to my bedroom door. "Teagan, I need you to meet two people tonight. They're *very* important to me," I said, before pushing the door open.

She nodded and swallowed hard.

I brushed the back of my fingers across her cheek to assure her. "You can trust me," I said softly. She *could* trust me because I would never lie to her.

We entered the room and Hannah was sound asleep in the center of the bed, surrounded by pillows so she couldn't roll toward the edge. I held my breath and watched Teagan's reaction.

"Is she your daughter?" she asked softly as she stared down

at Hannah. She turned and looked up at me, waiting for my answer.

I shook my head. "Not in the way you think she is. She's my goddaughter, and my niece. The woman who was here with her the day you came over is my sister, Zoey."

Her eyes filled with tears so I took her hand in mine again.

"I'm so sorry. I just assumed . . . you don't look anything like your sister. She was wearing a wedding ring, and was talking on the phone about a man doing something bad to her," she said quietly. She looked back down at Hannah. "She's beautiful."

"She is, isn't she? Her name is Hannah, but she's my Sweet Pea. I'd do anything for her."

Teagan squeezed my hand, and it gave me hope.

"Is your sister here too? I'd like to meet her and apologize for my behavior."

I nodded. "She's here with her husband, who you already met at the hospital. They're in the dining room."

We left Hannah sleeping on my bed and went to the dining room. I reintroduced her to Andy and then to my sister.

"Teagan, it's wonderful to meet you, officially," Zoey said.

"Hello, Zoey," Teagan offered her trembling hand to my sister in greeting. "Um, I'd like to apologize for the way I acted the day I came over here. I misunderstood the situation. I'm very sorry."

And because Z is the way she is, she hugged Teagan. "It's okay. I was being rude for staying on the phone, please accept my apologies."

After a bit of small talk with us, Zoey and Andy packed up Hannah, and went home. Teagan and I still needed to talk and I hoped she would stay. At least neither of us had been drinking this time and our heads were clear.

"We have a lot to talk about Teagan," I said. "I have an odd proposition for you, but I hope you'll say yes." *God, please let her say yes.*

She waited for me to continue. "Will you go back to your place and pack a bag and come back here for the weekend? You can stay in my room or the guest bedroom, by yourself obviously. I really want to get all this crap Cammie has done out in the open, so you'll know what's true and what isn't."

I honestly couldn't tell what she was thinking from the expression on her face. I only knew she was upset and overwhelmed. I had seen that look on my sister's face too many times not to recognize it.

"We can talk, hang out, and do whatever you want. I have a pool in the backyard—we can barbecue, and get to know each other. Take things slow. I'll give you a few minutes to decide. Here are the keys to my car. You can drive it to your place to get some clothes and anything else you want to bring over."

I set the keys on the table next to her. She looked down at them then back up at me. The ball was in her court and I had to live with her decision this time.

If this was the last time I was going to see her, I at least wanted a chance to say goodbye. I stepped over to her and wrapped my arms around her.

"Please . . . come back," I said softly into her ear and then I left her standing there because I couldn't stomach watching her walk out my door. I went to my bedroom and sat on my bed. I waited until I heard my front door close then went back and found my keys were still on the table.

She'd made her decision, and she wasn't coming back. I'd really lost her for good this time.

After flipping on the TV, I sat on the couch and channel surfed in a daze for two fucking hours before I finally shut it off. When I stood to get the tequila and a shot glass from the kitchen, I heard a soft knock at the front door.

I jogged over and pulled it open. Teagan was standing on my porch with a small suitcase in her hand.

She hadn't run away again. This time she'd come back to me.

Teagan

I'd been standing on Jeremy's doorstep for fifteen minutes trying to gather the nerve to knock. The last time I'd knocked on his door an unpleasant series of events, which held absolutely no truth, had happened. Cammie and her friend had told me so many lies about Jeremy, I hadn't known what, or who to believe.

I hadn't wanted to leave the bar with him, but I was glad I did. Granted, he hadn't given me much of a choice. My lips parted in a soft smile at the memory. But I'd felt like I was being stupid and stubborn at not giving him a chance to explain. Although not everything I had been told about Jeremy could be ignored, he had shown his honesty by bringing me to meet his niece and his sister. Now was the time for me to give him the benefit of the doubt. Through his window, I saw his flat-screen TV shut off, and figured he was getting ready to go to bed. It was now or never.

Within seconds of knocking, the door swung open, and Jeremy stood in front of me. His surprised expression told me he hadn't thought I was coming back.

"Teagan, you came back," he said. He let out a breath and ran his fingers through his hair. "Please, come in." He reached down and took my small suitcase from my hand as I stepped through the door.

A ton of questions needed to be answered, but one needed to be answered before I could accept his proposition. "Jeremy, what is the purpose of me staying here with you for the weekend when I'm not exactly your type of woman?"

His brows furrowed in confusion and he motioned for me to sit on the couch. "I want you here to talk about what's been going on without interference from anyone. I want you to get to know me, by talking to *me,* not other people." He took a seat next to me. "As for you not being my type of woman, you're wrong about that. You are exactly my type of woman." He breathed in then out slowly before he asked, "So can you stay and give us time to talk, really talk?"

Can I take the risk? Could I give him the chance he wanted? Even through all the lies, I was attracted to him and we had a connection I couldn't deny even if I'd wanted to.

Believing the girls at work without giving him his say wasn't fair to him. I knew Cammie and Jeremy had been in a relationship at one point. The truth about Zoey and Hannah had been revealed. I didn't know what to think about anything else that I'd been told, but by accepting his proposal, I could make up my own mind based on his actions and his explanations. "Okay, Jeremy. I'm in. I don't know what's going to happen after the weekend is over, but I do agree with everything you've said so far."

He smiled anxiously, but his shoulders noticeably relaxed. "Look, this is all new for me. I'm going to screw up, but I *am* trying to make this right. I swear I will never lie to you. I'll answer any question you have, even if I know you won't like the answer. I'd never intentionally hurt you, and I'm sorry for everything you've already been through because of me."

Straightening in my seat, I took a deep breath and let it out, hoping this was the right decision. "Alright, let's do this. What do we have to lose?" *Just myself . . .* "Where's my bedroom?"

He grinned then stood and held his hand out to help me off the couch. After I slipped my hand into his, Jeremy grabbed my suitcase and escorted me down the hallway past the bedroom I knew was his. He flipped the light on in another bedroom.

When we stepped in, my heart sank when I saw the room. It looked very familiar, and I didn't want to stay in there. "Um, can I stay in your room instead?"

"Sure, but what's wrong?"

He was confused, and had every reason to be.

"Can we hang out tonight and start our deal tomorrow, please? I'm exhausted and hungry and can't think straight right now."

He nodded, and I knew he understood.

"Anything you want, ask. I'm glad you're here." On the way to the kitchen, he set my suitcase inside the door of his bedroom. "Let's get some dinner. Zoey made enough to feed an army."

He took my hand again and led me to the kitchen. I loved how he always did that; it was a sweet gesture. I wondered if he had been like that with Cammie. I hated the thought of them together, so I pushed it from my mind. *I won't think about her again, tonight.*

He pulled the fridge door open, took out several covered dishes, and set them on the counter.

I felt like I needed to help, so I started opening cabinet doors looking for plates. "Are you eating too, Jeremy?"

"Yeah, grab a plate for yourself, my sister wrapped mine and put it in the fridge when I went to get you."

I noticed a plate on the countertop with a piece of plastic wrap covering the food on it. "You left your dinner with your family to come and get me?"

He nodded.

"Why would you do that?" This man was surprising me at every turn.

He turned and rested his hip against the counter. "Because I haven't seen you in weeks, and I couldn't figure out what I had done to hurt you. And . . ." He ran his hand through his hair. "I need to make everything right, so I can see if there can be something between us."

My mouth dropped open at his candidness, and it caught me off-guard. "Do you *want* there to be something between us, Jeremy? Is that your intention?"

"Yes. Ever since the day in the ER, I haven't thought of anyone but you. I've been going crazy since then because I didn't know your number, I didn't know your last name, and then the night you stayed here . . ." He crossed his arms over his chest.

Something was on his mind. I closed the distance between us. "What is it, Jeremy?"

"I need to apologize for my behavior that night. We'd both had too much to drink, and I shouldn't . . . um. Shit. What happened in the living room . . . I don't want to screw things up between us by moving too fast."

I felt my cheeks flush. "The day I went to your house and saw Zoey, I was coming to apologize to *you* about that. I'm sorry, I don't know what came over me, but I don't regret it. Please, don't blame yourself."

He nodded and a grin eased over his face. "Okay. I promise to be a perfect gentleman from here on out. There will be no more drinking for me so I can keep my head clear."

"Let's heat up our food so you can finish the dinner you left to come and get me." I raised my eyebrow to hopefully get a bit of the confidence boost I'd needed.

"I'd do it all over again, just to open my front door and see you standing there with your suitcase."

His sweet words were music to my ears, causing my face to heat and blush. I gave him a shy smile then pulled lids off the food containers. Everything looked and smelled great, and I was famished. Jeremy handed me a fork and knife. I placed a piece of chicken onto my plate and gave it to him to put in the microwave for me.

"You're not having mac and cheese?" he asked.

"Um, no thank you. It looks delicious, but I really shouldn't have any. I haven't been eating well lately and it's not exactly on my meal plan."

My response didn't faze him a bit. "It's not exactly in mine either, but I can't resist it. Zoey makes me a special batch with fat free cheese and milk so it's not as fattening. Oh, and she puts jalapeños in it for me."

"I don't mean to be nosy, but do you think you're overweight or something? Because I don't think you are." His body was perfect.

Jeremy laughed. "Not anymore. But I used to be. I'm just maintaining now." He took his wallet from his pocket and pulled out a photo.

When he handed it to me, I saw an overweight teenager with gorgeous olive skin and blue eyes. "I had no idea, and never would've guessed you'd struggled with your weight. I'm sorry for making assumptions." I handed the photo back to him then grabbed my purse from the living room. I gave him a photo of myself from my wallet. "Looks like we have a little bit more in common than I thought."

He scanned the photo. "Now it's my turn to be nosy," he said, handing the photo back to me. "I don't think your body could be any more perfect than what it is right now—and I think that body needs to try just one scoop of this mac and cheese. What do you think?"

Jeremy was right. Just a bit wouldn't hurt and he thought my body was perfect. I graciously accepted his compliment with a full-on smile. "Okay, just one scoop. Especially since it's jalapeño spicy."

He grinned and spooned one scoop onto my plate. "You like it spicy, huh?"

I shook my head. "No, I *love* it spicy." I was only halfway talking about dinner.

Swallowing hard, he turned away to heat my food. He faced the microwave until it dinged indicating my dinner was ready.

After his was heated, we sat in the dining room to eat. "Do you always eat in here?" My family sat in front of the TV while we ate dinner. We weren't very formal.

Jeremy looked around the room. "This is actually the second time I've eaten in here. Zoey only finished the room today."

"Zoey decorated your house for you?"

He nodded.

"She did a great job. Does she do it professionally?"

"No. She actually owns a business with Andy. But let's not talk about them tonight. Can we have a do-over Teagan, from the beginning?"

He was being serious. We needed a *major* do-over. Hopefully, a private talk and time spent together would do the trick. "From the beginning then," I laughed. "But can we do it without you getting stitches in your head this time?"

At that point, he laughed. Hard.

Apparently, I'd missed the joke. "What's so funny?"

"The note I wrote you . . . after I was at the ER. It said I'd like to talk to you again, but I'd rather not get stitches in my head again to do it."

I laughed with him. "Agreed. No more stitches. Hmm, where to begin . . . um, let's start with the basics. Obviously, my name is Teagan. Middle name, Shea—last name, Donnelly," I said, feeling like I was in the middle of an interrogation on *Law and Order*. "Age twenty-seven. I can't drive a stick shift, which is the reason I didn't take your car back to my house. Fortunately, I live three blocks away on Shasta Avenue, so it's not a long walk. I'm currently living with my parents and my sister Shannen."

His brows rose. "Three blocks away, huh? Well, I'm Jeremy Douglas James. I'll be thirty in November. I run a business with my three brothers and Zoey."

Holy crap, four boys? And Zoey? I imagined poor Zoey having to deal with four brothers her whole life and no sisters. "Tell me about your family, Jeremy."

"Zoey's been my sister for eleven years now. My mom and dad adopted her when she was fourteen. You know Andy and Hannah. I'm the only one of my siblings who is single. My brothers are all married, except Adam, but he has a girlfriend." He stopped to catch his breath. "My mom is Mexican, and my dad is white, but speaks fluent Spanish."

That explained his gorgeous combination of skin, hair, and eye color.

"Your turn, Teagan."

He'd been so forthcoming with me that I wanted to let him in just a bit more. "Okay, I am one-hundred percent Irish. My mom immigrated here with my nanna and papa when she was little." I didn't want to talk about my father now, so I only said, "My birth father isn't in the picture. Shannen's dad has legally been my dad since I was three. We're very close." I stood to clear our dinner dishes. "Let's take care of these." I didn't want to push things too much, too soon.

"Sure. That sounds good." Jeremy grabbed his dishes and followed me to the kitchen.

When we were finished, I was worn out and just wanted to relax. "Maybe we can change into our pajamas and watch a movie. How does that sound?" I felt silly. It probably wasn't his idea of a good night.

"I'd say it sounds like a perfect way to spend the evening," he replied with a grin.

Jeremy took my hand in his and headed to his bedroom where he pulled a pair of pajama shorts from his dresser then left me in the room, shutting the door behind him.

When I opened my suitcase, I realized in my daze while packing, I had only brought an old Ramones T-shirt to sleep in. My sleep shorts were still at home on my bed. I pulled the T-shirt over my head but kept my skirt on.

I found Jeremy on the couch trying to find a movie for us to watch. He looked at my skirt in confusion, causing me to giggle. "I sort of forgot the bottom half of my pajamas." I smoothed my skirt down.

"You can borrow whatever you need. Check my dresser and see if you can find something that fits. I like your shirt, by the way. Great band."

"Thanks, they were pretty badass. What's your favorite song of theirs?"

He thought about it then replied, "Pinhead."

I sang the song in my head and laughed when I came to the lyrics about the guy meeting a nurse he 'could go for.' "Very funny," I said.

He smiled up at me. "Very funny, but very true."

I shook my head and went back to his bedroom for something to wear. I found the pair of boxers I slept in before and pulled them on.

"What did you find to watch?" I was curious to see what type of movie he'd chosen. I took a seat on the couch next to him and glanced up at the TV.

"I found a few we can rent. You choose which one you want to watch," he said while scrolling through the pay-per-view channels.

"Oh, the scary one, please," I said when my gaze landed on the latest horror flick. I loved the suspense and the anticipation of being scared.

He laughed when I told him the plot of the movie then said, "Alright, but don't get mad at me if I crawl on your lap at the scary parts."

During the movie, I felt him jump a few times and I laughed aloud. Finally, I took pity on him and reached for his hand. Our fingers intertwined and it just felt *right*.

I awoke the next morning, alone in his bed. I vaguely remembered him picking me up and bringing me in here. I was almost back to sleep when he stepped into the bedroom and pulled a drawer open on his dresser. The clock on the nightstand showed it was almost seven.

"Good morning," I said quietly as I watched him rummaging through another drawer. "Are you going somewhere?"

"I'm sorry I woke you. I was getting some running clothes. Go back to sleep."

After sleeping so comfortably, a long, morning run sounded great. Besides, I hadn't been running since the day I'd gotten the wrong impression about Zoey and Hannah. Today would be the perfect day to take it up again.

"Can I come with you? I can be ready in ten minutes."

"Yes, of course. You can show me where you live."

I could hear the smile in his voice.

"I'll wait for you in the living room," he said then left the bedroom.

Less than ten minutes later, I was dressed, had my hair pulled back, and my teeth brushed. I walked into the living room to find him sprawled out on the couch flipping through channels.

"Um, are we running or watching TV?"

He smirked then smiled up at me. "I thought you'd take longer to get ready." He shut off the TV and tossed the remote onto the couch. "Let's go."

We ran in silence along the streets of our neighborhood, until we neared my house. My dad was in the front yard mowing the lawn, before it got too hot outside and my mom was on the porch swing watching him, or "supervising" as he liked to say. I slowed down to a walk because I was taking Jeremy to meet my parents. He just didn't know it yet.

"You tired?" Jeremy asked. He was barely out of breath.

"Nah, I'm good. I am thirsty, though. Let's go get a drink."

Taking his hand, I led him across the street to my parents' house. As soon as my dad saw us, he shut off the mower. Grass clippings littered his shoes and socks, and I knew my mom was going to gripe about it later when she did laundry.

"Hey, honey. What are you out doing this morning?" he asked. "Who's your friend?"

Since my dad and I were both already hot and sweaty, I hugged him. "We're just out for a run. Dad, this is Jeremy James. He lives a few blocks away. Jeremy, this is my dad, Lucas Jennings."

The men shook hands. "Nice to meet you, sir," Jeremy said.

"Likewise," Dad replied.

My mom came down the front steps with three bottles of water. She handed us each a bottle.

"Thanks, Mama," I said then introduced her to Jeremy. He was polite but seemed a little nervous.

To break the awkward bit of silence, I asked, "What are your plans for the day after mowing?"

"We're driving over to see Nanna. She's been asking for you," Mom replied.

Crap, I haven't seen her in almost a week.

"I'll go see her today." My mom smiled and looked relieved. "How is she doing?"

"About the same. Her therapy is going well and she asks about you every day." My mom's concerned expression told me she was worried about her.

I wanted to go see her before the weekend was over, and I hoped Jeremy didn't mind. "Let's get going, Jeremy."

He shook my dad's hand again, and we said goodbye to my parents.

About a block from my house, he slowed to a walk and stopped. "I've never met a girl's mom and dad before." He seemed bewildered, and it was cute to see him like that.

"Almost thirty and you've never met a girl's parents? Wow, Jeremy, should I be flattered or scared? Have you ever seriously dated *anyone?*"

He shook his head. "No, not really," he said. "Cammie was as close as I got."

Not wanting to talk about Cammie, I took off running and he followed. Running with him was easy because we kept the same pace. Much easier than running with Shannen, that's for sure. We were a block and a half away from his house when I had an idea.

"Last person to your house has to fix breakfast."

My challenge caught him off guard and I sped ahead of him. I heard him yell out "cheater" as I turned the corner. By the time he reached the corner, I was already down a cleverly hidden walkway between two houses.

I was positive he didn't know about the walkway because only people who lived in the neighborhood for years knew about it. As I ran, I looked behind me a few times, and he was nowhere in sight. I made it to his house and waited for him at the gate. He ran up a few minutes later, out of breath.

"Do you know I've been running past your house every morning since I moved back here in May?" I asked.

He shook his head, still trying to catch his breath.

"I've been watching the progress of the renovation for months. I considered trying to buy it when it went up for sale, but I couldn't afford it. I love the picket fence. It's my favorite feature," I reached out and touched the top of a picket then pushed open the gate and walked up the sidewalk. "So, what are you making me for breakfast?"

I heard him laugh as he approached. He pulled his key out and let us inside the house.

Later that morning after we'd both showered and dressed, I asked Jeremy to take me to see Nanna. He wanted to spend the weekend together to get to know each other, so that was what we were going to do. He'd already passed the parent test when I'd led him straight to my house to meet them without warning.

On the drive to Nanna's home, I said, "I have some

questions, Jeremy."

He turned down the radio. "I'm ready to answer them and have nothing to hide."

"Why don't we get the hard questions out of the way first?"

He agreed.

"Did you meet Cammie at the hospital when you went to see Zoey and Hannah?"

"Yes."

"Did you have sex with her in the parking garage when you left?"

"Yes, I did."

"Why?" Knowing he'd actually done that with her where I worked made me sick, but I needed to know he would tell me the truth no matter what.

He sighed. "I did it for a few reasons, but once I explain them to you, I need to tell you the repercussions that made me want to change."

He looked over at me, waiting for an answer.

"That's fair. This should be a two way street."

"I had sex with her because I could. I hadn't been with anyone in a while . . . I met her on my way to see Zoey, we kind of hit it off, and she gave me her number. We made a plan to meet after she got off work an hour later. I'd planned to take her out to see where things went, but when I met her after seeing Zoey, she didn't let things get that far."

"She's the one who instigated sex in the parking garage, not you?" My mind was officially boggled and I could never see myself doing something like that.

He nodded. "Yes, that's what happened."

"When was the last time you had sex with her?"

"It was a few days before I broke it off with her."

Jeremy downshifted his car to slow down then stopped at a red light. He glanced over at me while we waited in traffic.

"On the night I left you at Dub's, Cammie and Tiffany came into the bathroom. Tiffany told me you had a bunch of girls you were stringing along from their floor at the hospital. She said she was one of many. Is *any* of that true?" I felt stupid asking the question as soon as I said the words because it sounded so ridiculous.

His mouth dropped open. "Absolutely not, I don't know Tiffany, and the only person I've dated from the hospital was Cammie. Teagan, I promise I am not a cheater. I don't do shit like that."

"That night we met, I was sitting in my car and saw you leave Dub's with Cammie." The incident that night was something I'd seen with my own eyes, so he really needed to have a good explanation.

"I did, but it's not what you think."

The car behind us let out a long, obnoxious honk of their horn. "Oh shit, the light's green. Let me pull over." Once he'd stopped the car at a small park, he said, "When you said you were going into the bathroom . . . you were gone for so long I went to find you and I ran in to Jackie. She told me you'd left. Then Cammie came up and I had to take her home since I'd brought her to the bar with me, although earlier that evening, we'd gotten into an argument and I'd broken up with her—"

"Stop right there, Jeremy."

He'd gone from breaking up with her to talking and flirting with me all within the span of an evening? I couldn't think straight with his overwhelming presence inside the car. Flinging open the car door, I scrambled out and jogged toward the small duck pond in the middle of the park.

"Wait, please," he said, his voice pleading as he came up behind me. "When I broke up with her, I thought she'd left, but apparently, she hadn't. Then you showed up. I was so caught off guard seeing you again all I wanted to do was get to know you. After you left, I swear, I just drove her home."

"Can you give me a few minutes alone to think, please?" I glanced over my shoulder and saw the hint of panic and desperation in his eyes.

Nodding, Jeremy backed away and found a bench nearby.

The hot sun and heat made it hard to concentrate, so I lifted my long, light-peach colored dress above my knees, and kicked off my shoes. I slowly waded into the cool water. It calmed my nerves and cooled me off in the process.

Standing in the water, staring out across the pond at a duck and her babies, I thought long and hard about our conversation. When Jeremy said he'd tell me anything even if he knew I wouldn't like the answer, he had done just that. I believed I was getting exactly what I'd asked for.

Glancing over my shoulder at Jeremy, I watched him for a minute. He sat forward on the bench with his elbows on his knees and his hands in his hair, staring down at the ground. Clearly, the situation was unsettling for him.

Was I crazy for believing him? I wasn't sure, but I was willing to find out.

Suddenly, something brushed against my bare ankle under the water and I let out a yelp. It was gross and slimy. One quick glance down had me scrambling from the water with the grace of a drunken woman trying to run in hooker-heels. Jeremy was at the bank like a knight in shining armor to rescue me from the disgustingly large half-frog, half-tadpoles that had chased me from the pond.

He hoisted me into his arms.

And he was laughing at me.

"You'd think with that scream you just let out there was an alligator in the water or something," he said, with a playful grin.

Apparently, I'd disturbed an entire army of the creepy things, because now they were swimming around the edge of the water. Lifting my wet, grass covered feet higher, even though he was holding me off the ground, I wrapped my arms around his shoulders and gave the slimy creatures a glare for embarrassing me.

"Those things could've climbed up my legs! Ughh . . ." I shuddered and looked at Jeremy.

He let go of the laugh he'd been holding back.

"Shut up, hero."

"Make me," he said, his deep voice just above a whisper.

I pressed my lips to his, effectively putting a stop to his tormenting me.

When I pulled away, he sighed and pressed his cheek to mine. "Don't worry, pretty girl, I wouldn't have let them hurt you. I'd never let anything hurt you."

My heart felt light in my chest and my body fit perfectly in his arms, so I let Jeremy carry me to the bench he'd been sitting on. Carefully, he set me down then jogged back to the edge of the pond and grabbed my shoes. He retrieved a towel and a bottle of water from his car. Kneeling in front of me, he poured the water over my feet to wash away the grass and dirt. After he dried them off, he helped me back into my shoes, then pulled down the hem of my dress and held his hand out to help me stand.

He didn't let go after I stood. I loved it. And I trusted him.

"You know, Cammie said some awful things about you the day after we first met at Dub's. But, I believe everything you've told me today."

"Thank you. It means a lot to me. Do you want to get back on the road now and finish this conversation later?"

"Yeah, let's get to Nanna's." Hand in hand, we walked back to his car.

Jeremy

I was nervous as hell when we arrived at the home where Teagan's grandma lived. Unexpectedly, I'd met her mom and dad this morning and thought it had gone well although I had a feeling she'd planned to stop at her house.

The simple fact was I wanted to be with her and would do anything to make it happen. I would tell her my deepest, darkest secrets if that's what she wanted.

When I woke up in the early morning hours with her still at my house, she was all around me. Her sweet scent was in the air, her clothes and other personal items mixed with mine.

She completed me. As cheesy as it sounded, I'd never felt more whole and thankful in my life.

I needed her to see she belonged here, too. When she'd asked questions while we were in the car, I'd been sickened at the lies Cammie and her friend Tiffany told her. After our visit with Teagan's grandma, I would make sure we finished that discussion. I still needed to explain a lot to her. My story began long before I met Teagan, and I needed to show her I was trying hard to change my ways.

"Jeremy, can we talk about my nanna before we go in?" Teagan asked, pulling me away from my thoughts. I turned in my seat, giving her my full attention.

"She had a stroke in May and has some paralysis on her right side, so her speech is a bit slurred and it can be hard to understand sometimes. Her mind is quick and she knows what she wants to say, but she can't get her brain and mouth to cooperate when she gets excited or frustrated. She's in speech therapy and working her butt off to get better, but it's taking time."

"Thank you for telling me what to expect. I'll do my best to pay attention. Will you let me know if I do or say something I shouldn't?" I'd never known anyone in her grandma's condition and hoped I wouldn't do something wrong.

Teagan surprised the hell out of me when she leaned across the console and kissed me on the cheek. "You'll do fine. I just wanted to prepare you. Let's go."

We rode the elevator to the fourth floor and found her grandma's room. Since the building she lived in was a combination of home and hospital, the room looked like a typical bedroom, but with a few pieces of medical equipment blended in.

Teagan's grandma sat on her bed propped against a few pillows, staring out the window.

"Nanna?" She didn't seem to hear her, so Teagan moved closer and spoke louder. "Nanna?" The elderly woman turned. The left side of her mouth curved upward in a smile, but the right side remained almost motionless.

"Peaches," she said slowly when she saw Teagan.

I would have to ask about her nickname later.

"Hi, Nanna, I've missed you so much." Teagan hugged her grandmother then kissed her forehead.

"Me, too, Peaches," her Grandma said, and patted Teagan's arm.

Teagan turned and held her hand out to me. I walked forward and took her hand, interlacing our fingers. I loved the way her hands felt so perfect and warm in mine.

"Nanna, I'd like you to meet someone. This is my friend, Jeremy." Teagan turned and smiled at me.

God, she's beautiful.

"Jeremy, this is the original Teagan Shea Donnelly . . . my nanna."

"Hello, Mrs. Donnelly," I said to the woman with the same name as the woman who held my hand in hers. What an incredible honor for Teagan to share the same name as her grandmother.

Her grandma took a look at me, one side of her mouth turned up in a smile. "Oh, Peaches," she said. "Sinatra eyes—lovely blue."

Teagan laughed and glanced from her grandma to me. "Nanna has a thing for Frank Sinatra," she said with a smile.

"Handsome man with pretty blue eyes," her grandma said then looked from me to Teagan. I wasn't sure if she was talking about Frank Sinatra or me at that point.

While Teagan made small talk with her grandmother, I quickly noticed what she'd mentioned earlier about her grandma getting frustrated easily. When she wanted to say something, it took her several tries, but eventually, the word would come.

After the last sentence, Teagan stood and pulled a book from the small bookshelf next to the bed. She handed the book to me. "She wants you to read her a poem. Are you game?"

I read the title and found it was a book of poetry by Yeats. I smiled, pleased with the old, worn book I held in my hand, because I was a fan of the writer. "Yeah, I can handle this." I set a chair next to the bed and rested my elbow on the edge while I searched the book for the poem I wanted to read. When I found it, I began reading aloud, *"Beloved, gaze in thine own heart . . ."*

While I read, I would occasionally glance up to find Teagan and her grandma watching me closely. After I finished reading the last line, I peeked over at Teagan and she had tears in her eyes.

I hadn't noticed while I was reading, but Teagan's grandma had laid her hand in the crook of my elbow. She looked from me to her granddaughter.

Teagan stared at me in awe. "Jeremy, that was beautiful. Thank you." Her bottom lip quivered and all I wanted to do right then was kiss her.

"Peaches," Teagan's grandma said then waited for Teagan to respond to her.

I stood to put the book back on the shelf then lingered

there to give them time to visit. Teagan leaned closer to her grandma, and listened very carefully to the words the woman spoke.

After about ten minutes, Teagan straightened when their gradual conversation was finished. "Nanna?" She looked at me with an alarmed expression on her face.

"Is everything okay? Do I need to get someone for her?" I thought maybe something was wrong.

She shook her head and turned back to her grandma. "Are you sure, Nanna?"

Her grandma nodded without hesitation.

Teagan seemed taken aback by what her grandma had said to her. She rose to her feet as tears streamed down her face. She wiped them away with the back of her hand as her grandma peeked over at me, and then back at her namesake.

There was something very heavy and emotional going on between the two women and I didn't know what to do. I watched as she carefully unclasped a necklace from her grandma's neck then removed something from it. She put the necklace back on her grandma when she finished. Her grandma lifted her left hand and Teagan slid a ring off the woman's finger. "Nanna, please . . . are you *sure* about this?"

Teagan's voice was so intense with emotion it turned to a whisper as she finished her question.

Once again, her grandma nodded. "Yes. Peaches and Frank." She laughed and so did Teagan.

Teagan wiped the remaining tears from her cheek and motioned for me to come and stand beside them. "Jeremy, she's giving these to us." She held her hand out and I saw two rings lying in the palm of her hand.

My brows furrowed in confusion as I stared down at the rings.

"They're Nanna and Papa's Claddagh rings." She took a deep breath and let it out. "She wants to give you my papa's ring, Jeremy."

Holy shit. I didn't know what the rings symbolized, but because of her reaction, I knew this was a big deal. "What do you want me to do?" I asked quietly.

"You need to take it," she replied. Her grandma mumbled something, so Teagan leaned back in to listen. She looked at me with panic in her eyes. "She wants us to put them on each other."

Not wanting to upset Teagan or her grandmother, I held out my hand.

She offered me the smaller of the two rings then held her right hand out, her fingers splayed. "From what I remember, you're supposed to put it on my finger with the bottom of the heart pointed toward my wrist." She turned to her grandma who nodded her approval.

Without question, I did as she said; all the while, my heart was pounding out of my chest. The ring fit her dainty finger perfectly. As her grandma watched on, Teagan took the other ring, swallowed hard, and slid it on to my right ring finger. The ring fit my finger perfectly as well.

Teagan looked back over at her grandma, whose eyelids were getting heavier by the second. She kissed her on the forehead and whispered, "Sweet dreams, Nanna."

Once we were in my car, Teagan sat in silence, trying not to cry. I didn't know what had happened in there, and I didn't know what to say to her. All I knew was we were both wearing rings that held great meaning, which had upset Teagan to the point of crying.

"Teagan, say something, please. Do you want me to take the ring off?"

She shook her head and twisted the ring on her own finger as she stared down at it.

I finally looked at the ring on my finger. It was gold, and on the top of the band, two hands held a heart between them. There was a small crown on the top edge of the heart. I had never seen a ring like it before. The details of the ring were worn down by age, so I knew it was old. Teagan's ring looked much the same, but hers was very feminine, whereas mine was masculine.

"Do you want to talk about what went on in there?"

"Yes, we need to. Let's do it at home, though," she said.

I loved the sound of that.

Teagan shifted in her seat, angling her body toward me.

"Do you mind if we go back to the conversation we had on the way over? I kind of want to get that out of the way before we talk about what just happened with Nanna."

I nodded so she went back to asking questions.

"You mentioned repercussions and changes earlier. What did you mean?" she asked.

"When I went to the hospital to see Hannah for the first time, Zoey was alone in the room with her. She looked like she was at peace for the first time in her life—Z hasn't had it easy like the rest of us. She forced me to hold Hannah. She was so little and sweet," I said, remembering how tiny she was and how she took right to me. "That's why I call her Sweet Pea. Anyway, Z had been bugging me to settle down for months. Andy came in later, and I held Hannah while they ate dinner. They were always off in their own little world, but when Hannah was born, everything became *right* for them. Does that make sense?"

"Yes, it does," she replied. "It's like they weren't complete until she came along."

"Exactly," I agreed. "When it was time for me to go, all three of them were on Zoey's hospital bed . . . I don't know, the way they were together made me realize I do want that for my life." I paused, and I knew what I had to say next could possibly hurt Teagan. "Then I left, things happened with Cammie. A few days later, I called her and we were together for a while. I knew all along she wasn't right for me, and I'd finally had enough of her that night at Dub's, so I broke it off."

"Why did you think she wasn't right for you?" she asked.

I didn't think long about my response. "Because she's shallow, self-centered, fake, and we had almost nothing in common."

"Why were you with her for so long if you had nothing in common?"

Her gaze shifted to me and I couldn't say the words because I hadn't even admitted the reason to myself. I'd stayed with her for sex, plain and simple. The realization hit Teagan when I didn't immediately respond.

"Oh. Never mind. I get it." She looked down and twisted the ring around her finger.

"Teagan, that's not what I want from you. It's not like that with you," I admitted, hoping she didn't think I was a total pig.

"Then what is it like, Jeremy?" she asked, her voice monotone and uncertain.

Jesus, she wasn't holding anything back and I felt like I was being put through the wringer.

"Everything feels different when I'm with you. I want to do it all the right way . . . that is, if you plan to give me a chance after this weekend. I'm not perfect and I've never claimed to be, but I need to make sure I don't screw this up by doing something stupid."

This discussion was draining me dry, and I was wondering why people went through all the pain and suffering to be together when this shit was so hard. The outcome had to be worth the emotional risk I was taking, right? Honestly, I wasn't sure as the depression and uncertainty I was feeling about my future was freaking me the fuck out.

Teagan sat in silence until I pulled into the garage at my house. We got out of the car and she walked over to the Chevelle. "What happened to your car? Did you crash it?"

"It's not mine. It's Zoey's. This is what she was talking about on the phone the day you came to see me. Her ex-husband did it. She hadn't seen it until right before you came over."

Teagan frowned and let out a frustrated breath. She reached out and touched the dented fender of the car almost as if she didn't believe it was really there.

"I'm so freaking stupid," she whimpered as she rubbed over her eyes with the back of her hands. "Jeremy, I'm so sorry . . . for everything." She came over to me and hugged me. "Can we relax in the pool? This has already been a long day and it's not even noon yet."

She tilted her head back and looked me in the eyes. She seemed tired and stressed, and I would do anything to ease her constant worry. If I could take it all away forever, I would.

"Yes, we can do anything you want." I leaned in to kiss her on the cheek but she turned so my lips landed on hers.

Neither of us moved, or tried to intensify the kiss. We

didn't need to. It was simple, and natural, and perfect.

After going inside the house, we went our separate ways to change. As I was changing into my swim shorts, I thought about our conversations throughout the morning.

She had no reason to be apologizing to me. Her harassment at work was because of *me* and I hated the toll it was taking on her. I'd tell Cammie to leave her alone, but my guess was that would only make things worse.

I found Teagan already outside, with the pool net in her hands, skimming a few leaves from the surface of the water. She wore her sundress over her swimsuit. She was barefoot and beautiful, and seemed perfectly at home.

I went back inside, found us some drinks and snacks, and plugged my iPod into the stereo system I'd installed on the patio. I found a fully inflated air mattress and tossed it into the pool, laughing at the memory of waking face down with a deflated one between the concrete and me.

"What's so funny over there, chuckles?" Teagan asked as she put the net away.

I picked up the deflated air mattress. "Just thinking back to when my friends helped set up the garage and they brought tequila . . . I woke up on this the next day."

She laughed as she pulled her sundress over her head. Her dress caught on her hair clip and she pulled it free. Her hair spilled over her back and shoulders in beautiful, red waves. She was wearing a skimpy, emerald green bikini that left nothing to the imagination. Her peaches and cream skin was flawless, her body was perfectly curvy, yet fit, and she was definitely the most captivating woman I had ever seen.

I watched as she twisted her hair back into the knotted style she always wore. The way the muscles in her arms flexed as she twisted her long hair had my mind wandering to having her arms wrapped around me, and her hair spilling around us. I groaned inwardly as my mind and dick betrayed me, yet again.

"Jeremy, are you coming?"

My mind went straight to the gutter and I grinned. "Yeah, I forgot towels though. I'll be back." That wasn't a lie. I *had* forgotten them. Thank God I had because I needed to get my hard-on under control.

By the time I returned, Teagan was in the shallow end of the pool. She was so petite the water was almost to her chest. She turned when she heard me. I took off my shirt and tossed it onto the back of a patio chair. She glanced down at my chest, and a surprised expression came over her face.

"Jeremy, when did you get your tattoo?"

I thought back to when I went to the tattoo shop with Andy, Zoey, and Sweet Pea to commemorate my induction as a godfather. It was a monumental week in my life, the best week of my life, actually.

"It was a week or so after the night I saw you at Dub's, why?"

Her cheeks flushed and she looked mad. "Can you grab my phone off the table, please?"

I handed the phone to her as I set our towels down on the patio next to the pool. I sat on the side then dropped down in the water next to her. She scrolled through a bunch of pictures and when she found the one she wanted, she handed her phone to me.

On the screen, was a picture of me asleep in my bed. I knew it was mine because I recognized my bedding and headboard. Cammie was draped over me doing that gross duck-face she thought made her look sexy. She was topless and her fake tits were pressed against my chest. The text below the photo read: *Guess where your BF is while you're working. Lol.*

I was pissed she'd taken the picture without my knowledge, and furious she'd taunted Teagan with it. It made me want to watch Teagan jump on her and punch her all over again. She deserved it.

"I'm so sorry," I said. "Is this why you didn't want to sleep in the guest bedroom? Because of the bed?"

"Yes. I'm sorry—it's stupid. I didn't want to sleep where she had. Sorry for acting ridiculous."

"Nothing you do is ridiculous, Teagan. Don't talk like that. Just so you know, the mattress is brand new. I'm the only person who has ever slept on it, and you, Hannah, and I are the only people who have slept on the bed in my bedroom. When did she send this to you?"

She took the phone out of my hand and set it on the towels lying next to the pool. "A few days ago. But since you got the tattoo after you broke up with her, I know it's an old picture. By the way, your tattoo is adorable," she said as she checked it out again.

"Adorable, huh?" I asked. "Well, I happen to think you're pretty adorable too." Did I really say that? *I think my cheese-factor just hit an all-time high.*

She smiled sweetly, and her cheeks flushed again.

"I also think I need to know why your nickname is Peaches."

Her cheeks turned even redder and I suspected that her pretty skin was the reason for the nickname. She playfully splashed me then blatantly ignored my statement about her nickname.

Reaching out, she placed her hand over my tattoo. "Is this really Hannah's handprint?"

"Yep, it is." I told her all about the day they asked me to be her godfather and the day I got the tattoo.

"Everything you've been doing these last several months has been because of her?"

"Pretty much. That and I realized I'm too old to be doing the same crap I've done for years. It's time for me to grow up, I guess."

She laughed. "Yes, I'd say thirty is a good age to *finally* become a responsible adult."

"Now you're just being mean to me," I joked and backed away from her toward deeper water. "You're breaking my poor, irresponsible heart over here."

She splashed water at me again as I floated farther away. The water was now to my chin and I was standing on my toes. I exhaled all the air from my lungs, submerged, and walked backward across the bottom of the pool until I reached the side.

With three feet of water over my head, I watched as she lifted herself out of the pool. The next thing I knew, I felt an impact of someone jumping in, and she was under the water in front of me. She sank down until she was eye level with me. I pulled her close and pressed my lips to hers.

She wrapped her arms around my torso and pushed off the wall behind me, pulling me with her. We broke the surface of the water with our lips still pressed together, and her arms wrapped around me.

I wanted to deepen the kiss so badly, to taste her—but I needed to let her make the first move. Thank Christ she did. Her lips parted, inviting me in. I didn't resist. I didn't have the strength to. Her legs wrapped around my waist and I propelled us to the shallower edge of the pool where my feet touched bottom.

I couldn't get enough of her. Our hands were all over each other—bodies pressed tightly together, tongues and mouths in a frenzy of motion. Her phone rang from the side of the pool, interrupting our heated moment.

"Don't answer it," I begged as she released her hold on me and made her way across the shallow end to the pool steps.

"I need to. It might be about Nanna," she said breathlessly. By the time she got to her phone, it had stopped ringing. Within seconds, it was ringing again, and she answered it. "Reese!" she squealed. "I'm alright, how are you?" she asked the *Reese* person.

Was Reese a man or woman? From the one-sided conversation, I eventually determined Reese was definitely a man. A pang of what I assumed was jealousy, shot through my gut. Great, yet another new feeling for Jeremy James.

I waded to the steps and got out of the pool. It was past lunchtime and I was getting irritable from not eating.

After I dried off, I wrapped a beach towel loosely around my waist. Teagan wasn't paying attention to me so I pulled my wet shorts off from under the towel and laid them over the drying rack. I opened the French doors that led to my bedroom, and went inside and put on dry shorts.

I was in the kitchen cutting leftover lemon chicken in to chunks to toss onto a salad when Teagan came in.

"Why'd you leave?" she asked.

I turned around and found she was wearing her sundress again. "I was hungry and wanted to give you some privacy for your call."

She closed the distance between us, so she was standing

directly in front of me. "Reese is a good friend from Denver. He's moving out here next week and we needed to confirm our plans. The apartment won't be ready when he gets here so he's staying with me and my family until then."

I cringed inside. *There's that pang of jealousy again.* I didn't like it. "He's staying with you?" I asked just to confirm that I'd heard her correctly.

She smiled, and a hint of curiosity outlined the corners of her perfect lips. "Are you jealous, Jeremy?"

Hell yes I am. I didn't want him to come and take her away from me. I leaned against the counter. "Yes," I muttered as I stared at the floor. "I know I don't have the right to be, but . . . ."

She moved closer and pressed her body against mine, resting her cheek on my bare chest. "Don't be. Reese is very . . . gay." She looked at me, grinning. "Besides, after our visit with Nanna this morning, we're both officially off the market."

Huh? "I'm sorry, what?" I mumbled, shaking my head in confusion.

She stood smiling at me, and then laughed heartily. "You should see the look on your face, Jeremy. It's priceless."

"What are you talking about, Teagan?"

She was now doubled over holding her stomach because she was laughing so hard. "I thought you wanted to be my boyfriend," she said between laughs.

Duh, Jeremy, wasn't that the whole point of this weekend alone?

She pushed me out of the way and finished making our lunch as I stood there like an idiot. She took our plates to the dining room, sat down, and began to eat without me. After a few minutes, she came in and dragged me to the seat next to her. As she ate and I stared down at my plate, perplexed, she took my right hand and rubbed her thumb over the ring her grandma had given me.

I got the hint. "I guess you should tell me about the rings."

Teagan

Jeremy wanted to know about the rings Nanna gave us. I didn't know the exact history of them, but I knew what we were supposed to do with them and why she gave them to us. "They're my grandparents' wedding rings, Jeremy. They are over sixty years old."

He shifted anxiously in his seat and propped his elbows on the table. "Why did she give one to *me?*" he asked.

His questioning made me uneasy, and I found it difficult to tell him what she said to me. When she'd started speaking, I hadn't believed my ears because she hadn't spoken that many words in a row since her stroke.

My eyes stung from the tears forming in them. "She's eighty-one, Jeremy, and very old school. She gave them to us because she said she can tell we love each other as much as her and my papa loved each other."

"How can she know that if *we* don't even know it?" He ran his fingers through his hair.

"Call it Nanna's *intuition,* I guess. She's never been wrong about it before," I said. She'd seen it with my mom and Lucas, and she'd seen it with other family members and friends throughout the years. Why would I ignore it?

"I know it sounds crazy, but she's never been wrong about people before. In my family, the Claddagh ring is supposed to be passed from mother to daughter, but my parents already have their own rings. Nanna gave us the rings now because she said I didn't trust in us, but we were meant to be." I gestured between us as I spoke the last few words.

"What was the purpose of us putting on the rings the way we did, Teagan?" He swallowed hard.

"My mom once told me that wearing them on our right hands with the bottom of the heart facing toward our wrists means we're not available to be with other people. That we've found the person we're destined to be with."

He looked down at his plate, then back over at me.

"Holy shit, I'm at a loss here, Teagan. I don't know if I should take it off and give it back to you . . . or keep it and hope she was right by giving it to *me*."

My heart and stomach simultaneously flip-flopped inside my body. "I don't know what to do either." On one hand, I wanted him to take the ring off and give it to me, but was it because I was on the fence about trusting him? Or because of all the trouble with Cammie?

On the other hand, I desperately wanted him to keep it, and for Nanna's premonition to be correct. I wanted to be in love, but a trusting love. I wanted to be married and live in a house with a white picket fence. I wanted a bunch of babies to hold and to watch them grow. I wanted it all, but was Jeremy "the one" I was supposed to have it all with?

"Do you want her to be right, Jeremy?" I swore he was turning green right before my eyes.

He pushed his chair back and stood. "I don't feel so good," he said and left the dining room in a bit of a daze.

Obviously, he could use some time on his own, so I continued to eat. When he didn't come back in a few minutes, I went to find him. I found him lying face-up on his bed. A small fan on his nightstand blasted cold air on him while he stared at the ceiling.

"What's wrong?" I asked as I stood next to his bed.

As I waited for an answer, I stared at his gorgeous body. Physically, he was perfection. His dark brown hair was short on the sides and longer on the top. I loved watching him run his fingers through it. I would love to run my fingers through it. His dark, olive colored skin covered a slim but muscular body. My eyes drifted from his tattoo, down his body to a faint scar low on his abdomen. I guessed he must have had his appendix removed years ago.

The man definitely took care of himself. I scanned his torso where he had that sexy-as-hell V of muscle along his hipbones. The sexiest part of his body was the two thick veins that bulged above the waistband of his shorts, and wandered up his lower stomach. I hated to think of all the sit-ups and the ab workouts the man tortured himself with to get that V.

He still hadn't responded to me by the time I'd finished studying every inch of him. "Jeremy, what's wrong?"

"I think you should take the ring," he said without looking at me.

"Why?"

"Because, Teagan. I've told you how I feel about you, but you haven't told me anything. I've already caused you too many problems, and I can't promise you it's going to get any better. You don't deserve that."

He was right. He wasn't holding anything back from me, but I was. Since so many thoughts and feelings were on my mind, and I'd had many, many days to think about them, they all came out in a flood. "Jeremy, I love being here with you. I love being around you. I do think we have something between us. It's when we get out in the real world, and I go to work . . . that I get worried. Am I going to have to watch out for random girls you've been with, trying to do the same thing Cammie is doing? Every time we go somewhere, and you talk to a girl, do I need to wonder if you've had sex with her?" I placed my hand on his arm and gave a little squeeze to make sure he was paying close attention to me. "Do I need to worry about you cheating on me?"

He finally looked at me then rolled onto his side facing me. I laid down beside him, mimicking his position.

"I would never cheat on you, Teagan. That's not how I am," he said. "As for going out and running in to girls I've been with before, it's a possibility. I'm friends with some of them still, but only friends." He took my hand in his. "Besides, they don't compare to you—not even close. I've barely touched you, but I know you're so much more than what I deserve."

Not once had he taken his eyes off mine.

"What do you want to do, Jeremy?" I whispered. "Now that we've cleared up a lot of what's happened with Cammie, I want to give us a chance, but . . ."

"Teagan, what's happened with Cammie is not your fault. It's mine and I need to fix everything that she's done. I can't let it go on."

I shook my head. "I'm scared it's going to make everything worse at work. I already have two strikes against me, and I'm still on probation."

"Why are you on probation, and what could you possibly have done to get two strikes against you?" He was making it sound like I could do no wrong.

I explained how the probationary period worked, and then I went on to tell him about the disciplinary actions in my personnel file. "The pictures HR had were completely innocent, but I did break the rules by dating a coworker."

Jeremy reached into the pocket of his shorts and pulled out his phone. Once he found what he was looking for, he handed the phone to me. "Are these the pictures they showed you?"

When I looked at them, I saw Cammie had sent them. I felt like beating the crap out of her. Again. "Yes, they're the same. That morning, I'd visited Nanna before work and was upset about her condition. The guy consoling me is Jared and we dated for a month or so."

I swiped my finger across the screen to look at the photos again, but a different picture popped up. This one was of a shirtless Jeremy, and Hannah was sitting on his lap. The tattoo on his chest was very fresh looking.

"I love this." I smiled as I showed Jeremy the picture.

"Me too," he said. "Keep scrolling and you can see the rest of them if you want."

I scrolled through several more—pictures of cars or his family.

"Who is this princess?" I asked when I came to a photo of him with an adorable dark haired little girl with big brown eyes.

"That's Mya, Jason's little girl. She had her first birthday in June. She is a princess for sure. She was the only girl until Hannah came along. Spoiled rotten . . . both of them."

He smiled like the proud uncle that he was. From the high chair I'd noticed in his dining room, I knew he took his godfather and uncle duties very seriously.

I laughed at the next photo. "Uh, Jeremy . . . please explain this to me."

He took the phone and laughed with me. "*That* would be my baby brother, Adam."

"Is he duct taped to a pole?" I leaned in and looked closely at the picture.

"Yep, check this picture out." He flipped to the next picture, and Adam was wearing makeup and his hair was in pigtails. Jeremy had the biggest grin on his face as we looked at the next several pictures of his brother.

"You guys are so mean. What did he do to deserve that?"

Jeremy shrugged. "Hell, I don't remember, but I'm sure it was justified. We were in so much trouble with my mom after we cut him down, though. The duct tape ripped all the paint off the pillar and ruined his work uniform."

He laughed explaining how they left Adam taped to the pillar for over an hour and how they'd had to repaint it.

Jeremy suddenly stopped laughing and turned serious. "Teagan, you asked me a question earlier, and I didn't answer you. My answer is yes. I want your grandma to be right about us."

I was surprised by the sudden turn the conversation had taken. We didn't know each other well, but the time we had spent together felt like it truly meant something, and we'd also had fun together.

"What should we do?" I asked. "Everything is so complicated at work. What if I can't handle it?"

"I understand." He started to slide off my papa's ring. "Here, you need to take this back then."

"No, leave it on. You misunderstood me. We can have us here in your house, but until I find another job, I need to make sure that what we do isn't going to cause more problems at the hospital."

"So what you're saying is you'll be my girlfriend, but I get to be your dirty little secret while you're at work?" he asked, smirking.

I didn't think that was funny. In fact, it made me feel terrible that he'd even thought it.

"That's not it, Jeremy. If the girls at work find out we're together, I have a feeling they'll try to get me in trouble again. One more strike then I'm out on my ass—and I need my job. I live at my parents' house, and I'm too old to be doing that."

Sighing with frustration, I rolled onto my back. My mind bounced all over the place, thinking of all that could go wrong, but every time I glanced over at the man lying next to me, the more I wanted to take a chance with him.

But I was scared. Scared to risk myself, scared that it wouldn't work out, scared that deep down, he would see my insecurities as weaknesses. My biggest fear was history repeating itself. Cheating and betrayal from someone who should love me was not something I wanted to go through again.

"Teagan, can you put all this Cammie crap aside and trust that I won't let them hurt you."

I wanted to. I really did. *I do.* "Jeremy, I want to trust you, and I do, but you have to try to understand what I've been going through at work. You can't save me there. Between Cammie, her friends, and Jared, I'm in a really tough spot."

Jeremy ran his fingers through his hair then interlaced his fingers behind his head. "Is Jared the doctor in the picture? The one you dated?" he asked.

"Yes."

I told him about the incident in the residents' room and that Jared had met up with Tiffany later that day.

Jeremy slid his arm underneath me, and the next thing I knew, he'd rolled me over on top of him. I rested my cheek against his bare chest as he wrapped me in his arms. I didn't want to be anywhere else.

"I'm so sorry about everything," he said. "I want to make it stop. What do you want me to do? Do you want me to call Cammie and see if I can convince her to leave you alone? I'll do anything you ask."

If Jeremy talked to Cammie she'd know about us, which would only make matters worse. "Jeremy, I don't want you to talk to her."

"Why not?" He loosened my hair then untwisted and arranged it so it spilled over my back and his arms.

Loving the way he played with it, I decided I would wear it down when I was with him from now on. He stroked my back as his fingers combed over my hair. I'd never felt as close to anyone before, as I did right then.

"I don't want her to know about us. All she's going to do is cause more problems." Taking in a deep breath, I let it out and said. "I'm so sorry, Jeremy. I don't want you to be a secret, or go back to work there, but I have no choice. I need to move out and quit freeloading off my parents. In the meantime, I'm looking for a new job."

At that moment, I wanted so badly for Nanna to be right. I loved the self-imposed bubble Jeremy and I were in now, and I didn't want to leave it. We had our white picket fence surrounding us, holding us safely inside.

"I think I'll try to catch her before or after work and try to talk to her. If the conversation goes bad, I'll walk away," I said.

"Please, will you let me call her? I don't want you to get in trouble at work, Teagan. I hate the fact that my previous actions are affecting you," he said softly.

I heard the guilt in his voice and raised my head slightly to look him in the eyes. "It's not your fault, but I can't help but feel animosity about it. I hate that, but it's how I feel. Can you understand that?"

"I can, but it still doesn't make me feel any better. I want her to leave you alone. I want to tell everyone who will listen that I've finally found the woman I'm supposed to spend the rest of my life with, Teagan. I don't want to hide us, but I understand the need to for now."

His confession briefly rendered me speechless. "Are you serious, Jeremy? Do you really feel like you want to spend the rest of your life with me?"

He nodded his head shyly, never taking his eyes from mine. "I don't want to be without you now that I've found you."

I felt my eyes fill with tears. No man had ever spoken to me the way he did, and I never wanted him to stop. Right then, I also wanted to tell everyone I'd found the person I was supposed to spend the rest of my life with, but there was still that annoying doubt in the back of my brain. It was inescapable. For weeks, Cammie and her friends had been pounding stories, rumors, lies, *and* truths into my head and my heart.

I *wanted* to trust every word he said to me. I *wanted* to believe he was the man for me.

"Teagan, say something, please. I'm spilling my guts here for the first time in my life, and it scares the hell out of me," he said, squeezing me a little tighter.

"I'll try to speak to Cammie on Monday. The sooner she leaves me alone, or the sooner I can find a new job, the better. Can we try it my way first and see what happens? Then if that doesn't work, we'll go from there?"

He smiled and let out a quiet chuckle. "Yes."

He had the cutest smirk on his face, so I knew something was up. Like there was a story behind his short response.

I laughed. "After *all that* . . . all I get is a *yes*? Nothing else?"

"You get a yes, and one of these." And he kissed me.

I'll take as many of those as he wants to give me.

After the kiss, I had to go back to the whole *yes* thing, though. I sat up and straddled him, then pinned his hands up over his head.

"So, *my boyfriend,* what's this yes crap? Not that I'm opposed to you telling me yes all the time, but you need to let me in on the joke."

He grinned mischievously and shook his head. "No way, *my girlfriend,* it's a man thing. You wouldn't understand."

"Oh, are we back to doing it the hard way, Jeremy? I see how it is." I laughed as I kissed and nipped his neck. In between kisses, I whispered, "Tell me," but it didn't work. I let go of his hands, and he tangled his fingers in my hair, to pull me into a kiss. Things were escalating quickly, when he abruptly stopped.

"We need to get off this bed before I mess up, Teagan."

We were both breathing heavily, and I didn't want to get up. I was perfectly comfortable lying on my new favorite spot.

"Come on, let's go finish lunch and get back in the pool to cool off," he suggested.

He was really taking this seriously. And I appreciated that. I eased off him and stood from the bed.

After lunch, we walked hand in hand to the patio.

"Are we really doing this?" Jeremy asked, shooting me an expectant glance.

"Officially, you're my boyfriend?"

"Yes, if you'll have me."

"I will. How about my better half?"

"Sounds perfect, but I think you're the better half of us."

An uncontrollable grin spread across my face and I giggled. "Do you wanna be my sidekick? A dynamic duo like Velma and Shaggy from *Scooby Doo?*"

He laughed. "I'll be whatever you need me to be, Teagan. Just say the word. But, I am not smoking weed and driving that ugly-ass Mystery Machine."

I nodded with a satisfied grin on my face. We were doing this. *We are really doing this.* "Got it. No marijuana, no ugly van. I can agree to that."

"Then let's take this plunge together, shall we?" he offered.

I laughed heartily because I loved the idiom he used. We gripped each other's hands tighter, ran to the deep end of the pool, and jumped.

Sunday came, and we went running again. This time, when we got home, I made breakfast and we lounged around the pool.

"Will you go somewhere with me later?" Jeremy asked out of the blue, as we were sunning ourselves on an enormous two-person hammock.

I let out a quiet giggle before responding, because I needed to ask him another question. "Yes, I will go with you, but you owe me an explanation about something first."

He opened his blue eyes and glanced over at me with an inquisitive expression on his face.

"Tell me about Yeats." I'd been completely blindsided

when we'd visited Nanna and she'd asked him to read to her. Most men would have opened the book and read the first poem they found. Not Jeremy, though. He'd known exactly what he was reading.

He smiled bashfully, and his cheeks flushed slightly. "That's an easy answer," he said. "Remember the picture I showed you from my wallet?"

I nodded, thinking back to our matching chubby pictures.

"Well, I was quiet and shy back then, so I found other stuff to do with my time. Don't laugh, but I worked in the library all through high school. I read every book I could while I was there. I excelled in all my classes and had enough credits to graduate a year early."

I was in utter disbelief. "Not only is my boyfriend handsome, he is also very intelligent. That is a perfect combination." Carefully, I rolled to my side so I wouldn't flip us over in the hammock, and kissed his bare shoulder. "Where are we going later?"

"I want to take you to our weekly family dinner," he said as if he thought I was going to say no.

"That sounds great. Should I make anything to take over there?"

He smiled and shook his head.

Four and a half hours later, we were on our way to his family's dinner. He had plugged in his iPod, but left the volume barely audible. I didn't want to go messing with his stereo, but I wanted to see what music he liked.

"Can I check out your music?" I asked.

He handed me his iPod.

I scrolled through his playlists, finding a wide array of music. Most of it was music I listened to already. The rest was music I hadn't heard before. I scrolled until I saw a band I loved, selected the album, and pressed play.

When the music started, Jeremy glanced over at me with an enormous grin on his face. "I don't even know what to say right now," he said and shook his head.

"What?"

"This is my favorite band."

He turned up the volume, and drove all the way to his parents' house listening to *my* favorite band, In This Moment.

When we entered his parents' house, I was suddenly nervous to meet Jeremy's family. *What would they think of me? Would they like me?* I'd worn a cute, dark green sundress, and a pair of wedge sandals. I'd left my hair down, but tamed my long, loose curls with a smoothing serum to keep them under control, and applied a minimal amount of makeup.

We walked through a very colorfully painted house and out a large sliding glass door to where his family congregated. Apparently, we were the last to arrive at the house. Several surprised expressions greeted us from around the patio.

Eventually, I spotted a face in the crowd I recognized. Zoey smiled brightly and lifted herself from Andy's lap to jog over to us. She slammed into Jeremy and hugged him tightly, saying nothing. After releasing him, she turned to me.

"Teagan, it's great to see you again." She gave me a quick hug.

"Hello, Zoey. It's good to see you, too. There are a lot of people here." I glanced around again, taking in all the unfamiliar faces.

Zoey laughed. "Don't worry, everyone will love you. I promise." She looked over at Jeremy and smiled.

I sensed a silent conversation happening between them.

Finally, she gave him a sisterly punch on the arm, "I'll let you two make the rounds with the rest of the family," then went back to her husband.

Jeremy took me around and introduced me to everyone. His family was fantastic, and treated me as if I was a part of their family.

When dinner was ready, we sat down at the largest outdoor dining table I had ever seen. I sat next to Jess, Jeremy's sister-in-law. She had quite the baby belly going on, so we chatted about her pregnancy. She and Noah had wanted to start a family right away, and less than eight months after their wedding, she'd become pregnant.

Jess was very sweet, and we got along great. I found that Angie, Adam's girlfriend, was hilarious, and Heather, Jason's wife was all of the above. That woman could multi-task like nobody's business. Between taking care of her three children, she also helped prepare the food and made the rounds conversing with each person throughout the day.

While we were eating, I noticed Luisa, Jeremy's mom, watching us closely from the opposite end of the table. She smiled and said something to Jeremy in Spanish. Everyone at the table erupted in giggles and laughs.

"Jesus Christ, Ma! Did you have to say that in front of *everyone?*" Jeremy had a huge, embarrassed grin on his face, so I figured she was teasing him about something.

Looking around, the only other person who looked as confused as me was Andy. He smiled and shrugged. We were out of the loop, not knowing Spanish.

Jeremy scrubbed his hands over his face and whispered to me, "Please tell me you don't understand Spanish."

I shook my head.

"Thank God." He said something to his mom in Spanish, which made her laugh.

"What did she say?" I asked curiously.

"Nothing," he replied, but he was still smiling, which made me even more curious.

Adam leaned across Angie to talk to me. "She said that you and Jeremy will make pretty babies someday," he said, with a face splitting grin, that I knew was meant to poke fun at Jeremy.

Oh, my . . .

"Seriously, bro?" Jeremy said to Adam. "I was going to tell her later, and not embarrass her in front of everyone. You are such a prick sometimes."

Adam grinned mischievously at his brother.

Angie held her hand out to Adam, palm up. "Give me your phone and your wallet."

He did as she said.

A moment later, Jeremy pushed his chair back, and Adam was running across the patio. Jeremy caught up with him, threw him over his shoulder, and chucked him into the pool. I was surprised, but everyone continued eating as if nothing had happened.

"Don't worry," Angie said. "My poor boyfriend doesn't know when to keep quiet sometimes. You'll have to forgive him."

I agreed, and we laughed as we watched Adam climb out of the pool, and take off his shirt to squeeze the water out of it.

"I always bring him a change of clothes, just in case." She laughed, but didn't get up to help Adam.

Jeremy

Right after I returned to my chair next to Teagan, Adam bellowed at me. "Jeremy, get over here. *Hurry!*"

When I looked over at him, he was frantically digging in the pockets of his wet shorts. It wasn't like Adam to panic about anything, so I knew something was up and jogged over to him. "What's wrong?"

His face paled and he dropped to his knees, searching for something on the patio around us.

"It's gone. Oh, my God, it's gone!" he snarled. "You need to help me find it, *now*."

I took a hold of his shoulders, forcing him to calm down and look at me. "What's missing? I can't help you look if I don't know what I'm looking for." I was really getting worried about him. Adam didn't freak out about anything. *Ever*.

He leaned in close so only I could hear him. "Angie's engagement ring was in my pocket. I was going to ask her to marry me when we sat down for dessert, so it was out of the box already. Oh, God. It's gone. What am I going to do?" He scrubbed his palms over his face.

Shit . . . I had to find the ring. It was my fault it was lost. "Try and calm down, we'll find it."

Adam and I searched the ground around the pool area, but it wasn't there. It must be *in* the pool. Like a moron, I'd dumped him in the deep end, where the water was twelve feet deep.

Fuck me.

I hadn't brought swim shorts, but I wasn't about to ruin my brother's big day. I pulled off my shirt, stripped down to my boxers, and jumped into the pool. Adam jumped in right behind me, and we submerged ourselves to search along the bottom.

When we both surfaced for air, our entire family was standing at the side of the pool asking what we were doing.

"Something fell out of my pocket, and we're trying to find it," Adam muttered. He was glaring at me, and most likely plotting how he would murder me.

Shit, he was really pissed at me. I felt horrible and would do anything to find that ring. I dove back down to the bottom.

Adam joined me again, and we dove repeatedly for thirty minutes straight trying to find the ring.

On my last trip up for air, I had a hard time breathing from holding my breath for so long, and held on to the side of the pool to calm myself. Jess, Heather, Zoey, Angie, and Teagan were sitting at the shallow end of the pool soaking their feet and watching us.

All of the women were talking, except for Teagan. She caught my eye. Leaving her hands folded on her lap, she pointed to the area directly in front of her and tipped her head toward where she had pointed. I cocked my head to the side because I wasn't sure what she was trying to tell me. She spun the ring on her right hand and then casually pointed at the water in front of her again.

It finally dawned on me that she was telling me the ring was in front of them. I didn't know how the hell Teagan had seen it, but I nodded once, then dove back under and got Adam's attention. I pointed toward the shallow area of the pool where the girls were. We surfaced and I thanked God that we didn't have to search any longer.

"It's in front of the girls," I whispered to him. "Teagan can see it and showed me where it is."

"Your girlfriend is a life saver," he said as an extreme wave of relief washed over his face. "You better not fuck things up with her."

All I could do was nod in agreement. My entire body was

sore, my eyes were burning from the chlorine, and my lungs were on fire. I made my way over to Teagan to thank her as Adam sank under the water for the ring. Teagan had her sundress pulled up over her knees to keep it dry as she soaked her feet and legs in the cool water.

I stood in front of her and rested my wet hands on the top of her knees. She took my hands in hers and turned them over, palm up. "Your hands look like raisins. Let me get you a towel so you can get out," she said as she smiled down at me. She bent over and hugged me around the neck, so I wrapped my arms around her waist, and then realized I was getting her wet.

"Sorry, I'm getting your dress wet," I said to her and tried to pull away.

She pulled back and combed my wet hair away from my face. "It's only water. I won't melt." She kissed the scar below my hairline.

I let go of her and put my palms on either side of her thighs and pushed up out of the water, completely drenching her in the process. I balanced on my hands with my legs still in the pool. I was now eye level with the prettiest woman at the house. I pressed my lips to hers right in front of every single person in my family and didn't feel the slightest bit weird about it.

Apparently, she thought it was funny because she was laughing with her lips pressed hard against mine. Teagan wrapped her arms and legs around me and squeezed tightly.

I was glad she wasn't mad at me for getting her all wet. Cammie would've thrown a hissy fit. That's what I loved about Teagan. She was easy going, and didn't give a crap that her dress was soaked, especially in front of people she'd only known for a few hours.

She also didn't seem to mind my PDA, which was cool too. Not that PDA's were a big deal with my family because they all did it, even my parents. Nobody ever went overboard or anything, but they were affectionate toward their spouses.

"Can I get everyone's attention, please?" Adam called out from behind me.

The girls stayed where they were, and my brothers, along

with Andy, and my parents came to the pool with all the kids. I turned around to face Adam and rested against the wall of the pool in between Teagan's knees. She placed her hands on my shoulders, leaving just enough room for me to kiss the ring on her right hand.

Adam swam through the water then stood in front of Angie. He looked up at her and smiled. "Angie, this isn't the way I planned on doing this, but plans change." He glared over at me. Angie giggled then her eyes filled with tears as Adam said, "Angie, I love you. I want to spend the rest of my life loving you. Will you marry me?"

Adam held the diamond engagement ring up to her and waited for an answer. Angie held out her left hand, and Adam slid the ring on her finger.

"Yes, Adam! Absolutely, yes!" She quickly emptied the pockets on her shorts, jumped into the pool, and threw her arms around him. "I love you so much, baby," she cried as my family cheered around us.

Teagan bent over, wrapped her arms around my shoulders, and kissed me on the side of the neck. I rested my cheek against hers. "Thank you for finding the ring, Teagan. You just saved my ass. I would've felt like shit if I ruined his surprise more than I already had."

I watched as Adam and Angie hugged while Angie checked out her new engagement ring. Adam glanced over at me, and the look of relief on his face made me feel better, but I still mouthed "I'm sorry" to him. He nodded once and smiled a big, toothy grin.

Either he was forgiving me for tossing him in the pool and losing the ring temporarily, or that was a look letting me know revenge was coming. It could be either so I'd watch my back for the rest of the day.

Adam and Angie got out of the pool, and the rest of my family went back to the table for dessert, but I stood right where I was, feeling more comfortable and happy than I had in a long time. Teagan might be a feisty little thing, but she made me feel . . . *whole*. She filled the missing piece of my heart and completed my life.

Holy fuck, this is really happening to me. I wanted to

embrace every second of this relationship with Teagan because inevitably, I would screw up. The way I'd lived my life before I met Teagan was biting me in the ass. The trouble Cammie was causing was only a taste of what could happen. If I'd only known I would meet someone like her eventually, I surely would have done things differently.

"Hey, where'd you go just now?" Teagan asked softly. "You're thinking about something awfully hard. Is everything okay?"

I wanted to tell her what I was thinking, but the words wouldn't come out. I opened my mouth twice to speak . . . and nothing . . . I'd spilled my guts to her the entire weekend, and now I was mute.

I was scared shitless.

Flat out scared I was going to lose this perfect woman because of the way I used to be—someone I no longer wanted to be.

All I wanted was to be with Teagan.

I stared down at the ring she'd put on my right hand for several long seconds, before realizing Teagan was in the water in front of me, still wearing her pretty, green sundress.

"What are you doing?" I asked. "You're getting your dress wet."

"It's already wet, and you're kind of scaring me. Please tell me what's wrong." Her emerald eyes searched my face for a hint. Her soft hands slid up my chest and she locked her fingers together behind my neck. "Do you want to leave? Are you ready for me to go home?"

I shook my head and pulled her to me, wrapping my arms around her small body. "That's the problem. I don't want you to go . . . at all," I said quietly as I rested my cheek against hers again. "I like having you with me at my house. I like you here with my family." I took a deep breath and slowly let it out. "Tomorrow's Monday, and we both have to go back to work. I don't want this weekend to be over."

"Jeremy, remember what we said yesterday? Remember the decisions we made?" She looked me in the eyes again. "I'm not changing my mind about us." She pulled my right hand up out of the water and rubbed her finger over my ring. "This means we're together, no matter what. When I'm at work, when I am away from you for whatever reason . . . we're still together."

"I know. I've gotten used to having you around already. I like getting up every morning to go running with you . . . I like being with you." *God, I feel like a total bitch right now.* "I want you to stay."

"What do you mean *stay*, Jeremy?"

"Do you know that aside from the night when my friends and I got drunk and crashed at my house, the first night I spent there, was with *you?*" I asked. "The night I wasn't at Dub's was because I had been moving out of my apartment. The night you stayed, was the day I officially moved in." I laughed when I remembered the morning after the garage arranging party. "Oh, and I forgot one other person has slept on my bed."

Teagan looked at me curiously and narrowed her eyes at me.

"Don't worry, it was John."

"Do I want to know that story?" she asked then laughed.

I told her about finding his naked ass on my bed.

"Do you guys party like that all the time?"

"No, not anymore. Not for the last year or so, anyway. We only do the MMA nights now. That night was an exception. Like I said, I'm ready to settle down and be a grown-up now."

She seemed relieved then smiled at me. "You're doing a good job of that too, by the way. New house, new girlfriend, and you've become a godfather. I'd say you're well on your way to becoming a full-fledged grown up."

"Don't make me toss you into the deep end, Red."

She feigned innocence and batted her dark eyelashes at me. "You wouldn't. My hair would get all wet and I'd have to throw a fit and embarrass you in front of your family."

Knowing she couldn't care less if her hair was wet, I picked her up and tossed her. She squealed as she flew through the air before splashing into the water. When she surfaced, she laughed and splashed me in the face.

"Remember, Jeremy . . . payback's a bitch." She pulled the

bottom of her dress out of the water and wiped away the makeup that was running down her face then laughed.

Shit. She does get even. She proved that when I tossed her over my shoulder the other night and packed her out of Dub's. Now I had to watch my back with her *and* Adam.

Teagan swam up, slipped her arms around me, and kissed me quickly on the cheek.

I heard the sound of someone coming up behind me. I turned and found Angie bringing two dessert plates. She set them down at the edge of the pool. "Thought you might want this before there's none left."

I was opening my mouth to thank her and the next thing I knew, Teagan was yanking my freaking boxers down my legs. They were already past my knees before I realized what was going on. Angie was laughing, and my only option was to cover my dick with my hands so I didn't give my brother's new fiancée an eyeful.

I thought Teagan was going to leave my boxers around my feet. But no, she grasped my ankles and yanked my feet out from under me, submerging me, and taking my boxers in the process. I stood and turned my back to Angie but kept my junk covered because now I was facing Teagan.

I was fucking naked in the pool with my entire family within twenty feet. *Perfect.*

Teagan laughed as she tried to run-swim to the pool steps with my boxers in her hand. Her waterlogged dress was making it hard for her to move across the pool quickly.

"Teagan Shea Donnelly, if you don't bring those back right now, you're in big trouble," I said through gritted teeth.

"Adam, I have something for you!" she called out. She made it to the steps and tossed my boxers onto the patio at Adam's feet before she sloshed out of the pool.

He picked her up in his arms and swung her around a few times before setting her back on her feet. "Oh, Teagan . . ." Adam said enthusiastically, "I do believe I owe you big for this. Anytime you need a favor, you call me. I've got your back."

Since my spirited new girlfriend had forcefully unclothed me, I stepped back over to the side of the pool where Angie had set the dessert plates. I dug in to my dessert of whole strawberries with a side of fruit dip. It's not like I could get out of the pool now.

"Hey, handsome," Teagan said as she approached with two beach towels. Her green dress, saturated with water, hung heavily on her small frame and dripped a trail of water behind her. Her long, wet, red hair was plastered to her shoulders and arms. "Did you lose something?" She sat down and dropped her feet back into the pool, then picked up her dessert plate.

"Nope, I didn't lose anything," I said as I bit into a ripe strawberry. "Did you?"

She set her plate on the patio and looked herself over. "No, I don't seem to have lost anything. All of my clothes are still on." She looked over the edge of the pool at me. "You *definitely* lost yours though."

"Can you please hand me a towel so I can get out and get dressed? I've been in the water too long."

"Are you mad at me for that?" Her smiled turned to a frown. She quickly picked up a towel and went to stand.

I pulled her back down and held my hand out for the towel, which she handed over quickly. "No, but you have a slightly unfair advantage now," I said with a smirk.

I took my towel and walked to the steps to get out of the pool. I held the towel up as a shield so nobody would see anything, and wrapped it securely around my waist when I reached the top of the steps.

Teagan met me there. "What do you mean by *unfair advantage?*"

I moved in close to her so nobody could hear. "You've seen me naked, but I haven't seen you naked. It's just not fair." My eyes roamed over her beautiful, fully covered body.

Teagan burst out laughing and clapped her hands together in amusement. "Are you sure about that?" she whispered. "I seem to remember waking up in your clothes once, and I know I didn't change into them myself."

I gripped her around the waist and pulled her close to me. I rested my cheek against hers, so my mouth was close to her ear. The closeness of being cheek to cheek with her was quickly becoming my favorite thing. "For your information, it was dark in the house that night and my eyes were closed the entire time I was helping your drunk-ass change into my clothes . . . so technically, I haven't *seen* anything."

She pulled back and her eyes grew big with surprise. "You're joking."

I shook my head. "Nope, I'm dead serious."

I picked up my boxers then tossed them onto the drying rack. I left Teagan standing there stunned as I gathered my shorts and T-shirt from the patio and went inside the house to dry off and put on my clothes. I was glad Adam hadn't thought to hide them from me.

When I came back out, I found Teagan sitting at the table with my family finishing her dessert. She'd brought mine back to the table with her, so I sat next to her and resumed eating. I looked around the table at my family and every single one of them had a smirk or a smile on their face.

"What's up, everyone?"

When I glanced at my mom, my gut clenched because even though she had a smile on her face, the sudden uncertainty in her eyes had me second-guessing my abilities to be worthy of Teagan. My entire family thought I was a player with women and I'd never corrected them. Now I wished I had. Finally, I broke my silence. "I know what you're all thinking . . . I've finally met my match, and I swear I'm gonna try my hardest to not ruin it."

Teagan glanced at me with hope and reassurance in her eyes then squeezed my thigh under the table. I reached down, took her hand in mine, and made a silent vow that I would never let her go.

Later that night after we were back at my house sitting on the couch, trying to find something to watch on TV, Teagan took a breath to say something, and then changed her mind.

After a few minutes, she still hadn't said anything.

"What's wrong, Teagan?" I waited for her to tell me it was time for her to go home. I didn't want to hear her say it . . . I didn't want her to go.

"Are you sure you aren't mad at me for the boxer's prank?" she asked quietly.

I chuckled at the thought. "I'm not mad at you, but if you wanted to see me naked, all you had to do is ask."

She laughed and playfully smacked me on the arm. "What's wrong then? Things got all weird after that. Even with your family, it just felt tense."

When she pulled back, I caught her hand and faced her. "There's nothing to worry about with my family, okay? They loved you. I just don't want you to go."

"I can stay another night," she replied. "But why is my leaving freaking you out so badly?"

"Because, the last two times you left my house, I didn't think I'd ever see you again. Well, technically, the first time you left, you snuck out and ran away. And the next time, I thought you were gone for good because I saw my keys lying on the table," I admitted.

"I'm sorry . . . I really am. I was confused, and with all the crap going on with Cammie—I didn't trust you. That doesn't mean I didn't have feelings for you, because I did. I came back because I needed to see if you were the same person I met that day in the ER, and then at Dub's."

She scooted closer to me and moved onto my lap. *I am being a pussy, but shit happens.* The idea of her leaving and her friend Reese staying with her was unbearable. I knew he was gay, but he was still a guy, and I wouldn't have her all to myself anymore.

"When does your friend get into town?"

"Tomorrow evening sometime. He's on his way already, driving a U-Haul truck and towing his car all the way from Denver."

Fuck, that soon?

"You know, we can all hang out together, right?" she asked. "He's never been to California before, but since I have to work, he'll be going to check out his new job and meet his coworkers. He has a lot of things to do until the apartment is ready to move in to next week."

"Okay," I said. "I'll do whatever you want, as long as I don't have to wait another week to see you."

She pressed her lips against mine. "I'll miss you every second I'm away from you," she said when she pulled away.

I pulled her back to me and kissed her again. Our lips parted, our tongues tasted each other, and when I couldn't hold back any longer, a groan involuntarily escaped me.

Teagan let out a quiet giggle, and spun on my lap so she was straddling me. She was wearing one of my long T-shirts and it rode up her thighs. Feeling the heat between her legs through my shorts made me want to be inside her and I was horny as hell now.

Obviously, she wanted the same thing, because she suddenly slipped her hand past the elastic waistband of my shorts and boxers to grasp my rock hard dick. *Jesus, she went straight for the kill.* There was nothing between her soft hand and my dick. It was skin on skin, and if I died right then, I would die happy.

But, I didn't want it this way with her . . . it *had* to be different. My mind tried to send that message to my dick, but my dick blocked the message. *Does that mean my dick just mind-blocked me? Hmm, that's a new one.* Usually my mind does the blocking, not the other way around.

Teagan slowly stroked me, and I let her. She abruptly let go of me and gripped the waistband of my shorts and my boxers to pull them down.

It was just enough time for my mind to clear. "I can't believe I'm going to say this, but we need to stop, Teagan." I took hold of both of her hands and unhooked them from my shorts. I looked her in the eyes and she seemed a little hurt.

"I don't understand, Jeremy. Did I do something wrong?" The rejection in her eyes was obvious.

"No, you could never do anything wrong. I don't want our relationship to start out this way. I don't want to mess things up, and I think if we go any further . . ." I trailed off, hoping this was making sense to her. "I want to do this right—and now is not the time for us to take things to that level."

She straddled me again and rested her arms across my shoulders. "Thank you, Jeremy."

Teagan looked into my eyes with such sincerity I *felt* it.

"You're right," she said. "Especially with the way things have gone up until yesterday. We should take our time." She laughed. "But just so you know, I haven't had sex since last

September, so don't make me wait *too* long."

September? Holy shit. Poor girl. "September, huh?" More thoughts from previous conversations we'd had over the weekend came to me. "So you had a boyfriend until then?"

She frowned. "We broke up in January . . . his name was Gary. I lived in Denver with him for a couple years. I came home in January to find him in bed having sex with my best friend Katie. I'd been relieved from my shift early, because my patient died, and I came home to . . . *that*."

Holy shit, I wanted to kill the fucker for hurting her. What she told me after that, made me want to kill him again. That prick cheated on her more than once, and with more than one woman. How could he do that to someone like her?

Then, to treat her with such disrespect about her weight, and the job she loved so much, was unconscionable to me.

"Teagan, I'm sorry that happened to you. What they did was shitty. Is this why you've mentioned cheating a few times this weekend?"

She nodded and looked away. Gary and Katie's cheating had not only broken her heart but was still upsetting to her.

I gently took her chin in my hand and turned her head back to face me. "I'd never cheat on you. You know that, right? It's not the way I was raised."

She didn't respond and it worried me. *Did she think I would do that to her?*

"I've seen what it's done to people, and I would never cheat on you. *Ever* . . ." I hoped I was convincing her, but just in case I wasn't I explained further, "Teagan, my grandfather cheated on my grandma every chance he got. She divorced him when she found out about it. By the time he died, he had ten children with six women. His cheating was hard on her and my mom, so they've always pounded it into mine, and my brothers' heads that you don't treat someone you love that way. I'd never do that to you, okay?"

Shit, did I tell her I loved her, in a roundabout way? Fuck, I guess I did.

She still wasn't saying anything.

"Teagan, say something." Had my little slip up just screwed me over?

She hugged me tightly around the neck, still not saying anything. Eventually, she let out a long sigh. "Sorry, that was a lot to take in and a lot for me to tell you. I haven't talked about my situation much with anyone other than my family and Reese."

An odd expression came over her face. "Speaking of Reese . . . Jeremy, he and I were roommates after Gary kicked me out. I need to let you know he only had a one-bedroom apartment, so we slept in the same bed."

What the fuck? Slept in the same bed? "I'm sorry . . . when you say you *slept* in the same bed, do you mean you had sex?"

She laughed and then ran her fingers through my hair. "Reese is *gay*. As in, the *thought* of a vagina freaks him out . . . trust me."

She had the cutest grin on her face, but I still wasn't convinced.

"Where's he sleeping until his apartment is ready?" I asked.

She frowned and looked away.

"Oh hell no, Teagan!" I growled as I picked her up off my lap and set her on the cushion next to me. I rose from the couch and paced the room.

She was going to let him stay in the same bed with her. Fuck that shit.

"He can stay here next week, then," I offered, off the top of my head. "The guest room is all his, but he sure as hell isn't sleeping with you."

"Jeremy, calm down. He's gay for Pete's sake. My parents met him when they came to visit me in Denver and they don't care if he sleeps in my room. Besides, it's not like I knew I was going to have a boyfriend when he decided to move here," she said, clearly exasperated. "So, I guess now is a bad time to tell you I was planning on moving in with him."

"Please tell me you'll have separate bedrooms when you move in with him, at least." My stomach churned at the thought of them being roommates.

She burst out laughing, so I stopped pacing and stared down at her. "What the hell is so funny, Red?"

She laughed harder. "Are we already having our first fight?" Teagan covered her mouth to keep from laughing.

I shook my head while thinking about it. "Not if you count the three or four we've had since we've known each other." I joined in her laughter and all the jealousy left my mind. I sat down and she crawled right back on my lap.

"Would you really let him stay here because you don't want him sleeping in my bed?" she asked.

I turned and looked at her intently. "Hell yes. I don't care if he's gay or not. He's still a man and I don't want another guy sleeping with my girlfriend. How would you feel if the tables were turned?"

"You're right, I'm sorry . . . I'll change plans with him. On one condition though."

I raised my brows waiting for her terms.

"Can I stay here, too?"

"Yes," I said without even thinking because I wanted her to stay and wasn't about to say no.

She tickled the crap out of me. "You and your stupid *man yes's*," she said, laughing. I tossed her off me onto the couch and pinned her down with my body.

"Be quiet, my girlfriend. I need to kiss you now," I whispered and pressed my lips to hers.

Teagan

The alarm on my cell went off at five thirty so I could get in a run with Jeremy before I had to leave for work. My eight-to-five shift this week was going to work out well for us, especially with Reese getting into town.

A few minutes after my cell alarm had gone off, the most god-awful sound blared from across the hallway in Jeremy's room. Well, technically the guest room, since I was still using his. The noise echoed throughout the entire house. *Can he not hear it?*

Did he leave on his run without me and forget to shut off his alarm? If he had, I was going to kick his ass because running together was now my favorite part of the morning.

Holy crap. That horrid racket needs to stop.

I padded across the hallway, and flipped on his light. He was still sound asleep. I shut off the offending noise.

"Wake up, Sleeping Beauty." I shook his shoulder but he gave no indication he was waking up. I pulled his covers back and shook him again . . . nothing.

"Jeremy, wake up!"

I shook him harder and he still didn't budge. Thinking something was wrong with him, I rolled him onto his back, calling out his name again.

And then I went in to nurse mode.

With my fingers on his neck, I checked that he had a pulse and his chest rose and fell as he breathed. His color was good, there was no outward appearance of injury, and his skin was cool when I pressed the back of my hand to his forehead. I shook him again harder, and he finally groaned and stretched as if he were waking up the way he usually did.

"Jeremy, are you alright?" I asked, my voice trembling from the scare he'd given me.

"What's wrong?" he asked sleepily without even opening his eyes.

Seriously? Did he sleep like this every night?

"Didn't you hear your alarm going off? I heard it across the hallway. You scared me because you wouldn't wake up." To get my point across, I shoved his shoulder.

"Jesus, Red, is this how you're going to wake me up every morning?"

I tried to stand, but he yanked me down onto the bed and pulled the sheet up over us. "Just ten more minutes, please."

I giggled at his roughness and snuggled in close to his warm body. "You scared the heck out of me, Jeremy." My heart was still pounding in my chest.

"I was sleeping, how could I have possibly scared you?"

"Your alarm was blaring and you wouldn't wake up. I even took your pulse," I said.

He laughed. "You really took my pulse?"

"God, you're deaf and you sleep like the dead! Yes, I took your freaking pulse because you wouldn't wake up," I muttered against his neck.

"I'm sorry, Nurse Teagan. I didn't mean to scare you. You should know, though, I *do* sleep like the dead, I always have. Once I fall asleep, I'm out cold. My dad is the same way. It takes several minutes for me to hear my alarm after it goes off, so that's why I set it loud as hell."

He let out a deep laugh and his chest rumbled against mine.

"Thanks for the warning." I kissed his neck and pressed my body closer to his. There had to be a better way of waking him up each morning. I didn't know how long I could stand to hear his crazy alarm every day.

Jeremy sat up suddenly, throwing the covers back. "Shit,

I'm so sorry, I forgot you didn't want to be on this bed." He tried to move me off the bed.

"No, it's fine. You said it was new, and I was being childish. I'm sorry for that." It was just a bed. It's not like Cammie had lived with him or anything. She'd never even been to this house. Apparently, I'm the only girlfriend who had.

"Since we're up, let's get our run out of the way so I can fix my boyfriend a nice breakfast before he goes off to work."

"That sounds like a great plan." He kissed my bare shoulder.

We got up, and once we were both ready, we headed out the door for our morning run.

"I need to stop by my house to pick up some work clothes for today. Then tonight after work, I'll need to go home and pack more, now that I am staying for a week while Reese is here." I smiled and gave him a playful elbow to the ribs.

Jeremy shot me a grin as we jogged down the block. "This feels really weird to be planning out our day together."

He seemed nervous and honestly, a little clueless. Not in a bad way, but as if he really had no idea what it was like to be in a relationship. It was kind of cute.

"This is what normal couples do Jeremy," I said with a smile. "You're doing a great job for a rookie."

He laughed heartily. "Aren't normal couples supposed to exchange phone numbers too?" he asked with a sideways glance.

Crap, we'd been together since Friday, and I had never even thought about it. "You are correct, sir."

A thought passed through my mind, and I abruptly stopped jogging. "Jeremy, I forgot I was going to see Cammie today." He stopped running and came back to me.

"What am I supposed to tell her?" I asked. "Do I tell her we're together and hope she leaves me alone, or do I tell her we're only friends?"

"Honestly, I don't know," he replied. "I suppose you can see how it goes when you talk to her. Like I said, I'll do whatever you want. I don't want to lose you over this, Teagan. Not because of Cammie." He bent his knees and slipped his arms around my waist, picking me up. "I mean it, Teagan. I want you . . . I want to be with you. I'll go along with whatever you tell her."

"Okay. I'll let you know what happens as soon as I can." Tilting my head to the side, I kissed him, slipping my tongue into his mouth, and wrapping my arms around the back of his neck.

Strong hands roamed over my butt, to my thighs, lifting my legs to lock them around his waist. Jeremy deepened the kiss, moaning against my mouth. He pulled back and rested his forehead against mine. He groaned and pulled my hips forward, blatantly drawing attention to his erection, as if I didn't already know it was there.

I knew, and I liked it!

"You're making it hard for me to run now," he said.

I unlocked my legs and he set me down.

"I can take care of that for you real quick if you want to head back to the house." I brushed the backs of my fingers over his shorts along his sizeable package.

Jeremy took a step back and closed his eyes. "Don't make this harder on me than it already is," he mumbled.

"You started it and you're the one who keeps saying the word *hard*," I retorted, stepping closer to him.

He put his hands out and stopped me. "I mean it, Red. You have to stop teasing me, and I'll do the same. You need to do things your way when it comes to Cammie. Please, let me do this *my* way. I promise I'll make it worth the wait."

He chuckled and gave me a quick kiss on the cheek before he took off running.

After we stopped off at my house and picked up my work clothes for the day, I cooked our breakfast. Since Reese and I were going to be guests of Jeremy's for a week, I decided to go grocery shopping after work so we wouldn't be eating all of Jeremy's food. It was the least I could do for him letting us crash at his place.

As we were getting ready to leave for the day, I picked up his cell phone and called my cell so we had each other's numbers. I handed his phone to him and took mine out to add him to my contacts. I laughed quietly when I entered the name "Frank Sinatra" instead of his name.

I was paying homage to his gorgeous blue eyes, and how cute Nanna's reaction had been to him. Plus, I didn't want Cammie to realize I had his number if she happened to steal my phone. I wouldn't put it past her, and I was positive she wasn't smart enough to get my name joke.

Jeremy snatched the phone out of my hand and looked at the screen. "Nice." He grinned, picked up his phone, and started typing. "Nope, that's too long . . . hmm." He typed something else. "Shit, that won't work either."

"What are you typing, my boyfriend?" I asked, trying to sneak a peek at his phone.

He jerked it away and laughed. "Hold your horses there, Red," he said, while he typed. When he finished, he smiled and handed me his phone.

The words on the screen made me smile, because I knew he had chosen them from the Yeats poem he read to Nanna.

For my contact name, he had typed in "My Beloved."

"Why'd you have to go and get all sweet with my name? Now the one I picked for you sounds lame." I pouted playfully.

"Let's get you over to your house to pick up your car." Suddenly he pulled me into his arms and just held me. "Teagan, thanks for giving me a chance." He kissed me gently on the lips then we left.

Jeremy drove me over to my parents' house to drop me off. "Let me know how it goes today . . . as soon as you can so I don't worry about you."

I nodded and gave him a quick peck on the cheek. "Have a great day at work, dear," I teased as I opened the door and stepped out of his car. He shook his head, told me goodbye and left. I had no time to waste so I went straight to my Neon and headed to work.

As soon as I pulled into a space at the hospital, I spotted Cammie exiting her car a few rows over from me. *It's now or never Teagan.* I jogged toward her, "Cammie, can I speak with you, please?" I swear when she saw me jogging at her, I thought she was going to run. She must have had a flashback from when I jumped on her at Dub's.

"What do you want, you crazy bitch?"

Alrighty then, I guess we're going that route. Hmm, this could go several ways depending on my next words, so I needed to choose wisely. "Look, I wanted to talk to you about Jeremy."

She stopped walking and spun to face me. "Me and Jeremy are perfect, thank you very much. We had an amazing weekend together."

Clearly, she was delusional, so I'd let her live in her own world with her invisible Jeremy while I kept the real one all to myself.

"Cammie, I'm barely even friends with Jeremy, just so you know. My friends and his friends hang out sometimes so I only see him when he happens to be there." The breath froze in my lungs as I waited for her response to my lies.

"Then why did you attack me?" she asked.

Um, because you're bat-shit crazy!

"That had nothing to do with him. You were screwing with my job, and I found out about it. What you did to me is wrong, Cammie. You've got it in your head that I'm a threat to you somehow with Jeremy, and I'm not." I took a step closer and raised my hands to show I meant no harm. *Well, unless she kept messing with me.* "Will you please stop what you're doing to me? I haven't done anything to you, so I'd appreciate it if you would leave me alone. I really do hope you and *your* Jeremy will have a happy life together." *You know, the one who doesn't exist.* "I'll live my life with my boyfriend and won't give this another thought, if you just . . . stop." *God, I hope I find a new job soon.*

"You have a boyfriend?" she asked, being nosy. "What happened to Jared? I thought you were dating him."

*Crap . . ."*I dated him briefly, but it didn't work out," I blurted. *Think, Teagan. Think.* I needed to show her proof I had a boyfriend. Reese! *Jeremy, please forgive me for what I'm about to do.*

"I've actually reconciled with my boyfriend from Denver. He's driving here as we speak and we're moving into an apartment together." I lied as I'd never lied before and I hated it. I felt like I was betraying Jeremy, and he truly had become my dirty little secret. My stomach muscles involuntarily clenched at the thought.

Cammie eyed me curiously before she replied. "I'll stop, but you need to stay the hell away from my boyfriend," she muttered.

"Sure, not a problem." I'd stay away from her boyfriend, but I wasn't staying away from mine. Why did it feel like I was fifteen years old and in high school with this dumb bitch? *Oh that's right, because that's how she's acting.*

Cammie turned and walked away from me. I checked the time on my phone. With less than five minutes before I needed to clock in, I had no time to call Jeremy. I ran to the entrance, swiped my key card, and jogged to the break room to clock in, making it right on time.

I didn't want Jeremy to worry all morning, so once I checked my schedule for the day, I slipped into the bathroom to text him.

> *Our chat was interesting. No time to call you now so details will have to wait. Working in ER all day so I'll be busy. Miss you already. Have a good day at work. Xoxoxoxxxxx*

As soon as I silenced my phone and dropped it back in my pocket, it vibrated with an incoming text. I pulled my phone back out. I laughed when I saw the name on the screen. *Frank Sinatra.* My beautiful blue-eyed boyfriend.

> *XXXXOO, I miss you too. Call when you can. I'll be patiently waiting, my beloved. :)*

I smiled, crammed my phone into my pocket, and hurried to the ER to find a full house. Happy freaking Monday! I sighed, wishing the weekend was still here and I was lounging around with Jeremy without a care in the world.

By the time my lunch break rolled around, I was so flustered with how the day was going, I found myself doing a replay of Nat's head banging on the table routine from several weeks back. When she and Jackie showed up for lunch, my head was still on the table. They dropped into chairs on either side of me.

"Rough morning, Teagan?" Nat questioned. I raised my

head and groaned which caused them to laugh at me.

I took a deep breath in and let it out. "The ER is crazy today and it's only going to get worse," I said as I took my lunch out of the bag Jeremy had packed for me. A white piece of paper was taped to the top of the container. I pulled off the paper and unfolded it.

My beloved,

I wanted to tell you this was the best weekend I've had in a long time. I hope we have many more to come. Think of me while you enjoy your lunch. I'll be thinking of you until I see you again.

XX

He didn't sign the note with his name, and I was thankful for that. I didn't want Cammie getting a hold of it. I folded the note back up and tucked it safely into my pants pocket.

In my lunch container was a delicious looking turkey sandwich loaded with veggies. "Oh my God . . . yum," I mumbled around a mouthful of sandwich. I closed my eyes and savored the deliciousness. *Why do sandwiches always taste better when someone else makes them?*

Nat bumped my arm with her elbow to get my attention. "You got another one of those?" She nodded toward my sandwich.

"I don't think I've ever seen anyone orgasm from eating a sandwich before," Jackie said before bursting in to a fit of giggles.

Nat snorted when she laughed at Jackie's comment.

"Assholes," I teased before taking another bite. "Don't hate me because my lunch is better than yours."

Jeremy had been so thoughtful to make my lunch for me. What a surprise. Something so simple, but it showed he cared about me.

I quickly finished my lunch, and left my friends to call Jeremy. I had half an hour left, so I jogged out to my car and sat inside. His phone rang a few times before he answered, and when he did, he sounded like he had been running.

"Hey there," he said, out of breath. "How are you?" Over the phone, I heard many different noises from the shop. It sounded like they were busy.

"I'm doing great." The mere sound of his voice caused me to smile. "I just had the best lunch ever. How are you?" I sighed and patted my full belly, reclining my seat back to stretch out and relax.

"I'm good. Glad to hear your voice finally. Do you have time to tell me what happened with Cammie?"

"That's why I'm calling." I recapped Cammie's and my conversation and I sensed he wasn't happy about it.

"Teagan, I wish you would let me talk to her. I hate that she's lying to you about me. The only good thing is you *know* she's lying since you were with me all weekend."

"I know. Jeremy, I'm sorry I told her Reese was my boyfriend, but I think if she sees him taking me to and from work after he gets here, it will keep her off my back and buy me more time to get another job. I feel like the biggest jerk right now, but she really caught me off guard with her stupid story about her weekend. I'm so sorry."

"Teagan, stop apologizing. None of this is your fault. The blame is all on me because I didn't keep my dick in my pants before I met you. I'm sorry it's affecting you because it shouldn't be. I really think I should talk to her."

Listen to Nanna, Teagan. Trust in her. She's never been wrong. Staring at the Claddagh ring on my finger helped ease my doubts about mine and Jeremy's relationship.

I glanced at my watch. "Jeremy, I need to get back to work. Can we talk about this again later?" Tears pricked my eyes. I felt terrible and wanted to go back inside the bubble with him and never leave.

"Yeah," he said morosely. "Remember what I said this morning, please. You mean so much to me and I can't lose you over this."

He knew exactly what to say to make me feel better.

"I'll never forget, my boyfriend. I promise. I'll see you tonight."

The rest of the day was mild, but at a quarter to five, one of the administrators entered the ER to make an announcement.

"We need everyone working now to stay on shift for some overtime. We have a bus versus a delivery truck on Interstate Five, with an estimated twelve injured coming in about fifteen minutes. Call your families and let them know you'll be home when you can."

Crap! Reese had already sent me a text saying he'd be at Jeremy's in an hour. What was I going to do? I wanted to be there when he arrived because they didn't know each other and I felt bad about changing where Reese was going to be staying at the last minute. I pulled my cell from my pocket and called Jeremy.

He answered quickly.

"Jeremy, I'm so sorry but something's come up at work."

"Are you okay? What's wrong?"

"I'm fine, but I have to work late because of a big accident on the freeway. I don't know how long I have to stay here, so it's just going to be you and Reese for a while," I said. "I hope that's okay."

He breathed a sigh of relief. "Yes, of course. Jesus, Red, you scared me. I thought something was wrong."

"Sorry for scaring you, but they only gave us time to call home to let our families know we wouldn't be home for a while. Reese should be there long before I arrive."

He laughed deeply. "It's no problem. I'm off work in a few minutes. We'll be fine, I promise. I'll see you later."

"You're the most wonderful, perfect, sweetest boyfriend ever." I meant every word. Once our call ended, I shot off a text to Reese letting him know he was on his own with Jeremy until they let us out of work.

An hour later, I was knee deep in patients, charts, and concerned family members. While I ran to the supply room, I checked my phone and had a text from Reese.

Hooker-face! This man is H-O-T! He gets the Reese Junior thigh poke of approval! Hurry home before I steal him from you. Kidding . . . this boy only has eyes for you. Does he have any gay brothers? Love you, girl.

I laughed and replied to his text.

No, sorry. No gay brothers. I'll have to see about friends though. It's going to be hours before I get out of here. Hope you boys can find something to do while you wait for me. Hands off my man! Love you too.

By the time I made it to Jeremy's house it was after nine. I knocked on the door and Jeremy answered right away.

When he saw me, he smiled happily. "Why are you knocking, pretty girl?" He took my hand and pulled me through the door. "My girlfriend doesn't knock . . . ever. She can come right in."

I was happy to see him and thrilled to be back at his house away from all the drama. I threw my arms around his neck and he lifted me up from the floor. I laid a steamy kiss on him and tasted tequila on his tongue. "I missed you today," I murmured against his lips.

After I locked my legs around his waist, he carried me into the kitchen where I found Reese with a shot glass in his hand. Jeremy set me on the countertop and moved away so I could reunite with my friend.

As soon as Jeremy backed away, Reese was in front of me pulling me into a tight bear hug. "I missed you so much hooker-face." Reese squeezed all the breath out of me. "The apartment just wasn't the same without my snuggle buddy." He let out a long sigh and embraced me again.

I looked over at Jeremy and he was smiling at us. I knew right then he wasn't worried about the comment Reese had made. "I've missed you too, Reese. I miss you kicking my butt at the gym every day. I really do. Even those crunches you forced me to do."

Jeremy stepped forward. "Why don't you two go get caught up while I fix you something for dinner, Teagan. We already ate," he said.

"Actually, I'd kill for a shower, so if you boys can hang out for a bit longer without me . . . and I'd love dinner too."

Jeremy turned to the fridge and pulled out a container. "Is spaghetti good with you, Teagan? It's what we ate."

Oh, that sounded delicious. "Absolutely, I'm starving. I haven't eaten since that sandwich you made me for lunch."

"Let me get this straight," Reese said, shaking his head. "He fixes you lunch, dinner, treats you like the princess you are, and he's h-o-t. Are you *sure* he doesn't have any gay brothers?"

Reese and I laughed as Jeremy shook his head and turned to the sink to fill a pot with water. "No gay brothers, sorry, man. You're outta luck."

Jeremy was clearly amused by Reese.

I hopped off the counter, kissed the cheeks of two of my favorite men, and headed to the shower.

My body was exhausted from my long shift in the ER, but the hot water revived me a little. Since I'd had to work late unexpectedly, I'd had no time to go to my house to get more clothes. Fortunately, I tended to over pack when it came to bras, panties, and socks so I had enough to last me a couple more days.

I pulled some boxers out of Jeremy's dresser and then found a black T-shirt in his closet that had *James Racing* across the back. The shirt hit me about mid-thigh, so the boxer shorts were barely visible, but this was all I had to wear. I pulled the towel off my head and combed through my drying hair, then went back to the kitchen.

After dinner and visiting, Reese decided he was ready to go to bed after his long day of traveling. I was exhausted too, so we said goodnight, and he went to the guest room and closed the door. Jeremy and I hadn't discussed sleeping arrangements for when Reese was here, *other* than he was not sleeping with me.

Jeremy was in his bathroom when I entered his bedroom and crawled into his bed. A few minutes later, he came out wearing his pajama shorts. "If Reese could see you now," I joked, as I looked him over. He really was H-O-T, as Reese liked to say.

"I like seeing you in my shirts," he said, while pulling the extra blanket off the footboard of the bed.

I sat up and modeled it for him. "So, this is where you work, huh?"

He nodded then asked, "Do you mind if I stay with you instead of on the couch?"

"I would be honored if you'd sleep with me, Jeremy," I teased. I'd be thrilled if we were naked too.

He smirked and laid down on top of the covers, then situated the blanket over him and faced me.

I wished he felt comfortable enough to be under the covers with me, but I knew he had his reasons, so I didn't push him. I leaned over and kissed him. "Goodnight, Jeremy." I turned off the lamp and laid back down.

"Goodnight," he whispered from the darkness.

As soon as he was asleep, I slipped out from under the covers and eased under his blanket with him. I had missed our closeness all day and wanted to be wrapped in his warmth. I slid my arm over his side, nestled against him, and fell instantly to sleep.

Jeremy

Teagan thought she was being sneaky by slipping under my blanket with me after assuming I was asleep, but I wasn't. I let her though because I simply wanted to revel in the fact she was still here, and she would be for an entire week.

The first night she'd stayed with me when she'd been drunk, I didn't think I slept all night. I'd been too worried about her waking up and freaking out. Like a creeper, I'd watched her most of the night. When I'd woken after dozing off the next morning, I had been pissed and disappointed to find she'd left.

Now everything was being cleared up between us, I knew she wouldn't leave me again. I was happy she was staying here. I loved the fact she wanted to be near me, because I sure as hell wanted to be near her.

Unfortunately, I was sharing her for the next week, but she was still staying with me, and I wasn't going to complain. When she and Reese moved into their apartment together, I would probably feel differently, though.

As it turned out, Reese was a cool guy, and like a big brother to Teagan. When he arrived at my house, he came right up and introduced himself.

Lying in bed, with my arms wrapped protectively around my gorgeous redhead, I thought back to the conversation Reese and I had had about Teagan during dinner.

"Gary grabbed her and held her down on the bed by her

neck," Reese said. "She convinced me that it didn't hurt her physically, but he still scared her enough that she felt defenseless against him if he were to try anything else."

My anger had reached a boiling point by the time he'd finished his sentence. "I want to fly to Denver and beat the hell out of that guy."

He laughed and shook his head. "Don't worry, Teagan can take care of herself now. She took one of my self-defense classes and was very good at it."

I had a lot of respect for Reese and trusted him completely. He cared about her as much as I did, and I appreciated it. I knew she would be safe with him, and was safe because of him.

I woke the next morning to my two houseguests trying to wake me up in a very unconventional way.

Pretending to be asleep, I tried my hardest not to laugh at what they were doing.

"Thisss . . . is the *honey badger*," Reese said in the gayest voice I had ever heard. "Watch him sleeping all sexy-looking in his pajama shorts. Look at him, he just doesn't give a shit. He is dead to the world. Honey badger appears to be in hibernation. Typically, the honey badger hibernates for around eight hours per night, but not this particular breed. He definitely doesn't need his beauty sleep."

Teagan was giggling quietly, and I was dying, trying not to laugh. Reese's commentary grew louder.

"This honey badger needs to come out of hibernation soon so he can go out into the world in search of snacks. Look at that sleepy fuck. He just doesn't give a shit. Come on, wakey-wakey, honey badger!"

One of them poked me in the ribs, and I couldn't take it anymore. "Honey badger is awake, and you're both lunatics." I groaned and rolled onto my back. "I'm so happy my sleeping habits amuse you." God, it was like living with my brothers when we were kids.

Luckily, I'd watched the hilarious honey badger videos on YouTube, so I was able to play along. "Honey badger wants to know if this is how you're going to treat your host for the next week. 'Cause if so, honey badger don't take no shit from houseguests and you'll have to do all your—"

The next thing I knew, Teagan tackled me.

"No, honey badger!" she squealed. "Your houseguests are good badgers, not those nasty-ass mean badgers. *Please,* don't throw us out. We promise to be good, sweet honey badgers from here on out."

I laughed as she peppered kisses all over my face causing my morning wood to come back full force. Thank God she was lying on top of me, hiding it, but I knew she felt it when she pressed herself against me and gave me a very sinful grin.

All of a sudden, Reese laughed and yelled out "Honey badgers love Teagan sandwiches!" and jumped on top of Teagan, squishing her in between us on the bed.

These two were nuts, and between them, I had over three hundred pounds on top of me. I groaned as I tried to breathe, and my dick was being crushed under the weight.

"Honey badger needs you to get up. You're smashing his prickety-prick, and he can't breathe," I said in between gasps.

"This honey badger kicks ass!" Reese yelled and rolled off Teagan, landing on his back on the floor, laughing uncontrollably. "We should get shit-faced and watch honey badger videos tonight."

Finally, I could breathe. Jesus, that dude had to weigh two hundred pounds. Teagan stayed where she was and rested her cheek on my chest as she laughed. I caressed my fingertips up and down her back. "Are you ready to run?" I asked them.

They both said yes, so I rolled out of bed and went into the bathroom, grabbing my running shorts on the way. When I came out, they were camped out on my bed still talking in honey badger mode. "You are freaks. Now let's go run so you can make me breakfast when we get back."

Later that morning I arrived at work, still laughing at how Teagan and Reese had woken me up. I cringed when I thought about what they might do to me tomorrow. Those two living in the same house spelled trouble for me, although, very entertaining trouble.

I walked down the hallway past the office and saw Zoey already at her desk. Usually she came in later in the morning.

I poked my head through the door. "Hey, Z, you're early today. Everything okay?"

She spun in her chair to face me. "Yeah, I wanted to get this paperwork done early today. I'm going to take Hannah with me to get a mani-pedi. Maybe get her nails painted." She grinned as she looked over at my Sweet Pea, who was in the crib across the office playing with a stuffed unicorn.

I went over to her crib, and she raised her arms for me to pick her up. "Look at my big girl, sitting up and playing by herself," I said, picking her up. "Baby girl, you need to stop growing. You're getting too big, too fast." Hannah put her hand over my mouth to play our game and I kissed it.

"Someone's looking awfully happy today," Zoey said with a hint of curiosity.

I grinned from ear to ear. "Because someone is happy today, that's why. Teagan is still staying with me. Her friend Reese moved to town and is staying at my place until their apartment is ready."

Her eyebrows rose. "Is Reese a guy or a girl?"

"Don't worry, he's gay, so it's all good. He's her best friend, and seems like a good person, Z."

Zoey smiled happily. Two of her best friends, Justin and Will were gay and she adored them.

"Hey, do the three of you want to come out with us on Friday night, Jer? Hooligans bought an awesome karaoke system, and they're having a big party that night. They invited all of us to come and test it out. Wanna go?"

"Yeah, okay," I said. "Sounds cool. It's been ages since I've seen you on stage. Do Will and Justin have any single friends they can bring so Reese won't feel like a third wheel? I can bring John, Sonny, and Eric too. We'll make a night of it and invite everyone. It'll be fun."

"That sounds great, Jer. I haven't gone anywhere since Hannah was born and I'm ready for a night out." She laughed.

"Alright, it's a plan then. Should be a great night."

I realized then, I'd never actually gone out to a bar with my sister. I was going to need to keep my eyes on two women, and I was glad Andy and Reese would both be there.

I went out to my bay and picked up where I'd left off yesterday. Needing a socket wrench, I went to my toolbox. When I lifted the lid, I found several photos of Teagan and me at family dinner taped to the inside.

Zoey had taken them. Her camera had been attached to her ever since Andy had given it to her for her birthday. I examined each of the images. I hadn't noticed my sister taking them. My favorite was of me, balancing on my hands on the edge of the pool with Teagan's arms wrapped around me, her dress soaked and our lips pressed together.

My favorite moment from that day had been captured in a photo forever. I doubted I would ever forget that day, but regardless, the moment was there for me to look at and remember whenever I wanted. Studying the photos again, I realized even I could see what Teagan's grandma had known.

We loved each other. We may not have felt it yet, but the photos told otherwise.

As relationship challenged as I was, I noticed the way we looked at each other, the way we leaned in to each other, the constant smiles on both our faces, and the soft, gentle touches captured when we thought nobody was looking.

Zoey had even snapped a photo of me twisting a lock of Teagan's hair around my fingers. I didn't remember doing it, and I wondered how often I'd done it that day, without realizing what I was doing.

There was only one photo of us where we were actually looking at the camera. Zoey had asked us to pose and she'd taken it from across the table where she and Andy were sitting. Teagan and I were leaning in so closely to one another our cheeks were almost touching.

Hmm, Mom was right. We would make pretty babies. Holy shit, I don't feel so well.

What if this didn't work out between us? If it did, what if she didn't want kids? Would I even be a good dad? I had the uncle thing down to a science, but being an uncle gave me the liberty of either going home or passing the kids back to their parents if they got to be too much for me. I laughed out loud at the thought then shook off the unexpected feelings that had come over me, found the socket wrench I needed and went back to work.

Luckily, the day was flying by and I would be back home with Teagan in a few hours. While I was helping Jason lower a motor into the engine compartment of the car he was working on, Mandy, our receptionist, announced over the intercom, "Jeremy, you have a female visitor out front."

Fuck me. My brothers gave me shit, and Adam made it very clear that if there was a woman other than Teagan here to see me, he was going to make sure I was the one duct taped to a pole and tortured.

Jesus, I hated the fact they thought I was some sort of manwhore. I never gave a shit before, but now that Teagan was in the picture I wished I'd shut down that notion a long time ago. I jogged to the shop phone and called the front desk to get this over with.

"Yessss?" Mandy spoke into the receiver, knowing the drill where I was concerned.

"Hey, can you tell me who's out there?" I asked.

"Yep," she said. "Give me a sec, I don't recognize her." This wouldn't be the first time I'd asked her to identify the female in question, but I was concerned that Mandy didn't know her this time.

I heard her cover the phone and say, "What's your name again? They're trying to find him, but he may have left for the day." Not only was Mandy a wise-ass but quick on her feet. Personally, I thought that was exactly why Zoey hired her— because she could put up with my brothers and me.

"Teagan is here," Mandy finally said.

Teagan? Why isn't she at work? All I could think about was her being fired from her job or Cammie doing something so bad to her that she'd quit.

"Tell her I'm on my way up," I said then hung up the phone.

I jogged up to the front desk and into the lobby. Teagan was facing the window, with her back to me. She had her purse in her hand, but her arms were at her sides, so her purse was nearly touching the floor. I knew instantly something was wrong.

"*Red?* What are you doing here?" I asked, cautiously. *Please don't be here to break up with me already.*

The second she turned around and looked up at me, I wanted to kill someone. A bruise was on her left cheekbone and her face was swollen under one eye. She had a bandage on her forearm as well.

In two long strides, I was across the lobby and had her face cradled in my hands. "Who did this to you?" I growled. I was gonna find the fucker and kill them for hurting her.

She wrapped her small hands around my wrists and her thumbs moved back and forth across the top of my hands. "It was some cracked-out patient, Jeremy. Nobody I know," she said softly, instantly calming me down. She released my wrists and wrapped her arms around my waist, resting her uninjured cheek against my chest.

I put my arms around her and stroked up and down her back. "Are you okay?" I whispered. She nodded against my chest, and I held her tighter. "Tell me what happened."

Neither one of us moved as she explained what had transpired at work. "Right before lunch the police brought this woman in. She was high on something and was in handcuffs when she arrived. She passed out—well, she pretended to pass out, and then she faked a seizure. They took the handcuffs off so we could treat her."

She paused long enough to take a deep breath. "I reached out to pull her over on to her side and she punched me in the face. That caused me to lose my balance and I fell down, scraping my arm on the bottom of the gurney." She pulled back from me when she finished her story and her eyes met mine.

"Are you sure you're okay?" I asked.

She nodded. "Yes, they did an x-ray and nothing is broken. The ER doctor gave me some Vicodin and cleaned up my arm then my supervisor sent me home for the day." She grimaced. "Jeremy, that bitch rang my bell. *Hard*. I've never been punched in my life."

"I'm so sorry you were hurt. Did Reese get you from work and bring you here?"

"No, I took a taxi because Reese is checking out the new gym where he'll be working. After that, he was going sightseeing in Old Sacramento, so he won't be home until late tonight. I didn't have anywhere to go because I left my keys at your place. I hope you don't mind that I came here."

I smiled down at her because I was more than thrilled that she turned to *me* when she needed someone. "I'm glad you're here, and you're okay. Are you feeling well enough for a tour?"

She nodded happily. I introduced her to Mandy and then I showed her the office, the break room, and the customer lounge. When we were going into the shop, I glanced over and caught her wincing in pain.

"Can we go back to the vending machine so I can buy a bottle of water?" she asked. "I need to take a Vicodin. My jaw kind of hurts."

Taking her hand in mine, I led her back to the break room and grabbed a bottle of water out of the fridge, uncapped it, and handed it to her. She popped a pill out of a foil packet and swallowed it with a drink of water.

"Teagan, are you sure you're alright? Please tell me they're going to add an assault charge on top of whatever else that woman was arrested for."

"I'm sure they will, but it's a typical job hazard," she replied. "Kind of like when you got smacked in the head by the tailpipe." She reached up and rubbed her fingers over my fading scar.

I grinned at her. "Best thing that ever happened to me, because I met you." I held her close and kissed her lips carefully so I didn't hurt her.

When we went out to the shop, we stopped at each work bay so she could say hi to everyone. She had to explain the bruise to Andy, and each of my brothers.

I took her to my work bay last. "This is where I work," I stated with pride.

She looked around the shop, and at the car I had been working on. "I had no idea it was such an elaborate business, Jeremy. I mean, I knew you were a mechanic—but these cars—this is some high dollar shit!"

I held in a laugh when she cussed because she didn't do it often, but this time, she was very enthusiastic about it.

"Yes, they are," I replied honestly. I was proud to be a part of the family business and wanted to tell her about it.

"Some of the cars we build are several hundred thousand dollar jobs. We build cars for professional drag racers. Most are from California, but we get some from all over the country. Plus, we do smaller jobs for the local guys. Build motors . . . things like that. Each of us has a specialty. Jason is the motor genius, Adam is the electrical man, Noah can custom build anything, I do the custom exhaust and help Jason with motors, and Andy, he's our import guy."

She smiled proudly. "You're incredible," she said. "This family run business is the reason you and your family are so close. You should all be proud."

"Thank you, Teagan" I intertwined our fingers. "When my dad retired back in February, he gave us all equal shares in the company, so it truly is a family owned and operated business now. It's awesome."

"Oh, my boyfriend's a business owner too. Amazing."

My pretty girl swayed a little on her feet and grinned like she was tipsy. The Vicodin must be working.

"Come on, I think I need to get you home and in bed."

"No, don't leave work because of me. I'll just go sit in the break room and wait for you."

I took one look at her and knew she was going to fall asleep. Her eyelids were getting heavy, and she was relaxing *too* much. The break room would be too noisy for her, so I decided to take her upstairs to the apartment, which still had all the furniture from when Andy and my sister lived there.

I stepped inside the office and found the key on one of the hooks beside the door. "Come on, pretty girl, I'll take you someplace quiet and more comfortable."

As we neared the end of the hallway, the door swung open, and my mom, Zoey, and Hannah came in. Not surprisingly, Mom and Zoey got big shit-eating grins on their faces when they spotted Teagan.

And then they noticed her bruised cheek and the shit hit the fan. My mom frowned as she looked at me, then back at Teagan.

"Teagan, honey, what happened?" She took Teagan into the office to get a better look at her. Zoey followed them, and was as concerned as my mom. They listened as Teagan gave them the short version of her altercation.

"Come on you mother-hens," I said to my mom and sister. "I'm taking her upstairs to put her to bed until I can get off work."

Zoey shook her head. "No, it's too loud up there, trust me. You can hear everything that is happening in the shop. Take her over to my place and get her set up in the guest room."

"Oh, Zoey, thank you," Teagan said, surprised. "But I am covered with germs from the hospital, so I don't want to—"

"Don't be silly," Z said. "You're family now. Jeremy, you know the alarm code right?"

I nodded, knowing the code was Hannah's birth date.

Zoey took her phone out of her pocket and called someone. "Hey, Tara, can you do me a favor?" She waited a beat for Tara's response then asked, "Can you pull some small shorts and a small tank top off the rack and hold them for Jeremy? He's bringing his *girlfriend* over, and I want her to have them. No charge."

She had a shit-eating grin on her face as she spoke in girl-code with Tara for another minute before they hung up.

"There, now you don't need to worry about germs, and you'll have something comfy to wear," Zoey said as she smiled at Teagan. I mouthed "Thank you" to my sister.

"Thank you, Zoey. I really appreciate it," Teagan said. She was getting sleepier by the second. We said goodbye to my mom and sister and went next door to the store.

Tara was waiting for us with a small bag in her hand. I introduced her to Teagan then took the bag from her, and left. I would definitely ask Z about the girl-code conversation another day because Tara had the same shit-eating grin on her face.

"Where does Zoey live?" Teagan asked.

I pointed toward the upper level of the building as we stopped in front of the lobby door of Z's apartment. I slid my key into the lock and let us inside the building. I helped Teagan up the stairs and unlocked the apartment door. Once we were inside, I entered the code to shut off the alarm.

I turned to find Teagan with her mouth hanging open, and

her eyes wide, taking in the apartment around her. "Wow," she said in surprise. "This place is insane. Are those real surfboards hanging on the wall? What's an All Black?"

I chuckled as I tried to remember everything she'd asked. "It used to be two apartments and they remodeled it, turning it in to one. Yes, those are real surfboards, and the All Blacks are a rugby team from New Zealand where Andy is from."

Taking her hand, I led her to the guest bedroom to lie down. I had to help her out of her scrubs and into the shorts and tank because her arms and legs were like rubber from the Vicodin. Once she was changed, I pulled back the covers, and she sat on the edge of the bed.

"I'll get back to work so you can get some sleep. Are you sure you're going to be okay?" I asked.

She got a wicked gleam in her eyes and untucked my shirt from my pants. "I'll be better if you stay."

Note to self: Teagan should not take Vicodin. It makes her loopy as hell . . . and apparently, horny too.

While I was making that note to myself, she unbuttoned and unzipped my pants and pulled them slightly down my hips. I glanced down at her, and she was staring hungrily at my stomach.

"You know," she said, her voice slurring. "These veins right here . . ." Her fingers traced the two visible veins on the lowest part of my torso. "They are, by far, the sexiest thing I've ever seen in my life."

Before I knew it, she'd pulled my hips forward and licked my skin over one of the veins. And then she ran her tongue up the other one. Dear God, why did she have to be on mind-altering meds right now? She was killing me, and I was weakening for her. I didn't know how much longer I could last without touching her again.

I dropped to my knees in front of her, cupped her pretty face in my hands, and kissed her goodbye. "Lay down, sleepyhead," I said soothingly. "I'll be back to get you after work." She did as I said, and I covered her up. She was out just after her head hit the pillow.

I gently kissed her bruised cheek, and then smoothed down her hair. "Sweet dreams," I whispered.

After fixing my pants and shirt, I watched her sleep for a moment before leaving. She'd had a rough day, and I wanted to make it better for her. I texted my sister telling her I had a few errands to run, and that I'd be back to finish up for the day.

I had some shopping to do for my woman.

Teagan

My entire body tingled as a warm hand slid over my back and bare shoulders. My eyes slowly opened and I found myself in a room I'd never seen before. The space was beautifully decorated, neither feminine, nor masculine, but bright and sunny—where the heck was I? And who was massaging my back?

A few memories from my day came flooding back to me. Ah yes, I was at Zoey's in her guest room because some crack head had punched me in the face, and my boss had sent me home from work.

The strong, warm fingers belonged to Jeremy. Taking in a deep breath, I stretched and slowly rolled over to face him. He was kneeling next to the bed, nearly eye level with me, with a sweet smile on his face.

"There she is," he said softly when I made eye contact with him. "How was your nap, pretty girl?"

I loved when he called me that and instantly it made me smile. "It was wonderful." Knowing Vicodin usually had a strange effect on me, especially since I'd swallowed it on an empty stomach, I asked, "So . . . what did I do to embarrass myself after my Vicodin kicked in?" I tried unsuccessfully not to cringe.

He smiled. "You did something that nobody else but me knows about so don't worry."

Oh, what had I done? I cocked an eyebrow at him.

"Jeremy . . . tell me. *Please*. That stuff makes me act weird."

Jeremy hovered over me and brushed his lips across my bruised cheekbone. "You licked me," he whispered as his mouth passed over my ear. He pressed a kiss to my hair then pulled away.

Well, that was a new one. I hadn't licked anyone the last time I'd taken it. Although, the last time was when I'd had my wisdom teeth surgically removed, so my mouth hadn't been in any condition to be licking anyone.

"Oh God, I'm sorry." I slapped a hand over my eyes briefly as I sat up to swing my feet over the side of the bed.

Jeremy, standing in front of me, brought back the memory of me licking him, making me laugh. "Never mind, I'm *not* sorry about licking you." My face flushed, but I *loved* those veins on his stomach and the sexy V along the edge of his hips.

"I'm not sorry you did it either, Teagan," he said with a lustful grin on his face.

I glanced down at the tank top and shorts I was wearing. My shirt had the James Racing name and logo emblazoned across my chest. "Where did I get these clothes?"

"Zoey gave them to you. She sells them at her store. We stopped there to get them because you didn't want to wear your work clothes on her bed."

That made sense. The ER was a nasty, nasty place. "Are you off work now?" I asked and he nodded.

"It's after five, so we can leave whenever you feel up to it."

Feeling pretty good after my nap and the Vicodin, I knew we had errands to run and should probably get going. "I'm ready, but I want to go grocery shopping and stop at my parents' house to get more clothes."

He held his hands out to me and helped me up from the bed. My legs felt rubbery, but I quickly recovered. I slipped my arms around his waist and hugged him.

"Thank you for taking care of me and for being here when I needed someone," I said against his chest.

He hugged me and kissed the side of my head. "I'll never be anywhere else, and I will always be here for you, Teagan. *Always*."

Why did it feel like he sincerely meant every single word he'd just said to me? We were still too new, and all the thoughts and feelings from the last several weeks still weighed heavily on my mind.

So why did I feel the need to grope and tease him constantly? Because I wanted him badly, and I wanted him to want me, too.

Granted, I didn't do one-night stands or anything like that, but I wasn't a prude by any means. He was my boyfriend now, right? I could try to blame my actions on the Vicodin, but that wasn't the reason. I've had my hand down his shorts and touched him multiple times without the assistance of meds, but he had told me repeatedly how he didn't want our relationship to move too fast.

So what had I done? I'd freaking licked him.

Twice.

Perfect, I was acting like a horny teenage boy. At least neither of us was sorry about it.

"Teagan, what just happened here?" Jeremy asked, brushing his hand over my hair, while his other arm stayed locked tightly around my waist. "Your entire demeanor changed."

Did he really notice that? Wow, I was impressed with his intuition. Even though he was inexperienced at being in an actual relationship, he'd read my body language like a book.

"I'm sorry, Jeremy. I was thinking how you've asked me not to tease you, yet I keep doing it." I tilted my head to look at him, glad to find him smiling and not upset with me.

"I said I'm not sorry you did it, Teagan. It was very hard to leave you here and go back to work, but I swear I'm being good with our relationship. I can't mess it up. If I do, I'll never forgive myself." He let out a breath to ease his tension, but it didn't make me feel any less guilty for being so forward with him when he was trying to change his ways. *For me.*

"Look, I have no idea how I'm supposed to do this relationship thing, but—"

"Jeremy, this is new to me too. I've never had a boyfriend who is doing it all backward. It's usually the other way around and the man is the one waiting on me. I'll be honest, I am physically attracted to you in a way I've never been with anyone else, and it's making me act differently than I normally do. I'm really sorry for torturing you, and I will try to stop."

Jeremy laughed and scrubbed his hands over his face. "I do believe this is the craziest conversation I've ever had." He paused and took a step back. "Let me also point out I've never been more attracted to anyone in my life, Teagan."

"Alright, now that's out of the way, let's get out of here and go grocery shopping. I'm restocking your kitchen for putting up with Reese and me for a week."

I turned around to put Zoey's bed back together. Hearing Jeremy chuckle from behind me, I turned back to him. "What are you laughing at, Mr. James?" I cocked an eyebrow at him.

He grinned at me guiltily. "Is it too early in our relationship for me to express an observation about your tits and ass?"

"Please, feel free to speak your mind. This has to be good if you're asking first."

Jeremy spun me around to face the bed. "Lean over and put your hands on the bed." He spoke in a hushed tone, his breath in my ear. Bending at the waist, I placed my palms flat on the bed.

God, I loved it when he was close to me, talking so only I could hear him. Every word from his mouth meant for me, and *only* me. His arms went around me then he dragged his fingertips gently across my breasts, directly over the logo on my tank top. My nipples hardened immediately from his soft touch.

Leaning over me, pushing his pelvis against my butt, I could feel his erection through his pants. He gripped my hips tightly and moved his hips from side to side, his body pressing against mine. He stopped abruptly but didn't back away.

"I want to let you know how seeing my last name scrawled across your perfect tits and ass has made it *hard* to concentrate since I left you here earlier."

My panties were officially soaked now. Jeremy gave me a hard smack to my right butt cheek and my lady parts ached for his hands to make their way there for a little special attention too.

"That's payback for what you did to me this morning on our run," he said before nipping my shoulder and running the tip of his tongue up the side of my neck.

Oh that was a dirty trick! *But I liked it . . . a lot . . .*

I turned and faced him, looking him straight in the eyes. "It's on now you big tease—you'd better watch your back."

Making sure to brush my "perfect tits" across his arm as I went, I walked over to the full-length mirror in the corner of the bedroom and checked out my James Racing gear. The tiny shorts I was wearing also had the James logo scrawled across the butt.

"You're right, my tits and ass do look great in this outfit. Now, let's get to the store so I can show the whole neighborhood how *magnificent* they are."

His mouth dropped open and he stepped over to the closet and pulled the doors open. "There's got to be a jacket in here somewhere," he muttered so quietly I barely heard him as he searched the closet.

"Come on. Your name is on my shirt and shorts so I'm pretty sure everyone will know I'm yours." I kissed his cheek and closed the closet doors. Taking his hand, I laced our fingers together and grabbed my purse from the bed. We left Zoey's place and Jeremy drove us to the grocery store near our houses. The same store I'd seen him and his sister shopping with Hannah. That day was horrible, so I quickly pushed it from my thoughts.

Jeremy's little tits and ass stunt earlier—*which I very thoroughly enjoyed*—gave me an idea.

First, we hit the produce department. While Jeremy was filling a plastic bag with bell peppers, I picked up a small zucchini. *"Psst, Jeremy . . ."* I whispered loudly across the aisle.

He turned toward me, and I held the zucchini up to inspect it and then very deliberately looked between it and his crotch several times.

His mouth dropped open and he shook his head adamantly. *"You're insulting!"* he whisper-growled back across the aisle at me, but he had a sly grin on his face as he said it.

Laughing, I dropped the zucchini and a few more into a bag and moved on. I was picking out a few tomatoes when Jeremy tapped on my shoulder. He was standing so close I was squished between him and the cart, and unable to face him.

"Hold out your hand, you brat," he said.

I held out my hand, and he dropped a giant cucumber onto my palm, then turned and walked away.

I burst out laughing. *Oh, this is fun!*

The next time I saw him, he was holding a lemon in one hand and a lime in the other hand, pretending to size them up with my boobs. I was a full C cup, so I knew he was getting me back for the zucchini joke.

I picked up two oranges, and traded him for the lemon and lime. "These are more accurate," I said as I turned on my heel and walked away. I heard him chuckle as I made my way back to our shopping cart.

For the next few minutes, we actually shopped like normal people would. Then Jeremy disappeared. I finally found him in front of a bin of peaches. He had one bag full already and was filling another bag.

"Do you have a thing for peaches?"

A mischievous grin lit his face when he put both bags of peaches in the cart. He stepped behind me and pushed the cart, his hands on the handle next to mine. Jeremy leaned in close and whispered, *"I fucking love peaches."*

For some reason, the way he said it made my entire body heat and my face flush, not to mention send a jolt of pleasure straight to my girly parts.

"What's so special about *peaches?*" I asked, waiting to see how far he was willing to go. The anticipation was killing me.

Jeremy leaned in close to my ear again. "They're sweet and juicy for starters. Secondly, I love the way they taste. But, my favorite part of all is how the juice drips down my chin while I *eat* them."

Well, now, that is quite possibly the dirtiest, but most delicious description of a peach I'd ever heard in my life.

"Isn't that a little . . . *messy?*" I whispered back as we pushed the cart.

"Nah, I just lick and suck it all off. I don't want to waste a drop of that sweet nectar," he said in a low voice.

"You are a dirty, dirty boy, Jeremy James." I flicked my tongue out to lick his neck.

He groaned, and his body stiffened behind me.

I stopped in front of the sausage and bacon section of the meat department. "Can you grab a couple packs of bacon?" I asked, setting him up for my next teasing session.

He walked away and looked over the bacon selection thoroughly before finding the kind he wanted. He came back and tossed them in the cart.

A moment later, he was standing behind me again as I scanned over the assortment of sausages.

"Can I help you find something, *Peaches?*" he asked, snaking his arms around me.

It's go time!

"They don't sell what I'm looking for." I pretended to be upset about it.

"What are you looking for?"

I was struggling to get my next words out, without laughing because I was sooo not good at this dirty talk business. "I was trying to find some Mexican sausage or maybe some meatballs, but they don't seem to have any." I paused a moment then reached behind me and cupped his crotch. "Oh, wait, I think I found what I was looking for." I gave him a gentle squeeze.

Jeremy sucked in a sharp breath. "Fuck yes, you found them. Jesus Red, you're evil. I think you win this round."

I rubbed him, feeling him thicken beneath his pants. Standing so closely together, nobody could see what I was doing to him.

"Fuck," he panted against the side of my head. "Fuck, I'm gonna come right here if you don't stop."

I didn't stop.

He grabbed my hand.

I turned to face him. His eyes were closed as if he were trying to calm the unrestrained hard-on I'd given him. *In public.* It didn't seem to be working well with the tent still pitched in the front of his pants.

His eyes blinked open and his gaze met mine. "In a battle of dirty talk at the grocery store, you are clearly victorious, Teagan."

My brows rose with curiosity. "What's my prize?"

He shook his head and adjusted himself in his pants. "That's for me to know and you to find out." He walked away from me and took the shopping cart with him, no doubt to block the view of his erection.

I laughed to myself and jogged to catch up to him.

"You totally cheated, pretty girl," he said after I ducked under his arm to walk between him and the cart.

"No rules were discussed at any time during the game, therefore, I could not *possibly* have cheated," I said. "Besides, you're the one who started all of this by doing your little bump and grind against my ass earlier."

He laughed heartily. "If that's how you want to remember it that's fine, but you still win, and you'll still get your reward later."

Excited to see what my reward was going to be I picked up the pace. I looped my arm through his and rested my cheek on his upper arm. He kissed the side of my head and we finished our shopping.

Back at his house, while we were unpacking the groceries, Jeremy said, "I have a surprise for you. Stay right here."

He left the kitchen and went into his bedroom. When he returned, he had a big grin on his face. "Since you had such a shitty day at work, I did a little something to make you feel better. Come with me . . . but close your eyes."

After he made sure I closed my eyes, he picked me up in his arms and carried me to what I assumed was his bedroom. He set me down on the bed. "Keep your eyes closed."

I was nervous and excited all at the same time. I listened to the noises around me, and I could tell he'd gone into the bathroom.

"Okay, it's ready, but keep your eyes closed." Taking my hand in his, Jeremy led me to the bathroom. "Open your eyes."

When I opened them, I was standing in the middle of his giant bathroom. He'd run me a hot bath in the enormous Jacuzzi tub and a gorgeous vase full of flowers was sitting next to the sink.

"What are these for?" I asked. "Are they my reward?"

He shook his head. "No, they're not. That'll come later." He took my hand and pulled me over to the flowers. "The day I sent you flowers at work and you never got them . . . these are exactly what I sent you. Do you like them?"

"I love them, Jeremy. They're beautiful, but you didn't need to buy me new flowers."

"Yes, I did. You didn't get the flowers I sent you, and I want to atone for everything that's gone wrong."

"That's not necessary, Jeremy, because Cammie and her stupid friend made my life hell, not you."

"I *need* to make this right, Teagan. Will you let me?" The sincerity in his voice and the determined look on his face left me with no choice.

"Of course I will," I said and suddenly after the crappy day I'd had at work and what he was doing for me now, I was teary eyed. I wrapped my arms around him and held him tight. "So how'd you do all of this if you were at work?" I asked when I noticed the array of girly soaps and bath products along the rim of the tub.

"My job was actually almost finished when you showed up, so as soon as you fell asleep I went shopping and dropped everything off here, then went back to work."

"You're sneaky, Mr. James."

"I want you to take a nice, long bath and relax while I cook you dinner. Do you want a glass of wine or water?"

"Oh, wine sounds yummy, but I'd better stick with water and another Vicodin." My jaw was aching again from all the laughing I had done at the grocery store.

Jeremy grinned. "Get your sexy ass in the tub and I'll go get it for you."

I laughed and pulled my tank top over my head, revealing my black, lacy bra. "Can I bring my tits into the tub with me too?"

He nodded then turned the jets on in the bathtub. And then he added half a freaking bottle of bubble bath.

"The only body part I want to see when I come back in here is your pretty face . . . no more teasing me tonight, Red. You hear me?" he asked, with a smirk on his face.

"I hear you loud and clear. I'll be on my very best behavior."

He gave me a quick peck on the lips and left the room.

I stripped off the rest of my clothes and dropped them onto the floor. The tub was going to be nothing but foam from the amount of bubble bath he'd added. He'd done it so he wouldn't see me naked.

After testing the water temperature, I slid down in the tub and relaxed, letting the water run until the bubbles were up to my chin. I shut it off just as Jeremy knocked on the door.

"Everything is completely covered, just as you asked," I called out. "It's safe for you to come in." I'd teased him enough today, so I was going to give the guy a break the rest of the night.

He opened the door and peeked around it to make sure I wasn't lying to him. He came in and handed me a pill and a glass of water. "I'm going to make dinner, enjoy your bath," he said then left the room.

Forty-five minutes later, I was out of the bath and drying off. Whatever he was cooking for dinner smelled delicious, and I was anxious to see what it was. After I went into his bedroom wrapped in a towel, I realized I'd forgotten to have him make a stop at my house for more clothes. Once again, I was dressed in a pair of his boxers and a shirt when I went into the kitchen.

He was just coming through the French doors with two steaks on a plate. We sat down and enjoyed a mouthwatering dinner together.

During our meal, Reese sent me a text.

Meeting a few of my new coworkers at a pub for dinner and a beer. Hope my sweets is feeling better and letting her H-O-T man take care of her.

He's taking extra special care of me. Have a good time tonight. I am in good hands.

I bet you are, hooker-face! JEALOUS!!

I laughed at his response and put my phone away. After dinner, we cleaned up the kitchen and Jeremy told me it was time for my reward. He took my hand and led me to the bedroom Reese was using, sat me on the bed, then left. He finally returned wearing a beach towel around his waist.

"What are you doing?"

He didn't answer, but held his hand out to me instead, which I more than willingly accepted. He led me through his bedroom and out the French doors to the pool. The lights were off outside, so the patio was dark, with the exception of the light coming through the French doors.

We stood at the top of the pool steps not saying anything. For some reason, he seemed nervous. Finally, Jeremy came in for a kiss. This was no ordinary kiss, though. He kissed me as if it was the last time he'd ever kiss me. His tongue tasted like peaches; it was intoxicating, and I wanted more.

While our tongues and mouths explored each other, he took my hand in his and placed it where his towel was tucked in to keep it in place. Did he want me to remove it? Crap, I wanted to remove it so I gave the towel a tug, and it fell to the patio.

My eyes were closed, but when I slid my arms around his waist, I realized he was completely bare. I pulled away from him and gave him a once over. Dear God, he was naked, and I wished it wasn't dark outside so I could see every gorgeous inch of him. Was he my reward? *Oh please, let him be my reward.*

He didn't say anything to me, just turned and went down the steps into the pool. I didn't know what to do. I watched him walk through the water, but he stayed in the shallow end. He stepped over to the side of the pool and called to me quietly. "Come here, pretty girl."

At that point, I would do anything he said, so I rushed to where he was and found a beach towel spread out on the patio next to the pool in front of him.

"It's time for your reward. Sit down."

I sat on the towel as instructed and waited impatiently. With him in the pool and me sitting on the edge with my feet in the water, we were eye to eye with each other.

"I didn't say you could wear my clothes, take them off," he instructed, tugging at the hem of his shirt I was wearing.

Whatever game he was playing with me, had me intrigued and horny as hell. I yanked his shirt off and tossed it over my shoulder. He curled his fingers around the top of the boxers I was wearing, and I lifted up for him to take them off me. I didn't hesitate to let him pull my panties off with them. I reached around, unsnapped my bra, and slid it down my arms. It joined his shirt behind me on the patio.

I felt daring to be completely exposed outside in Jeremy's backyard, but also exhilarated. The air was warm, and with the darkness and the high fence around the yard, I doubted anyone would see anything.

"Teagan," Jeremy whispered. "If you're uncomfortable we can go inside."

"No way, I am *very*, very ready for my reward."

He chuckled. "Good, 'cause I'm more than ready to give it to you."

His hands traveled up my bare thighs, gripped my hips, and pulled me closer to him. The water was cool on the hot skin of my legs. I took in a deep breath as Jeremy kissed my neck, while he pulled my hair out of the clip, letting it spill over my shoulders. In the next breath, all I smelled was Jeremy and another scent . . . was it *peaches?*

The surprise of something very cold and wet against the side of my neck caused me to gasp in surprise. "What is that?"

He trailed the object down my neck and stopped above my breast. "Open your mouth and find out."

I willingly complied, and he held the object to my lips. I took it into my mouth, and licked the juice from his fingertips while he licked the trail of juice from my breast, up my neck. *Mmm . . . sweet peaches were truly sinful when Jeremy James was involved.*

Jeremy pressed another chunk of cold peach against my nipple. He circled the fruit around then popped the piece into his mouth. He fed me another bite while he sucked and licked the peach juice from my sensitive nipple.

When he had licked me clean, he moved on to my other breast while feeding me small bites of peach. He was overwhelming my senses and my entire body hummed with pleasure. His mouth was on mine again, and he was pushing me over backward to lie on my back.

"Lie still," he said, backing away from me.

Not a problem, I didn't think I could move even if I wanted to. Which was good, because I didn't want to. I was going to let him do whatever he wanted to me because I had no doubt I'd enjoy every second of it.

My eyes fluttered open to view the dark sapphire blue of the California night sky. Stars twinkled as the moon made its way across the horizon.

A cold, wet trail from the fruit in Jeremy's very skillful fingers, slowly made its way up my thigh, followed immediately by his hot tongue warming my skin as he licked off the juice. Just when I thought he was going to make contact with my center, he veered to the right, and up over my hip.

I whimpered at his blatant neglect, and my hands instinctively seized his head. I gripped his hair tightly, wanting to direct him to where I craved him most.

Jeremy let out a low chuckle. "All in good time, pretty girl," he whispered.

He placed another piece of peach on my stomach then sucked the chunk of fruit into his mouth. Another piece appeared in his hand from somewhere—this time half a peach. He squeezed the fruit, dripping the cold juice over my stomach. The liquid warmed quickly as my skin was ablaze from Jeremy's delicious torture.

"Jeremy, please," I crooned.

His mouth made contact with my hot skin, his tongue licking away the peach juice. He kissed and nibbled his way down my stomach, then pulled away from me. My body ached with the need for him to touch me again.

Finally, he pushed apart my knees "Are you ready—"

I gave his hair a yank.

"Easy, Red," he said. "You can pull it as hard as you want just make sure it stays attached to my head."

The next thing I felt was cold peach juice dripping down between my legs, and his mouth was on me, licking and sucking. He gently blew his hot breath against me then teased my clit with his tongue. He moaned against me, and my body betrayed me. Crying out his name in pleasure, my back arched and my fingers tightened in his hair as an intense orgasm rocked my entire body.

While my body and mind drifted into complete bliss, he roamed my body placing gentle kisses, one of his hands following the path his lips made. Goose bumps broke out across my blazing hot skin from his touch.

When he groaned against me, I realized where his other hand was and what it was doing. He was stroking himself to his own climax.

My body shivered with its final release as Jeremy came and let out one of the most carnal noises I'd ever heard in my life. Breathing heavy, he rested his cheek against the inside of my thigh and I released my hold on his hair.

After nipping the inside of my thigh, he raised his head and gently ran his hand between my legs, startling me.

"Absolutely beautiful, Teagan. I wish I could see you better out here. You're perfect, smooth and soft, just like a peach," he said in awe.

It felt like my entire body flushed. Thank God it was dark, and he couldn't see how red my cheeks were.

I sat up and dropped down into the pool with him, pulling him into a kiss. He tasted like peaches and me. It was erotic and I desperately wanted to give to him what he had given to me, but it was too late.

"Why didn't you wait for me to get you off?" *Where did that come from?* All the teasing and dirty talk from earlier this evening must have made me comfortable enough with him to be more assertive.

"Tonight was all about you, not me," he said. "I'm good, really."

I'd take care of him another time. *When he was ready to give in to me.*

After we'd dried off, he picked me up and took me into his bedroom. Neither of us bothered with pajamas. For the first time since I'd started staying at his house, Jeremy slipped under the covers with me, and we fell into a deep, satisfied sleep.

Jeremy

When I opened my eyes the next morning, the first thing I noticed was that it was already daylight outside. Normally, on a workday I woke up while it was still dark. My alarm should've gone off by now, but the house was dead silent. The second thing I noticed was my body was hot, a little sweaty, and . . . *sticky?*

That's when I realized Teagan was draped over me. Naked. Not wanting to move, but knowing I had to, I shifted to look at my alarm clock. It was ten minutes after seven. Shit, neither of us had turned on an alarm after we'd come in from the pool last night.

"Teagan!" I shook her, trying to wake her. "It's after seven and you have to be to work soon."

She curled closer to me and mumbled something about peaches, causing me to reminisce briefly about the previous night. Rather than get out of bed, I wanted to crawl between her legs, and bury myself inside her all morning, but even after last night I wasn't ready for that yet.

After peeling a very sticky Teagan off me, I shook her again. *Looks like I missed some peach juice after all.* "Teagan, it's after seven. You need to wake up, pretty girl. You're going to be late for work."

That got her attention because she quickly sat up and threw the sheet off us.

"*Crap!* It's after seven?" She jumped out of bed and ran

toward the French doors buck-naked. "I don't have any work clothes!" She went outside then came back in with the clothes she'd been wearing last night.

Jesus, she was even more beautiful now that I'd seen her in all her naked glory in broad daylight. Her red hair was wild and curly, and her peaches and cream skin was flawless. Her body was both tight and curvy at the same time . . . *sheer perfection.*

"Jeremy, what am I going to do?" She was freaking out and here I was, sitting on my bed sporting wood, unable to think about anything but the naked woman in front of me.

"Jeremy?" she said again, giving me a shove on the shoulder to get my attention.

Now would be a good time to tell her that I'd done her laundry yesterday when I'd come home to drop off the flowers and bath soaps.

Averting my gaze away from her nakedness, I concentrated on her eyes. "Get in the shower. I washed your clothes yesterday."

She stared at me, unmoving, like a deer in headlights. Since she needed to be at work on time so she wouldn't get in trouble, and she still wasn't moving, I took matters in to my own hands.

I stood and tossed her over my shoulder then took her into the bathroom. Carefully, I set her on her feet in the shower and turned on the water. Teagan sucked in a sharp breath and covered her mouth to quiet her screaming. She danced around in the ice-cold water as she reached down to adjust the temperature.

"Thanks a lot for the cold shower, but it looks like you need one more than I do," she kidded as she pulled the shower curtain closed.

I glanced down, and my dick was still standing at full attention. With no time to take care of it, I went back to my bedroom to get ready for work. Once dressed, I went into the bathroom and stuck my head under the tap in the sink to wet my hair because it was sticking up all over. I combed my hair down, washed my face, and brushed my teeth then went and grabbed the basket from the laundry room with her folded clothes.

Just as I set it on the bed, she came flying out of the bathroom with a towel wrapped around her hair and one around her body. Stopping when she saw the basket full of clothes, she seized the front of my work shirt in her hands and yanked me toward her to plant a hard kiss to my lips. "You are the best boyfriend, ever," she breathed out after she pulled away from me. "Thank you, Jeremy."

Teagan dropped the towel from her body and searched the basket to find a bra and panties. Droplets of water still trickled down her shoulders as she dressed and I had to stop myself from licking them from her skin. After she pulled a clean scrubs top over her head, she turned to go back to the bathroom, catching me blatantly staring at her.

"You better stop staring at me like you want to *eat* me." She grinned then picked up the towel from the floor and snapped my leg with it. "We need to get to work."

I just sat on the bed staring at her like a love-struck idiot with a big, stupid smile on my face.

Taking the towel with her, she went into the bathroom, shutting the door behind her. My girl was getting good at the dirty talk and I smiled as I thought about our grocery store outing and poolside activities.

It seemed silly to do that next to the pool, but I'd needed to be where she wasn't able to touch me. I knew I wouldn't be able to stop if I'd let her. I'd hardly been able to contain myself as it was and had only stroked my dick a few times before I came.

Five minutes later, Teagan was back out and ready to go. She grabbed her purse and we ran out the door. We gave each other a quick kiss goodbye then hopped into our respective cars. I waited for my girl to leave first, but she suddenly jumped out of her car and was at my passenger door. I rolled down the window to see what was going on.

"My car won't start," she said in a panic. "It's just making a clicking noise."

"Dead battery," I replied. "Get in, I'll get you to work on time."

We had a twenty-minute drive ahead of us, and only fifteen

minutes until she needed to clock in. She hopped into my car and I backed out of the driveway. "Buckle up tight, Red. This might be a scary ride."

She grinned and put on her seatbelt as I shifted to first gear and peeled out down the street.

"Are you going to stop completely at *any* of the stop signs, Jeremy?" Teagan asked as I drove out of our neighborhood, hauling ass toward the freeway.

While speeding down the on-ramp to get on to I-5, I shifted quickly through the gears. "You do realize we're in California right?" I merged into traffic. "Where do you think the term *"California Stop"* came from? We don't actually *stop* at the signs. It's more of a pause, roll, then stomp on the gas kind of thing." I shot her a grin across the car, but she seemed nervous.

Then she laughed while gripping the armrest on her door and seat for stability. I gunned my car up to ninety to get past a few slower cars then took the exit to the hospital. I drove as fast as traffic would allow, the final two blocks to her job.

"Jeremy, pull around to the front instead of the employee parking, please," she said, a frown marring her pretty face.

Shit, she didn't want anyone to see me dropping her off. I agreed, but my stomach dropped from her reminder of how I was her secret at work.

Pulling up to the curb, I stopped in front of the entrance. She was halfway out of the car, yelling goodbye to me before I had a chance to say anything to her. All I could do was give her a half-hearted wave as she ran around the front of my car. She shot me one last glance before making her way through the front doors of the hospital.

This sucks.

I called the shop and let my mom know I was running late because I'd unexpectedly had to take Teagan to work. Once I was off the phone, I took my time driving to work. I needed some time to think before dealing with people and noise.

Jesus, I was a pussy. Why did I let Teagan keeping me a secret get to me?

All she was thinking about was her job and avoiding another strike. I was a total dick for letting that offend me.

By the time I pulled into the parking lot at the shop, I had two texts waiting for me. One was from Reese and the other from Teagan. Reese was thanking me for getting Teagan to work for him and told me he'd take care of changing her battery. She was supposed to wake him up for our run, but since we'd overslept, he hadn't woken up until after we'd left. The text from Teagan was long, but it restored my bruised ego after I read it.

> Thanks for getting me to work on time. With your kick-ass (yet somewhat scary) driving skills and California stops, I was one minute early. Extra special reward for you later, and it will definitely involve Peaches! You have been my hero many times this week, and I don't know what I would have done without you. I'm sorry about the front entrance drop off, I really am. Everything is going perfectly for us and I don't want anyone to ruin it. I'm sorry if I hurt you, because that was never my intention. Please trust in me, and my feelings for you, and know they are pure and true. I'll see you after work. XOXO

Fortunately, I wasn't too late for work and nobody gave me shit about it. I went straight to my toolbox and popped the lid to look at the pictures taped to the inside. My mind needed to see us together, and to see that what we had was real. After I brushed my thumb over Teagan's cheekbone in the photo, I closed the lid and went to work.

Noah had been in a shitty mood all day because he couldn't get the motor he was working on finished. His deadline was two days away on Friday, but he needed to finish today so he could put it on the dyno for testing to make sure everything worked properly. If something went wrong, he'd have time to fix it before the customer came to pick it up Friday afternoon.

"Dude, if you force it, you're gonna fucking break it," I said, trying to calm him down. He was doing a simple task now, but it was a pain in the ass if you were frustrated and in a shitty mood.

Noah glared up at me. "No shit. See if you can do any better, dickhead." He handed me the piston and rings and I assembled it easily. I set the completed piston aside and picked up the next one.

"Fuck you," Noah grumbled and walked off. He went into the break room and called someone on his cell phone.

Deciding to help my brother out, even though he was being a prick, I sat down on the stool in front of his workbench and assembled the rest of the pistons for him. Right at five, he came back out and didn't seem to be in a better mood.

"What is your problem, Noah?"

The James brothers didn't beat around the bush with each other. If there was an issue, we addressed it, fixed it, and moved on.

"I'm freaking out. Jess is due in six weeks. I'm going to be a *father,* Jeremy." He paced the floor of the shop, both hands making wild gestures the more agitated he became. "What if I fuck up? All Jess wants to do is get the nursery ready and be prepared for when our little girl gets here. I can't even concentrate on that, so Z's helping her."

He propped himself against his toolbox waiting for me to say something. Holy shit, I never thought I'd see Noah, of all people, freaking out about something like this. I actually felt bad for him.

"Why don't you go home and speak to your *wife* about this. I'll stay and finish the motor," I suggested, before realizing I was giving up an evening with Teagan by working late. I was still not used to the fact that I had a gorgeous woman living with me.

"Are you serious, man?"

I nodded and forced a smile because there was no way in hell I could rescind my offer. "Get the hell outta here before I change my mind," I said. "Just for the record, you're going to be a good dad, Noah. Jess is smarter than you and wouldn't have let you knock her up if she didn't believe you couldn't handle it."

Noah clapped me on the back, called me an asshole, and thanked me before he practically ran out the door. Shit, there went my night with Teagan. However, I was helping my anxious brother out. He needed to get his mind straight, and a nursery finished before his daughter was born.

Taking my cell out of my pocket, I called Teagan to let her

know I wouldn't be home any time soon. She was understanding, and told me to call on my way home so she could have dinner ready for me. I agreed and we ended our call.

My phone rang as soon as I hung up with Teagan. Cammie's name and picture appeared on the screen. I didn't want to talk to her, but now was the chance for me to tell her to fuck off.

"What do you want, Cammie?"

She let out an irritated huff into the phone. "Why are you always such a jerk, Jeremy? I was calling because I miss you."

"How many times do I need to tell you we're through before it sinks in? We're no good together, can't you see that?"

"Don't say that. Our relationship was amazing. We had lots of good times together."

I shook my head, even though I knew she couldn't see me. "It's not true and you know it. All we did was fuck and fight. That's not a relationship, and not what I want."

"It's all because of that redheaded slut, isn't it?"

"I'm assuming you mean Teagan. We're friends Cammie, but that is none of your business anyway, because you and I are not together. Why can't you go find someone else and leave me alone?"

"Because, I don't want someone else, Jeremy. I want you back. I miss you."

"Not gonna happen. Goodbye, Cammie." I hung up on her. She called right back.

"Look, I don't have time for this anymore," I seethed when I answered. "I'm busy with work and have a lot of shit to do. Please, stop calling me." I ended the call, blocked her number then left my phone on the workbench. I needed to stay focused on the motor.

When I finished, I glanced up at the wall clock. *A quarter to midnight? Not good.* I had completely lost track of time, but at least the motor was ready for the dyno test tomorrow.

I washed up and when I picked up my phone, I saw I'd missed a couple of texts from Teagan asking where I was. I hadn't heard my phone go off because I had been making quite a bit of noise. I didn't text Teagan back because she was probably already asleep and I didn't want to wake her.

She wasn't in my room when I got home, but the TV was on in the guest bedroom. I found Reese and Teagan asleep in the center of the bed, Teagan pressed up against Reese's back with her arm thrown over him. I was jealous, but not because my girlfriend was in bed with another man. Reese was undoubtedly gay and I trusted them. No, I was jealous because I wouldn't have her sleeping next to me tonight. Teagan needed her sleep and I needed mine so I turned off the TV and went to clean up.

After my shower, I pulled on boxers and crawled into bed alone. This time I made sure to turn on my alarm clock, in case Teagan had forgotten to turn hers on before she'd fallen asleep.

Sometime during the night, I woke to find her sitting next to me on the bed staring down at me. My eyes adjusted to the light from the lamp next to the bed and even though I was half-asleep, I knew she was upset.

"What time is it?" I asked her.

"It's three-forty. Where were you?" she asked, staring down at her clasped hands in her lap. "I was worried. You said you would call on your way home and you didn't. I sent you texts and you didn't respond."

I'm too tired for this conversation right now. "Can we talk about this in the morning? I'm exhausted." My eyes involuntarily closed and I drifted off again.

"I'll see you tomorrow morning," she said with a hint of irritation in her tone. She rolled from the bed, turned off the lamp, and left the room. When she went into the other room, I heard her and Reese talking.

Teagan was upset and once again, it was my fault. Grumbling, I forced myself out of bed and went into the other bedroom.

"What's wrong?" I asked from the doorway. I was met with silence from both Teagan and Reese. *What the fuck?* I could see the outline of them on the bed, and they were lying in the same position they were in when I'd come home.

I walked over and slipped in behind Teagan. I was tired

and just wanted to sleep after working over fifteen hours.

"Where were you, Jeremy?" Teagan asked from the darkness. She rolled over to face me.

"I'm going to go in the other room so you can talk," Reese said, throwing back the covers on his side of the bed.

"You might as well stay since it seems you already know what's going on here. Besides, I have nothing to hide," I said with a sigh.

As Reese settled back in, I found Teagan's hand. "I was at work Teagan, like I told you when I called earlier. Where do you think I was?" She obviously thought I was somewhere I wasn't supposed to be.

"I don't know, Jeremy. All I know is you said you would call me and didn't. And you ignored my texts. I was worried about you."

"I'm sorry, I lost track of time. I wasn't ignoring your texts intentionally. I put my phone on the workbench because Cammie kept bugging me until I blocked her, and then I didn't hear your texts come through because I had the air compressor on and wasn't near my phone."

I heard her sigh with frustration. "Did you talk to her?"

"Yes I did. Then I hung up on her, blocked her number, and went back to work. When I finished the motor and realized what time it was, I came home, *to you*."

"What did she say?"

"The same shit she does every time she calls. I told her again we were over. She asked if it was because of you. I told her you and I are *just friends*." I let out a sigh when the words left my mouth. I hated hiding us, and even though I'd agreed to it, it was getting to me. Being the secret man in a relationship just felt all sorts of wrong now. "Teagan, it really sucks that it has to be this way."

Suddenly I didn't want to be in the same room with her. She didn't trust me. Was it going to be this way every time I worked late? I tossed the blanket off and got out of bed.

"I'm sorry, Jeremy," she whispered.

Taking a deep breath, I closed my eyes as I turned toward the door to leave. "Yeah, me too."

When I stepped into the hallway, I heard Reese tell Teagan she needed to go after me. At least someone was on my side.

I just wished it were Teagan.

As soon as I was in my bed and comfortable, I felt the mattress dip slightly as Teagan slipped in behind me. She wrapped her arm around my waist and kissed my back. It felt like she was shivering, so I rolled over and pulled her closer.

"I'm scared," she whispered.

The raw emotion in her voice broke me.

"I'm sorry, Jeremy. I can't help it. I am trying to work everything out in my head, but it's hard considering all that's happened."

"I know it is. But I promise I was at the shop. Noah was having a bad day and I took over his job. Sometimes I'll have to work late because of our deadlines. It might be once a month, or once a week. There's nothing I can do about it."

"Is Noah okay?" she asked, scooting even closer to me.

It was cool that she was concerned about my brother. "I think so. He's freaking out about the baby. Jess is due in six weeks and it's stressing him out."

"I bet it is. Being a parent is a huge change in his life, so it's understandable to feel that way."

"Teagan, I'm sorry I didn't call you on my way home, but it was almost midnight when I finished and I thought you'd be asleep. Next time I say I'll call, I swear I'll do it. Sorry I worried you."

In the dark, her hand found my bare shoulder then made its way to my cheek. She rose up on her elbow and her sweet lips found mine. "Thank you," she whispered, and kissed me again. "I'm kind of attached to you."

"Goodnight, pretty girl."

"Goodnight, my boyfriend."

Reese and I were sitting on the couch, all dressed up waiting for Teagan to finish getting ready. We were going out to dinner before meeting up with Zoey and some of our friends at Hooligans for the christening of the new karaoke machine.

When Teagan made her appearance in the living room, my jaw hit the floor. She was wearing my favorite color on her—emerald green—in the form of a silky . . . tank top?

Holy fuck, what was she wearing? It was sexy as hell, whatever it was. It hit her about mid-thigh and was cinched around her waist by a gold, metal, chain-like belt. My eyes traveled down her gorgeous legs and found her feet wrapped in gold, strappy stilettos.

My gaze moved back up her body, and the tiny dress she wore hugged every curve. My girl's tits and ass were going to be on display, but she looked amazing, and I'd be more than honored to have her on my arm all night. Her hair hung loose in perfect curls and she was wearing more makeup than I'd ever seen her wear.

She looked like a goddess.

"Oh man," Reese elbowed me to get my attention. "You're so lucky I'm gay."

I snapped out of my Teagan induced trance and looked over at Reese, who was still ogling the stunning woman standing in front of us.

"Quit drooling over my woman, you twat," I grumbled.

Teagan burst out laughing and Reese gaped over at me with a big, surprised grin on his face. "Did you really just call me a twat?" he asked, before erupting in laughter.

"Yes, I did." I grinned. "And I'm not lucky you're gay, *you* are. And you need to find a new roommate because I'm not letting you have my girl."

"But she was my girl first."

"She's mine now."

Teagan stood watching Reese and I go back and forth.

"He's a mean, nasty-ass honey badger tonight, hooker-face," Reese said to Teagan.

Ignoring Reese, I stood and took Teagan's hand, spinning her so I could admire the rest of her. I let out a whistle as she turned. When she stopped, I leaned in, kissed her cheek then whispered in her ear, "Absolutely perfect, Red."

"Are you sure it's not too much?" She pushed her hair back away from her face, revealing large, gold hoop earrings.

Teagan seemed uncomfortable with what she was wearing, but she was the most beautiful vision I'd ever seen in my life.

"Hooker-face, your man and I are going to be the luckiest bastards in the room tonight," Reese said while I ogled her like an idiot.

After dinner, we arrived at Hooligans to find my sister, Andy, Jess and Noah, along with Zoey's friend Sasha and her boyfriend, Ben, sitting with Sonny. Zoey's friends Justin and Will couldn't make it, and John and Eric had declined my invite, saying they were going out to find "some pussy" since there wouldn't be any single women at the bar with us. Something was definitely up their asses ever since I'd moved into my house and found Teagan.

Once I'd introduced Teagan and Reese to everyone we took our seats. Since my sister was a friend with the owner, he had given us front row tables right near the stage. Sonny switched tables to sit with Reese, Teagan, and me. Looking around the bar, I had to admit the place was insane. The sound system made it seem like we were at an actual concert, not at some cheesy karaoke bar.

Nearly four hours later, Teagan was missing, off somewhere in the bar with Sasha. Those girls had turned out to be two peas in a pod, leaving Sonny, Reese, and me to hang out together. I felt like a third wheel with Reese and Sonny because they'd been talking non-stop.

Worried about the girls being gone for so long, I was getting ready to get up to find them, when the bar's owner, Jerome, took the stage to announce the next act.

"Ladies and gentlemen, are you havin' a good time out there?" Jerome yelled into the mic, eliciting deafening screams from the enormous crowd. "I don't even know what to say about this next song, but once you see these two sexy-ass ladies, shit's gonna get crazy! I just watched them practice backstage, and these chicks are gonna set this place on fire! May I present to you, Miss Sasha and Lady Teagan."

Jerome took a bow and placed the mic back on the stand. The stage went dark, but I saw Sasha take the stage up front near us, while Teagan stayed at the back. I had no clue what they were doing, but when the music began to play my curiosity was definitely piqued.

Reese smacked me hard on the arm a few times because he was so excited. "Wait till you see what your girl can do. She's amazing!" he yelled over the noise in the room. He leaned toward Sonny and reiterated Teagan's awesomeness.

A spotlight came on over Sasha's head right before she started singing "Beast Within" by In This Moment. Halfway through the first verse, a spotlight came on over Teagan's head, illuminating her gorgeous red hair, and she joined Sasha singing, swaying her arm back and forth in the air.

I could not believe what I was seeing and hearing. As Sasha finished the second verse, Teagan took over singing. No, she wasn't singing, she was doing the screaming part of the vocals. Holy fucking hell. She sounded exactly like the singer from the band.

How the fuck did I not know my petite girlfriend had enough rage inside her to scream like that? It was definitely a far cry from her usual sweet and calm voice.

The girls pulled their mics from the stands and joined each other in the center of the stage. Together, they traded off vocals as if they'd performed the song a hundred times. They were flawless. Teagan turned, Sasha stepped up behind her and they did a sexy bump and grind dance. Teagan turned to face Sasha and they did their dance again.

I didn't know about the other guys, but my pants were getting pretty snug around my dick region. I'd never seen something so hot in my life and couldn't look away even if I'd wanted to.

When they finished the song, the crowd went insane. People were on their feet, mostly men, calling out for them to do another song. The girls agreed and the music for the song "Adrenalize" came pumping through the speakers. Oh damn, this was gonna be good.

I stared in awe as the girls gave another flawless, nearly X-rated performance that once again had every man in the room going nuts.

A minute before the song was over, Ben tapped on my shoulder. "I don't know about you, but I am going to get my girl from backstage. I am not about to let her walk out here by herself with all these horny assholes around."

Shit, I didn't want Teagan walking back out here by herself either. Leaving Reese and Sonny at the table, I followed Ben backstage. We found our girls in a dressing room gushing over nailing their songs.

Teagan saw me and launched herself into my arms, locked her legs around my waist and her arms around my neck. Ben and Sasha quickly left the room, shutting the door behind them.

"What did you think?" Teagan's body was vibrating with excitement.

Pulling her hips forward and centering her against my dick, I was certain she knew exactly what I thought. "Mmm, I fucking loved it," I groaned as I crushed her lips to mine and backed her up against the door.

"Jeremy," she moaned. "I feel like doing something crazy right now. That was so liberating."

"What do you want to do?" I asked, nibbling gently on her lips and grinding myself against her. I wanted to rip her panties off and take her right here against the door.

But, I couldn't.

I wouldn't.

Our first time wasn't going to be in the back room of a bar. Jesus, I needed to get my head screwed on straight.

"Jeremy?"

"Yeah, Red?"

"I want you . . . right here, right now."

Fuck me. I wanted her too.

And, we were back to square one. Like the first night she'd come home with me, I wasn't going to have sex with her, but I wasn't going to leave her hanging either.

Unlocking her legs from around me, I set her on her feet. Dropping to my knees in front of her, I slid my hands up her thighs, and under her dress. Oh hell, she was wearing the panties that tied at her hips. I made quick work of the ties, pulled her panties off, and shoved them into the pocket of my jeans.

Reaching up next to her, I locked the door as she tangled

her fingers in my hair. "Spread your legs for me, pretty girl." She widened her stance a bit and my fingers curled around her ankle. Picking up her foot from the floor, I situated her leg over my shoulder, and went in for the kill.

I licked her hard, and flicked her clit with the tip of my tongue. She attempted to rock her hips toward me but couldn't with only one foot on the floor to balance her. Without stopping what I was doing to her, I moved back just enough, and lifted her other leg over my other shoulder. She let out a squeal when she slid down the door a few inches.

Chuckling against her, I gripped her ass in my hands and pulled her hips away from the door so she could move freely against my mouth. I thrust my tongue inside her and slowly turned my head from side to side, ever so slightly, delving deeper.

Teagan let out the most beautiful moan for me as she squeezed her thighs together in ecstasy. I licked, sucked, and teased her until she came undone. In true Teagan fashion, she gripped my hair hard while she came, and I fucking loved it.

19

Teagan

Halloween Day

"Wake up, sleepyhead." I shook Jeremy as I straddled him on the bed then ran the palms of my hands up and down his toned chest. "It's time to get up so I can take you out and scare the pants off you."

As Jeremy woke, a grin slowly eased across his face. "How are you supposed to scare the pants off of me if I'm not wearing any, Red?"

Stifling a giggle, I scooted back and laid my naked body on top of his. Kissing his chest, I yanked the covers over us and descended his body to find the tip of his dick poking out the waistband of his boxers. I gave it a kiss as I tugged on his boxers. He groaned quietly and lifted his hips for me so I could take them off.

"Evil woman," he mumbled as I licked him from base to tip then took him inside my mouth. I released him quickly and moved back up his body, pretending I was going to stop.

"So you don't want your favorite wake-up call this morning?" My face hovered over the veins and V on his lower stomach that I loved and lusted after so much. Planting kisses and licking them while I purposely let my hair fall over his dick would answer my question quickly.

Hearing him laugh quietly, he put his hand on top of my

head, preventing me from moving any farther.

"That's what I thought," I said before pulling my hair over one shoulder. I looked him right in the eyes and licked the head of his dick before taking him into my mouth. The next thing I knew, he'd bolted upright and his fingers were tangled in my hair.

"Come here," he said, gently urging me to release him.

Sucking hard and slow as I pulled my mouth away from him, he let out a long hiss of breath until I let him go. As soon as he was free, he spun me so my feet were near the top of the bed and rolled me to my side. He pushed my legs apart then rested his head on my inner thigh. He bent his knee at an angle, giving me a place to rest my head on his inner thigh while he pulled my other leg over his shoulder. He'd arranged us into a very comfortable, sideways sixty-nine position.

"I'm gonna eat some Peaches," he said with a laugh before moving my leg higher and diving in.

His lips and tongue consumed me within seconds, and I cried out from the sudden pleasure. I took in several breaths until I could function enough to grasp him in my hand. I stroked his dick briefly before taking him into my mouth.

He groaned against me, the vibration causing me to moan, and my eyes fluttered closed. Stroking the base of him while sucking and working the rest of his perfect dick with my tongue and mouth, I cupped his balls in my other hand, kneading them lightly the way he liked it.

My body was hot and my blood was racing through my veins while he teased me relentlessly with his tongue and fingers. Jeremy pulled away to bite and mark the inside of my thigh as he stroked my G-spot, sending me over the edge.

God, he's good at that.

Letting out whimpers and moans of pleasure, I came with him still in my mouth. He cursed and slowly rocked his hips, pushing and pulling himself in and out of my mouth. He never went overboard and I trusted him completely to be easy with me.

Jeremy easily shifted us around again so that he could watch me. He propped several pillows behind him, and I maneuvered my body between his legs to give me the best access and him the view he wanted. I leaned forward knowing he loved it when my hair spilled over him. As I teased him with my mouth and hand, his fingers weaved into my hair. Within seconds, he moaned my name and his body stiffened with his release.

I loved trying new things with him sexually, because he still refused to actually consummate our relationship. We were, however, having an energetic time finding new and exciting ways to please and surprise each other. Sometimes they worked to benefit us, and other times we'd end up on the floor laughing at our failures.

Nearly a month and a half had passed since I came to stay with him. I hadn't left because he didn't want me to go. And I didn't want to go because I loved being with him. So, I'd pretty much moved into his house. He refused to take money from me for rent, so I did the majority of the cooking and cleaning, and kept the fridge and the rest of the household supplies stocked.

Reese had moved into our apartment weeks ago, but hadn't decided if he was going to rent out my room or keep it for me, just in case.

I wasn't worried about the "just in case" because I was truly happy for the first time in years, and in a relationship with someone who treated me the way I wanted to be treated. Jeremy continually surprised me with his caring and loving ways.

Even though Jeremy hated the picket fence, he'd kept it after he'd noticed my disappointment when he'd mentioned ripping it out one day over breakfast

I had been so giddy about keeping it I'd dressed in grungy clothes, and scraped as much of the old flaking paint off as possible. After going to the store and buying new paint, I'd spent the rest of the weekend painting the entire fence.

"Come on, let's get in the shower," I said, as I hopped out of bed. "I'll take you to breakfast before we head out to the corn maze and haunted barn."

"Are you trying to kill me by scaring me to death?" he asked jokingly.

"Don't worry, my boyfriend, I'll protect you from the

zombies and chainsaw wielding murderers in the corn maze."

He was such a chicken when it came to *anything* horror. He blamed Adam for scaring the crap out of him when they were little. Every time they would watch scary movies, Adam would grab him or scream when the scary parts came on. I got the impression that being the baby of the family, Adam had been quite the troublemaker as a child.

Halloween was my favorite holiday, and since I didn't have to work, Jeremy had taken the day off too. We had the whole day planned to do all my favorite Halloween activities.

Once we were ready, we stopped for breakfast at a small café on the way out of Sacramento. At the farm with the corn maze, I practically skipped to the entrance to pay our way in because I was so excited.

Jeremy laughed as I dragged him behind me. "Jesus Red, you're acting like a kid on Halloween."

"You're the one acting like a kid, 'cause you're scared, you big sissy." I wrapped my arms around him and planted a kiss on him. "Don't worry, I'll protect you."

"You better, pretty girl. You'd be sad if you lost me in there, wouldn't you?" He tipped his chin toward the looming corn maze behind me.

"You know I would. But, today is the only day of the year I get to act like a big kid, so you had better be prepared. This is gonna be so much fun."

He smirked and rolled his eyes at me, but the big grin on his face was the icing on my metaphorical Halloween day cake. I hadn't been to the farm since I was a kid and I wanted to share a bit of my favorite things with him. Unlike Gary, Jeremy never berated me or made fun of the things I liked or did, and I'd never appreciated it more.

"Let's get on with you scaring my pants off me already."

Later, when we were officially lost in the maze . . . well, he was lost . . . I wasn't. I had a map and knew exactly where I was. Two rows over from me, Jeremy walked toward the next turn. I snuck quietly between the corn stalks, jumped out, and grabbed him when he walked past.

He easily caught me around the middle and planted a kiss to my forehead and then another to my lips. "You're lucky you didn't get punched, Red. The last time Adam pulled that shit with me, he ended up with a black eye and a busted lip."

Doubling over with laughter, I reached out and tried to take his hand in mine, but he pushed my hand away. "Aww, you're not mad at me are you?" I could see he was trying not to smile.

"Yes, I am. I think you need a spanking," he said low enough so nobody except me heard.

Grinning, Jeremy took a step closer to me and I backed away. He jumped at me unexpectedly and tossed me over his shoulder like he had so many times before. As soon as I quit squirming, he smacked me hard on my butt cheek.

"Oh, do it again," I said loud enough for everyone around to hear. "Spank me harder, you dirty, dirty beast!"

He spanked me one more time just for good measure then bent forward and dropped me back to my feet. "You're such a shit, Teagan," he said with a laugh.

Taking his hand in mine, we hurried out of the corn maze using my trusty map. "Time for the haunted barn," I said, dragging him behind me.

"Fabulous," he groaned and followed me toward the building of doom.

At the haunted barn, we waited at the end of a long line of people. We were talking about the zombies wandering through the corn maze and how creepy and realistic they were when someone called out Jeremy's name.

"Jeremy James? Is that really you out here on a *farm?*" a female voice asked from behind me.

Jeremy looked past me and his expression became guarded.

Turning around to see who called out to him, I found a blonde woman approaching us. She was gorgeous, not surprisingly, and exactly the kind of woman I'd imagine Jeremy with if I weren't in the picture. Jeremy took my hand in his, holding it tightly.

"Nicole," he said when she stopped in front of us. "How are you?"

"Good, and you?"

"Never better."

"I can see that," she said, glancing at me then at our entwined hands.

My guard instantly went up, sensing something had once been between her and Jeremy. Nicole surprised me by reaching her hand out to me.

"Well, it seems that Jeremy's not going to introduce us," she said, her smile teasing, but friendly. "I'm Nicole. I've known Jeremy for years."

Taking her extended hand in mine, I said, "Hi, I'm Teagan, Jeremy's girlfriend. It's nice to meet you."

"Sorry," Jeremy said, "I was just surprised to see you here, Nic." He let out a breath and relaxed.

She released my hand and I let it fall to my side.

"It's wonderful to meet you, Teagan. Are you two going into the haunted barn?" she asked. Her eyes drifted between Jeremy and me, waiting for one of us to answer.

"Yes," Jeremy finally spoke up when I squeezed his hand. "Teagan's been waiting all day to get me in there."

Nicole laughed, a knowing expression on her face. "Ah, still a big scaredy cat is he?" she asked me.

"Most definitely," I replied with a laugh. Regardless of what had once been between them, clearly they were only friends, now. Surprisingly, that didn't make me uncomfortable. "Are you going into the barn?"

She shook her head. "I wanted to, but I'm here with my sister and nephew. He's too little to go in and I didn't want to go by myself. We were sitting down to have a snack when I glanced over and spotted Jeremy. I just came over to say hi."

"Why don't you go in with us," I blurted out.

Nicole's eyes grew big and Jeremy shot me a "what the hell" look.

Grinning, I shrugged my shoulders. "Nicole wants to go inside, but doesn't want to go alone. Since we're going in she won't have to miss out on it if she goes with us."

Here I was extending an olive branch to someone I knew Jeremy had been with, but Nicole seemed normal, not like crazy Cammie. I could be the bigger person in this situation since Nicole posed no threat to us.

"Are you sure you don't mind?" Nicole's eyes darted between Jeremy and me.

Again, Jeremy answered, meeting my eyes for reassurance. "I'm okay with it as long as Teagan is."

"I am totally fine with it." The fact that Jeremy was on board with my decision to invite her along with us showed that I trusted him to be around an ex. Well, one that wasn't Cammie. And in that situation, I trusted him, but not her.

Nicole grinned at me, her face alight with surprise and a bit of confusion. "Let me run over and tell my sister. Be right back," she said and turned back the way she'd come from.

"Teagan . . ." Jeremy stared down at me, obviously not knowing what to say.

"Look Jeremy, I'm not blind. I know there was something between you two at one time, but she seems nice, and it's obvious that she's not interested in you like that anymore." I giggled when he let out a sigh of relief.

He pulled me close and took my face in his hands; his stormy blue eyes stared into my green eyes. "Do you even understand how much this means to me?" He pressed his lips delicately to mine before wrapping his arms around me. "Thank you for trusting in me."

A minute later, Nicole joined us again. "You two make a really cute couple, you know?"

Jeremy and I pulled apart and he took my hand in his again. "Thanks, Nic."

"I'm really happy for you, Jeremy," she said, just as our group was called to go into the barn.

He gave my hand a squeeze and the three of us entered the barn together.

We weaved our way through the barn, and I had a feeling that I was leading Jeremy through with his eyes closed because he kept running in to the props. He stayed silent and close to my side. Nicole led the way, and I screamed with fright when the biggest, freakiest looking clown jumped out and grabbed both of us. Although Jeremy was a chicken, Nicole and me had a scary-good time as we made our way through the rest of the tour. At the end, we were ushered out the door and back into the bright sunlight.

"I'd better get back to my sister and nephew," Nicole said as we let our eyes readjust to the light. "It was good to meet you, Teagan. Thank you for inviting me to go in with you."

She turned to Jeremy to say goodbye. "You've got yourself a keeper here, Jer. Take good care of her."

"I know—and I will. It was good to see you, Nic. Take care of yourself."

After saying our goodbyes, I spotted our next activity for the day in the form of two giant horses pulling a hay wagon. "Hayride!" I squealed. "Come on, let's get on and go pick out our pumpkins."

I reached out for Jeremy's hand and he pulled me close. "Teagan, I meant what I said earlier. Thank you." He rubbed his fingers over my Claddagh ring. I nodded as his hands came up to cradle my face. He kissed me sweetly, making my lips tingle. "Now, let's go find my beloved woman the biggest pumpkin in the patch."

Once we had picked our pumpkins, we played a few games, split a bag of kettle corn then decided to call it a day. We had an hour-long drive home, pumpkins to carve, and a ton of candy to pass out to the trick-or-treaters.

When we arrived home, we were filthy dirty from goofing around at the farm. We carved our pumpkins old-school style, with triangle shaped eyes and noses, and toothy grins. *Somebody* thought it would be funny to throw a handful of his pumpkin guts down my shirt while I was bent over gutting mine. That caused a huge gut fight between the two of us.

Thankfully, we were on the patio in the backyard when it happened and not inside the house. We took a quick shower together because I had pumpkin guts in my hair and couldn't get them out on my own. At least that's what I told Jeremy.

After our shower, I dressed in my Halloween costume and fixed my hair. The kids in the neighborhood always used to love it when I dressed up to pass out candy at my mom and dad's. Because I was a redhead, this year I dressed as Princess Merida from the kid's movie *Brave*. Yes, I knew she was Scottish, and I was Irish, but the kids wouldn't care either way.

"Look at you, sexy lady," Jeremy said when I entered the living room and twirled around in my dress. He had the bowl of candy for the trick-or-treaters on the couch between his knees and was picking out a few of his favorites. He set it aside then pulled me down onto his lap. "And who are you supposed to be?"

Because I couldn't master a Scottish accent, I stuck with the Irish accent I had mastered while growing up listening to Nanna and Papa.

"You fool, I am Princess Merida. Don't make me shoot you in the ass with my bow and arrow."

He laughed at my awesome acting skills and snuck his hands under my long dress, sliding them up my legs. When he hit the top of my thigh highs and garters, his eyes grew big and he lifted my dress.

"Holy shit, Red. What do you have on under your dress?"

"It's my Ariel costume, but it's for your eyes only after everyone leaves," I said. The look of confusion on his face was priceless. Jesus, had he never watched *The Little Mermaid?* "You cannot tell me you've never seen *The Little Mermaid,* Jeremy."

He shook his head. "I had all brothers growing up, Teagan. Zoey didn't live with us for very long before I moved out, so I never saw movies like that."

That made sense.

To give him a little preview of later tonight, I clutched the hem of my dress and slowly began to reveal my tiny costume underneath. Jeremy's eyes and hands traveled up my legs as I pulled up my dress. He got impatient after he spotted my garters and pushed the costume up to my waist. When he saw my tiny, sequined panties that resembled the turquoise, scalloped detail of Ariel's mermaid tail, his jaw dropped.

"Fuck me," he mumbled. "Can I see the rest, please?"

Laughing, I slowly dragged the dress up higher intending for him to see my matching seashell bra, but the doorbell rang. He'd have to wait until later to see that.

"Our first trick-or-treaters!" I fixed my dress and jogged to the door, yanking it open to find Andy, Zoey, and Hannah on the porch.

"Come in, come in," I said, ushering them inside.

"You have the worst timing ever," Jeremy told them when they came in.

"Did we interrupt something important?" Zoey asked as she looked between Jeremy and me.

"No."

"Yes."

Zoey and Andy laughed when Jeremy and I gave different answers at the same time.

"Don't worry, we won't stay long," Zoey said to her brother with a knowing grin on her face. "We just wanted to bring our little ladybug out for her first Halloween."

Jeremy jumped up off the couch and went to get Hannah. She held her arms out to him and started jabbering on about something only she could understand.

"Happy first Halloween, Sweet Pea," Jeremy said as she snuggled down in the crook of his neck, her little, black antennae hitting him on the chin. "Look at you in your pretty ladybug costume." He kissed her on the cheek and my heart melted the way it did every time he held her and said adorable things to her.

Then Jason and Heather showed up with Jake, Alex, and Mya. The boys were dressed as Batman and Robin, and Mya was dressed as a princess. After they all left, Jeremy and I spent the next few hours passing out candy until it was gone.

"Now what do we do, Miss Halloween?" Jeremy teased.

After locking the front door, I flipped off all the lights and he followed me down the hall to the bedroom. "Now we hide from the trick-or-treaters and watch scary movies in bed."

"Hmm, I love the bed part of your idea," he said, quickly ridding himself of his clothes and dropping them onto the floor. "I think I need to see that other costume of yours right now though."

Shaking my head, I stepped into his closet and brought out the adult treats I'd put aside for us earlier. I set the tray containing two shot glasses, his favorite tequila, and snacks on the bed.

By midnight, we were both drunk and he was still trying to

get under my dress. Finally, I gave in and jumped off the bed, ripped the dress off over my head and tossed it at him.

"Your tits have she-sells on them," he mumbled, moving to sit on the edge of the bed. "I mean she-shells. *Fuck*. Seeee-shells . . . I fucking love your bra. Lemme see your ass now."

I spun around, struck a pin-up pose, and wiggled my hips for him. Jeremy snaked out his arm and caught me around the waist, pulling me backward onto the bed. He rolled me onto my back and kissed me like he was a man possessed.

My mind was swimming with tequila, lust, and love for him. His hand slid down my leg and he unsnapped the garters from my thigh highs as he kissed me. I sat up, took off my bra, garter, and thigh highs, and tossed them onto the floor.

Jeremy pulled my panties off, licked between my legs, and continued kissing upward until he reached my mouth. I pushed his boxers down with my hands, and he kicked them the rest of the way off. I took his dick in my hand and caressed him while he centered himself between my legs.

His mouth was on mine and his hands were in my hair, then all over me, stroking, gently squeezing, and rubbing every part of my body. He was everywhere all at once, my body, my heart, and my mind.

Letting go of him, I wrapped my arms around him. His weight rested on me as I stroked his bare back. We kissed frantically for what seemed like forever before he pulled away to tease my nipples with his mouth and tongue. I wrapped my legs around his thighs and pulled him back up to kiss me again.

I needed him closer.

Over the last month, I had fallen in love with him, and desperately wanted to be with him.

When he finally came to rest on top of me, his hand traveled down my stomach, between my legs. He massaged tight circles on my clit as he slid his fingers in and out of me.

"Teagan, you're so beautiful. You make me so happy," he said quietly before crushing his mouth to mine again.

My legs instinctively squeezed and pulled him closer. Close enough so the head of his dick was pushing against me. He rocked his hips so the tip of him slid through my wetness.

"Jeremy," I whispered, unsure of whether I should tell him now how I felt about him.

"Hmm?" He hummed in response against my neck.

"I love you."

He pulled back and looked me in the eyes briefly, before smiling and devouring me again. His hips slowly thrust against me, and within a second, he was pushing himself inside me. My mind and body instantly went into a frenzy because this was *finally* happening. I tilted my hips up to meet his and take him in. Once he was fully inside, we moved together, our bodies already connected and well acquainted with one another. Our soft moans and whispers filled the quiet room.

As we made love, all the bad memories from the past left my mind, and Jeremy's sweet words and soft caresses took their place. My life never felt as right as it did in this moment. Jeremy stilled long enough to take my hand in his, entwining our fingers.

"Teagan," he murmured repeatedly, thrusting slowly and gently. His pace picked up after a few minutes and the familiar tingle began low in my belly.

"More," I pleaded, and he thrust harder, pushing me to my release. My body constricted around him, and he hardened inside me. His breathing quickened and the sexy moans I loved to hear from him became louder. As my orgasm subsided, Jeremy let out a ragged breath, and his body shuddered with his release.

Neither one of us moved afterward.

Waking up less than an hour later, nearly sober, with Jeremy sleeping curled protectively around me, I really needed to use the bathroom. Knowing he wouldn't wake up, I untangled myself from his arms and legs.

As soon as I stood, I felt the wetness between my legs and realized we hadn't used a condom.

Oh, crap.

I ran into the bathroom and cleaned up. I'd been completely horizontal for nearly an hour after he came inside me. I woke up Jeremy to tell him.

"What's wrong?" He sat up and rubbed his eyes.

"We didn't use protection," I said as I paced next to the bed.

"Teagan, I've never had sex without a condom before and I've been tested."

Granted, I'd been tested too because of Gary's cheating ways. And because I'd always made him use a condom, I hadn't bothered with birth control pills. I shook my head and sat on the bed next to him.

"Jeremy, I'm not on the pill . . . God, how could I be so stupid?"

"It's not your fault, Red, okay?"

What if I get pregnant? I took in a deep breath and let it out, unable to form a coherent response.

Jeremy moved close to me and began rubbing my back. "Shit, I'm sorry. Neither one of us was thinking properly. If you get pregnant, we can take care of it."

Take *care* of it?

"Jeremy, I don't believe in abortion," I whispered, and moved away from him to look him in the eyes.

"Hey, that's not what I meant," he corrected. "I meant take care of the *baby*, Teagan. Together, as a family."

"You'd really want to do that with me?" I asked, surprised at his admission. *He'd really give me the family I'd always dreamed of?*

Gary had made it clear he'd never wanted children and now this man next to me, who I'd only been with a short time was telling me that if I ended up pregnant, he'd stick around and take care of me and our baby. He was so much more of a man than my cheating prick father and Gary.

"Yes, I would. Without a doubt," he said, twisting a lock of my hair around his fingers. "You're everything I've ever wanted, Teagan, and a family with you would be an added bonus. Until you, I never pictured a future with a family, but now I do."

I stared in awe at the man who'd just told me he would never do to me what my father had done to my mother when he'd found out she was pregnant with me. Jeremy wouldn't leave if we'd happened to make a baby together just now.

Those realizations made me love him even more. And I was everything he'd ever wanted—I was his—and he was mine. I crawled under the covers with him and we entangled ourselves together once more.

"Thank you, Jeremy . . . I love you," I whispered against his neck.

"Me too, pretty girl . . . me too."

The next day before I headed off to my new, crappy shift at the hospital, I gave Jeremy *very* firm instructions to go to the store and buy condoms. Lots and lots of condoms.

Later in the day, I received a text from him. He'd sent a picture of several boxes of condoms set out on the bed, and his text simply said: *enough?*

I counted six boxes in the photo. After laughing my butt off, I texted him back.

That might get us through the weekend.

I laughed, but then felt bummed as I dropped my phone back into my pocket. John and Eric had convinced Jeremy to let them throw a Halloween party at his house tonight since it was Friday, but I was going to miss it because I wasn't off work until midnight. In fact, I was working swing shift for the next couple of months. I was still applying for jobs in hospice, but hadn't caught a break yet.

Throughout the night, Jeremy sent me random texts so I'd know what was going on at the party. Reese was there as were Nat and Jackie, which made this shift a quiet and lonely one.

A little after eleven, Jeremy sent me one last text telling me he was going to bed to wait for me and he would have plenty of condoms on stand-by for when I arrived home. I laughed at his text, but truthfully, I was just as excited as he was to make love again. *Sober this time . . .*

Once my work shift ended and I made it home, I let myself inside, setting my purse and keys on the table. The house was dark except for the light he'd left on for me.

The bedroom door was open, and I entered quietly because Jeremy might have fallen asleep. But, when I heard a familiar moan and heavy breathing, I froze. The words that followed broke my heart and shattered my world.

"I love you," Jeremy murmured in the dark room.

It took me a second to gather my senses and flip on the light. While my eyes adjusted to the brightness, I heard shuffling from across the room.

"What the fuck?" Jeremy yelled, pulling the blankets up to cover himself and the girl who was in bed with him.

The girl who wasn't me.

Oh God . . . not again.

He hadn't even looked over yet to see who'd turned on the light. He was still trying to cover himself and his *friend*.

"Jeremy?" I said, barely loud enough for him to hear me.

His head whipped around to face me. "Teagan, what are you doing over there?" His face contorted in confusion and a second later, it morphed into an expression I'd never seen before. "Oh fuck, no! No, no, no . . ."

His usual olive colored skin turned as white as the sheet he held in his hand. Jeremy looked down at the bed and tossed the sheet off him.

The girl on the bed was still giving him a blowjob.

"Cammie!" he growled. "Get the fuck off me! What the hell are you doing? How did you get in here?"

So he was going to play it like that? My hand went up over my mouth and I choked back a sob as my eyes filled with tears. Cammie sat up on the bed and smiled over at me.

She wins. I give up.

I needed to get the hell out of here. Turning around, I ran down the hall and out the front door as I heard Jeremy calling for me. I'd never run so fast in my life. When I stopped at the gate, I fumbled with the latch because it was dark and my eyes were too full of tears to see. Knowing Jeremy was going to be right behind me, I kicked the gate hard instead, completely unhinging it.

I took off running again. In my rush to leave, I realized I'd left my purse and keys on the table. I wouldn't be able to drive away so I hauled ass running down the street. I was a block away when I heard Jeremy calling me, yelling at me to stop.

But I wouldn't.

I had to get as far away from him as possible.

He was catching up to me, so as soon as I rounded the next corner, I ducked into the secret walkway between the houses.

Jeremy was getting closer, so I dropped down behind a trashcan. By that time, I was sobbing uncontrollably.

I'd been cheated on.

Again.

So here I was hiding behind a gross, smelly trashcan from the man who just shattered my heart by doing something he promised he'd never do to me. I covered my mouth to silence my sobs as Jeremy came to a stop less than ten feet from me.

"Teagan!" he yelled out. "Oh God, what the fuck happened?" He bent over and rested his hands on his knees, trying to catch his breath.

"Jeremy, come back to the house. She's gone," a female voice said to him. "We can pick up where we left off."

Fucking Cammie.

I squeezed my eyes shut as a fresh wave of tears spilled down my face and anguish rolled through me. I wanted to cover my ears too, so I didn't have to overhear them, but I knew if I took my hands off my mouth, they would hear me crying.

"Why did you do this to me?" Jeremy growled at Cammie.

"We can be together now, Jeremy. You said you loved me, so I know you still want me," she said.

"You make me sick, Cammie. There is no way in hell I knew it was you and you know it. I thought you were Teagan, you stupid bitch. I would never touch you because I love her. I love Teagan, not you. I will never love you. I will only ever love her."

"You don't mean that," she whined.

"Yes, I do. I wish I'd never fucking met you. You've ruined my entire world."

Jeremy pushed past her and made the trek back to his house, with Cammie hot on his heels, begging him for forgiveness.

As soon as they were out of range to hear me, I pulled my phone from my pocket and called my sister.

"Teagan, what's wrong? Why are you calling so late?" she asked as soon as she answered her phone.

"Sh-Shannen," I cried. "Please, you n-need to come get m-me."

"What happened?"

"Please Shannen, run over to Jeremy's and get my purse and keys off the t-table and pack me a bag as quick as you can. I just caught him in bed w-with C-Cammie."

"That piece of shit motherfucker," Shannen muttered. "Where are you?"

"In the walkway between the houses, please hurry."

"I'm on my way. Stay right where you are. I love you, Teags."

Twenty minutes later, my Neon pulled up near the entrance of the walkway and the passenger door flew open. "Get in. Hurry!" Shannen yelled from the car.

As soon as I was in the seat and the door shut, she was speeding off down the street.

"Teags, what happened?"

"I can't talk about it right now," I sobbed out.

"Where do you want me to take you?"

There was only one place I wanted to be and one place he wouldn't look for me.

"Take me to Nanna's, please."

20

Jeremy

9 days, 7 hours, and 16 minutes since my happy life ended.

If someone had told me how painful it was to lose the one you love, I would've called them a liar.

Nobody could've prepared me for this kind of agony.

I was a worthless piece of shit, smeared on the bottom of a dirty fucking shoe then dragged through the filthiest places on earth.

My life was now hollow. A shell of what it was. Yet, every day, I woke up alone and pretended I was living. Only I knew how unhappy I was inside since Teagan had left.

The worst part was I deserved it.

My body had committed the cruelest act of betrayal against the only woman I'd ever loved. When I said my body, I really, truly meant my body. It should've known the woman who'd crawled into bed with me wasn't Teagan.

Why the fuck hadn't I known it?

Some small part of me had to have known, right? When I had gone to bed that night, I'd dozed off willingly because I knew Teagan would wake me up when she came home. We'd had big plans for one another.

Getting drunk Halloween night had been unplanned, and I had done something incredibly stupid because of it. We'd had sex. She'd told me she loved me, and I hadn't said it back.

Why hadn't I said it back?

Please tell me why I didn't say it back.

Because I do love her.

I loved her more than the stars loved the night sky.

I loved her more than every breath I took.

Teagan hated me, and I deserve it. I deserved to die a thousand deaths at her hand.

I couldn't even *try* to fix this. I didn't deserve her, or her love.

The last time I saw my girl, she had been running away from me because I'd committed the ultimate betrayal. Not on purpose, but still it had happened, and she'd witnessed it.

Before Teagan had come home that night, I'd kicked all the people out of my house, I'd cleaned up the messes they'd left then had gone to bed completely undressed after taking a shower.

My plan had been to make up for the night before the party when I shouldn't have had sex with her when we'd been drinking. I hadn't wanted our first time to be like that. But when she'd told me she loved me, something had changed. I hadn't been able to stop myself. I hadn't said it back because I'd wanted to *show* her I loved her.

Now she would never know how much I loved her. All she would know is that I didn't say it back. Less than twenty-four hours after we had been together for the first time, she'd come home from work to find my dick in Cammie's mouth and to hear the words "I love you" said in the dark to the wrong person.

In our bed. In the house I'd bought to make a home for my future wife and family. In my eyes, the house was as much hers as it was mine. It wasn't a home without her in it.

Half the people had been dressed in costume that night. Cammie must have snuck in that way.

All I knew was that I had been asleep then woken up by a small, warm body under the covers with me. Her hands had been on me, stroking my dick as my mind had slowly woken up. My body had definitely been awake and reacting to being touched.

The scene played constantly in my mind.

Since Teagan had run away from me, I'd called and I texted her relentlessly. I'd even gone to her job. I had acted like a crazy person trying to find her, but she had been nowhere to be found. She hadn't gone back to her parents' house, and even if her family and friends had known where she was, they sure as fuck weren't telling me.

Well over a week later and still no contact with Teagan, I was forcing myself to return to work. I drove in a daze. Once I arrived, I went straight to my workbench. The second I lifted the lid of my toolbox I regretted it. The images of a happy couple stared back at me. I pulled them from the lid and took them out to my car.

On the way back to the shop, Z called me into her office. Not wanting to talk to anyone, I kept walking.

"Jeremy? Please don't ignore me," Zoey said from the doorway behind me.

"What do you want, Z?" I turned. "I'm not in the mood to talk. I just want to work and go home."

She frowned, but the pity in her eyes pissed me off. I didn't need anyone's pity. I was getting exactly what I'd deserved. My past had reared its ugly head and taken a piece of my life that I'd never get back.

"Have you talked to Teagan?" Zoey asked.

"No."

"Are you still trying, Jer? You can't give up—"

"What the hell do you think I've been doing since she left, Zoey?" I yelled. "She's gone!"

"Don't yell at me," she whispered. "I just want to help."

"Yeah? Well, I don't need your fucking help. I need you to mind your own business."

Zoey's eyes grew as big as saucers about one second before the shove came from behind.

Big hands slammed against my back and propelled me a few feet down the hall. The same big hands grabbed me and spun me around, shoving me against the wall.

The blue eyes of my brother-in-law came in to focus as he inched closer to my face. "Don't you ever fucking talk to her like that again, Jeremy," Andy growled. "Do it again, and we'll have problems."

I nodded. He let go of me and I turned to my sister. "Sorry, Z." It had been a dick move, but I didn't know what else to say to her. She gave me a curt nod and went back into her office with Andy right behind her, and I went to work.

Two days later and everyone was still treating me differently. They barely spoke to me. My own family knew what a piece of shit I was. I drove home in the darkest mood only to find Teagan's belongings gone.

I immediately grabbed a bottle of Patrón and made him my new best friend.

My phone rang, but I let it go to voicemail. I didn't want to speak to anyone. I opened my eyes, and my vision was blurry for some reason. Teagan's face was in front of mine, resting on her pillow. I blinked rapidly, trying to clear my vision to see her better, but when it finally cleared, she was gone.

She was never there. Yet, she was everywhere in this house.

I saw her in the kitchen cooking. I saw her lying beside me in our bed, and on the couch next to me as I stared blankly at the TV on the wall. As soon as I blinked, she was gone.

I'd been drinking most of the day.

Shit, I wouldn't lie . . . I'd been drinking nearly every day for the last two weeks.

I had ruined something so perfect and precious I was physically ill. I rolled to my side and pulled Teagan's pillow close, breathing in the scent of her shampoo that was rapidly fading. It was all I had left of her. Her white pillowcase didn't match the new black bedding I had bought after I ripped off the other set and set fire to it in my backyard fire pit. Results of another evening spent with my new best friend Patrón.

I closed my eyes and drifted back into my self-induced tequila coma.

Uncertain of exactly how much later it was, I was woken up by someone pounding on my front door. I ignored them because I didn't want to see anyone. Whoever was at the door would get tired of waiting for me to answer and leave.

Unless they had a fucking key.

I heard voices in the living room now, and my sister called out for me. I didn't answer. *Please, go away.*

A moment later, Zoey stepped inside the room and I made eye contact with her. Again, with pity in her eyes.

"Jeremy, please," she begged. "You need to get up. It's not healthy for you to keep doing this to yourself. What happened was not your fault."

Boy, she didn't know how wrong she was. I rolled the other way on the bed so I didn't have to see her because her gaze of pity had turned to sympathy.

I didn't deserve it.

The mattress sunk down behind me as Zoey sat on the bed. In the next second, she was lying behind me, hugging me so tightly I didn't know what to do other than apologize for upsetting her.

"I'm so sorry, Jeremy," she said. Then she got up from the bed and walked toward the doorway. "He's in here. Do it."

I didn't know who she was talking to, or what they planned on doing, but more people came in my room. The next thing I knew, Andy, Noah, and Jason were carrying me to the bathroom. Zoey turned on the water and the three assholes set me on my feet, and pushed me into the shower fully clothed. The water was freezing cold, but I didn't care. I stood and let it rain over me.

After a few minutes, I was shivering from the cold, but still, I stood there.

"Jeremy Douglas James," Zoey called from the other side of the shower curtain. "If you don't take a proper shower and get rid of the awful fucking stench you've got going on, these three are going to strip your ass naked and help you. And I *know* you don't want that."

A slight smile creased my face at the thought. Those fuckers would do it too.

"Yes, Mother," I muttered, turning the water to hot and stripping off my smelly work shirt. "Get the hell out of my bathroom. I promise not to drown myself."

The shower curtain moved quickly toward me, and someone from the other side of it punched me.

"Don't ever say that again, Jeremy," Zoey growled.

I can't believe she just punched me.

"You hit like a girl, Z," I said, because that's what I told her every time she hit me.

"Screw you. I am a girl." She punched me again. A lot harder this time, to get her point across.

"Alright, alright, I'm shutting up. Now, get the fuck out of my bathroom. I am not showering with all of you in here."

The door closed and I was finally alone in my own bathroom. I pulled the rest of my wet clothes off and tossed them to the tile floor.

Once I was clean and out of the shower, I felt a little better. I definitely smelled better.

Apparently, wallowing in your own stench, along with wallowing in shame and misery, was a bad combination. Honestly, I didn't remember when my last shower was.

Gross.

During my destruction mode, Sonny had dropped off tequila on my doorstep after I'd called and begged him to. He wouldn't even come inside the house because somehow he'd found out about the Cammie incident. When I did eat, I'd called and had take-out delivered and had probably gained ten pounds from all the garbage I'd ingested.

Once dressed, I pulled all the bedding from my bed, except Teagan's pillowcase and tossed them in the washer.

I found three of my four unwanted visitors in the living room watching TV. Zoey was in the kitchen doing something, so I poked my head through the doorway to see her cleaning out my fridge. She popped the lid off a plastic container, took a whiff of whatever was inside, gagged, and tossed the whole thing into the trash.

Whatever, I didn't care anymore.

"Why are you here?" I asked nobody in particular, after sitting on the couch staring at the wall for almost an hour.

Zoey came into the living room when she heard me talking. "We're going out to dinner *as a family* for your birthday, Jeremy. You do realize it's today, right?"

No. I didn't. I would rather forget about it and go back to

bed. That reminded me that my sheets were still in the washer. Saying nothing, I left the room and put my sheets into the dryer. I would be going back to bed shortly, so I'd need them, even though I had several sets in the closet.

As soon as I turned around to leave the laundry room, Andy blocked the doorway.

"What?"

"You need to get your shit together, brother," Andy said.

Well, considering I was a piece of shit, that should be a piece of cake, right?

"My shit's together, *brother*," I said as I tried to squeeze between his body and the doorjamb.

He blocked me and I glared at him. "What the fuck, man?"

"Jeremy, you're going to get your shit together and go out to dinner with your family. Then you're going to eat the birthday cake your sister spent all morning baking and decorating for you. And you're going to pretend to enjoy every bite of it. You feel me?"

Well shit.

Andy didn't stop there. "You're also going to meet your new niece Chloe tonight for the first time, since you didn't go to the hospital when she was born."

Fuck. Fuck. Fuck.

I counted back and realized I'd missed the first six days of my niece's life and I didn't even know what she looked like. I gave Andy a curt nod.

"Can you send Noah down here please? I need to speak to him."

Why don't we add being a horrible brother, uncle, and all around general fuck up to the ever-growing reasons of why I hate myself? If not going to the hospital to see Jess and Chloe wasn't bad enough, I just now learned my new niece's name.

There were three reasons why I hadn't gone to the hospital when Jess went in to labor.

One- Teagan

Two- Cammie

Three- I was a piece of shit

I had been worried about running in to either one of them while I was there. Scared that the mere *sight* of me would cause Teagan more pain and angry enough that if I saw Cammie, I would do something to be arrested.

"You wanted to see me?" Noah said from the doorway, breaking my train of thought.

Swallowing hard, I stepped over to my brother and hugged him.

"I'm sorry, Noah," I said, my voice gravelly and remorseful. I expected him to push me away because he was pissed at me, but he did the exact opposite.

He hugged me back.

"I know." He released me. "Jer, nobody is mad at you. I know you think that, but it's not true. Nobody knows what to say to you, especially after you blew up at Z."

Guilt filled me again. "I shouldn't have done that. And I should've been at the hospital when your baby girl was born. Can we go see her now?"

Noah nodded and we rejoined the others in the living room. With more people to apologize to, I walked straight up to Jason. "Thanks for coming, bro. Sorry if I was being a dick at work and you had to take care of my jobs."

"It's all good," he said, pulling me into a hug. He slapped me on the back a couple of times before releasing me.

Next, I moved on to Zoey. She was a hugger, so I wrapped my arms around her and squeezed. Out of everyone in my family, I'd probably hurt her the most during the last two weeks and she hadn't deserved one bit of it. "I'm sorry, Z. I know you were only trying to help, but I don't know what I'm doing. My life is a mess."

Zoey nodded and I knew she understood exactly what I meant. "I know, Jer. We've all been where you are, and know how badly it hurts. I'm sorry I upset you the other day."

I released my sister and Andy was immediately at her side. He pushed her hair away from her face and they had one of their silent conversations. Zoey smiled and Andy pulled her in close, kissing the top of her head. He shot me a look and offered me his hand. I took it, knowing it was his way of letting me know we were good.

I followed the four of them to Rico's pizza where the rest of my family was waiting for us. I made my rounds, apologizing to everyone. I met my new niece, who was absolutely adorable, and my Sweet Pea showed me how she could now stand with her mom holding on to her hands.

After we'd eaten dinner and cake, Zoey brought Hannah over to me. I cradled her against me, breathing in her sweet baby scent. I had missed her so much, and she instantly wrapped her tiny arms around my neck, snuggling into the crook.

I swore her cuddling brought tears to my eyes. She let out a sigh and I didn't know how, but this tiny girl, who was almost nine months old now, seemed like she knew how I felt and wanted to comfort me. I rubbed my hand up and down her back to soothe her until she fell asleep.

Andy motioned for me to bring her over and I handed her off to him. He smiled down at her and kissed her cheek.

Suddenly, it hit me that I may never find that for myself. And the mere thought of Teagan being pregnant because we hadn't used protection made me want to vomit. I prayed that she wasn't, because having *my* child after everything that had happened would only cause her more pain.

I need a drink.

Looking toward the small beer and wine bar, I considered going to get a pitcher of beer, when I spotted familiar, bouncing red curls in the distance. The air whooshed from my lungs, and within an instant, I was on my feet chasing after her before I even knew what I was doing.

Why was I chasing after her when I wasn't worthy of her?

Because, I was out of my fucking mind in love with her and I needed to tell her how sorry I was.

She entered the hallway that led to the restrooms, and I followed. Pausing outside the women's restroom to gather my thoughts, I finally pushed open the door and slipped quietly inside.

"Teagan?"

She gasped from behind a bathroom stall and I knew I'd scared her.

"*Jeremy,* is that you?"

"Yes. I'm sorry for following you in here, but . . . I don't know what the hell I'm doing."

She actually laughed, catching me off guard. "You realize you're in the ladies room, right?"

For the first time in two weeks, I laughed. "Yes, I'm aware."

"Jeremy, I don't mean to sound rude, but I really need to pee and I can't do it with you in here. Can you step outside?"

Fuck no. There was a window in here, and if I knew her, she'd be jumping out of it as soon as I left the room. Thinking quickly, I turned on every faucet in the bathroom filling the space with the sounds of running water. "There, I can't hear anything now."

Leaning against the wall, I waited for her. She came out of the stall eventually and my heart clutched in my chest at the sight of her. She was dressed up and looked beautiful.

She stepped over to the row of sinks and shut off all the faucets except for one. After she washed her hands, she turned to face me. Her eyes shot to my right, and I realized I was leaning on the paper towel dispenser. I righted myself, pulled several towels out, and handed them to her.

"Thank you," she said quietly, staring up at me.

Her eyes were tired and she looked unhappy. But, she was still the most beautiful creature to walk on this Earth.

"You look like shit, Jeremy."

That comment should have hurt, but it didn't. She was right. "That's because I am shit."

The look on her face was sad and bewildered by what I'd said. Teagan tossed the paper towels into the trashcan and inched closer to me. Her hand came up to my face so fast I closed my eyes and prepared for the slap I deserved.

I would gladly take it and a thousand more, if that was what it took for her to show me how much she hated me.

The slap didn't come.

Instead, she placed both of her hands on my face. My arms quickly reached around her, pulling her close to me. She draped her arms around my neck and pressed her cheek on my chest, and in an instant, I was in heaven.

"I'm so sorry, Teagan. I didn't know it was her, I swear to

you—on my life—I didn't know. *I didn't know.* I'm sorry I never told you I love you, because I do. I love you so much, and I know everything is screwed up—"

She jerked away from me, her eyes filled with tears. They were my undoing. I couldn't stand to see them so I forced myself to look away.

"It still doesn't change anything, though," she whispered.

My eyes met hers again and I couldn't tell what she was thinking. To my surprise, she rose up on her toes and brushed a kiss across my lips.

"I need to go, Jeremy. I'm here with someone, and I should get back," she said.

Oh God, she's here with someone? A date? It's not your business, asshole. You ruined everything . . .

Stepping aside, I let her pass and she walked out the door and out of my life again.

My body went numb and what was left of my heart crumbled. I exited the restroom and headed out the restaurant door to my car. I didn't tell anyone in my family I was leaving, I just left and drove straight to the bar.

By last call, I had drowned my sorrows with tequila and brushed off every woman who had attempted to speak to me. I vaguely remembered responding to one of Zoey's phone calls asking where I was, so I wouldn't worry her.

"Jeremy," Sam, the bartender, said from across the bar. "I called you a taxi but they won't be here for thirty minutes. You gonna be alright waiting for it outside?"

"Yeah. Thanks, Sam," I mumbled as I crammed my phone and car keys into the pocket of my shorts. I wasn't in any condition to be driving anywhere and I knew it, so I went outside and leaned up against the building to wait for the taxi.

I didn't wait outside for long before I nearly froze my ass off, dressed in shorts and a T-shirt in the middle of November. *Fucking moron.* I decided to sit in my car to wait for the taxi because I was so cold. I fired up my car and turned on the heater full blast. Once I started to warm up, I leaned my head on the headrest and closed my eyes for just a minute.

Unfortunately, I dozed off and was woken up by someone tapping on my window. Looking over, I was blinded by a flashlight shining through the glass and the bright flashing of red and blue lights in front of my car.

Fuck me.

Thirty minutes later, I sat cuffed in the back of a cop car on my way to jail for DUI. Even though I hadn't been driving, I'd still been arrested. Apparently, sitting in your car with the motor running while being drunk, was not legal.

Who knew?

The humor of it all was I'd been freaking delirious and unable to stop laughing during the entire episode. Tears had been dripping down my face, and I hadn't been able to wipe them away because my hands were cuffed behind my back.

First off, the cop on the passenger side of the car had been a dick. He'd already accused me of being a drug dealer because I drove an expensive car. Next, he'd called me a "spic" because I *"look like a Mexican." No shit, I am Mexican.* He went from calling me a spic to renaming me *Jose.*

It hadn't ended there. Apparently, I'd left my wallet inside the bar, because I hadn't been able to find it. So what had I done? Because he was being a total douchebag and I really had nothing more to lose, I'd fucked with him right back.

Yeah, I'd called him a pig. He'd asked me my name and what had popped out of my mouth?

Frank Sinatra.

Next, they'd located my car registration in my glove box and had seen my real name on it. They'd found it unbelievable because I was a *spic,* and the name on the registration wasn't Mexican. The business cards I carried in my car for James Racing also indicated that I was, in fact, a business owner, and *not* a drug dealer.

So then, they'd assumed the car was stolen and hadn't been reported yet. They'd impounded my baby and the last time I'd seen her, she was being pulled onto the back of a tow truck.

Now, Douchebag cop on the passenger side dug through the bag that held my personal belongings and pulled out my cell.

"Let's see what we have here, Jose," he said, sounding exactly like Lieutenant Jim-fucking-Dangle from the show *Reno 911.*

My laughing stopped and I sobered right up when he asked, "Do you know you've missed sixteen texts, Jose?" He scrolled through my phone, reading off the names. "Zoey, Andy, Mom, My beloved, Noah. Whoa, what was that? My beloved?" He turned in his seat and smirked at me. "This ought to be good."

Fuck! Teagan texted me?

He read her text to me. *"Where are you? I came by your house and you weren't there. I've thought about it since we ran in to each other earlier, and I think I'm ready to talk. Can you meet me?"*

Fuck my life.

I glared through the cage separating the front and back seats. That dirty motherfucker was typing out a response to her. "What the hell are you doing?" I yelled, struggling against my restraints.

He laughed and read to me what he'd typed. *"Sorry, can't meet. With someone. Go fuck yourself."* My phone made the swooshing sound when the fucker sent her the message.

I leaned over onto my side and kicked the back of his seat as hard as I could. "You fucking prick! You have no idea what you've just done!"

My phone chimed with an incoming text and he read it back to me. "Oops, looks like you're in lots of trouble back there, *amigo*. She says you're cruel and she's leaving for Denver tomorrow."

Oh, shit . . . no. She's going back to Denver?

My pulse was pounding so loud in my ears I barely heard him when he said, *"Have a nice life."* I watched helplessly as the bastard typed the words into my phone then hit send.

I'm gonna beat the shit out of this dickhead.

When we arrived at the jail to go through processing, he roughed me up as we walked, causing my feet to tangle together. I wasn't taking what he did to Teagan lightly. Before I hit the floor, I swept my leg out and knocked his feet out from under him. He crumpled like a sack of potatoes, and I laughed.

"Stupid asshole," I muttered, and watched him pick himself up. The other officer yanked me up from the floor by my arm and shoved me down on a hard chair.

That stunt got me shackled around the ankles and chained to the chair for several hours. Oh well. If I was going to jail, might as well make it worthwhile, right?

Wrong.

Two long days later, someone finally came to tell me the charges had been dropped, and I was being let out. I had no idea what was going on because when they'd offered me my phone call, I'd told them to fuck off.

Once I was processed back out of jail, I found Zoey and Andy waiting for me.

Shit. I am so dead.

Andy was scary when he was angry, and I made a vow then never to piss him off again. Neither of them uttered a word to me as I walked behind them out the door. Zoey headed straight to her Tahoe, climbed inside, and left.

When she backed out, I spotted my Caddy next to where she'd been parked. Andy held his hand out to me, palm up. "Keys," he said angrily, and I couldn't get them out of my pocket and into his hand fast enough.

He dropped into the driver's seat of my car and started it up, so I went around to the passenger side and got in. Andy pulled out of the parking lot and drove in the opposite direction of my house.

Fuck. I silently prayed he hadn't brought a shovel with him because as angry as he was I wouldn't be surprised if he had plans to take me out to the country, kill me, and bury me.

"You know," Andy said, "if I had it my way, we would be on our way to see my lawyer and get your stupid ass removed as Hannah's guardian."

Oh, shit. I couldn't say I blamed him, though.

"For some reason, your sister still believes in you, so I won't do it. *Yet.*"

He glared over at me, and I took his warning straight to what was left of my heart. *I can't lose my Sweet Pea. I just can't.*

"Okay. I'm sorry, Andy. I'll get it together, but please don't take her away from me, too."

Andy sighed. "You owe your sister a shitload of money for getting your ass out of jail, and you better kiss the ground she walks on after this."

"How did she get me out?" *Not to mention getting the assault on an officer and DUI charges dropped.*

Andy turned down a side street and flipped a U-turn, heading back the direction we'd come from. *Guess we're not going to the country.*

"She called Kyle when someone from the police department called to see if anyone in the family was missing a Cadillac CTS-V."

Ah, yes, Officer Kyle Sherman. Andy's good friend.

"It would've been a lot easier to find you if you'd given them your real name when they arrested you." He actually smirked. "Frank Sinatra? What is that all about?"

I laughed. "You don't want to know. All I am going to say is it involves Teagan."

Oh shit, Teagan went back to Denver. I dug my cell out of my pocket and scrolled through the texts the prick officer had sent her. I fired off a text to her to apologize, and it came back as 'undeliverable'. What the fuck? I called her phone, and it was no longer in service.

Son of a bitch.

Andy pulled into my driveway next to Zoey's Tahoe. He shut off the engine, tossed me my keys, and got out. I stepped out of my Caddy and he glared over the roof at me. "Get your shit together, Jeremy. I won't hesitate next time, no matter how much your sister believes in you."

Once they were gone, I ran into my house to do everything humanly possible to find Teagan. I couldn't let her go back to Denver. I had to get her back, no matter the cost.

Teagan

December 2013

"Hooker-face? You ready?" Reese called from the bathroom as Sonny and I sat on his bed, my stomach in a ball of knots.

"Yes . . . no! No, wait, I'm not ready. Oh, God." I sat for a few more seconds wondering if my life would be changing with the words Reese was about to say. "One, two, three, go!" I yelled.

Gripping Sonny's hand tightly, I closed my eyes and cringed.

"Negative!" Reese shouted. "All ten of those bitches."

Opening my eyes, I let out a sigh, and then suddenly burst in to tears. Sonny put his arm around my shoulders and pulled me in close. I didn't know why I was crying. *I should be happy that I'm not pregnant, right?*

Ten pregnancy tests proved it. Yes, ten tests were probably a bit much, but I'd had to be sure. My period never came in November, but I was definitely not pregnant. All of the stress since the night after Halloween was the most likely culprit.

So why was I crying? Did I want to be pregnant with Jeremy's baby?

Don't be silly, Teagan, your life is a mess.

All I knew was I still loved him and missed him like crazy.

Reese sat next to me on the bed and pulled me onto his lap. Wrapping me in his strong arms, he comforted me. "Shh, Teagan. Calm down. Everything is okay," he whispered then kissed my head. "I'm sorry. I don't know what to say right now to make this any better or easier for you."

That made two of us.

I wiped the tears from my face with the backs of my hands. "I really thought he was the one person I could trust." I took a deep breath then let it out. "I miss him so much, Reese."

"I know you do." He consoled me while Sonny sat quietly, probably not knowing what to do since he was Jeremy's friend. "Do you think you'll ever talk to him and find out what happened that night?"

I shrugged my shoulders. "That's the hard part. I *was* willing to talk to him and sent him a text telling him I was ready . . . and then he sent all those horrible texts back. I'm even more confused because that is so out of character for him. What I *do* know for sure, is that I can't un-see what I saw with him and Cammie."

Remembering that night still made me sick. The sight was ten times worse than catching Gary and Katie in the act because I truly loved Jeremy. I had loved Gary at one time in my life, but he had ruined that along the way with the cheating and the insults regarding my weight and job. What Gary hated about me were the things that Jeremy loved the most and that made me love him even more.

He accepted me for who I was inside and out.

"Reese, Sonny, I think I need to be alone if you don't mind."

Reese hugged me tight and kissed my head.

"Let us know if you need anything. I'm going to the store to get a bunch of junk food and find a chick flick for us. We'll have a night in to snuggle before you go back to your cousin's tomorrow."

"That sounds like a perfect night. I love you, Reese. Thank you."

He turned to Sonny and asked, "You wanna come with, or stay home?"

"You go ahead. I have a couple things I need to get ready

for work next week, but I'll be done by the time you get back," Sonny replied.

When Reese went to leave, I noticed the sweet smile Sonny gave him as he passed. When Reese had told me a month ago that Sonny had agreed to be his roommate, I had been thrilled for him and myself. Reese had finally settled in Sacramento. He loved his job, his new friends, and I loved having him so close.

Sonny gave me a nervous wave then followed Reese out of the room to go to his bedroom.

I pulled the covers back on Reese's bed, slid in, and yanked them up over my head. My life for the last month had been a whirlwind of both good and bad events, and I needed some time to think.

I'd only been alone for a short time, when a light tapping on the bedroom door startled me. "Who is it?" I called out, just in case . . .

"It's me, Sonny."

"Come on in."

Sonny entered the room, his expression uncertain. His eyes went to the floor as he asked, "Can I talk to you for a minute?"

Sitting up on the bed, I made room for him and motioned for him to take a seat.

"Is everything okay?" I asked.

He shifted and ran his fingers through his hair. "Look, Teagan, this is really hard for me . . . Jeremy's my best friend and, well . . . Reese . . ."

Poor Sonny. He was understandably torn between his long-time friendship with Jeremy, his new living situation with Reese, and now I was inserting myself right into the middle of it just by being here. But I knew he had deeper-seated issues than just these.

"You like him a lot, don't you?" I asked, knowing what he was attempting to tell me. "Sonny, I've known Reese a long time, and he told me how hard it was to finally speak up and trust the people closest to you with your secrets. Especially if you think it's something the other person might not want to hear, but I'm not that person. You can tell me anything and I will never judge you."

His lips pursed and his light brown eyes drifted up to meet mine. "I guess I don't have to tell you I'm gay since it seems you already know."

"I've known since the night you met Reese, but it wasn't my place to say anything, Sonny. It's your business and your story to tell if and when you are ready."

"Thank you, Teagan. I do like Reese, and I think the feeling is mutual. We'll just have to see how it goes. But, he's really helped me to put a lot of things into perspective. I'm almost ready to tell my family and friends. I know I'll lose some of them and that hurts, but I can't keep hiding who I am . . . I just want to be free."

Tears filled his eyes and spilled over when I reached out and squeezed his hand.

Sitting up on my knees, I wiped the wetness from his handsome face. "Well, my friend, I am proud of you and I really do wish you and Reese all the best."

The slamming of the front door startled us and we hurried to the living room to see what was going on. As soon as we spotted Reese, we heard loud banging on the door, causing all three of us to jump.

"I know you're in there, Reese!"

Oh, holy crap. Jeremy was here.

"Open the door, please . . . please tell me where Teagan is."

"What should I do?" Reese asked. "He was waiting for me in the parking lot and I ran like hell the minute I saw him."

"Reese!" Jeremy yelled again, his voice muffled by the door. "*Please* tell me where she is."

Sonny's expression was complete panic, as was mine.

"Shit, both of you go hide. I'll figure something out," Reese said as he waved us toward the hallway.

Sonny and I went into Reese's room and locked the door. With our ears pressed to the door, we listened as Reese opened the door to Jeremy. "She's not here, man. Wait, you can't come in!"

"You're her best friend, Reese. Where else would she be? Please, let me see her."

"I don't know what to tell you, Jeremy. She's not here."

"Did she really go back to Colorado?"

He was clearly distraught from the sound of his voice. My arms ached to hold him again and my heart skipped a beat because he was just on the other side of the wall from me.

"Yes, but it was only for a couple of days. One of her former patients passed away and she went for the funeral. She's back, but she doesn't live here."

"Her phone's been shut off. Why?" Jeremy asked.

"She lost it at the airport and just hasn't gotten a new one yet."

"Okay . . . okay. Please tell me where she is. I need to talk to her, man. I love her and need to see her."

For several minutes, we only heard silence from the living room and I imagined the two men staring each other down, unwilling to give up. Sonny and I backed away from the door and I accidentally bumped Reese's dresser, knocking over his bottle of cologne. We turned to each other and cringed at the noise.

"What the hell, Reese?" Jeremy muttered. "Teagan, please come out and talk to me, or I'm coming in there."

Knowing he'd break down the door, I decided to reveal myself and get the confrontation over with. I turned the lock, but in one swift and sneaky move, Sonny slipped into the hallway, yanking the door closed behind him. I tried to pull the door open, but he must have been holding it shut.

"Hi, Jeremy," Sonny said.

"Sonny? What are you doing here?" Jeremy asked.

"I live here. Can we talk?"

He had just sacrificed himself to save me. *Oh, Sonny.*

"What the hell is going on here?" Jeremy asked, the confusion in his voice obvious.

"I've been wanting to tell you something for a while, and I think now's as good a time as any, but first let's go sit down in the living room," Sonny said.

"Is someone going to tell me what's going on?" Jeremy asked. "Why are you here, Sonny?

After they moved into the living room, I opened the door a

crack and took a seat on the carpeted floor.

If Sonny was going to come out to Jeremy, the next several minutes were going to be very hard on both of them. I wished I were out there to support Sonny and Jeremy because their friendship was about to be changed forever.

"Like I said—I live here," Sonny reiterated, his voice surprisingly calm and collected.

"You're roommates," Jeremy commented, but I heard the question in his voice.

Reese kept quiet knowing this was Sonny's time to talk.

"Yes and no," Sonny said. His voice quavered a bit, and I silently urged him to let it all out.

"What does that mean?" Jeremy asked.

"Remember when you moved into your house and I shoved John for the comment he'd made about being gay?" I assumed Jeremy confirmed because Sonny continued, "You said I could tell you anything . . . this isn't easy for me to say, so I'm just going to come out and say it . . . I—I'm gay, Jeremy. I've known I was different since I was little . . . that time on the playground when we were in third grade and you pulled those three kids off of me—they were calling me a fag, Jeremy. They were kicking the crap out of me, calling me a fag. I was eight years old and didn't even know what that meant."

"Fuck . . ." Jeremy said as the breath left his lungs.

My heart hurt for Sonny now, and for the torment he'd gone through as a child.

For several seconds, nobody said a word. I couldn't stand the silence. Sonny had just told his best friend his deepest, darkest secret and Jeremy's response angered me. He'd helped an eight-year-old child being bullied and beaten by his classmates, but he wasn't saying anything now? From my seat on the floor, I inched open the door and poked my head out to see what was going on in the living room.

Jeremy was standing in the middle of the room with his back to me. He was looking down at Sonny, who was sitting on the couch with his head in his hands. Suddenly, Jeremy reached out and set a hand on top of his friend's hand. Sonny took it and Jeremy pulled him up from the couch.

I held my breath.

Tears flooded my eyes as Jeremy pulled Sonny into a tight, bro-hug, and hung on to him as if his life depended on it. My faith in Jeremy revived . . . at least with regards to his friends.

Finally, Jeremy smacked Sonny on the back, like I'd seen him do so many times and said, "This doesn't change a thing, man. You've been my friend for more than twenty years and no matter what, I've got your back."

When Sonny's tough façade finally cracked, I couldn't watch anymore. The last image I saw was the two of them releasing each other, and a look of relief on Sonny's tear streaked face. Quietly, I pulled my head back into the room and shut the door to a crack again.

The two of them talked a bit longer about Sonny's revelation while my butt grew sore from sitting on the floor for so long. Just when I was about to return to the bed, Reese did the unthinkable.

"What happened the night of the Halloween party, Jeremy?" he asked. "If you have any chance of getting Teagan back, you're going to have to spill it . . . and I mean everything. Did you cheat on our girl?"

"No!" Jeremy said. "I love her and would never cheat on her. What happened that night was one big cluster fuck caused by Cammie."

"Teagan needs to know the truth. Tell me everything that happened after I left the party, right now, and I promise to talk to her. What she does with the information after that is up to her. Deal?"

"Hell yes," Jeremy replied.

Suddenly I was no longer pissed that Reese was asking Jeremy about that night without my permission because he was doing it for my benefit. I wanted to run out there and kiss him.

By the time their hour-long conversation was over, I knew Cammie had snuck into the house unnoticed and crawled into our bed with Jeremy. He'd thought it was me, just like he'd told Cammie that night when he'd run after me.

And he'd thought I'd been on a date the evening I'd seen him at Rico's pizza, but I'd been there with Ed and Rita Dixon, the owners of Nanna's home, having a spur-of-the-moment job interview. Because of this simple misunderstanding, he'd left his thirtieth birthday dinner with his family and landed himself in jail. I was livid when I found out how the police had treated him, especially with the texts.

Seeing Jeremy, looking like hell, broke my heart. Now, I knew for certain he hadn't lied about not knowing Cammie was in bed with him that night. However, I still couldn't be with him as long as Cammie continued to play her games. She knew where he lived. And I was convinced she wouldn't stop harassing him. Thankfully I was free of her—now that I was working at Nanna's facility.

Once Jeremy left, I jumped back into bed and Reese came into the bedroom with two bags full of junk food, a now-cold pizza, and a DVD from his collection.

"You ready for company?"

"I am. Thank you for talking to Jeremy about what happened, Reese. I have a lot to think about. And I'm going to take some time to see what Cammie does."

"Just take your time, hooker-face. If he loves you as much as he says he does, he'll wait until you're ready."

Smiling at him, I sat up on the bed, arranging our food and drinks, while he kicked off his shoes and changed into basketball shorts. After starting the movie, he hopped into bed with me.

"Is Sonny joining us?" I asked.

Reese grinned and scooted to the center of the bed, making room. "Sonny! Get that cute booty of yours in here. It's time to introduce you to chick flick night."

Sonny came in and made himself at home on the California king-sized bed with us. He let out a laugh when Reese told him we were watching *Fried Green Tomatoes*.

"I love this movie. Kathy Bates is epic." He grabbed a handful of popcorn then settled in to our new group of three.

Halfway through the movie, Reese's cell phone rang. After looking at the screen, he said, "It's for you," and handed me the phone.

"*Holy shit balls, Teagan,*" Jackie whispered excitedly. "You are never gonna believe this."

"What am I never going to believe, Jacks?"

"There's a cop here, and he's talking to Cammie. It doesn't look like a social call, if you know what I mean."

Cammie is being questioned by the police? "Get your butt closer and see what they're talking about," I told her. "I want to know what's going on."

"I'm on it. Let me sneak over there."

I waited on the line while Jackie found a way to hear what the officer was saying to Cammie. The whole time, she trilled the theme song to *Mission Impossible* and it was hard not to laugh at her.

"Okay, Teags. I am closer, but it's hard to hear them."

"Thank you, Jacks. I owe you for this."

"Alrighty, he just said that she could be charged with trespassing, for starters. Oh, you should see the look on her face. Now he says what she did is a felony. Oh crap, he moved and I can't hear him."

There was a long pause on the line before Jackie spoke again. "Um, he just asked her what would happen to a man if he snuck into a woman's house and did the same thing. Holy shit balls, Teagan, she is freaking out. I don't think I've ever seen a fake tan fade that fast! She's turning as white as a ghost."

Holy crap, I wished I could see what was happening. "Now what's going on, Jacks?"

"Shit, they almost caught me. I've got to get out of here before they see me. Hang on."

Dead silence filled the air before she came back on the line. "Sorry Teags, I didn't want to get busted."

I snickered at my sneaky friend. "You've done more than enough, girl. Don't get in trouble on my account."

"It's all good, I'm safe," she laughed. "The last thing I saw was Cammie crying as the cute, baby-faced cop mentioned felonies and jail."

Baby-faced cop? Is it Kyle, Andy's cop friend? It has to be.

"Thank you so much, Jackie."

"That's what *real* friends do for each other, Teags. By the way, Nat and I are missing you like crazy. Can't wait to see ya when we go for our night out."

"I miss you guys, too, but I am so happy to be out of that hospital."

After we hung up, I set Reese's phone down on the bed. "Sorry everyone has to call your phone, Reese. I can't believe I lost mine."

"It's fine hooker-face, my phone is your phone as long as you need it." Reese put on a pouty face. "I don't want you to go back to Brit's tomorrow." He threw his arms around me and pulled me closer. "Snuggle with me right now, hooker-face."

Sonny laughed at our antics.

But, of course, I snuggled the hell out of Reese.

The next morning, I woke up to a thigh poke from Reese junior before I hopped in the shower. Later that morning, I had several errands to run, a new phone to buy, and to make a trip to the bank. After I'd attended the funeral for Eloise Larsen, my final patient while working for Denver Home Hospice, her estate lawyer had approached me, because apparently, she'd left me something in her will. I laughed, thinking it was the *Duck Dynasty* DVD collection I had sent for her birthday. She had been obsessed with the show and I'd endured hours of watching it with her.

Boy was I wrong. *Well, partially wrong . . .*

When I'd taken my seat on the plane home, I'd had the *Duck Dynasty* DVD's *and* a check in my purse for fifty thousand dollars.

At my new job, I was paired up with the patients who were extremely ill because of my hospice experience. I worked my rotations with Dr. McGuinness, who was brilliant. She knew how to treat her patients, the staff, and how to dress.

Seriously, that woman worked a pair of five-inch heels and a pencil skirt like nobody's business. I didn't know how the heck she wore those heels every single day. Depending on what I was doing, my feet barely made it through a day wearing my expensive and well-padded nurse's shoes.

To celebrate surviving my first week at my new job, I was

on my way to Dub's to meet Jackie and Nat. I knew Jeremy might be there and a part of me hoped he would be.

Every day, I woke up missing him more and more. I wished things between us were different, but with Cammie still around, I couldn't risk sacrificing the peace and quiet I'd found through my new job by becoming involved with him. But most of all I couldn't be with Jeremy because of the vision of him and Cammie together. Once that vision of them in our bed popped into my head, I struggled to banish it.

I hated it.

I hated what it did to me and how it made me feel.

I hated that because of it, I couldn't get my life with Jeremy back.

Because that's what I wanted—him in my life, but that couldn't happen until I could get the vision of him and Cammie out of my head.

I needed time—lots of time to recover from this. After seeing Jeremy and Cammie together, I'd realized how deeply all the cheating in my life had affected me, Gary's as well as my cheating prick father's.

Arriving at Dub's, I found my friends waiting for me with a tray full of tequila shots. I dropped down on the couch next to Nat and noticed she had a cat-that-ate-the-canary look on her face.

"What happened now?" I asked, knowing it had *something* to do with Cammie.

Nat wiggled excitedly and clapped her hands with a huge grin on her face. "She's gone. Today was her last day!"

Holy crap.

"Where did she go?" I asked, still unable to believe what I was hearing.

"Rumor is she's been in and out of HR all week, so I'm not sure what happened. All I know is she's moving to Portland where her dad lives."

I turned away to hide the tears that pricked my eyes.

She's leaving town. But not to go to jail where she belongs. Jeremy must not be pressing charges. I wondered why, but it was his decision, not mine.

Would my misery finally be over with her out of the state? I picked up a shot of tequila in each hand and slammed them back quickly.

"Teags, you okay?" Jackie asked me.

"Honestly, I don't know."

Suddenly, I was angry. "That *stupid bitch* has fucked up my life for months and ruined what I thought was going to be—" I was so mad, I slammed back two more shots of tequila then I took several deep breaths. "I thought Jeremy and I were going to be together . . . then her stupid ass swoops in with her fake tits and craziness, and in five fucking minutes, she's taken everything away from me. She's ruined the lives of two people and is getting off scot-free by moving away."

Jackie spoke up first. "Teags, do you really think it's ruined? If you and Jeremy love each other, you can get through this."

"Easier said than done, Jacks. All I can think about is what I saw that night. I know in my heart he is a victim of Cammie's, but I still see them on the bed as clear as day. I can't get it out of my head. Will I ever be able to?"

"I don't know, sweetie," Jackie replied, her eyes full of sympathy. "All I know is you love him, and he loves you."

After a few moments of silence, Nat voiced her opinion on the matter. "Personally, I think we should hop in the car, drive over to her house and cunt-punt her to fucking Siberia where she belongs."

As I laughed, Jackie asked Nat to show her how to perform said "cunt-punt" while I covered my ears because I hated the C-word.

"Why did you have to say that word? It's so gross!" I yelled.

"Well, when *she-who-rarely-curses* starts dropping F-bombs and calling people bitches, I thought it was fitting," Nat said with a devious grin on her face.

"Come on bitch, show me how to cunt-punt!" Jackie begged Nat. "I am definitely on a need to know basis."

Nat jumped up from the couch, danced around, and then pretended to kick a field goal before she and Jackie jumped up and chest bumped each other.

Oh my God, my friends are nuts.

"What the *hell* was that all about?" asked a voice from beside the couch. The three of us looked over to find Eric and John watching us.

"That was me cunt-punting Cammie to Siberia," Nat said, still dancing around like a boxer in the ring waiting for his fight to begin.

"Stop saying that word! I can't take it anymore." I yelled and covered my ears again to the amusement of my friends.

Finally, Nat calmed down and took a seat on the couch.

"It's good to see you back here, Teagan," John said.

It is good to be back here.

"Thanks John." I glanced toward the door hoping to see Jeremy, but I only saw Sonny making his way over to us.

Eric pulled me up off the couch into a bear hug. "Red, glad you're back. Maybe now Jeremy will stop walking around like a damn zombie."

He set me down and I sat next to Sonny. I gave him a sideways glance and said my hellos. Maybe Jeremy wasn't coming. I picked up another shot and slung it back to hide my disappointment.

Soon, the fights were underway. As we watched, John's phone rang and he had a quick conversation with someone. It was amusing to watch, because whoever was on the other end of the line was getting short answers of "yep" as John refused to take his eyes off the TV.

Half an hour later, I had downed a couple more shots and was really in to the fights. The two competitors were going at it and everyone in the bar watching, was standing on their feet, cheering and yelling at the TV's. And I was right there in the middle of them.

"Oh shit, here we go again," John said loudly.

Someone blocked my view of the TV. I opened my mouth to ask him to move. Then I realized it was Jeremy.

After looking at him for a few seconds, I noticed he didn't look right.

In fact, I wasn't quite sure how he looked.

He appeared pissed, relieved, miserable, and . . . happy?

The next thing I knew I was tossed over his shoulder, and he was stalking out of the bar.

"Jeremy, can you put me down, please? I can walk, you know?"

"No."

Alrighty, then.

He didn't put me down until we were around the side of the building. Then he pinned me against the wall with his body and caged me in with his forearms on either side of my head.

"Do you still love me?" he asked. He was obviously wound up by the way his eyes glowered.

"What are you do—"

"Do you still love me?"

Yes, I still loved him, but right now, he was a little intimidating. "Jeremy, please calm down. You're scaring me," I whispered.

He relaxed and eased back, but left his arms against the wall.

"I'm sorry." His shoulders slumped slightly and he rested his cheek against mine. "Teagan, *please* . . . I need to know. Do you still love me?"

"Yes, Jeremy. I do, but—"

"Please, come home," he whispered, his mouth so close to mine I could feel his breath, cool against my skin. He was breaking my heart.

"I can't."

"Please . . . I can't be in the house without you. When your text said you were going to Denver . . . I swear I fucking lost it. Then I called and your phone was disconnected and I couldn't find you anywhere. Then I went to Reese's to see if you were with him and got the surprise of my life when I found Sonny living with him instead of you."

"I know . . . I'm happy for those two."

I felt him smile against my cheek as he nodded.

"I've been living with my cousin, Brittany. I went to Denver to attend the funeral for a former patient . . . and to just get away for a few days. Jeremy, when you saw me that night at the pizza place, I'm sorry I confused you. I was there on a job interview. I don't work at the hospital anymore, but at Nanna's home."

"Does that mean you'll give me another chance?" he asked.

The hope in his eyes broke my heart.

Jeremy kissed my cheek and twisted a lock of my hair between his fingers. "I'm so happy you're home. I love you so much, and it's driving me crazy not being with you."

"I miss you too, Jeremy . . . but I can't be with you right now. I need time. Please, just give me a while. Every time I close my eyes, all I see is you and Cam—"

"Stop, *please*. Please, don't say her name. I'm so sorry about everything. I should've known it wasn't you, Teagan. *I should have fucking known.*"

"Jeremy, I understand, and I don't want you apologizing again for it. It's all Cam—*her* fault. Reese told me everything you told him." I wouldn't admit to him that I had been there and had heard his explanation with my own ears because I didn't want him to be mad at Reese and Sonny.

"Can I tell you how sorry I am about Halloween night? I didn't want it to be like that, Teagan."

His words went straight to my heart. "Are you saying you regret us having sex?"

He shook his head. "No, pretty girl, I would never regret making love to you. I wanted it to be different for us . . . *special*. I wanted to take you away for the weekend, some place private and quiet."

A strange look came over his face, and he reached down and rested his palms on my stomach. "Are you pregnant?"

"No."

"Are you sure?"

I chuckled at the memory of ten pregnancy tests laying in a perfect row across the top of Reese's bathroom counter. "Yes, I'm positive. I took ten freaking tests to be sure because I was so late, Jeremy." And I'd gotten my period yesterday. *Finally.*

He pulled me away from the wall and wrapped his arms around me. "I'm so sorry I wasn't there for you."

"Jeremy, you've *got* to stop apologizing for everything. You know you're as much of a victim now in this whole situation as I am, right?"

He released me and took a step back. "It doesn't make me feel any better."

"What's it going to take to make you feel better?"

"Please, come home," he said, embracing me again.

"I can't, Jeremy. I said I need time."

"How much time?"

"You're very impatient, you know?"

He laughed against my cheek. "Only when it comes to you, pretty girl. I love you so much and want to go back to the way we were before."

"Me too. Please give me time, that's all I'm asking for."

He took a step back and looked in to my eyes. "I'll be waiting. *Impatiently,* but I'll still be waiting. For as long as you need me to."

Jeremy cupped my face in his hands and kissed me gently on the lips. "So, I'll see ya when I see ya?"

Nodding, I couldn't help but smile. "Yeah, you'll definitely see me."

Without another word, Jeremy turned and walked away. He stood at his car door and looked back at me one last time.

"Jeremy?" I called out to him. "I love you."

"I love you, too, Teagan."

Jeremy

March 2014

"Jeremy, wake up!" Through my exhausted brain, I heard Zoey's panicked voice as she shook my shoulder and smacked me on the arm so hard it stung.

"Where is Hannah? She's gone!"

"She's not here, Zoey," Andy growled and I knew right then that my life depended on my ass waking the hell up.

On her knees next to the couch, Zoey smacked me again just as I opened my mouth to speak. "She's with Jay and Heather. Quit hitting me!"

Z backed away from me and dropped onto the floor in relief next to the coffee table.

"What time is it?"

"It's two-twenty. Why is she with Jason and Heather, Jeremy? Was she too much for you to handle?" Andy asked, his glare aimed right at me.

"No, not at all, she was a perfect angel. They dropped by to take her out for ice cream with them and the kids. I'm surprised you didn't pass them on the road because they just left."

Shit, I had only slept for twenty minutes.

"Why didn't you call and tell us, Jeremy?" Andy asked, the

accusation in his tone deliberate.

Jesus, they really didn't trust me, did they?

"I didn't call because you said you were going to be home by two-thirty. I knew you wouldn't mind them taking her and planned to tell you when you came home. I didn't intend to fall asleep."

Andy still glared at me, but Zoey had a relieved expression on her face.

"I'm sorry," I said as Andy burned holes in my face with his icy glare. "You can trust me with her, Andy. I would never let anything happen to her."

He finally relaxed, and I hoped it was because he realized I would die for that little girl. She would always be safe with me.

Today they'd asked me to babysit her so they could go to lunch and a movie. While they were gone, my Sweet Pea and I had picnicked on the living room floor, played, and watched *The Little Mermaid*.

I hated that movie because it reminded me too much of Teagan and a much happier time.

Happy.

An emotion I hadn't felt over the last month.

"Jeremy, are you okay?" Zoey asked, concern dancing in her blue eyes.

Hell no. I'm not okay. I am miserable. I can't sleep and I can't believe Teagan still needs time.

"Yeah, I'm good. Still trying to wake up, that's all."

She didn't believe me, but she didn't push. We'd come to an understanding now about her getting on my case regarding Teagan.

"I'm gonna go, I guess. I've got shit to do." The lie fell easily from my mouth. I didn't have jack shit to do. Not until tonight, anyway.

After helping Z off the floor, I stood to leave. "Jay and Heather said they'd be back by four with Sweet Pea."

Still getting the impression that I had done something wrong by not calling them, I apologized again. *Why am I constantly apologizing to everyone? Am I that much of a fuck up?*

"Jeremy, it's okay. We freaked out when we went in to see her, and she wasn't in her crib like we were expecting."

"Sorry I fell asleep, Z. I'm so tired all the time because I can't sleep at night."

She nodded like she understood and hugged me. While she held on to me, she whispered, "Maybe you should see a doctor, Jer, and get a prescription for sleeping pills or *something.*"

I pulled away from my sister and stared down at her because of the way she said the word *something.* "What do you mean?"

She hesitated, and I knew I wouldn't like what she was going to say. "Do you think you need an anti-depressant?"

Shit, no. What I *needed* was for time to pass a hell of a lot faster. "I'm fine, Z. I just really need to sleep."

"Why don't you take a vacation?"

That actually made me laugh. Who was I going to take a vacation with?

In the past three months, my friendships with Eric and John had become strained since Sonny had told them he was gay and seeing Reese. I backed Sonny one hundred percent and because of that, John and Eric, who weren't thrilled with Sonny's news, had stopped asking Sonny to hang out with us. I'd distanced myself from them because if they wanted to be dicks about it, I wanted no part of it.

"Yeah, Z, I'll think about it. Maybe once we're not so busy at the shop," I said to placate her.

After I left Andy and Zoey's, I began my drive home.

Home. What a joke.

I resided there, but I sure as fuck didn't *live* there.

On the drive home, I thought about all that had happened since the night I'd finally spoken with Teagan at Dub's. She told me she'd call when she was ready . . . and she had. It had taken her until after the new year, but she'd called. We'd decided to do the dating thing, which was what we should have done from the beginning, not move in together. Not that her moving in had been planned—she'd just never left after Reese moved into the apartment they were supposed to share.

Because I'd been thinking with the brain in my pants and not the brain in my head, I'd fucked up . . . again. And because of it, Teagan and I hadn't spoken in a month. Up until then, things had been going great. We'd go on dates to Dub's for fight night, and we'd texted or talked to each other daily.

But one night, it changed.

Teagan had come over to my house for the first time since the Cammie mess after the Halloween party. I'd cooked her dinner, and one thing had led to another. With her legs wrapped around me, I'd carried her down the hallway toward my bedroom. Being far too long since we'd been together, neither of us was thinking properly as we kissed all the way to my room.

Had I not been so consumed by her at the moment, I would have known the huge mistake I'd made by taking her to that bedroom. I tossed her onto the bed and she playfully scooted up against the headboard. Standing at the end of the bed, I pulled my shirt over my head and said, "Teagan, what are you doing over there?"

The happy, playful expression disappeared from her beautiful face and morphed in to heartache.

When I realized the question I'd asked her was the exact same question I'd asked her the night she found Cammie with me in bed, I'd felt like the biggest prick in the world. Apologizing profusely, I'd gone to her, but she'd pushed me away and ran from the room crying. I followed her to talk about it, but as she'd walked out my door, yet again, she'd said she needed more time.

Time. She was the cruelest bitch I knew. She made the days pass achingly slow. Time didn't ease the pain—she only made it worse. She caused sleepless nights to last far longer than they should. The time for me was almost up. I couldn't wait much longer for Teagan because it hurt too much.

If she didn't make a decision soon about us, I would need to try and move on. I couldn't keep doing this to myself, and if she couldn't get past what had happened and come back to me, then she needed to move on as well. Zoey was right.

Living like this wasn't healthy.

When I got home, I left my car in the driveway so I'd have extra space to work on the Chevelle. I'd started the project in December to keep busy now that I lived alone.

Repairing the Chevelle was my way of coping. My life was at a standstill and broken just like that car. As I had taken it apart, the guilt that had consumed me since November finally ebbed, and my need to fix the car had flowed. Almost as if I needed to repair it while I worked on getting myself back together.

Rob had smashed the ever-loving shit out of the car, so the body panels were pretty much fucked. He was a crazy bastard, but I could see how smashing the hell out of something might ease the pain for a short time. I'd considered doing the same thing, many times.

Now, I unbolted the seats Rob had shredded with a knife and set them aside to take them to be reupholstered on Monday. The carpet was full of burn holes and God knew what stained it. Not about to touch it with my bare hands, I pulled on a pair of rubber gloves and peeled the carpet out of the car. Laying it flat on the concrete where my car normally sat inside the garage, I rolled it up so I could take it to the shop and throw it away. As soon as I let go, the carpet unrolled itself.

Whatever had been spilled on it had stiffened it so it wouldn't stay rolled. Duct tape was in order for this job. If it could bind Adam to a beam for over an hour, it could keep the carpet rolled up. I popped the top of my toolbox open, and came face to face with one of the photos I'd taken from my toolbox at the shop—the picture Zoey snapped of Teagan and me sitting across the dinner table from her.

Seeing it hurt and pissed me off.

After slamming the lid shut, I pulled each drawer open trying to find a roll of duct tape. I searched my messy workbench too. I lifted up a box, finally finding the elusive roll of tape sitting right next to my crowbar.

Glancing between the two items, I knew I should be picking up the tape, but instead, I picked up the crowbar. The cold metal was heavy in my hands as I gripped it tightly.

Without thinking, I walked over to the already mangled

Chevelle, and raised the crowbar into the air to take a swing. I couldn't do it. Instead, I went back to work on the car because I knew taking my anger out on the car wouldn't do any good.

After I wound duct tape around the carpet, I smirked when I realized it looked like a body wrapped in a rug. I thought of what would happen if I were pulled over by the cops while it was in the back of the shop truck. Officer Douchebag would love seeing that.

After what felt like hours of work, I glanced up at the clock on the wall, checking the time.

Fuck, there she was again.

Time.

I pulled my cell out of my pocket and made the same call that I did every Saturday around this time.

"Hey, Jer," the cheerful female voice said when she answered.

"Hey you, just checking to see if we're still on for tonight." I prayed she was going to say yes.

"Absolutely. See ya around ten?"

"Yep. Same place?" I asked, knowing she understood my piss poor joke.

She laughed. I knew she was worried about me, yet she was the only person I could fully count on right now. I felt like everyone else was judging me.

"I'll see you at ten."

"See you later, Nic."

Right on time, I sat down on my usual barstool at Sam's bar, my old stomping grounds. Sam poured me two shots of tequila.

"First two are on the house." He set them on the bar in front of me.

"Thanks, man," I said before he walked off to help a customer at the other end of the bar.

Glancing around the room, I didn't see Nicole anywhere, but I knew she was here because she worked here. Every Saturday for the last month, after Teagan had run away from me once again, I'd been meeting her after she got off work.

After running in to Nic on Halloween, I'd told Zoey about how well she was doing and that Teagan seemed cool with her. Zoey hadn't approved, of course, but she'd said if Teagan was okay with Nic and I being friends, she had nothing to say about it. Whether she felt that way now that Teagan was out of the picture, I didn't know because I hadn't asked.

Something brushed against my arm then Nicole kissed my cheek. "You made it." She took a seat on the barstool next to me.

"I was beginning to think you were going to stand me up," I said with a smile.

Sam came over and dropped off a Coke for Nicole. She stood on the rungs of her barstool and leaned over the bar to give Sam a kiss.

"Thanks, baby," she said.

"My pleasure, gorgeous." He shot her the smile of a man in love.

Nicole and I had been going to Sam's bar for years, but she and Sam had never really talked aside from small talk when she'd ordered something at the bar. When Nic had applied for a job at the bar last summer, she and Sam had hit it off and had been together for a few months now.

She'd been clean from meth for over a year and had completely turned her life around. I was so damn proud of her. She was healthy, happy, and had really changed her life for the better.

Nic and I sat the rest of the night watching a game on the TV that hung on the wall behind the bar. I swallowed shot after shot of tequila, while Nicole stayed sober so she could drive me home later.

After last call, I handed my keys over to Nicole and she drove me home in my car while Sam shut down the bar. Once he was finished, he would pick her up at my house. Nicole always made sure I had arrived home safely and made a joke of actually tucking me into bed.

Once we arrived at my house, Nic wrapped an arm around my waist and pulled one of my arms over her shoulders to help me inside, since I'd had a few more drinks than normal.

She flipped on the light in the kitchen to see where she was going. When we passed by the dimly lit living room, Nic stopped walking abruptly. I wasn't paying attention and kept walking, almost pulling her over.

We fumbled around briefly before I finally righted myself. "Sorry, Nic—"

"Jeremy, you have a visitor."

I glanced over at the couch and saw the vision of my pretty girl sitting there. "She's not real, Nic," I slurred. "If you blink a couple times and wipe away the blurriness, she'll go away. She always fucking does."

Nic released me and I shuffled down the hallway to the bathroom. As I shut the door, I swore I heard Nicole talking to herself. Great, now this place was making her crazy too.

Once I was finished in the bathroom, I stripped down and fell into bed. Nic came into the guest room and handed me a glass of water and three ibuprofens.

"Take these. You know the drill," she said as I took the glass and pills from her hands.

I tossed the pills in my mouth and drank the entire glass of water. "Thanks again, Nic. You're a good friend," I mumbled as my head hit the pillow. She covered me up and ruffled my hair. A few seconds later, the room went dark.

Late the next morning, I woke after having crazy-ass dreams of Teagan. I dreamt that she came into my room and slipped in bed behind me. She laid close, resting her cheek against mine, holding me tight. The dream was so real I could feel the tears dropping from her cheeks to mine.

In the dream, she told me how much she loved me, but had come to the decision to let me go. She said I shouldn't have to wait for her, and I needed to move on.

Dragging my ass out of bed, I went on my run around the neighborhood. I purposely skipped the street where Teagan's parents lived. On occasion, I ran by there, only to be stopped by either her mom or dad to talk. I hadn't been down their street since the last time Teagan had run out on me.

Once I was home from my run, I ate breakfast and went to the garage to work on the Chevelle. Later that day, I drove over to the shop and parked my car inside, then drove one of the shop trucks over to my parents' house for the Sunday family dinner. I would load up the Chevelle seats and everything I needed to throw in the dumpster, and take it in to work with me tomorrow.

I played a few games of poker with my dad and brothers, losing my ass as usual. I didn't know why I bothered playing, honestly. I sucked at poker. Tired of losing money, I went and found my Sweet Pea. We sat in the middle of the living room floor and I helped her stand. Keeping hold of her hands, I backed away, encouraging her to walk to me.

Each time I backed away from her a little bit, Hannah became more confident and adventuresome. She'd even let go of my hands at one point to stand on her own with no support of any kind.

"Come see me, Sweet Pea." I held my hands out to her. She appeared unsure, but slowly took a wobbly step toward me.

Naturally, I got excited, but she dropped down on her butt before I could call my sister and Andy in to watch. I picked her back up and told her what a good job she did as I cradled her close.

"Zoey, Andy, come watch this," I called out to them.

They came in from the dining room, and Sweet Pea and I gave them a repeat performance of her taking a step on her own.

Z went a little overboard and started clapping. "Hannah. Look at you."

Zoey startled Hannah. She fell back down on her butt and started crying.

"It's okay, sweet girl," I said, picking her up and setting her back on her tiny feet. "She didn't mean to scare you."

Zoey came and sat on the floor and tried to get Hannah to walk to her, but she wasn't having any of it. All she wanted to do now was sit on my lap and pull my hair.

When my mom yelled for us to come and eat, we sat down in the dining room for dinner. Noah sat next to me and put a beer next to my plate. "No thanks, bro. I'm not drinking today," I said, as I cut into my piece of chicken.

"Today?" Noah asked. "What, you have certain days you drink now?"

Yes, as a matter of fact. "I don't want it, that's all, but thank you for bringing it to me."

"You probably had enough last night anyway," Adam chimed in from across the table. "You look hung over."

Here we go again. This is why I don't tell anyone anything.

"Have you talked to Teagan?" Adam asked.

"Adam, stop," Zoey said.

"Why? He's being stupid," Adam said.

"You know what? Go to hell, Adam. You don't have any clue what's going on with me, so don't pretend like you do," I said, getting more pissed off by the second.

"He's right, Jeremy," Andy said quietly.

Andy didn't usually speak up when it came to issues or any drama within the family, so I turned my head to look at him.

"Please," I said, glaring at my brother in law. "Please, tell me how I'm a total fuck up. How I'm doing everything wrong—as if I didn't already know." I couldn't give a shit about his answer so I went back to my dinner.

"Someone once told me what a coward I was being Jeremy. Open your eyes and real—"

The loud clatter of Zoey's fork dropping from her hand to her plate stopped Andy from finishing his sentence.

Now I was irate and feeling very singled out. Every person in this room knew what had happened and blamed me for Teagan's absence.

"She doesn't *want* me! Don't you get that?"

"When was the last time you talked to her?" Andy asked.

Fuck this. *I am done with this shit.* "It's none of your damn bus—"

"Enough!" Zoey yelled. She was sitting between Andy and me so she was right in the middle of the argument.

She stood and pushed her chair away from the table.

I was about to lose it, so I needed to go. "I'm outta here." I tossed my napkin onto my plate and glanced around the table making eye contact with everyone who hadn't started shit with me. "Sorry for ruining your dinner."

"Mijo," my mom said. "Please don't go. We're just worried about you."

"Sorry, but I really need to leave. Everyone's uncomfortable now, and I'm done talking about Teagan. She doesn't want me. What is, or isn't going on with us is my business, and nobody else's. I would appreciate it if everyone kept their opinions to themselves from now on where she's concerned. It's like you think this is my choice, but it's not. If I had my choice, she'd be sitting right here next to me, but as you can see . . . *she's not.* I don't know what the hell you expect me to do about it."

Jesus, I didn't think I'd spoken that many words in a row in months.

Looking around the table again and seeing the way my family was looking at me only made me feel worse. "Goodnight." I turned and walked out of the dining room.

As I turned the knob to open the front door, Zoey called my name.

"Not now, Z," I said, without turning around to look at her. I pulled the door open and slammed it shut after I was outside.

Once I was inside the truck, I sat in silence trying to calm down. Remembering that I had added a bunch of new music to my iPod while Hannah was napping the day before, I plugged it in. Zoey usually took care of updating my music, so I honestly had no idea what I had been downloading when I'd connected my iPod to her computer.

With her musical ADD, who knew what I was going to be listening to. I scrolled through her playlists, which had very blunt yet appropriate names. When I came across a playlist titled "songs to cry to," I let out a huff and pressed the play button.

Why the hell not?

By the time I arrived home, I'd heard songs about lost love, people dying, and my personal fucking favorite—things a couple would never have because they'd broken up. The lyrics even mentioned white picket fences.

That was the final straw for me.

Putting the song on repeat, I hooked a chain from the

trailer hitch on the truck to the picket fence around my front yard. For the next thirty minutes, I yanked every post from the ground. Pickets and boards were splintered and scattered around the yard and the sidewalk in front of my house by the time I was finished.

But the fence was gone.

Just like the woman who had loved it so much was gone. She'd spent an entire weekend scraping the aged paint away and giving it a new coat of bright, white paint. Now it lay broken all over the place.

I pulled the truck into the driveway and sat there. Several neighbors had come outside to see me yank down the fence. Knowing I was about to have a breakdown, I shut off the truck and went inside my house.

I had to get her out of my system.

I went into my old bedroom and flopped down on the bed. Plugging my iPod into the dock, I listened to the entire playlist again. Every song on the list ripped my heart out of my chest and stomped it into the ground. I understood why Z named the playlist "songs to cry to." I wanted to cry, but the tears never came. I was too numb.

At some point, I fell in to a deep sleep, and when I woke up, it was time for my morning run. I'd slept through the entire night. When I went out the front door, I came face to face with what I'd done the night before. That's when I dropped to my knees and knew what I had to do.

This was it.

I wasn't doing this to myself anymore.

I couldn't fucking take it.

Nic wanted to set me up with her cousin, and I needed to get over Teagan. I made the decision right then to call Nic after work and set something up.

Rather than go on my run, I cleaned up the fence mess. While I picked up broken pickets and chunks of fence, the song from the night before kept running through my mind. It was hard to let go of the fence even though I'd originally hated it. It was just another reminder of Teagan. She was gone and now so was the fence. Eventually, I loaded the destroyed wood into the back of the truck so I could take it to work and toss it in the dumpster.

After I showered and dressed for work, I sat down and picked at my breakfast. While I was washing my plate, I realized I'd forgotten to do something very important last night. For the last month, I had been going to visit Teagan's grandma on Sunday nights. I never stayed long when I visited her. Just long enough to read her a few poems from her Yeats book.

She was always happy to see me, but every time she mentioned Peaches, my heart sank. I didn't know what Teagan told her about us, and I didn't know what to tell her. She never stopped asking though. All I could tell her was that I loved Teagan. I didn't know what else to say.

I arrived early to work to toss the fence before anyone could catch me doing it. Unfortunately, Zoey saw me from the window of her apartment and came down. She didn't say a word; she just grabbed a spare set of gloves from the truck and helped me. Picket by picket, we tossed the fence into the dumpster until the truck was as empty as my fucking life.

By lunchtime, I was free to go home because my job for the day was finished. I popped into the office to tell Zoey I was leaving for the rest of the day. When I entered the office, I found my sister sitting at her desk holding a newspaper in her hand. She was close to tears.

"Z, what's wrong?" I asked, kneeling at her feet.

She held the folded up newspaper out to me and let out a shaky breath. I took it from her, and my gaze shifted from my sister to the paper. The page was full of obituaries and death notices.

My eyes landed on a familiar name in the death notice section and the breath froze in my lungs. The notice didn't list a date of birth so I couldn't be sure if it was her or her grandma. Either way, my knees gave way, and I sat on the cold tile floor of the office as I read the notice over and over.

Teagan Shea Donnelly — died February 28, 2014

Teagan

She's gone.

I can't believe she's gone.

When I'd come to work on Friday, she'd been awake and alert. She'd had three minor strokes in the last month, but the damage had been minimal. I'd spent every weekday evening with her after work, visiting and devoting every spare second to her, because I knew in my heart, her time was limited.

She was my rock, and I knew that once she was gone, I could never get her back.

During my lunch break on the day she'd died, I'd sat next to her bed, using her table. As I'd slowly eaten a salad, I'd read poems to her from her Yeats book. Once I'd finished reading The Two Trees, she'd reached out and put her cool hand on my arm. I'd covered her hand with mine and turned to face her.

"Peaches," she'd said as her hand fell from my arm. Then her eyes had gone blank and her breathing had stopped.

"Nanna?"

No response.

"Nanna?" I'd jumped from the chair, sending it flying backward and immediately started CPR. I'd pressed the button on the bed to call for help, but I'd known she was gone. When Rose and one of the doctors had rushed in, they'd found me cradling my sweet Nanna in my arms for the very last time.

Working in home hospice while living in Denver, I'd had to be the bearer of bad news many times. But this . . . this was excruciating. On autopilot, I'd called my mom.

"Mama, I'm so sorry," I'd said, before bursting into tears.

"Baby, what is it? What's wrong?" she'd cried.

"Nanna's gone, Mama. She's gone . . . I'm so sorry."

Wracking sobs had come over the line as my mom had broken down. My dad must have been close by because he'd come on the line. "Teagan? What's going on?" he'd asked, as my mom sobbed in the background.

"Nanna just passed away," I'd whispered. "Please come here."

After hanging up with my dad, I'd broken down. I knew this had been coming, but it didn't make the pain any less.

Alone in Nanna's room waiting for my parents and sister, the one person I had wanted to talk to was Jeremy. My finger had hovered over the call button on my phone, but I hadn't been able to press it. Since I'd run from him a month ago, we hadn't spoken.

Not that I hadn't wanted to, because I had.

I do.

But my family had shown up and we'd spent the rest of Friday saying our goodbyes to Nanna.

Now I faced Saturday evening and I needed a break after spending the entire day with a swarm of grieving people at my parents' house. I headed out for a walk around the neighborhood and found myself at Jeremy's house. He didn't answer when I knocked at his door, but I couldn't bear to leave without talking to him so I let myself inside with the key I still had and waited for him.

I wasn't trying to be nosy, but I wandered around the house that had been my home. When I walked into Jeremy's bedroom, I knew just by looking around he'd moved out of it. The mattress was bare and the bedding was folded up and sitting on the bed while the furniture was layered in dust.

I pulled drawers open on his dresser, finding them all empty. I walked around the bed and pulled the top drawer open on his nightstand, only to find the six boxes of condoms he'd jokingly sent me a picture of, unopened in the drawer.

Without Jeremy around to witness my humiliation, I sat down on the bed as an experiment. *It's only a bed, Teagan, a piece of furniture that holds no bearing on your relationship with Jeremy.* I still got sick to my stomach as the visions came back and I left the room crying.

Why was I still having such a hard time with this?

Jeremy had done nothing wrong.

He'd said he loved her, thinking it was me.

He loved me, not her.

Me, me, me.

Not Cammie.

All I wanted was to be with him.

But how could I do that if I couldn't even be in our bedroom without running away from the memories of that night?

Not having an answer to any of my questions, I walked around the rest of the house and found Jeremy had moved into the guest room. But why? Because I'd run away from him? The guilt overwhelmed me and I sat down on the bed. The scent of Jeremy's shampoo and cologne wafted around me when I sat, so I pulled the bedding back on the bed.

I noticed the pillowcases were mismatched. One was white, the other black. The white pillowcase was from the sheet set we used to sleep on in the master bedroom. That's when I realized the bedding folded up on the bed in that bedroom wasn't *right*. It wasn't white. It was a light shade of gray.

I jumped up and went back to the bedroom to confirm what I already knew. The bedding was different. I'd never seen it before. I went to the closet in the hallway and found all the other sets but the white one. Had he thrown it away?

Oh my God, he had.

Except one pillowcase.

I jogged back to the guest bedroom. The pillow with the white pillowcase was on my side of the bed. Why had he kept it?

Because he still loves you, idiot. And he can't let you go.

Like you can't let him go.

I sank down on the bed, and hugged his pillow against my body. It smelled like him, and I knew instantly why he'd kept mine.

Memories flooded my brain. Thinking about our time together hurt and I let my mind drift to Nanna. I laid down on the bed and cried. I cried because my life was out of control. I cried because my sweet Nanna was gone and I'd never hear her call me Peaches again. *Her last word* . . . I'd never curl up on her bed and read to her again.

I wiped the tears from my face with my right hand and felt the cool metal of my Claddagh ring brush over my cheekbone. I wondered if Jeremy was still wearing his, and hoped he was. Losing Nanna proved to me just how short life was and if the person you loved the most wasn't in it, it wasn't worth a damn thing.

Eventually I heard the garage door open, and Jeremy's car pull inside. Quickly, I jumped off his bed, ran to the living room, and sat on the couch. When I heard a woman's voice as he entered the house, my heart sank. He'd brought someone home with him. I was too late, and he'd moved on. I sat as still as possible and hoped they would pass by without seeing me then I could sneak out the front door.

I realized the woman was Nicole a split second before she saw me. When she informed Jeremy he had a visitor, he looked right at me and said, "She's not real, Nic. If you blink a couple times and wipe away the blurriness, she'll go away. She always fucking does."

He didn't believe I was here. That's when I realized how miserable he was.

I watched in silence as he turned and left the room.

Was he seeing Nicole again?

"Hi, Teagan," she said politely. "I need to take care of him, but can you stay? I'd like to speak with you before my boyfriend comes to get me."

Boyfriend?

I nodded my head and relaxed, knowing she had a boyfriend. She and Jeremy weren't together.

Nicole went into the kitchen and came back out with a

glass of water and a bottle of ibuprofen. She gave me a sympathetic smile as she passed and walked down the hallway to the guest bedroom Jeremy had gone into.

She stepped back into the hallway, shut off the bedroom light, and quietly closed the door behind her. She came and sat next to me on the couch. "How are you?" she asked, keeping her voice low.

I shook my head. "My grandmother died yesterday."

"Oh, Teagan, I'm so sorry."

She seemed sincere, but my thoughts were only on the man in the other room, now that I'd seen him.

"Does he do that all the time?" I asked.

Nicole followed my glance down the hallway. "Every Saturday night."

"Is it because of me?"

Nicole didn't respond. She didn't need to, because I already knew the answer.

I'd broken him.

I freaking broke him.

"Teagan, why are you here?"

That's when it dawned on me that I was here for my own selfish reasons. I wasn't here because I wanted to come home, even though I did. I was here because I was grieving, and needed to lean on him.

"Teagan?"

I felt ashamed for being so self-centered I couldn't answer her.

"Look, can I be blunt with you?" Nicole asked, her eyes filling with tears.

I nodded.

"If you're not here to stay, you need to let him go. That man in there . . . is not the Jeremy James I've known for years. He's miserable, and I don't even recognize him anymore. You can't keep stringing him along."

She was right. I had to let him go. I needed time to grieve for my nanna, and it wasn't fair to make him wait any longer. With all I'd put him through, he needed to be free of me.

"Thanks for taking care of him, Nicole."

Headlights lit up the living room, and Nicole looked out the window. "There's my boyfriend, so I need to go. Go easy on him, please." She tipped her chin in the direction of the guest room.

I nodded, and Nicole left.

It took me some time to gather my thoughts before I went into Jeremy's bedroom. When I opened the door, I left it ajar, so the light from the hallway allowed me to see him. He was asleep on his side, so I crawled onto the bed behind him.

He didn't stir when I wrapped my arm tightly around him and pressed my cheek to his. The tears started before I spoke a word.

"Jeremy, wake up."

When he mumbled my name and took my hand in his, the words I'd never wanted to say spilled from my mouth.

"Jeremy, I'm so sorry for everything I've put you through these last few months. Don't ever forget how much I love you. I guess the time wasn't right for us. I'm sorry for hurting you and pushing you away . . . if I could do things differently, I would. But I can't change what's happened. You shouldn't have to wait for me anymore. It's not fair to you and I want you to move on—be happy. I'm sorry I let you down, Jeremy. I love you too much to let you continue down your path of self-destruction because of me. So this is goodbye. I love you."

His hand jerked away from mine, and he reached up to wipe my tears from his cheek.

After I eased off the bed, I knelt on the floor in front of him just to see his gorgeous face one last time. I wished I could see those beautiful blue eyes, one last time, too. Suddenly, they opened and he stared at me for a moment before he rubbed his eyes and closed them again. They blinked back open and he rubbed them again. He opened his mouth to speak and I held my breath.

"Please go away," he mumbled, blinking rapidly. "Why aren't you going away this time?"

Jeremy's eyes closed again, and they didn't reopen. He'd fallen back to sleep.

I rested my palm on his cheek then combed my fingers

through his hair one last time. I wanted to kiss him goodbye, but I didn't deserve to.

I walked out of his house and didn't look back, hoping he would remember I had been here and what I'd said to him.

The days after Nanna passed away, and I had officially let Jeremy go, were the darkest of my life. In less than forty-eight hours, I'd lost the two people I held closest to my heart. But Monday was here, and my mom and I had spent all morning going over arrangements for the funeral. As I was preparing lunch for my family, my cell rang.

"Oh, thank God," Jeremy said as soon as I said hello to him. "Teagan, are you okay?"

"I'm doing alright at the moment." Tears pricked my eyes for the hundredth time since Friday.

"I'm so sorry about Nanna, Teagan."

He'd never called her Nanna, but her name rolled off his tongue easily as if he'd called her that all his life.

"Thank you. I appreciate your calling to check on me. How are you?"

He took in a deep breath. "Better, now that I've heard your voice."

"It's good to hear from you, Jeremy. Did Sonny tell you about Nanna?"

He let out a sigh. "No, I haven't talked to him lately. Zoey saw her death notice in the paper and told me. It didn't list her birthdate—"

Oh no, he thought it might have been me.

"Jeremy, I'm so sorry you had to find out like that. I should've called to let you know she died."

"It's alright, pretty girl. I'm glad you answered your phone right away . . . *so I knew.* Do you need me to do anything for you? Do you want to talk?"

My broken heart ached. I wanted to be with him, and for him to wrap his arms around me and never let me go. But, us being together even to talk wouldn't help either of us move on.

"I'm getting by, Jeremy, but thank you."

"Do you mind if I come to the service?"

"Not at all, Nanna loved you. She would want you there. It's on Thursday at two. I can text you the address of the church if you want."

"Yeah, I'd appreciate it. Are you sure I can't do anything for you?"

I did need something. My mom wanted someone to sing at the funeral, but I wasn't finding the time to work out the details before the service.

"Red, you still there?"

"I'm here. Jeremy, do you think Zoey, Jess, and Sasha would sing a song at the service?"

"Let me ask Z, she's right here, hold on a sec."

I heard them talking quietly before Zoey came on the line. "Hi, Teagan, I'm so sorry about your grandma."

"Thank you, Zoey."

"Jeremy said you wanted us to sing a song. We'd love to help if we can. What's the song?"

I took a breath and because of the title of the song, I almost started crying again. "It's called 'Do Not Stand at my Grave and Weep.' There's a unique version of it on YouTube that we love, but we didn't think we could find anyone to learn it and sing it on such short notice. We were going to play the song from a CD we found, but it's just not the same."

"Teagan, please don't worry about it. We won't let you down, I promise. Text me the link to the video and we'll get as close to it as possible," Zoey said, her voice reassuring me.

"Thank you so much, Zoey. You have no idea what this will mean to my mom."

"You're welcome Teagan, and please, if you need anything else don't hesitate to ask."

I heard her hand the phone back to Jeremy.

"Hey, pretty girl, you get everything squared away?"

Everything except my life . . . God, I missed hearing him call me "pretty girl" every day.

"Yeah, I think so," I said, as the tears streamed down my face. I wanted to tell him how much I loved him and how I wanted to come home, but I'd done the right thing by telling him to move on.

"Jeremy, I need to go, but thank you for calling to check on me. It means so much."

"You're welcome. Goodbye, Red."

His goodbye seemed so final, but I knew things had to be this way. I would see him in a few days at the funeral, but I needed to get back to taking care of Mama. She had taken Nanna's death very hard, and I needed to stay strong for her.

The next couple of days slowly dragged by. My parents' house was the main hub for my grieving family to get together. My aunt flew in from New York to stay with my mom, so I felt better going back to Brit's apartment every night. I needed time alone in my own room to think.

On Thursday my family gathered at the church for Nanna's service and greeted people as they came in, taking time to speak to each person. As I stood talking to a friend of Nanna's, Shannen tugged my elbow to get my attention.

"What's going on, Shannen?"

The worried expression on her face did not go unnoticed by me. Something was definitely up.

"Teags, freaking Gary is here."

Gary? Why on earth is he here?

"Where is he?" I asked as I glanced around trying to find him.

"He's up by the podium."

I turned around and saw him standing by the podium, dressed in a suit and wearing the stupid smirk on his face that I always wanted to smack. I marched up to the front of the church, stopping inches from him.

"You are not welcome here, Gary. Please leave," I muttered angrily.

"Not a chance. You've been ignoring my calls for months, and now I finally have you cornered," he said.

"What the hell do you mean?"

"It means . . . if you don't agree to get me the money you owe me, I am going to cause a scene right here in front of God and everyone."

Taking a step back, I glared at him. "You wouldn't do that to my family, Gary. This has nothing to do with them."

"I don't give a flying fuck about your family, you crazy bitch. You took money from me and I want it back."

He was nuts. The money I had taken was *mine*. Yet, I knew he would cause a scene, and I couldn't do that to my mom. Not at Nanna's funeral.

"Fine. We'll go to the bank after the service, and I'll get it for you, but please . . . *please* don't ruin this for my nanna, Gary. She doesn't deserve that."

"Good girl," he said smugly, and I wanted to slap the bastard right across the face.

When I turned around to go back to where my family was, he reached out and grabbed my arm, pulling me back to him.

"What the hell are you doing?"

"I don't trust you not to take off after the service is over, so you're staying with me."

"Are you kidding me? I need to be with my family."

"Then I'm coming with you. Just smile and pretend like we've cleared the air between us."

Not wanting to cause my distraught mother any more stress, I agreed. But I intended to make him regret it later.

As I turned around to walk back to my family, I ran in to Jeremy. He looked between Gary and me curiously before speaking.

"Hey, pretty girl," he said, wrapping me in the warm and comforting embrace I'd missed so much. When he kissed the side of my head, I felt his fingers brush through my hair before he let go of me. "Who's your friend here?"

I painted on a fake smile. "This is Gary." I watched Jeremy's face fall as I said the bastard's name.

"I see," Jeremy said. "I wanted to come by and say hi, but I can see you're busy. I guess I'll see you later."

Nodding, I apologized to him with my eyes, hoping he would see how sorry I was.

"Why didn't you introduce me to your *friend*, Teagan?" Gary asked, his voice dripping with spite.

"Fuck you, Gary."

What I wouldn't do right now to give him a nice throat punch! My family, along with Reese and Sonny had arrived at the front of the church and were taking their seats. I walked away from Gary and took my seat on the front pew of the church. That son of a bitch sat down right next to me.

The service got underway, and my sister and Reese kept shooting curious glances in my direction, no doubt wondering why Gary was sitting next to me. I swore Reese had smoke coming out of his ears because he was so pissed.

When the pastor was finished speaking, he invited Zoey, Sasha, and Jess up to the front of the church where they were handed microphones.

My mom looked over at me, as Zoey gave a short speech, thanking me for giving them the honor of singing. The three women sang the song beautifully, a cappella. With the way they sang and harmonized together, they didn't need music. The three had such distinctive sounding voices, yet complimented each other well. Clearly, they'd been singing together for ages.

When the song was over, Zoey stayed at the front of the church while the other girls went back to their seats. I wasn't sure why she stayed. She noticed me shoot her a questioning look, so she announced she was going to sing another song. The woman really knew how to work a crowd, and even though her next song was unplanned between us, nobody would've guessed it.

Andy showed up next to her, with two acoustic guitars as Zoey attached her microphone to its stand. They each slung the straps over their shoulders and began to play. When I recognized the song, I knew it was Jeremy's doing.

One thing Jeremy and I always had in common was our favorite band. Andy and Zoey played their guitars, as Zoey sang a very subdued, acoustic version of "The Legacy of Odio," by In This Moment.

Jeremy couldn't have picked a better song for me. I turned in my seat and searched him out in the crowd. He was sitting near the back, and to my surprise, the entire James family was surrounding him. Jeremy was holding his Sweet Pea, who was asleep on his shoulder. He made eye contact with me, and I mouthed "Thank you" to him. He gave me a half smile and tipped his head as if to say *you're welcome*.

Looking him over, I noticed his demeanor had changed since I had seen him earlier. His shoulders were slumped, his head was down, and he wouldn't look at me again.

"Turn the fuck around, Teagan," Gary growled in my ear.

I turned and concentrated on the rest of Zoey and Andy's song.

Gary is going to get it later, if it's the last thing I do.

When the song was over, some of Nanna's friends went up to share a few stories and give their condolences. When they were finished, the pastor asked if anyone else would like to speak. His attention was drawn to someone approaching the podium. "Yes, young man, please step forward and share your kind words with the family."

Jeremy thanked the pastor and stepped behind the podium. His sad, blue eyes immediately sought mine.

"Last year, I met the wonderful woman we're all here grieving for today. The very first time I met her, she asked me to read to her from a book of Yeats poetry. I agreed, because my brother-in-law, Andy, once told me the easiest way to make a woman happy was to just say yes. That day I had two women I wanted to make happy. So I said yes."

The corner of his mouth turned up just enough for me to notice. Finally, I had the answer to his secret "man yes" code of honor that he refused to tell me about.

"So today, I'd like to read two poems for her one last time. Every Sunday night for the past several weeks I've been going to read to her, and these two were her favorites."

At that moment, I swore the love I had for the man at the podium tripled. I had no idea he'd been going to see her. I thought back to the times when I had gone into her room and her Yeats book would be on her bed, or placed in a different slot on her bookshelf. Rose swore she hadn't been moving it, and said someone from the weekend staff must have been moving it.

It had been Jeremy all along.

Jeremy unrolled a piece of paper and began reading. The first poem was The Two Trees, which he'd read to her every time we'd visited her together—and the last words she'd heard before she passed.

The happenstance wasn't lost on me. *Beloved, gaze in thine own heart* . . .

The next poem he read, I didn't recognize. When he was finished reading, he rerolled the paper and slipped something over it to keep it from unrolling. Jeremy walked along the front of the church to my nanna's open casket and laid the roll of paper inside with her. He touched her hand gently and walked toward the back of the church where his family was sitting.

When the service was over, I walked straight up to the casket to see my nanna one last time. I was the first one there since I was only ten feet away from her. I kissed her on the cheek, whispered that I loved her, and straightened to look at her. That's when the sun glinting through the stained glass window of the church gleamed off of something inside the casket.

My heart sank at the sight of my papa's Claddagh ring. That was the item Jeremy had slipped over the paper to keep it rolled up. I burst in to tears as I shoved the ring and paper into the pocket of my jacket.

Right then, I realized I couldn't let Jeremy go. The ring belonged to him, and so did my heart.

The mourners filed out of the church, and I went to find him. Gary followed me, but I didn't care. Almost everyone was gone, but I wouldn't hesitate to knock Gary on his ass if he tried anything.

I looked for Jeremy everywhere, but he was nowhere to be found. Luckily, I saw Andy loading his guitar into the back of Zoey's SUV. I snuck away from Gary when someone he knew came up to talk to him and hurried over to Andy.

"Hey, where's Jeremy? I need to see him," I said, as Gary jogged toward me.

"He left the church right after he spoke." Andy said, with compassion in his eyes. He pulled me close and hugged me as Gary slid to a stop next to us. "Do you need help with this asshole?"

A giggle burst out of my mouth, and I squeezed Andy tightly. "As a matter of fact I do. Can you distract him for two minutes?"

Andy gave me a nod and let me go. I pulled him back down and kissed his cheek, then whispered, "Hurt him if you need to." Andy gave me a knowing grin.

He turned to Gary and held out his hand, and with a very American accent, he said, "Hi, I don't think we've met. I'm Joe, Teagan's friend, and you are?"

Gary took his hand and introduced himself. He tried to pull his hand away from Andy, but Andy tightened his grasp. Gary winced from the crushing pain of Andy's grip.

"Get outta here, Red," Andy said with a smile, firmly holding Gary in place by his hand.

I didn't stick around to find out what was going to happen next. I ran to my car and got the hell out of there.

The month of April brought on changes. Spring was in full force, flowers bloomed, and life had moved on. Nanna had been gone just over a month, her room emptied out, and a new resident moved in. I had given myself time to mourn for her and made several other decisions about my life. The day of her funeral, I realized I couldn't be without Jeremy.

He was the one for me.

I didn't know if my realization was from Nanna's intuition coming true or the glint off my papa's Claddagh ring in the church at just the right moment, I only knew I didn't want to spend another day of my life without him. I didn't know if he would ever forgive me for putting him through hell, but I had to try.

After the funeral, I'd called and texted, but he'd only responded saying he didn't have time to see me. His rejection hurt, but I understood. I decided to give him some space and time, and didn't go by his house and try to see him. I owed him that much after the way I'd treated him. Thankfully, Mama and I had been busy since the service, taking care of Nanna's estate and moving her possessions from the hospital, which helped to keep my mind off of Jeremy.

Before Nanna passed, she had given Rose specific instructions that the Yeats book was to be given to the handsome, blue-eyed man who read to her every Sunday evening. So now, I was on my way to deliver the book to him and to see if he would talk to me. His ring was in my pocket, just in case.

Driving to his house, I found the street lined with several cars and had to park halfway down the block. When I approached, I realized his house was the center of attention.

When I reached his property line, I also noticed that something was missing. He had ripped out the fence. Then I saw the "For-Sale" sign in the yard. At the top of the sign was a smaller sign, advertising an "Open House."

No!

No, no, no. He couldn't sell his house! I marched up the sidewalk and through the open front door. Inside, I found couples strolling around, opening cabinet doors, closet doors, and listening to the real estate agent go on and on about the recent renovation.

Every piece of furniture Jeremy owned was still in the house, and people I didn't know were sitting on it as if it belonged to them.

I want these strange people out! They don't belong here!

In the bedroom, the bed was nicely made with the bedding that had been sitting on it the last time I'd been here. I scurried into the guest bedroom and pulled open several drawers of his dresser, only to find them empty.

Like a mad woman, I pushed my way through the sea of people to our bedroom again and threw myself down on the bed. I would force myself to stay on it, no matter how many visions of Cammie and Jeremy popped into my head.

This is our bed, in our bedroom, in our house. This house is for us, and nobody else.

I couldn't let him sell it. Realizing I had to move quickly, I called the one person I knew would help me.

She answered right away. "Teagan is everything okay?"

"No, it's not. I'm at Jeremy's house. I need your help. I can't let him sell it. Will you please help me?"

"Absolutely, can you meet me at Rico's right now? I'll do whatever I can to help you, and him."

I breathed a sigh of relief. "Thank you, Zoey. I'll see you soon."

Jeremy

April 2014

Life was getting better.

Seeing Teagan with Gary at the funeral had pissed me off. I knew there had been something going on between them, although I knew it wasn't something she had wanted. Especially with the look she'd given me when she'd told me who he was, and then hadn't introduced us.

She might not have noticed, but I had been keeping an eye on her during the funeral. When Andy and Z had been playing their song, and Teagan had turned to thank me, I had seen that piece of shit Gary whisper something to her. She'd looked like she was ready to punch him when she turned back around.

When the pastor had asked if anyone wanted to speak, I'd made an impulsive decision to, but I'd really wanted to check on Teagan. I'd barely been able to see her from where I sat at the back of the church with my family. I hadn't been prepared to speak and hadn't had anything written down to say, so I'd improvised.

During the service, I'd nervously rolled my funeral program up and still had it in my hand when I walked to the podium. Once I'd made sure Teagan was okay, I'd unrolled the paper and recited the poems from memory. I'd already planned to give the ring back to Teagan, but as I was standing there, I realized since her grandmother had been the one to give it to me, I wanted to give it back to her.

Sliding the ring over the rolled paper, I'd slipped it into Nanna's casket when I'd said a final farewell to her. I'd placed it where Teagan or her mom could see it if they wanted to take it and keep it. With no other reason for me to stay at the funeral, I'd left. Teagan had made it obvious she wanted me to move on when she came into my room the night Nicole had brought me home from Sam's.

Yeah, I was shocked to find out that Teagan slipping into my bed and telling me to move on that night wasn't a dream. Nic had called me the day before the funeral to check on me. That's when she told me Teagan really had been at the house. Not the usual vision I saw of her when I was shit-faced.

Now, I was taking her wishes seriously and moving on, quitting my "path of self-destruction" as Teagan had called it. Well, if I was on a path of self-destruction, Teagan was the fucking tour guide. Yes, I was angry with her, but I'd finally accepted that we were over.

I was tired of being miserable. Tired of not sleeping, and tired of being in my house alone. As soon as I'd gotten home from the funeral, I'd packed all of my clothes and personal shit I used every day, and had gone to stay at the apartment above the shop.

Since the apartment was fully furnished I hadn't needed to bring anything from my house. All the furniture and everything else could stay there for all I cared. Which, in turn, made me feel extremely guilty after all the work my sister put in to making my home perfect.

With the apartment being quiet and containing nothing familiar to me, I'd finally started to relax for the first time in months. The place held no reminders of Teagan, no reminders of Cammie, and no reminders of the house that I loved so much but which I knew I wouldn't be going back to.

I had tried to live a normal life. I had tried to make a home. I had tried falling in love and making a life with someone.

I had fucking failed.

Miserably.

I had to sell the house.

My decision to sell didn't come easily. In fact, it was probably the second hardest decision I've made in my life. The hardest decision of my life was to let Teagan go, and move on. She wanted me to be happy, and my house was not making me happy.

In fact, every day I'd stayed there without her had depressed me more and more.

The first week I'd lived at the apartment, I'd actually slept. A full night's sleep. Every single night. I'd been amazed at how much better I'd felt just from being rested.

After that first week, I'd spoken to Z about selling my house. She'd freaked and hadn't spoken to me for three days. She hadn't even been able to look at me. Every time I'd tried to talk to her, she'd glared at me and walked off. I knew she'd come to her senses eventually. She always did.

The day after I had ripped the fence out, I decided I was going to meet Nicole's cousin, Joanne. She had recently come out of a long-term relationship with a man in the Army, and wanted to try dating again. Tonight, I was taking her out for the first time. We'd talked on the phone a few times and she was easy to talk to.

When I arrived at her house and knocked on the door, she answered right away. I was pleasantly surprised with the gorgeous woman who answered the door. Nicole said she was pretty, but she was wrong. Joanne was stunning. She had long, sun-kissed brown hair styled in loose waves, flawless porcelain skin, and the biggest, brown eyes surrounded by thick, dark lashes.

Her body was slender, with perfect curves and gorgeous, long legs. She was wearing heels, so she appeared tall, but I would have guessed she was around five-six without them. Joanne was dressed casually in a simple floral, yet sexy dress, with a tattered jean jacket over it.

Based on the way she was dressed, she seemed both carefree and confident. A great combination in my opinion.

"Joanne?" I asked after I stopped ogling her.

She gave me a sweet smile, showing off her perfect teeth and lips. "Hi, Jeremy," she said. "It's nice to finally meet you in person."

She held out her hand to me and I shook it . . . and I felt nothing.

Not a goddamn thing.

Sure, Joanne was beautiful, and I definitely liked her and the way she looked. What man wouldn't? But when I touched her hand, I felt nothing.

There was no heart stopping moment and no instant response to her the way that there was with Teagan.

"Jeremy, are you ready to go?" she asked as she stepped out of her house, pulling the door closed behind her.

"Yes, I am. Sorry, just got lost in thought for a sec," I admitted. I took her hand in mine and walked her out to my car, hoping my initial reaction to her was some sort of a glitch, and that if I kept hold of her hand, something would spark.

As I opened the passenger door for her, I told her she looked pretty, because she did, but the words felt foreign coming out of my mouth when directed at someone other than Teagan.

"Thank you," she said, as she took a seat in my car.

Jesus, she doesn't even look right in my car. This is too weird.

On the ride to the restaurant, we talked and she asked me about my work. I told her as much as I could without boring her. Nic mentioned Joanne was super smart, and a bookworm, so I wanted to find out more about her.

Once we were at the restaurant and seated, she ordered a glass of wine, and I ordered a beer before we scanned our menus.

"Nic tells me you manage some sort of a blog, is that right?" I asked.

"Yes, it's a book blog. I review books, interview authors, and do features on new books coming out. Basically, I help indie authors get the word out about their books so readers will buy them. That's just for fun though, really. I work as a copy editor for my day job," she replied.

Having no idea what a copy editor was, I asked.

Joanne laughed. She had a genuine laugh. "Trust me, it's very tedious and dreadfully boring at times. I spend all day reading and making sure writers use proper grammar, have their facts straight, and all that other junk," she said with a smile. "See, I get so tired of making sure the writers are doing their jobs correctly, sometimes I can't stand to talk about it."

"As long as you enjoy your work, that's all that matters. I'm guessing you like it though, since you do it for a living, and then you manage your blog in addition," I stated.

Joanne frowned slightly before taking a sip of her wine. "Being the girlfriend of a military man leaves you with a lot of spare time. A few years ago, I realized I was reading *a lot* and giving very candid reviews of the books after reading them, and that's when I decided to start the blog."

Shit, did I upset her?

"Sorry, I didn't mean to bring up a bad memory," I said honestly.

"No, it's okay, Jeremy. Is it just me or does it feel weird being out on a date?"

Oh, thank God. I thought I was the only one feeling off about tonight. Letting out a laugh, I finally relaxed.

"It does feel weird. This is my first date since my break-up."

Joanne noticeably relaxed, too. "Well, this is the first date I've been on in years." She smiled. "Now at least that's out of the way . . . how long were you and your girlfriend together?"

"Not long actually, but we had a real connection. Then everything went to hell. Are we supposed to be talking about our exes on a date? Isn't that bad dating etiquette?"

She let out a hearty laugh. "You know what? Let's talk about them. Get it all out in the open and out of the way. You game?"

By the time we left the restaurant, I knew her story and she knew mine. It felt good to talk about it without getting in to an argument with someone about my being stupid.

"So, what next?" I asked when we were inside my car. "We didn't make a plan for after dinner, but I don't really feel like going home and getting the third degree from my sister."

"Hmm, let's go hang out at my house," Joanne said. "We can watch a movie or continue to dwell on our exes. It's kind of liberating to talk about it, isn't it?"

"It is," I admitted as I started my car and shifted to first gear.

By midnight, we were pretty much talked out. We watched a movie on TV and hung out. I still felt nothing between us. In fact, the more I talked about Teagan, the more I missed her.

"What's going on in that head of yours right now, Jeremy?"

Crap, what do I say?

She narrowed her eyes at me as if trying to read my mind, and bit her lip before she spoke. "Let me guess. You're thinking I'm a nice person and we can be friends, but there isn't a spark between us. You're also thinking about Teagan, and how much you still love her."

My mouth dropped open, and I quickly shut it. Joanne burst out laughing and placed her hand on my knee. "I'm right, aren't I?"

"Yeah, you are. I won't lie to you, Joanne. This dating thing is unfamiliar to me." Shit, I'd only ever dated Cammie and Teagan. Dating was still a fairly new venture for me.

"Well, don't feel bad, okay? We're in the same boat, I think. After talking about my ex all night, I've realized I'm nowhere near being over him either."

"Friends, then?"

"Yeah, we can definitely be friends. You're a good person, Jeremy. I can see why Nicole speaks so highly of you."

"Thanks. I guess I should get going then," I said and stood to leave.

Joanne walked me to the door and hugged me.

"Thanks for dinner, Jeremy. I had a great time, and it was nice to have someone to talk to. Maybe we can get together again, just to hang out."

"Absolutely. Thanks for listening to me and for being cool about . . . the lack of spark."

She laughed. "Goodnight, Jeremy."

After that first date, Joanne and I hung out together often. We would meet for lunch or dinner, hang out at the bookstore to read and get a cup of coffee, or watch movies and cook dinner at her house. I didn't dare take her to the apartment.

Not with the prying eyes of my sister next door.

Since Z had found my house for me, she convinced me that she should also be the one to get rid of it for me. I agreed, but only because I couldn't stand to look at it anymore. She told me to leave all the furniture so the potential buyers would have a better visual of the house as a home.

Besides, at the time I didn't have a clue what I was going to do with all of the furniture, other than move it to a storage unit.

We argued about the price of the house and Zoey got pissed at me when I told her to sell it to the first person that offered what I owed on it. That was right after I put it on the market near the end of March.

Since then she had changed her mind, and the house was in the process of being sold. Someone from the open house was buying it *and* all the furniture because they loved the way it was decorated. Whatever. When escrow closed, it would all be over. Then I'd never need to worry about it again.

Several days later, I was working on a motor with Jason when Zoey called me into the office. I sat down on the chair next to her desk, and she pushed a few papers in front of me.

"Here, sign these," she said, holding a pen out to me.

"What is it?"

"They're the final papers for your house. Once you sign, it's gone. You know this, right?" she asked, irritably.

"Yep," I responded then scribbled my name on the lines highlighted in yellow. I tossed the pen on the desk when I was finished signing and stood to leave.

"You're a stubborn, fucking ass, Jeremy James," Zoey muttered.

"Thanks," I replied before walking out the door.

I made a right down the hallway and walked outside instead of going back to work. Signing those papers was the last thing I wanted to do, but it was done. Taking the stairs up to the apartment two at a time, I slammed the door behind me once I was inside.

Suddenly, I felt like breaking something or drinking an

entire bottle of tequila. But, I knew neither of those options would change anything. I took a few minutes, got my shit together, and went back to work.

The rest of the week dragged by, and I'd thought I had a handle on my decision about selling my house. I was wrong—dead fucking wrong. I couldn't believe after all the good shit I had done the last year, I had come full circle. I was back living in a small apartment and the only thing I owned was my car.

For a short time, I'd had everything.

Everything.

I'd had a great girl, a nice home, and a perfect life. Now it was all gone.

Every part of me wanted to go out to the bar and fuck any woman who wanted to take me home with her. But, I couldn't even think that without Teagan's face popping into my head. *Besides, that's not who I am anymore.*

Teagan had tried to contact me several times, but I was so pissed at her I wouldn't answer my phone or text her back. Probably a dick move on my part, but I had to move on.

So here I sat at my apartment alone, on a Friday night. There was no TV here because Andy had never bought one. I hoped the person who bought my house was enjoying my TV because I sure as hell hadn't found the time or energy to shop for a new one. Bored as hell and feeling a bit lonely, I gathered my laundry basket full of dirty clothes and headed next door to see if Z would let me use her washer and dryer.

When I knocked on the door, Andy answered. "Hey, Jeremy, what's up?"

Andy and I had patched things up after our argument during family dinner, but all my sister would give me now was the cold shoulder. Personally, I thought she was fucking with me half the time, because something wasn't right about how she had been acting toward me. That's Z for ya though.

"I was gonna see if you'd let me do a load of laundry if you guys aren't busy." *Please don't let them be busy . . .*

The door swung open farther, and Zoey stepped next to Andy. "No morons allowed," she said with a snarky smile on her face.

Bratty little shit.

"Why's Andy in here then?" I retorted.

He laughed, pulling the door open all the way, and walked off. "You assholes leave me out of your brother-sister feud, eh?" Shaking his head, he went and sat on the couch.

"Use the Laundromat down the street, Jeremy. You're the one who sold your house," Zoey snapped at me.

"Come on, Z, don't be like that. I couldn't stay there and you know it. Don't try and tell me if the roles were reversed you wouldn't have done the same thing."

She glared at me because she knew I was right. "Fine, you can do your laundry . . . on one condition."

"What?"

"You let me set you up with somebody." Her eyes begged me to say yes, and it was hard to tell her no. Plus, I really didn't want to go to the nasty Laundromat again. The last time I was there, this creepy lady with no teeth kept hitting on me. I shuddered at the memory.

"Fine," I said, pushing past her and into their apartment.

"Don't you want to know anything about her, Jeremy?"

"Nope. Can I go wash my clothes now?"

Z let out an irritated breath and joined her husband on the couch. She turned around and flipped me off before I left the room.

After tossing my clothes into the washer, I slipped quietly into Sweet Pea's bedroom to check on her. She'd kicked off her blanket, so I covered her back up and kissed her goodnight. Joining Zoey and Andy in the living room, I sat on the couch and watched a rugby game with them while waiting for my laundry.

"We're having a double date tomorrow night," Zoey said, as I was leaving with my basket full of clean clothes.

"Just tell me what time and where I need to go," I said, jogging down the stairs.

"Be here at seven. And dress nice!" she yelled as the lobby door closed.

The next day, I spent working on the Chevelle. Again. The seats were finally done, and the new carpet kit was first on my to-do-list for the day. Taking the carpet to the parking lot, I unrolled it and laid it in the sun to warm it up so it was easier to work with.

Back inside the shop, I unwrapped the seats from the protective plastic covers. I went to my toolbox to get the tools I needed to install them. I lifted the lid and came face to face with a photo of Teagan. *Freaking Zoey.* I'd removed the photos long ago so this new one had caught me completely off guard.

Why did I still love her so much, but hate her at the same time? She'd dismissed me from her life and hadn't even had the nerve to do it to my face. *Well, not to my sober face, that is.*

I grabbed the tools I would need for later, and slammed the lid shut. I put the seats on a flatbed cart and wheeled them outside.

After cleaning and prepping the floor of the Chevelle, I laid the carpet inside the car and went upstairs to find something to eat. When I was finished with lunch, I finished the carpet and installed the seats, then decided to take the rest of the day off and relax.

When six o'clock rolled around, I figured I should probably get ready for my double date with Zoey, Andy, and the mystery girl. Who would Z set me up with? She had a tight group of friends and hadn't mentioned anyone new.

I showered, shaved, and then went to my closet to try and find something nice to wear since Z said to dress up. I wasn't a dressy kind of guy, so I pulled on my nicest jeans and one of the few dress shirts I owned.

After I was ready, I suddenly felt nervous for some reason. Like tonight might be a game changer for me. If my *sister* was setting me up with someone, it might actually work.

Not surprisingly, my mind drifted to Teagan. Fuck this. She wanted me to get on with my life, and I wanted to get on with my life, so that's what I was going to do.

I walked across the courtyard to Zoey's. When I went around the side of her building, I noticed a red, Chevy Cruze that still had paper plates parked next to the building.

I opened the door to the lobby, then went upstairs and knocked on the door. Andy answered, and I instantly noticed the hesitant look on his face.

"What did my sister do?" I asked, knowing Z was up to something.

"Sorry, bro, I didn't know what she was planning," Andy said as we walked toward the kitchen.

Apparently, we were having our double date at the apartment because the smell of food cooking drifted from the kitchen. When I entered the room my feet froze in place the second I saw *her*.

I couldn't believe my sister had done this to me. I watched as the two women talked and laughed while they prepared dinner.

The two women being my sister—and Teagan. What was she doing here?

Andy cleared his throat to get their attention and both women turned. I was too stunned to say anything. All I could do was stare at her.

She looked beautiful. Her hair was pulled back in a low ponytail, with several wavy tendrils loose around her face. She was wearing a pretty, green dress and her favorite shoes. The same pointy shoes she'd been wearing last year when she'd kicked me in the shin. I almost smiled as I thought of that night and how feisty she'd been.

But then Teagan took a step toward me. "Hello, Jeremy. It's good to see you."

Ignoring Teagan, I turned to my sister. "What were you thinking, Zoey?"

Her face immediately fell because she knew I wasn't happy about the situation. "Jer, please don't be mad at me. You're both unhappy and you belong together—"

"*Stop*, Zoey. You had no right to butt in like this. She stopped talking to me then decided to tell me to get on with my life while I was passed out drunk. I'm not doing this. I'll see you later."

"Jeremy please, don't leave," Teagan said as she stepped toward me again. "I'm so sorry for everything, can we talk?"

I took a step backward, away from the woman I still loved.

"No, we can't. I am so fucking pissed off right now because

both of you went behind my back. I'm leaving. Enjoy your dinner."

When I reached for the doorknob, I heard Teagan let out a sob and tell my sister, "I knew this was a mistake. He hates me."

If she only knew how wrong she was. I wanted to speak to her, but I felt deceived by my sister and Teagan. I just wanted to get away from them. I pulled the door open and left.

Halfway across the parking lot I heard Teagan call out for me.

"Jeremy, please talk to me."

Still fuming, I spun around to face her. "What Teagan? Have you finally had enough *time?* Are you expecting me to forget about you not speaking to me for weeks? It's also pretty chicken-shit for you to dump me while I'm passed out drunk."

She hung her head and her shoulders shook as she cried.

"Stop crying, Teagan!" I yelled. Seeing her upset and crying was killing me, but she'd broken *my* fucking heart, not the other way around. She wasn't the one who should be upset.

"Jeremy, please, I'll do anything to get us back to the way we were."

I wanted that too, but I couldn't forget the last few months of me sitting around waiting for her to get her shit together.

"Do you have any idea what you've done to me? I've never had my heart broken in my life until you, Teagan. I sold my damn house because I couldn't be there without *you!* How pathetic is that?"

"It's not, Jeremy. I'm so sorry for everything I've done to hurt you, but if you give me a chance, I'd like to explain. I've done a lot of thinking lately, especially since Nanna died. Please talk to me. I still want her to be right about us. I *need* her to be right. I still love y—"

"Stop! Don't fucking say it! You're not allowed to say that to me, Teagan. Not anymore."

She covered her mouth with her hand and stepped back as if I'd slapped her. Her eyes welled up with tears again, and she took a deep breath after letting her hand drop to her side.

But she didn't give up.

"Please . . . *please*, forgive me. Please talk to me. That's all I'm asking, Jeremy. If you don't like what I have to say, I'll leave and never bother you again."

Tears trickled down her pretty face as I stood and stared at her. "I'm sorry Teagan, but I can't forget what you've done to me for the past few months. All this started with me punishing myself over what Cammie did to us, and even though you *know* what really happened, you continued to punish me by stringing me along."

"Jeremy, *please*," she cried and attempted to reach out for me.

"Teagan if you want to speak to me, you need to give me time, now. You and Zoey springing this date shit on me was a bad idea. I'll call you when I'm ready to talk. Please leave."

Not waiting to see what she was going to do, I turned and went inside my apartment and locked the door. I shut off all the lights and went to bed.

After an hour or so, my cell phone rang. It was Zoey. I ignored her call and the ten others after that. My cell rang again, this time it was Andy, so I answered.

"What?" I growled into the phone.

"Look, I know you don't want to talk to your sister right now, but she was calling you for a good reason."

"You're right, I'm pissed at her. What does she want?"

Andy sighed. "I understand, but are you aware that Teagan is outside your door?"

What the hell? "No, what is she doing?"

"Jeremy, just go and get her. It's cold outside."

After we hung up, I pulled on my jeans, shirt, and shoes. When I opened my front door I found Teagan curled up on the welcome mat on the landing. She'd pulled her legs up under her knee-length dress in an attempt to keep warm.

"Teagan, what are you doing? You're going to freeze out here." She was wearing only a thin dress and the spring evenings in Northern California were still cool when the sun went down.

"I'm not running away anymore. Not from you, not from anything," she said quietly, without moving to get up.

She was shaking, so I knew she was cold. I jogged to my bedroom and pulled a hoody from my closet. When I went back to the door, she was sitting up with her arms wrapped around herself trying to get warm. I sat down next to her and pulled the hoody over her head. As she slipped her arms into the sleeves, I brushed her hair away from her face.

My fingers grazed her skin and our connection was there, stronger than ever. And just like the first time I touched her, my heart stopped. I lifted her onto my lap and held her tightly to warm her up. I wanted to take her inside, but I couldn't. I needed her to leave. If I let her inside, all I would see is her, like I did at my house.

"Teagan, you need to go home. Give me some time to think about this, please."

She nodded hesitantly and stood. I followed her out to the street and she walked up to the red Cruze outside Z's apartment.

"You bought a new car."

"Yeah, my Neon, uh, bit the dust last week. I used the money Nanna left me to pay for it. Do you like it?"

"It suits you, Red. Now, get out of here. I'll call you, I promise."

"I'm really sorry about tonight, Jeremy. I didn't mean to make you mad," she said as her bottom lip quivered.

I hugged her then let her go. She got into her new car and left.

I hopped into my car and went straight to Sam's bar.

Teagan

A week had passed since Zoey had set us up, and Jeremy still hadn't called yet. Now, I regretted every single second of time I'd asked him to give me, and every single second we'd spent apart. Because of those seconds, I feared I had lost him for good. *I can't lose him . . . he's everything to me.* Why had I been so stupid and horrible to him?

While I'd been doing everything behind the scenes to get him back, he'd been drifting further away. But, I hadn't been able to let him know what I was doing because I needed to prove to him how much I loved him. The only way I'd known how to do that was to set up our future for us, and pray he'd want it too.

So I'd bought his house.

I'd bought his freaking house!

Our house.

The morning of the open house, Nanna's will had been read. She'd left each of her five grandchildren twenty-five thousand dollars. She left Jeremy her Yeats book, per Rose's instructions, and because of the book, I'd gone to see him and found his house for sale.

When I'd met with Zoey at Rico's, she told me her deal with Jeremy about selling it to the first person who offered him what he owed. My heart had broken knowing he'd just wanted to be rid of it.

Zoey had honored Jeremy's wishes about taking only what

was owed on the house for me because she wanted us to be back together as much as I did.

I'd used the money from Eloise for my down payment on the house, and banked the money from Nanna. Luckily I had, because my poor Neon had finally died.

Well, technically, someone had killed it when it had been parked at the grocery store. Somebody had hit the gas pedal instead of the brake pedal on their car and crushed my poor Neon between their car and a big truck. The insurance company had written my old Neon off as totaled, so I had been forced to buy a new car.

Now I had a new house and a new car, but no Jeremy.

He was the one thing I couldn't do without.

As soon as I was allowed to, I moved into Jeremy's house. I had since gotten over everything Cammie had done and I slept in Jeremy's bed every night.

Now all I needed was for him to come home. *But he hadn't called.* I knew he'd gone out on a date with someone Nicole had set him up with, but I also knew it hadn't worked out. They were still friends though and frequently spent time together.

I needed him back and didn't want to wait anymore, even though I knew I'd put him through hell waiting for me.

Screw this waiting crap! It sucks. No wonder he's so angry with me.

Tonight was fight night at Dub's. I didn't know if he was going, but I had to make a move before I lost him completely. All the guys had finally come around about Sonny and Reese, and were going to fight nights together again. If I called Reese or Sonny while they were at Dub's, they would probably out me as soon as they answered their phone, so I picked up my cell and called John.

"Yep," he said as a greeting.

God, he was so predictable and exactly the reason I'd called him over anyone else.

"John, it's Teagan. Is Jeremy with you?"

"Yep."

"Is he by himself?"

"Yep."

Good, he didn't bring his new friend.

"John, I am coming to see him, don't tell anyone."

"Yep."

"John, do you know any other word than yep?"

"Yep."

"Bye, John."

"Yep."

What a tool!

After my call, I drove like a crazy woman to Dub's.

Everyone was sitting at their usual couch watching the fight when I entered the TV room. I was nervous to be there, and had no idea what my plan was. Reese spotted me and grinned. He sneakily elbowed Sonny and a smile grew on his face as well. They knew exactly why I was here.

I had put Jeremy through hell, and my mission tonight was to make it right and show him we belonged together.

Taking a deep breath, I held it then slowly let it out. I walked over, stopping directly in front of him. I lowered myself to my knees and stared at his Sinatra-blue eyes.

A smile touched his lips, and he tilted his head to the side, curious as to what I was doing.

"Hi," I said quietly, as I rested my hands on his knees. My heart felt like it was going to beat out of my chest.

He placed his hands on top of mine and for a brief second, I thought he was going to push them away, but he didn't.

"Hi, pretty girl. Whatcha doing here?"

His using my nickname for me made me smile. *Good sign? I hope so.*

Glancing over at his friends, I found them observing us. While Reese and Sonny knew I'd bought his house, nobody else did. They were all watching and waiting for me to make my next move.

Thinking back to all the times Jeremy had hauled me out of here over his shoulder gave me an idea.

Here goes. "Jeremy, I have a proposition for you."

His eyebrows rose and his hands moved, lightly massaging

the tops of mine.

"I want you to come home with me so we can talk," I said.

"What if I have nothing to say to you yet?"

My stomach clenched. He was going to make this hard on me. Quite rightly. I'd gladly accept everything he might do or say to me, because I was so, so wrong about how I'd handled things with him.

"Please, Jeremy. I'm done running. I swear it. If you come and talk to me we can work this out."

His expression softened, so I stood and pulled his hands to see if he would stand too. He didn't, but kept hold of my hands. I stared at him, trying to figure out what he was thinking. His face remained the same, so I decided to use his own tactics against him.

"We can do this the easy way, or the hard way, Jeremy. You decide."

A smile eased over his face, and he laughed. He rose from his seat, challenging me. "What are you gonna do, Red? Toss me over your shoulder and haul my ass outta here?"

"If I have to," I countered and raised my chin defiantly.

He let go of my hands and lifted his arms out to his sides, as if to say 'bring it on.'

So I did.

I bent over, wrapped my arms around his thighs, and tried to lift him over my shoulder. Yeah, it didn't work and everyone laughed at me. I took a step back and blew my hair away from my face in frustration.

Now what?

Jeremy crossed his arms over his chest and stared at me, waiting for my next move. I froze. I had no idea what to do. We stared at each other for a moment before his arms dropped and he walked away. I followed him.

"Where are you going?" I asked when I caught up to him.

He laughed. "Since the hard way didn't work, I thought I'd let you off the hook and do it the easy way."

He's coming with me?

"You're coming with me?" I asked, surprised.

"What do I have to lose, Red? I can't lose you again since I don't have you."

He pushed the door open and headed for the parking lot. Jeremy walked straight over to my car and stood at the passenger door.

I pressed the button on my key fob to unlock the doors and he got in the car. When I reached down to pull open my door, he hit the lock button.

I doubled over in laughter then glared at him through the window only to find him smiling at me. "Okay, wiseass, you paid me back." I hit the unlock button again and reached for the door handle.

Jeremy locked me out *again*.

"Jeremy James! Quit being a shit!" I yelled from outside my own car.

He hit the lock button again, unlocking the doors.

I opened the door and got in. "Alright, I know I deserved that, but are you going to give me crap all night?"

"Maybe," he said, grinning. God, I loved his smile.

"What happened to your Neon?"

"It was totaled," I said, pulling out of the parking lot.

His head whipped toward me, a worried expression on his face. "Were you hurt?"

"I wasn't inside it when it happened," I said, then went on to explain how it had met its demise.

Jeremy reached over and took my hand, interlacing our fingers. "I'm glad you weren't hurt, Teagan."

I had a hard time containing my emotions when he took my hand, and a tear rolled down my cheek. I was slightly overwhelmed now, because when I'd gone to Dub's, I'd truly thought I would be going home alone.

Crap! How was I going to tell him I'd bought his house? *Think Teagan. Think!*

"Jeremy, do you trust me?"

"Do you want me to?"

"Yes, I do, but I'll understand if you don't."

"I want to, but you haven't made it easy on me, Red."

"I'm so sorry . . . about everything. But I need to tell you something important, and I'm not sure how you're going to take it. Everything I've done is because I love you and want us to be together. I want back everything we had. All of it, and I hope you do too."

"What have you done?"

"If it's okay with you, I'd rather show you." I glanced over at him and took a deep breath.

"Fine."

The closer I drove toward the house, the more nervous I became.

"Teagan, where are you taking me?"

Crap!

I didn't answer him.

"Teagan . . ."

At every stop sign, I did a California stop. I had learned from the master on how to execute a perfect one, and right now, they were coming in handy.

"Are we going to your parents' house?"

I didn't answer because we were approaching the street where his . . . my . . . hopefully our house was. Right at the last second, I slammed on the brakes and made a sharp right turn on to my street. Halfway down the block, I hit the button on the garage door opener, and hoped we were close enough for it to open.

I pulled into the driveway as the garage door finished lifting. I brought my car to a screeching stop inside the garage and hit the button to close the door.

"What's going on?" Jeremy asked, staring over at me in complete confusion.

Cringing, I closed my eyes and took a breath. "I bought your house." I let the breath out.

"I'm sorry, what? I swear you just said you *bought* my house."

"You heard me correctly, Jeremy. I bought your house. Because I love you and I want to be with you, here . . . in our home."

There, I'd said it. It was all out in the open. Well, what I wanted was out in the open. I still didn't know if he'd take me back.

"You bought my house?"

His stare was intense and I couldn't tell if he was angry along with his surprise, or if he was so shocked, he didn't know what else to say.

I needed to get him in the house so he would see that I'd changed.

"Will you come inside?" I gathered my purse and pulled the key from the ignition.

"You *bought* my house . . ."

I laughed and got out of my Cruze. He wasn't going to come inside on his own, so I went around and opened his door for him. I held my hand out to him and he didn't hesitate to take it. He stepped out and opened his mouth to speak. Most likely to say, *"you bought my house"* again.

"Yes, I bought your house, Jeremy. But not for me, I bought it for *us.*"

With his hand in mine, I walked to the door leading to the kitchen. He followed me inside willingly, and looked around. I hadn't changed a thing inside the house.

Our first stop was the bedroom—the place where everything had gone so wrong and the place where I wanted to start over.

I'd forced myself to sleep in that bedroom without him every night since I'd moved in. The first week had been torture, but eventually I'd gotten over the devastating memory.

I led him to the center of the room, kicked off my shoes, and sat on the bed. "Lie down with me," I said quietly, taking his hands in mine.

He hesitated and looked away. For a minute, I thought he was angry, but then I realized he was looking around the bedroom, taking in everything. Apparently, he needed to let my news sink in.

After I let his hands go, I turned on my new iPod to the playlist Zoey had made for this moment. I watched Jeremy stroll around the room looking at everything. He even flipped on the light in the bathroom and looked inside.

He opened drawers on the dresser, he looked inside the

closet, and then he looked in the nightstands. Amused, I relaxed against the pillows and watched him. When he was satisfied with whatever thoughts he had going through his head, he stepped over to the bed.

"Teagan, I don't even know what to say," he said, contemplating me on the bed.

"Will you stay and talk to me?"

He rubbed his hands over his face a few times, and then pushed his fingers through his hair. I missed doing that. I rolled to my side to face him and patted the bed next to me.

"Please?"

Jeremy pulled off his shoes and crawled onto the bed with me. He propped himself on his elbow and just stared at me.

Instinctively, I reached out and rested my hand on his cheek. "I've missed you so much, Jeremy. Will you let me explain why I needed time?"

He pressed his lips to mine unexpectedly then pulled away. He moved closer to me and draped his arm over my side.

"What do you want from me, pretty girl?"

"Everything. I want you to move back here with me. I want you to wake up with me every morning and go running, but most of all . . . I want your forgiveness. Will you ever forgive me, Jeremy? I'm so sorry for stringing you along."

"Why did you do it, Teagan?"

"I didn't mean to. Initially, it took me a while to get it through my head that you didn't do anything wrong, that it was all Cammie. Then everything in my life got so out of control. Moving in with my cousin and starting a new job. Then we began dating which started out great, and we were doing things the way we should have from the beginning."

Jeremy rolled to his back, and pulled me with him, so I was lying on top of him. He carefully took my hair out of the loose bun I'd put it in after my shower this morning, and combed through the strands with his fingers. I could feel the steady thump of his heart beating beneath my cheek, and I finally felt like I was home.

But I knew I needed to continue.

"Everything was going good for us and we were taking our

time, not moving too fast. But I'd never really dealt with all the cheating Gary had done. Or my cheating prick father for that matter. I know neither have anything to do with you, and I'm sorry if I made it seem that way. The night when you brought me in here after dinner, all I saw in my mind was you and *her,* then Gary and Katie."

His hands stilled on my back. "I don't need to know about all that because it doesn't matter, but, why did you stop talking to me, Teagan?"

"I have no excuse. The only thing I can say, is two days after I left here, Nanna had another stroke. In my heart, I knew she didn't have much time left, so my mind reverted to when my dad had cancer. She was my best friend, Jeremy. I needed to spend as much time with her before she left this life."

Tears spilled from my eyes and landed on his shirt. I lifted my head to wipe them away and he kissed my forehead.

"Every day I went to work early, and I took my breaks and lunch in her room. Then every night after work, I stayed with her until she fell asleep. On the weekends, I had to take care of everything I'd neglected during the week . . . laundry, pay my bills, clean the apartment, and spend time with my family. Jeremy, I'm so sorry. I should've told you. Time just got away from me. I was exhausted and basically shut everyone out except Nanna and my family. She had two more strokes after that, but she seemed okay. Until the Friday she died."

Jeremy wrapped his arms around me and kissed my head again. "I'm so sorry, pretty girl. I didn't know about the strokes. She seemed a little different each time I visited her, but—"

"I was with her at the end Jeremy. You have no idea how much that meant to me." Tears rolled down my face at the memory of her last day. "The last words she heard on this earth came from me as I read her The Two Trees. I'd just finished the last sentence when she reached out to me—just like she did to you the day you met her—and placed her hand on my arm." I had to stop because my tears were quickly turning into sobs and I couldn't speak.

Jeremy pulled me closer as my sobs grew louder. "Let it all out," he whispered. "I've got you."

When my sobs had finally quieted and I had no more tears to shed, I finished. "She looked me in the eyes and said 'Peaches.' A second later, she was gone."

"Teagan . . . I'm so sorry." He kissed the top of my head and wrapped me in his embrace again.

Nanna's final wish suddenly popped into my head. The book. I needed to give him the book. I leaned over and kissed him, loving the way his soft lips felt against mine. Sitting up quickly, I braced my hands on either side of his head.

"She left you something, Jeremy."

"She did?"

I hopped from the bed and went to get the book. When I came back into the room, Jeremy was sitting up against the headboard waiting for me. I climbed back onto the bed with him and tucked myself in to his side before handing him the book. He smiled and ran his hand over the worn cover the way he always did when he held it, then wrapped his arms around me.

Sometime later, Jeremy finally spoke. "I'm sorry I tore your fence down," he said quietly.

"What made you do it?"

"A song."

Pulling away from him, I watched Jeremy's expression turn guilty.

"Did Zoey put these songs on your iPod?" he asked.

I nodded. Zoey had told me how much music helped her, so I'd let her load my new iPod with music, thinking it would help me clarify my thoughts. I had to admit it really did work.

Jeremy took my iPod off the dock and scrolled through the music. He found the song he wanted and reconnected it.

I listened closely as the song played and could see why the lyrics would have thrown him into a mood to tear out the fence. I probably would've done the same thing. I climbed on to his lap, straddling him. Holding his face in my hands, I was prepared to beg him to stay with me.

I didn't want this song to be our last love song. I wanted it to remind us of what we'd had together, and what we could get back.

"Jeremy, I understand why you did it. But in the song she lists everything they won't have, we *can*. We can have all of it and so much more. Please, come home. This house isn't my home without you in it. It's ours. It's always been ours . . . don't you see that? Even before you bought it, I wanted it. I *still* want it . . . and I want you."

He pressed his fingers lightly against my lips, shutting me up. "Can you take me back to Dub's to get my car?"

Was he saying no? I reached up and pulled his hand away from my mouth.

"Jeremy?"

Panic ran through my entire body and my eyes filled with tears. He was saying no. Jeremy didn't want to be with me.

Suddenly he sat up and embraced me so tightly it was hard to breathe. His body was shaking with emotion as badly as mine. "I love you so much, pretty girl. Don't ever leave me again, promise?"

I sat back and stared at him. "You're staying?" I asked, wiping the tears off my cheeks.

"Not to be a total dick for not saying anything sooner . . . but you had me convinced when you said you bought my house," he admitted with a smile.

I leaned forward to kiss him, but he reached out and stopped me. "I still needed to hear everything we've talked about since we came inside, though. I had to see that you really wanted *us* back." He smiled. "Can we go get my car so she doesn't have to spend the night at Dub's? She misses her garage."

After I told him yes and kissed him, I jumped off the bed and slipped my shoes back on. "Jeremy, I'm on the pill now."

His brows rose and a smile eased over his face. "You're telling me this why?"

I took his hands in mine and pulled him off the bed. "Because when we get back here, we're going to christen every room in *our* house."

He sat back down on the bed and pulled me to him. "My car can wait. We're christening this room right now."

Jeremy yanked my shirt over my head as I slipped my

shoes back off, simultaneously pushing my jeans and panties down my legs. We were in such a frenzy of undressing while trying to kiss one of us was going to get hurt.

His shirt came off and I pushed him back on the bed. My hands made quick work of his jeans and boxers. As soon as they were on the floor, I crawled back onto the bed and hovered over him. As I kissed him, he unsnapped my bra and pulled it off then tossed it aside. He licked and sucked my nipples as I reached down to guide him inside me.

He didn't move as I eased down onto him. When I was ready, I moved. Jeremy gripped my hips and moved with me. He thrust upward as I lowered myself down his length.

My entire body felt him inside me. He was everywhere all at once, consuming my senses and dulling the ache in my heart. We were falling in love all over again, and it felt right.

Finally, I felt free of Gary, Cammie, Katie, and their betrayals.

Jeremy pulled me down to kiss me, and rolled us so I was on my back. He stilled over me and brushed my hair away from my face.

"Teagan, open your eyes," he said softly.

My eyes opened and met his blue gaze. I reached up to pull him into a kiss, but he hesitated.

"Is something wrong?"

"Tell me what you see, Teagan. Inside your head, *right now,* what do you see?"

Understanding what he was asking, I answered him honestly.

"I see you, Jeremy. I see you and me in our house, in our bedroom. I see us getting married and making lots of pretty babies. I see us raising those babies and growing old eventually. But what I see *right now,* is how much I love you and how much you love me."

His eyes filled with tears and he pressed his cheek to mine. "I love you, Teagan," he whispered and began moving inside me.

We made love as if it was our first time. It felt like it was the first time for us, even though it wasn't. I wrapped my arms around him and kissed him, as we loved each other.

"You feel amazing. I missed you so much," he murmured against my cheek, his hips thrusting harder.

My hands moved over his chest and back, into his hair, then down to grip his ass and pull him harder and faster against me. I didn't want this feeling to end, but ultimately, my body gave in, hurling me over the edge into the abyss. With my body clenching tightly around him, Jeremy came with me.

We lay there until he rolled us to our sides. We faced each other while I studied his gorgeous eyes, wondering what he was thinking.

"What are you thinking about, pretty girl?"

"Just wondering what you were thinking right now."

He propped himself up on his elbow and played with my hair. "I was thinking about the day we met, and how I thought it was the best day of my life. But I was wrong. Today is the best day. The next best day will be the day you say you'll marry me, and the day after that will be the day you say '*I do*.'"

"What then?" I asked because I loved where our conversation was going.

"The next best day after that will be the day you bring our first child into the world. But for right now, I'll settle for today being the best day of my life. The day you came home to me."

"I love you, Jeremy."

"I love you too, Teagan."

"I love it when you say you love me," I teased.

He kissed me quick on the lips. "Get used to hearing it, Red. I plan to tell you every day for the rest of my life that you're the best thing that's ever happened to me. You will never go another day without hearing how much I love you."

We stayed wrapped around each other for a while longer before I remembered something else I needed to give him. I went to my jewelry box for it.

When I turned around to face the bed again, I found Jeremy grinning from ear to ear.

"You have a great ass, Red. Your tits are amazing too."

Shaking my head and laughing at our inside joke, I sat next

to him on the bed.

"I want you to have this," I said as I held my hand out. My papa's Claddagh ring lay on my palm.

Jeremy sat up on the bed and stared at my hand in awe. "You found it?"

I nodded. "I did, and I want you to take it back. Will you accept it?"

He didn't say a word just thrust his right hand in my direction, his fingers splayed.

"I'll take that as a yes," I teased as I slipped the ring back on his finger.

"Absolutely. Thank you, my beloved. Now, let's go get my car so we can come home and get to work christening the rest of the rooms in our house."

The next morning, I slept in later than I had in ages. When I woke up, I reached out for Jeremy, but his side of the bed was cold. I sat up quickly and rubbed my eyes. Glancing down, I found a piece of paper on his pillow. I unfolded it and read his short note.

> *Teagan,*
>
> *I have something important I need to do. I'll be back as soon as I can, but it might take most of the day. I'll see you soon. I love you,*
>
> *Jeremy*

When he'd said it might take most of the day, he'd meant it!

It was midafternoon before I heard a car pull up outside. I glanced out the window to find one of the James Racing trucks in front of the house with a flatbed trailer attached. The trailer was stacked with what appeared to be some sort of lumber.

I walked outside and found Jeremy unloading boxes from the truck. He set a box down and saw me just as I stepped up to him. He instantly smiled and pulled me into his arms.

"Hey, pretty girl, did you miss me?"

"Only the entire time you were gone," I replied as I brushed my lips against his. "What is all of this?" I motioned to the boxes.

"Well, all the boxes are filled with my clothes and shit from the apartment. And this . . ." he trailed off. He took my hand and led me to the trailer attached to the truck. "*This* is going to be a white picket fence when we're done with it."

I slapped my hand over my mouth to cover the happy sob that was about to escape. Tears streamed down my face as I stared at the stacks of posts, pickets, and bags of concrete.

"But you hated the fence," I said when I stopped crying.

He shook his head and grinned at me. "Turns out I'm a white-picket-fence-kind-of-guy after all."

I flung my arms around his neck and kissed him as he lifted me off the ground. I wrapped my legs around his waist and kissed all over his face until we were both laughing.

"Let's get started on the fence right now," I said.

"No way, Red. First, we're going to take care of the boner you just gave me, and then we're going to unpack all my shit, and christen every room in the house, *again*. Tomorrow we can work on the fence. Sound like a good plan to you?"

Taking a page from his book, there was only one answer I could give him.

"Yes!"

"Good answer." He chuckled and carried me toward the house.

Our house.

Epilogue

Jeremy & Teagan

18 Months Later...

We ride up the elevator to the fourth floor of the hospital with our hands full of baby stuff. When the doors open, we both try to step out at the same time, but we're carrying too much and we bump in to one another. We look over at each other and laugh.

We're both excited that the time has finally arrived.

Jeremy carries two car seats, and I carry a diaper bag full of necessities and baby clothes.

We make our way to the nursery to pick up our babies. They were born early and had to stay in the hospital for two weeks after I was discharged. But now they're ready to come home.

Neither of us have twins anywhere in our family histories. When we went in for my first sonogram and the doctor found I was carrying twins, we were shocked.

But thrilled.

We didn't know until they were born via C-section we would be blessed with a boy and a girl.

"Are you ready for this, Jeremy?" I ask, because he's looking a bit green all of a sudden.

He smiles, and I know he's okay. "Ready. Let's get our little ones checked out of here and take them home."

We get our paperwork processed and go to the nursery to pick up our babies. Once we have them dressed in their outfits to take them home, we thank the nursing staff for taking great care of them.

Jeremy scoops our baby girl, Brenna, from her bassinet, and carefully arranges her in her car seat. While I strap her in, he picks up Lucas, who we named after my dad, and settles him in his car seat. Jeremy straps him in and picks up both car seats. I grab the diaper bag, and we make our way back down to our super roomy mini-van with our twins. Yep, we bought a mini-van after seeing how much baby stuff Jeremy's siblings carried around for their kids.

And Luisa was right; we did make pretty babies, just like she said we would.

I drive us home while Teagan sits between the babies in the back seat of the mini-van. She's small and fits perfectly between the car seats. Occasionally, I glance in the rearview mirror to see my beloved wife staring down in awe at our twins.

Every single day, Teagan amazes me.

She carried our babies inside her as long as she could, but when they wanted out, she had to have a C-section. Andy tried to prepare me for it, because Z had one with both Sweet Pea, and their son Kieran, but seeing my wife cut open like that scared me to death.

As soon as each baby was out and crying, the relief on Teagan's face helped me to relax. If she was okay, I was okay.

I pull our van inside the garage and one by one, I carry the babies in their car seats inside the house. Teagan isn't supposed to lift anything heavy yet, and I make sure she follows the doctor's orders.

I carry them into their shared bedroom, where Teagan sits in one of the two rocking chairs. I hand a hungry Brenna to her so she can nurse her.

Lucas is still asleep, so I carefully lift him from his car seat and sit in the other rocking chair. I rock my sleeping son while his sister nurses. Of course, as soon as Brenna has her fill, Lucas is awake and ready for his turn.

We trade babies and I burp Brenna and rock her back to sleep.

Teagan and I work great together and have this down to a science now. I am taking six weeks off work to spend time with my babies and my wife. I'm not going to miss a second of time with them.

Our families are awesome. They helped with everything from cooking us meals, to my brothers taking over my work when Teagan and the babies were in the hospital.

Once they are asleep in their bassinets, we quietly leave the room and go into our bedroom. We settle ourselves on the bed facing each other like so many times in the past.

"I'm so happy they're home, Jeremy," I say quietly. "I hated being away from them every night."

"Me too, pretty girl," he replies. "I think Brenna looks like you more and more every day. Don't you?"

I nod, because I know he's right. "You know Lucas is going to be a little heartbreaker don't you? It's crazy how much he looks like you."

"He won't be a heartbreaker. I won't let him. I am going to teach him how to treat girls with respect," he says.

I laugh, because I know our son will be as gorgeous as his daddy. Brenna's hair is already turning the same shade of red as mine. We each have a mini-me now.

It's going to be rough raising two babies at the same time, I think. But we love them, and we love each other more every day, so I know we can get through anything.

Jeremy rolls over, opens the top drawer of his nightstand, and takes something out. He sets a small black box down on the bed between us and pushes it toward me.

"I bought you something to remind you every day how proud I am to be your husband, and the father of our babies."

I sit up on the bed and open the box. Inside is a beautiful Claddagh ring. It's unlike any ring I've ever seen. The hands are holding a heart-shaped topaz, which represents the month in which our babies were born. The tiny crown holds a diamond, and the band of the ring has three more diamonds on either side of the hands.

"Jeremy, it's gorgeous. Thank you so much. I love you," I say before he takes the ring from me and slides it onto my finger. It fits perfectly.

"I love you too, Red. Now, we should probably get a nap before those two wake up. I have a feeling we won't be getting much sleep for the next year."

We wrap our arms around each other, kiss, and close our eyes. In our bed, in our home, with two tiny babies sound asleep in the bedroom next to ours.

If there's one thing we've both realized, it's that life is so much better when you're running toward it, not running away from it . . .

The End

About the Author

Jen Andrews was raised in a small town in Northern California, and still lives in the same county where she was born. She is a self-proclaimed music and lyric addict. She grew up in a 'car family' so her life has been spent around old hot rods. She and her husband, Jake, even have a few of their own. In her spare time, Jen loves to travel wherever she can. She finally lived her dream of traveling to New Zealand to see her favorite rugby team, the All Blacks, play. Jen loves to do photography as a hobby and continues to write.

Find Jen here:

http://www.goodreads.com/author/show/7762025.Jen_Andrews

http://www.facebook.com/AuthorJenAndrews

http://www.facebook.com/jenandrewsauthor

http://www.goodreads.com/book/show/20755729-the-reason

http://www.goodreads.com/book/show/22585630-just-say-yes

http://www.goodreads.com/book/show/24312326-beautiful-with-you

http://www.goodreads.com/book/show/25746537-running-away

http://twitter.com/jennysnowflakes